The Sky-Blue Wolves

The
Sky-Blue Wolves

A NOVEL OF THE CHANGE

S. M. STIRLING

ACE
NEW YORK

ACE
Published by Berkley
An imprint of Penguin Random House LLC
375 Hudson Street, New York, New York 10014

Map by Jade Cheung

Library of Congress Cataloging-in-Publication Data
Names: Stirling, S. M., author.
Title: The Sky-Blue Wolves: a novel of the Change / S. M. Stirling.
Description: First edition. | New York, New York: Berkley, an imprint of Penguin Random House LLC,
2018. | Series: Change series; [15]
Identifiers: LCCN 2018025781 | ISBN 9780451490681 (hardback) | ISBN 9780451490698 (ebook)
Subjects: | BISAC: FICTION/Alternative History. | FICTION/Fantasy/Epic. | GSAFD: Alternative
histories (Fiction). | Fantasy fiction.
Classification: LCC PS3569.T543 S58 2018 | DDC 813/.54—dc23
LC record available at https://lccn.loc.gov/2018025781

First Edition: November 2018

Printed in the United States of America
1 3 5 7 9 10 8 6 4 2

Cover art by Larry Rostant

To Jan, as always!

ACKNOWLEDGMENTS

More, but not enough.

Thanks to my friends who are also first readers: Steve Brady, Markus Baur, Scott Palter, Brenda Sutton, Pete Sartucci.

Thanks also to Kier Salmon, insufficiently credited collaborator, for once again helping with the beautiful complexities of the Old Religion, and with . . . well, all sorts of stuff! Including, in this book, a suggestion for a scene that solved a problem for me, and for the loan of BD.

To John Birmingham, author of many excellent SF works, including the Axis of Time and Disappearance series, and the excellent story "Fortune and Glory" in my anthology *The Change*. Thanks for help with Aussie stuff, and the loan of Pete and FiFi and Jules. He's also King Birmo of Capricornia in an alternate history, and does a boffo job of that, too!

To Diana L. Paxson, for help and advice, and for writing the beautiful Westria books, among many others. If you liked the Change novels, you'll probably enjoy the hell out of the Westria books—I certainly did, and they were one of the inspirations for this series; and her *Essential Ásatrú* and recommendation of *Our Troth* were extremely helpful . . . and fascinating reading.

To Dale Price, for help with Catholic organization, theology and praxis.

And to Walter Jon Williams, Emily Mah, John Miller, Vic Milán (still present in spirit), Jan Stirling, Matt Reiten, Lauren Teffeau, S.E. Burr, Sarena Ulibarri and Rebecca Roanhorse of Critical Mass, our writer's group, for constant help and advice.

Thanks to John and Gail Miller, good friends, for many useful discussions, for lending me some great books, and for some really, really cool old movies.

Thanks again to Russell Galen, my agent, who has been an invaluable help and friend for more than a decade now, and never more than in these difficult times.

All mistakes, infelicities and errors are of course my own.

The Sky-Blue Wolves

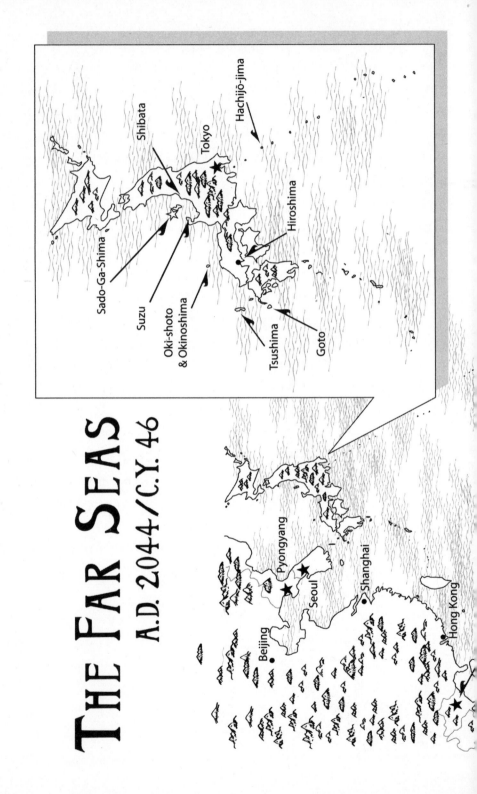

THE FAR SEAS
A.D. 2044/C.Y. 46

Hachijō-jima

Shibata

Tokyo

Hiroshima

Sado-Ga-Shima

Suzu

Oki-shoto
& Okinoshima

Tsushima

Goto

Pyongyang

Seoul

Shanghai

Beijing

Hong Kong

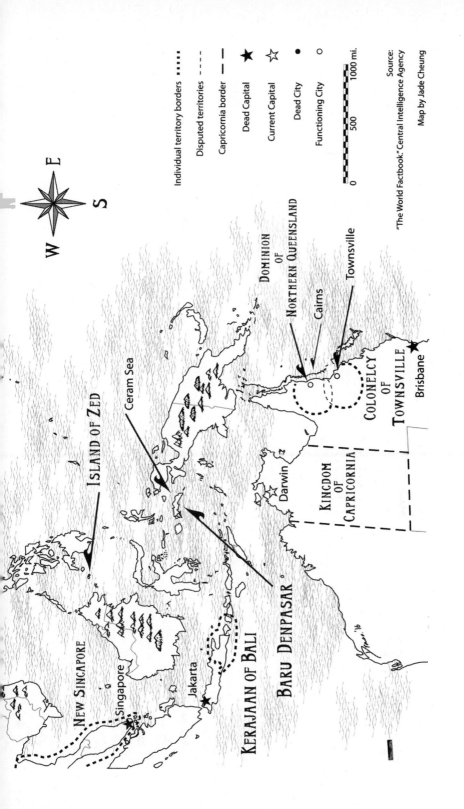

W · N · E · S

Island of Zed

Ceram Sea

New Singapore

Singapore

Jakarta

Kerajaan of Bali

Baru Denpasar

Darwin

Kingdom
of
Capricornia

Dominion
of
Northern Queensland

Cairns

Townsville

Colonelcy
of
Townsville

Brisbane

Individual territory borders ·····
Disputed territories − − −
Capricornia border ▬▬
Dead Capital ★
Current Capital ☆
Dead City ●
Functioning City ○

0   500   1000 mi.

Source:
"The World Factbook." Central Intelligence Agency

Map by Jade Cheung

CHAPTER ONE

*T*UUNNNNGGG.

Órlaith Arminger Mackenzie felt the massive frame of the frigate *Sea-Leopard* quiver beneath her feet as the fourteen-shot broadside cut loose, the catapults on the gun-deck below shaking the thick Douglas fir and Garry-oak structure of the warship as it sailed parallel to the coastline and across the land-breeze with a slow rocking-horse motion. The three masts and their stripped minimal shapes of battle-sail towered above her, and the other five frigates of the Montivallan Navy squadron traced a line behind her that might have been drawn with a ruler, white wakes against the cerulean blue of the ocean.

A little farther out from shore were the smaller, less drilled ships of the allied fleets, the navies of Hawai'i and Dai-Nippon, and the transports and barges that bore the troops who would storm ashore to put right the sneak attack and invasion. It was the task of the warships to soften their way.

Bolts and eighteen-pound roundshot arched out, a near-flicker as they left the launching troughs, arching away into invisibility with distance. That drew a merciful veil over what would be happening on shore as they slashed into the massed ranks of the Korean invasion forces, the dense black mass on the white beach, sparkling here and there with edged metal. They raised their square shields in a futile gesture against missiles designed to shatter the thick timber frames of warships or the stone of fortress walls.

What was it Da said? Órlaith thought grimly. *Yes, that it's a great pity that fighting evil* starts with killing evil's conscripted farmers.

Odors of tarred rope and wood, hot canvas and sweat and metal oiled with canola gone slightly rancid in the mild warmth overwhelmed the scented breeze off the land, that itself was tainted with the smoke of burning homesteads where the invaders from the east had harried among the Hawaiian workshops and settlements around Pearl Harbor. Behind the Montivallan ships some smoke still rose from the ocean itself, where the enemy fleet had met its fate five days ago and was now mainly drifting wreckage . . . and bloated bodies feeding the gulls. Sweat ran down Órlaith's flanks into the padded arming jacket and trews beneath her suit of plate, light and flexible though that titanium-alloy marvel of smithcraft was, but this wasn't nearly as bad as some desert summers she'd worn it through back home.

Still, when she took a dipper of water from the scuttlebutt with a murmur of thanks to the sailor, it slid down like the pure product of a mountain spring, stale and warm and tanged with the chemicals that kept it safe as it was. You had to be careful about things like that, though: it occurred to her that if she made a casual joke and asked if there wasn't cold beer instead, some officious twit might run around in a panic trying to find *actual* cold beer and getting in everyone's way.

While she was off looking for the Grasscutter Sword with Reiko—and dodging the people her mother the High Queen had sent to drag her back if they could—she'd gotten used to being around only her core of followers who knew her well and were friends as well as vassals. It was irritating to readjust to people who saw only the rank, though she couldn't really blame them, since that was all they could know.

"Time to get closer," Admiral Naysmith commanded quietly, standing at ease in her white linen tropical-service uniform jacket and gold-braided epaulettes and fore-and-aft cocked hat. "Apparently they use all their artillery as dual-purpose, and they didn't have time to dismount any from their fleet. Which they didn't expect to lose, of course. Unwise to be so specialized."

Empress Reiko of Dai-Nippon spoke . . . in her own language, though her originally indescribable and purely book-learned English was reasonably understandable now after most of a year of dogged effort:

"The *jinnikukaburi* navy is built for landing raiding troops and taking them off again. Fighting at sea is secondary for them."

Órlaith translated, since she had perfect modern Nihonjin courtesy of the Sword of the Lady she bore, though she tactfully gave post-Change coinage of *jinnikukaburi* as *the enemy*.

The literal rendering was something on the order of *human-flesh cockroach* or possibly *cannibal bug monsters*.

Considering what her folk's scant survivors had suffered since the Change from the reavers who came across the Sea of Japan, Reiko's attitude was understandable, and she had a mild case compared to most of her countrymen. Particularly since the enemy *did* eat the flesh of those they killed . . . and one another, when they were really hungry or someone was being punished. They didn't always kill you first, either.

But Montival wanted to keep it plain they were fighting Korea's demon-ridden sorcerer tyrants, not the land or the people, however much they'd been corrupted by that tyranny and however theoretical the distinction most of the time. Distance made that easier. Reiko had admitted the usefulness of the distinction, but rather grudgingly; most of her subjects simply wanted to kill them all.

Naysmith gave a respectful salute.

"Thank you, Your Majesty, that explains a good deal," she said to Reiko, and added: *"Domo arigato,"* with a pronunciation Órlaith's ear caught as just as bad as Reiko's English had been when they first met.

Then the Royal Navy commander went back to watching the beach through a leveled telescope, her square blocky face calm beneath the small blue brand-scar of the Bearkiller A-List between her brows. Only the observers in the tops or held aloft by great man-bearing kites cabled to the sterns of the repeater frigates had a better view. If the enemy troops pulled back from the beach the allied assault could come ashore uncontested beneath its shelter . . . but if they didn't, they had to stand under the hammer.

As Órlaith's mother had said to her once, battle was always a set of choices, and the mark of a really good commander was to present the other side with a series of choices that all amounted to: *damned if you do, damned if you don't*, each set worse than the last until they ended up with no alternatives between *surrender* and *die*.

And Da had laughed and marked out some maneuvers he'd seen on the table with crusts and saltshakers and gravy boats and wineglasses and added:

And never, never give them the gift of time to recover from a mistake.

His finger had stirred the improvised markers; she remembered the big long-fingered hands vividly, the scars and nicks and battered look of them and the way the red-gold hairs stood out against the weathered tan and the thick swordsman's wrists that hardly dimpled in at all from the forearm.

Looks easy here, does it not, my darling girl, here when we're cool and collected and can see it all? And you say, How could this captain or that have blundered so? *But ah, when your heart is pounding and there's dust in your eyes and much depends on the next decision and everyone's screaming at you for this or that . . . then it's hard, hard. Any fool can hit, timing is much less common, so it is. The same punch can break your knuckles or his face, depending on when you throw it. And waiting because you can't decide . . . that's a decision too, and* always *a bad one.*

Naysmith went on: "Switch to napalm shell. Open up the fleet and tack in succession, conforming to *Sea-Leopard*. All ships keep full lookouts on each other. Minimal sail, dead slow, just enough to keep steerage way, prepare to strike sail and drop anchor on the word of command. Captain Edwards, you will take this ship in about another three hundred yards closer to shore for our next pass to establish the bombardment line."

"Aye-aye, Admiral," he replied.

She'd just made a vote of confidence in his ship-handling skills and those of the other frigate-captains, since it was the sort of maneuver that looked easy and stately . . . unless it ended in disaster. The local pilots their new ally King Kalākaua had supplied were a help, but the Montival-lan frigates were also deeper-keeled than anything they were used to. And since there was no time to do their own surveys they'd just have to hope the charts were accurate, which so far they had been.

"Then make it so."

The *Sea-Leopard*'s captain echoed the command, and signal flags re-layed it to the rest of the allied fleet. The ship came about as the four hands at the helm spun the fore-and-aft paired wheels, the view past the distant bowsprit circling with ponderous certainty, land and then sea again as the third officer pointed with his cane and called:

"Thus . . . thus . . . very well, thus!"

A volley of commands via speaking-trumpet ran upward as the sails were adjusted by the crew aloft, and deck-teams hauled away and cursed the men-at-arms of the Protector's Guard and the kilted ranks of the High Queen's Archers who crowded into their working-space.

Órlaith could look down from the quarterdeck through a hatchway and into a part of the ordered confusion of sweating backs heaving at the levers of the hydraulic pumps that cocked the massive springs of the throwing weapons. Now they rushed to the other broadside as if the shrill twittering of the bosun's pipe were playing directly on their nervous systems, adding to the slight canting of the deck. Behind them the port-side catapult-ports slammed shut like so many doors, sending the gun-deck into darkness for an instant before the ones on the starboard snapped open and threw their shafts of light into the gloom.

The catapult-captains were gingerly laying the fireballs in the troughs of their machines with swift cautious motions, using tools like a giant version of kitchen-tongs to lift globes of ceramic or thick glass filled with a sticky mixture that would cling and burn inextinguishably. Each was wrapped in skeins of cord soaked in the same to act as fuses, and the shells were carried up from the metal-lined magazines below the water-line in sets of four, encased in rectangular steel boxes that could be slammed airtight-shut.

Napalm shells on wooden ships made *everyone* safety-conscious. The hulls of the Montivallan vessels had salvaged sheet aluminum covering to protect against fire on the outside, but within it was just timber.

A uniform fourteen-fold touch from fire sticks set the wrapping around the shells afire, flickering yellow and trails of black smoke, and the gunners gripped the lanyards as the last adjustments were made to the elevation and traverse wheels. They watched as the officer at the ladder in the rear sounded his whistle and slashed his cane down.

TUUNNNNGGG, as the springs—salvaged from the suspensions of pre-Change mining trucks—drove the paired throwing-arms forward *whap!* into the rubber-padded stops, so fast that there was no apparent time between the release and the stop, just *here* and then *there.* The frames slammed backward violently, slowed and then stopped by the hydraulic recoil cylinders that recovered the energy for the cocking mechanism, and then the pumpers were at their violent labor again. The whole was as choreographed as a ballet, and had to be, when forces of that strength were unleashed around vulnerable human flesh.

The ship shuddered again, and this time the broadside's missiles trailed smoke and fire all the way to the shore hundreds of yards away. Some burst too soon and left arcs of yellow fire in the air, but more cracked open just over the enemy's ranks and sent spraying gouts of liquid flame into their faces. More still ploughed into them and shattered and scattered burning gobbets that clung and ran down beneath armor to turn men into torches that ran and screamed and then fell to smolder and stink.

The enemy formation heaved and split, then settled down again with an almost inhuman discipline.

Or supernatural, Órlaith thought. *This is not just a contention of kings, or tribes fighting over borders like wolf packs over their hunting-runs.*

That could get bad enough; humans were a quarrelsome breed. This . . .

She laid her hand on the pommel of the Sword of the Lady, moon-crystal cradled in antlers . . . or at least something that looked like that to human eyes and felt like it to a human palm, just as the double-lobed hilt appeared to be black staghorn veined with silver and the crescent guard and the long two-edged blade looked like layer-forged steel. All might simply have been a masterpiece of the bladesmith's art, making any experienced hand long to whirl it for the joy of feeling its perfect supple balance.

But if you looked more closely, the layer-forged metal turned into recurring shapes that vanished into each other and drew your eye in and down, down and in. . . .

The Sword had been forged beyond the light of common day, to embody the land of Montival and the line of her blood. Her parents and their sworn companions had made the Quest of the Sunrise Lands a generation before, sought and fought and followed dreams and portents, to find it in a place even her father couldn't describe . . . because language itself buckled beneath the burden. He'd believed it wasn't a thing of matter at all, but a thought in the mind of the Triune Goddess given shape and form and palpable substance, a thing possible only in the modern era, after the Change began to open doors in the walls of the world that had been long closed.

It didn't give her that indefinable sense of *connection* here that it did back home in the lands and on the waters of Montival. These islands in the midst of the Mother Ocean were the domain of Powers wholly other than those she knew, wild and fierce and *strange*.

As she raised her gaze she sensed a woman-form with eyes that glowed like lava turning to look at *her*, like a ghost-wave of heat across her face. That One abode in the white-tipped blue of the mountains inland, or perhaps She *was* those mountains and the earth-fires at their hearts on all these islands born of upwelling rock meeting the sea in cataclysms of steam and flame. In the blue, blue waters alongside, a grim seaborne male-ness snatched at the land with every retreating roar of surf, rode the waves with fin and devouring shark-sharp tooth. And beyond those were others, a kaleidoscope of forms up to a terrible fourfold majesty. But They weren't unfriendly; not to her, far from it. She felt Their burning wrath that foreign men had dared to land with weapons in hand, to bring fire and killing among the folk who honored Them. Their hand was over Their people . . . and gave leave to anyone fighting alongside them against the same foe.

Above the enemy . . . a flat louring darkness, a taste of the absolute cold and motionless stasis at the end of all things, when the very atoms of being had decayed, and a stillness that hated and *hungered*. But strong, strong with a strength that had eaten the cosmos itself in other turns of the Wheel.

And the Sword *did* give her an intuitive sense of where her own people were—as if she carried all the maps and files and notes in her head, continually updated, and could recall them perfectly. The information was just *there* when she needed it, as if remembered; her father Rudi Mackenzie, the first High King, had told her that when you bore the blade forged beyond the world to war it was like having the world's best general staff living in your head. And like much of what the Sword did it was a little . . . disturbing when it popped up at the back of your mind all of a sudden. It didn't do things *for* you so much as made it possible for *you* to do things that wrung every ounce of the possible out of you, and a little more besides.

Through it she could feel what her followers felt. As any commander needed to do that and could . . . but through the Sword it came sooner, and more definitely. Fear of course, but also anger—her father had been much loved as a ruler and a man. The foe ahead were the ones who'd come to Montival and killed the High King, a gross offence to their pride and sense of themselves. Hence the grim resolve she sensed, a driving need to avenge his blood and the realm's honor.

Better still was an iron determination not to fail comrades whose respect mattered more than life: shields locked with a file-mate whose family had the farm next to theirs, the playmate and workmate of all their years; the bow-line who were village neighbors and blood relations and initiates of the same Mystery; the men-at-arms who had proudly knelt and put hands between those of a lord and pledged loyalty unto death for all to see.

Each one knowing those who survived would return home to tell their kin of their honor or their shame.

. "The enemy are very determined, but they won't stand and take that for long," Naysmith said clinically.

The elite of her people, the Bearkillers, selected what they called their A-List for merit and trained them to think as well as fight, and the Royal Navy recruited from all Montival on the same basis.

"They'll pull back to regroup and reinforce, maybe dig in behind field fortifications once we're committed to a single landing zone and we can't keep making them run up and down the beach trying to get ahead of us anymore. But here and now they're tired and they've taken heavy losses. Hitting them immediately will cut our butcher's bill, even if our landing-troops have to fight with their feet wet, and it gives us most of the day to fight."

Órlaith glanced at the two monarchs who flanked her on the flagship's quarterdeck, King Kalākaua of Hawai'i and *Tennō Heika* Reiko of Dai-Nippon. Each gave her a very small crisp nod, which was possibly a historic record for brevity and efficiency as far as coalition warfare was concerned. Montival had the bulk of the strength, but she had to tread carefully around the pride of her allies; not just the monarchs, but those behind them who they had to heed. And both of them had things to contribute that she and the realm needed badly.

Kalākaua was a big handsome brown-skinned young man of a few years more than her mid-twenties, glistening with coconut oil and lightly garbed in stout strapped sandals, a scarlet-and-yellow malo loincloth twisted around his waist and ending in a panel before and behind, and a short semicircular cape of the same color. He wore a light armor jacket of coconut-fiber woven with stainless-steel strands, similar guards on his muscled forearms, and a crest of yellow feathers across his round helm from brow to neck. There was a heavy nine-foot battle-spear in his hand, a short chopping sword and knife at his waist, and he was raging-eager to punish this attack on his people.

And she knew from things he'd said how bitterly he regretted all the sweat and toil lost as well as the lives—resettling an Oahu devastated and depopulated when the Change stopped the world-machine had been a work he and his father had pushed at all their lives. Much would have to be done over again, after the waste of war.

She thought Reiko had the slightest ghost of a smile on her lips as well, or perhaps only in her narrow dark eyes. Her left hand rested on the hilt of *Kusanagi-no-Tsurugi* tucked through the sash that girt her set of *Tosei-gusoku* composite armor, a new design that drew heavily on the legacy of the Sengoku, the Age of Battles. Two of her samurai stood by ready to hand her the flared seven-plate kabuto helmet with the chrysanthemum *mon* on its brow, or the long *higoyumi* bow and *naginata*; altogether she looked like some *kami* of war from her people's long, long past, down to the fact that her five-foot-six made her as towering for a Nihonjin woman as Órlaith was among her own people.

She'd recovered the lost Imperial sword, one of the three great treasures of her dynasty, with Órlaith's help . . . very personal help, since it had been only the two of them at the last, there in the haunted castle in its little bubble of otherness in the Valley of Death. Órlaith had held the doorway and Reiko fought within against perils not altogether of this world to reclaim a plundered inheritance brought there in the great wars of the last century. *Absorbing* the shattered fragments of the Grasscutter from within the bodies of her enemies and into her Masamune heirloom sword as it cut her foes down, to make the sacred Imperial blade anew in a different form.

Which is rather grisly, when you think about it. And if I find custom and ceremony irksome . . . for Reiko going back to it after a taste of freedom must be like being buried in living cement, though she'll never complain. My dynasty began with my mother and my father; hers is thousands of years old and claims to have been started by the son of the Sun Goddess Amaterasu-ōmikami . . . and that claim may be literally true. Cer-

tainly the Immortal One Shining In Heaven reached down and claimed her, that day on the beach at Topanga.

They were close friends, as far as their respective obligations allowed. They were of an age, and they had shared things no others did, starting with the fact that their fathers had been slain by the same enemy within an hour of each other. And going on to what they both bore at their waists, in shapes that only seemed to be steel. The Grasscutter had its own powers, and they'd both seen them. . . .

"Admiral, I think the assault wave should go in now?" Órlaith asked, a little rhetorically.

Admiral Naysmith snapped her telescope shut and meditatively raised a fist to her lips, touching them for a moment to a ring that bore three interlinked triangles in a knot.

"My thoughts exactly, Your Highness," she said, nodding slowly.

Sometimes I feel a bit irked when she's surprised I'm doing the right thing. Yes, I am a lot younger, but I was raised and educated by the people who won the Prophet's War, Admiral Grim-All-Business, with the Valknut on your ring. Why is it that people who follow a God who's a notorious trickster are usually so . . . so serious? The Thurstons out in Boise are that way too. But it's a party every night in Valhöll. To be fair, those among the Bearkillers and Boiseans who are Christians are like that too.

Bearkillers tended to think that Mackenzies were incurably light-minded, and that Associates were playactors too concerned with dressing up in fancy garb and ancient titles to be taken entirely seriously. They were like Boiseans that way, only more so. Órlaith qualified in both categories, in a way, even if she was a niece to their Bear Lord—he was her father's half-brother, on the other side of the blanket.

And I do carry the Sword of the Lady.

"Signals, my compliments to General Thurston, and pass the order to the first wave to commence the assault as per the operational plan," Naysmith said. "All warships, prepare to elevate to maximum range to avoid friendly fire when we have boots on the beach, but not before, and then to cease fire on order."

The flags moved again, and far above them the kite-rider released a grenade that trailed bright-red smoke all the way down, visible for miles . . . and to all the ships where eyes were kept constantly on that dot in the sky, connected to the repeater frigate by a long curve of cable. Nothing would happen immediately. There was a lot of waiting in war, another irritating instance of what her elders had told her turning out to be true.

You want the waiting to be over. Then it is, and you don't.

"Oh, I think I recognize that expression you're wearing," a voice murmured behind her.

It ran beneath the background noise of the crowded ship, everything from the creak of flexing timber and the thrum of wind in the rigging to the hundredfolds slapping of the crews' bare feet and the constant ratcheting clatter of the catapult pumps and the shanties the crews chanted in unison, like a surf that never ended. That meant you could have a fairly private conversation, if you were careful. Anyone who'd grown up in a tight-packed village learned to speak that way, or gave up any hope of privacy, and it was worse around Court and castles and manors where your rank made everyone want to eavesdrop on you all the time.

Nobles learn the jailhouse whisper as sure as convicts do.

The voice went on in the slightly staccato accent of the north-country; you could close your eyes and know the speaker had been born after the Change, in Association territory and not far from Portland.

"It's the expression my liege's family gets on their faces when they're about to do something very *brave* and very *noble* and very very *stupid*."

That was Lady Heuradys d'Ath, her sworn knight, Chief of Household and girlhood friend. Órlaith looked over her shoulder, which involved rotating herself a bit at the hips when wearing a suit of plate with the bevoir that shielded jaw and chin in place and laced tightly to her breastplate. Especially when the four-foot elongated teardrop shape of a knight's shield was slung over her back point-down.

Heuradys d'Ath already had hers on her arm, ready to sweep between Órlaith and harm, blazoned with the arms of Ath—*sable, a delta or on a V argent*—quartered below Órlaith's crowned mountain and sword crossed with the baton of cadency. She was two years older than Órlaith's quarter-century, and stood an inch shorter than the Crown Princess' five-foot-eleven, with amber eyes and dark-auburn hair, her regular features a little blunter than Órlaith's chiseled looks.

As she spoke she held out Órlaith's helmet, with the arming-cap and gauntlets in it; strictly speaking that was squire's work, but they'd never stood on formality. Órlaith sighed and pulled the knit wool and chamois leather of the cap over her braids, drew on the gauntlets and gave a slap of fists into opposite palm to settle them. Then she took the helm and settled it firmly and fastened the chin-cup and straps; the constriction of the felt-and-sponge pads around and on top of her head infinitely familiar, and she began the slight automatic motion of the head every so often that compensated for the way the sides of the broad sallet cut into her peripheral vision.

It was much worse with the visor down, of course, but then you were covered from the crown of your head to your toes. It didn't make you invulnerable, but it did limit the feasible targets on your body very sharply. At close range there was nothing in the world more dangerous than a knight who knew their business, and nothing harder to stop.

"Da never hung back from a fight," Órlaith said to her. "Are we going to have this conversation *again?*"

Heuradys helmed herself likewise and flicked the visor up with one gauntleted finger so that it shaded her face like the bill of a baseball cap. Her suit was of the same rare alloy and matchless craft from the Crown workshops, a gift given for her knighting and a signal mark of favor. Even the Crown Princess hadn't gotten one until she reached her full growth.

"By the Dog of Egypt, we most certainly are! Yes, he never hung back . . . and he died only a couple of decades older than you are now, leading the charge in a skirmish," Heuradys added with a bluntness few others would have dared.

They both had tall sprays of feathers mounted on either side of their helms, Golden Eagle for Órlaith since that was the sept-totem that had appeared to her on her vigil, by the Mackenzie custom she followed; her visor was drawn out a little and had the point curved to suggest a beak when it was down. Heuradys had northern Snowy Owl plumes of black-flecked white in the same place, and their like etched thinly into the surface of her helm, to mark the Goddess to Whom she gave her first worship.

Associate nobles were mostly Catholic Christians, like Órlaith's own mother and half her siblings, but *mostly* wasn't the same as *all*. Half the d'Ath family were pagans, and considered eccentric in other respects as well.

"It was by treachery *after* the skirmish he died, coming between me and the knife," Órlaith said. "And there was a prophecy he wouldn't live to see his beard go gray."

The smaller details of her father's death didn't alter the general point. Heuradys had been there too . . . and she had loved him, too, both as a long-time honorary uncle, as her family's patron and her personal benefactor, and as her King. Órlaith forced a warrior's lightness in the face of death into her tone. That too was part of grieving.

"And that prophecy was given him by Gangleri the Wanderer."

In a dream when he slept in a cave on the Quest, out in the Sunrise Lands, she thought

"Oh, a *prophecy* from a *god* that he'd fall in battle before he was old," Heuradys said. "That was like needing divine intervention to tell you that the sun would *probably* rise in the east next Friday. And you're the same way. He was the best master of the blade I've ever seen—even better than my Mom Two—"

Who was known as *Lady Death*, in a pun on her title of Baroness d'Ath. She'd been one of Rudi Mackenzie's tutors in his youth; in fact, Tiphaine d'Ath had been ennobled and endowed by the first Lord Protector of the Portland Protective Association when she captured Rudi and held him hostage for a while as a child, during the Association Wars, before the High Kingdom was formed. Órlaith had heard Lady D'Ath say that Heuradys was as good with a blade as she'd been in her prime . . . though she'd never said it *to* Heuradys, because, as she put it, vanity was a leading cause of death.

The scolding went on: "—But as the wise man said, even Hercules can't fight two, and a random crossbow bolt through your visor-slit is no respecter of persons and doesn't care how good you are with a sword . . . even *that* sword. Here's a *prophecy* from a mere humble worshipper of Athana: you won't make old bones either if you don't remember that a monarch is supposed to *command*. You've got plenty of people . . . people like me . . . to do the hack-and-slash."

"I'm not reckless!"

"Remember how you had us steal a sack of ramen and run away at night so we could set out on a Quest to find the Superman in his Solitary Fortress of Ice at the north pole . . . when you were *eight*? Gray-Eyed One witness I knew in my heart it was dumb even then, but you always could talk the birds from the trees or a honeycomb from a bear. And you're just as good at convincing *yourself* that it's a splendid idea to do what you want."

"No harm done that time, sure."

"So you *don't* remember the trouble we got in after Bow-Captain Edain dragged us back by the ears?"

In point of fact Órlaith *did* vividly remember how sick she'd gotten of ramen, which had been served up for her dinner every single day until the sack they'd filched from the Guard armory was finished, and by then she retched at the sight and smell of it. The stuff still repulsed her.

"It'll be the First of Never and two days more before you let me forget that little bit of mischief, am I right?"

"I'm going to have it put on my gravestone, along with, *Here lies Lady Heuradys d'Ath, peerless knight, who died shouting bitterly:* It's all your fault you mad bitch! *at her BFF.*"

"And you yourself being so timid, Herry dear."

Heuradys raised one eyebrow. "I'm your household knight and heir-vavasour to three quite theoretical manors out in the Palouse with nothing on them yet but a few peasant families and about six thousand sheep munching on bunchgrass and crapping wherever they please. *You're* the heir to Montival. It's just a bit of a bigger responsibility."

"And I have four siblings after me. . . ."

"Three if you don't count the one who managed to get washed out to sea and is She-knows-where."

"Four siblings, so there's more than one spare wheel to the dynastic wagon . . . *There they go!*"

The assault battalions finished clambering over the rails and down the nets on the sides of the transports, and the barges pushed off with a row of oars flashing like the legs of a salt-water centipede on either side; there were local pilots in each, fishermen and sailors born with a foot in these waters and an instinctive feel for them. But the crews and the troops were her people, come here at her call, and she bared her teeth with the aching need to be with them and share their peril.

Not yet, not yet; Herry's right that far. The monarch doesn't charge at the forefront more than once per battle and that at the crucial point, she thought. *I can feel them, through the Sword . . . can they feel me with them? Yes, at some level, I think so . . . the veterans all swear that in the Prophet's War they could sense Da's hand on their shoulders somehow.*

Heuradys handed her a pair of binoculars and she leveled them, adjusting the focus and compensating for the ship's roll. The first wave was a brigade of heavy infantry from the United States of Boise, in what the old world had called Idaho. Some very conservative elderly people there still called it simply the United States *of America*, though the Thurston line of Generals-President had quietly abandoned that claim when they swore allegiance to Rudi Mackenzie. Fred Thurston, their current ruler, had been with her father on the Quest in a complex sequence of events that had involved his elder brother in parricide and usurpation . . . and probably demonic possession.

The Boiseans wore armor of bands and hoops of steel plate joined by polished brass clasps, helmets with flared neck-guards and bills over the eyes like jockey caps and hinged cheek-guards, big curved oval shields in their left hands and heavy javelins with long iron shanks behind the points in their right. An officer was the first to leap down as the barges grounded in near-unison, shin-deep in the low surf; you could tell his rank by the stiff upright crest of red hair from a horse's mane mounted across his helmet from ear to ear and the vine-stock swagger stick in his hand. Beside him was a standard-bearer with a wolfskin cloak and the flayed head of the animal snarling above his brow, who was carrying a tall staff with the Stars and Stripes below a spread-winged gilded eagle.

He was too far away for Órlaith to hear what he shouted, but she could hear the answering call from his troops: a long deep guttural snarling:

"HOOOOOOOORRRAAHHH!"

It carried as well as a drumbeat, and stirred something primal that coiled under her breastbone and made the little hairs on the back of her neck try to stand under the constriction of her arming-doublet.

As they gave the Republic's battle cry they leapt over the bows and sides of the barges, some of them neck-deep as they waded shoreward with their shields and javelins held over their heads. A few had to be rescued by their comrades and crawled ashore coughing, heaving and spitting up seawater, but the rest formed up quickly, crouching with shields up and covering them from eyes to the greaves on their shins. They needed to be; despite the constant stream of roundshot and bolts going by overhead, arrows were already coming back from the enemy ranks, standing quivering in the sheet-metal facings of the plywood shields marked with a black stenciled spread-wing eagle and crossed thunderbolts. More shafts came every moment, and the Korean forces used a powerful composite bow of horn and sinew. Here and there a man fell still or writhing, an arrow in face or arm or thigh showing you could meet your own personal ill-fate regardless of how the battle went overall. The rear ranks dragged them out of the way and back to the stretcher-bearers and medics and merciful morphine, and a new man stepped into each vacant place with stolid speed.

Another order, this one carried by the hoarse screaming of brass *cornu*, coiled trumpets Boisean signalers wore like sashes. She'd known the Boisean battle-calls even before the Sword came to her—that one meant *form standing testudo*.

The front rank went to one knee with their javelins point out and butts stamped into the sand, shields braced on the ground edge-to-edge like a wall bristling with spines; the second rank held their shields up to make the wall more than man-high, and the third and fourth snapped theirs up overhead to form a roof. The whole took mere seconds, in a rippling unison like a living machine, and full of a deadly menace and promise.

More arrows sleeted down on them, but the formation stood. Just offshore now were more barges, keeping station as the empty ones threaded through and headed back out to load more troops. That second wave was full of archers in kilts and light open-faced sallet helms and green brigandines marked with a silver waxing crescent moon between black stag-antlers.

"Oh, the kilties do love to sing and chant," Heuradys said; those were the Clan Mackenzie's archers. "It's a pity they're too crowded to do a sword-dance first. They'd rather dance than fight any day . . . well, so would I."

Behind her Karl Aylward Mackenzie and his brother Mathun—young men now of her household, and alike clansmen from Dun Fairfax—made small rude noises as they leaned on the cased staves of longbows made of yellow mountain yew from the Cascades, taller than a tall man and still unstrung, with grips and risers of black-walnut root and tipped with nocks carved from elk antler. The others in the small band of Mackenzies they led sniggered quietly.

One of them—Órlaith didn't turn her head to see which, for dignity's sake, but the voice was female, she thought Boudicca Lopez Mackenzie— began to murmur along with the men and women raising their bows closer to shore, and she could feel her wish to be there like the tension on a drawn bowstring:

"We are the point
We are the edge—
We are the wolves that Hecate fed!

We are the bow
We are the shaft—
We are the darts that Hecate cast!"

Not even Mackenzies, who were a people of the bow and raised to it all their lives, could shoot accurately from a barge rolling in the low waves near shore. They didn't have to—their target was a black mass of thousands of men and spearpoints drawn up in plain sight and only about a hundred paces away . . . and there were thousands of the clansfolk, too. Thousands of the clothyard arrows flew upward at a forty-five degree angle for maximum range. They slowed to the top of their arch, twinkled slightly like stars on a rippling night-time sea as the honed edges of the heads caught the sunlight when they turned, and plunged point-down towards the enemy formation with a rushing whistle that was audible even here.

It didn't end, either, continuing like the sound of steady rain on a tile roof, punctuated by a multifold hail-drum as the points struck shields and helmets, armor and dirt . . . and human flesh. The enemy staggered under the blow and began to crumple, like a sandcastle in rain.

"*Maith thú*, and doubly well done! Good shooting!" Karl said. "*Mackenzie abú!*"

Another volley and another rose, regular as a metronome, until six or seven were in the air at the same time, and twelve left the strings in the first sixty seconds alone. At that angle a longbow shaft of dense straight-grain Port Orford cypress-wood from an old-growth tree, with a head beaten, cut and ground from the head of a pre-Change stainless-steel spoon, was moving three-quarters as fast when it hit as it had when it left the string . . . and that was very fast indeed.

In the old wars with the Association, charges of knights had been stopped dead in their tracks by that arrow-storm. And at the Battle of the Horse Heaven Hills the death-sworn fanatics of the Prophet's red-armored elite guard had died in windrows before the Clan's section of the battle line, men and horses piled four-deep, weakening them crucially for the charge that broke the power of the Church Universal and Triumphant forever. The Koreans weren't nearly as heavily armored as either of those foes had been.

"*Nock . . . draw wholly together . . . let the gray geese fly . . . Loose! Nock . . .*" one of the clansfolk behind her murmured.

That echoed what the bow-captains in the barges would be shouting. Mackenzies prided themselves on being a free people, with no lords but the Chief of the line of Juniper Mackenzie they hailed themselves, governed by their assemblies where any crofter or crafter could stand and vote and speak their mind to anyone, including the Mackenzie Herself Herself. One of the reasons that boast was largely true was that anyone in the *dúthchas* could cut a dozen yew staves in a single autumn day and put them to season in the rafters of their cottage, and a year later a skilled bowyer could turn that seasoned stave into a longbow in an afternoon at modest cost. Long chill, rainy winter afternoons in the Black Months were often spent making arrows.

Naysmith made a gesture with her telescope: "Ships to cease fire."

The clamor of the broadsides ended, a stillness running down the line of battle from *Sea-Leopard* to *Wave-Witch*. In that—relative—silence another brass snarl from the *cornu* rang clear, and the Boiseans began to move forward, opening up their formation into a checkerboard, boots pounding in unison and right hands cocked back with the javelins—the pila—leveled until they were thirty paces from the foe.

Then at another signal each of the front line took a skipping sideways step and threw. The heavy spears flew out in flat arcs at close range, their narrow heads slamming into bodies and faces and penetrating armor of lacquered leather and steel lamellae like a metalsmith's hammer-driven punch. Where they hit the heavy square shields with hard *crack* sounds they slammed through the outer layers of hide and wood, and then the shanks of soft iron bent to let the wooden shafts drag on the ground, making the shields useless . . . and making it impossible to pull them out and throw them back. She could see the enemy making that nasty discovery themselves, shaking their shields or wrestling and hammering at the embedded weapons while their officers screamed at them to keep ranks.

"USA! USA!"

A huge unified crashing bark from the whole Boisean brigade, and the front rank snapped out the short leaf-shaped thrusting-swords worn high on their right sides and charged at the run with shields advanced. The rows behind threw in sequence, three thousand spears in thirty seconds, then moved up behind their comrades in the dance of the maniples; taking spear-thrusts on their big shields, their helmets and shoulder-armor shedding the overarm slashes that the enemy's point-heavy sabers delivered, punching the shield-bosses into faces like a twenty-pound set of brass knuckles and smashing the steel-shod lower edges down into feet hard enough to snap bone or into a fallen enemy's neck to finish him. Crowding close and stabbing, stabbing, stabbing at face or groin or gut or armpit, sometimes bending under a shield held like a roof to aim a hocking backhand cut at an enemy's ankle or knee.

Officer's whistles trilled, and the front rank stepped back as the second rank stepped forward sword in hand to replace them, letting the tired men at the enemy's forefront face opponents who were always fresh. The effect was rather like the endless teeth of a circular saw in a water-powered timber mill ripping into one log of tough wood after another.

Though wood doesn't scream in quite that way . . . Órlaith thought.

Behind them the barges bearing the Mackenzies moved in and grated on the sand of the beach, and the whooping clansfolk leapt free, holding their precious bows and quivers overhead.

The savage wail of the bagpipes sounded then; the pipers of each contingent playing the skirling menace of "Hecate's Wolves Their Howl" in unison as they assembled on the beach. Lambeg drums began their inhuman hammer and the tall upright carnyx horns bellowed through mouths shaped like the heads of boar and wolf and tiger. True howls and ululating banshee shrieks ran louder still from contorted faces painted for war in jagged designs, sept totems or sheer fancy in red and black and green and yellow.

Some of them *did* dance a wild whirling step or two as they landed, or just flipped up the rear of their kilt and slapped their buttocks in the enemy's direction.

Those on board tossed loads of fresh arrows down in a rain of thirty-two shaft bundles before the sailors pushed off and started back out. The archers shook themselves out into their bands by Dun and sept or oath-bond, trotting up with wolfish springy strides to spread out on the flanks of the heavy infantry. This time they delivered aimed fire at close range, slower but even more deadly, with the eye-punching accuracy of lifelong practice, and *eóghann*—helpers, teenage apprentices not yet old enough for the bow-line—ran back and forth with bundles of shafts, or got the wounded to the rear and began first aid beside the healers.

From about the age of six on, Mackenzies shot at the marks most days, for training and the public pride of making a good score. More, they rarely set foot outside their villages—*duns* in Clan dialect—without a bow in hand and a quiver on their back, because they hunted even more often for food and hides and fur. And to protect their crops and orchards and truck gardens from the nibbling hosts of deer and elk and boar and rabbit and bird, and their livestock and children from the hunger of wolf and cougar and tiger the year-round, in a world where humans and their tame fields and beasts were scarce again, and unpeopled forests and marshes and savannas many and broad.

Órlaith nodded, feeling what her folk did, knowing what they knew.

"It's time," she said. "Admiral Naysmith, send in the rest of the force— we have enough of a perimeter now not to get tangled up."

A question was in the glance she got, and she explained:

"The enemy is bringing their first wave of reserves forward to try and push the Boiseans back into the sea by main weight while they're fully engaged."

Then she looked at her allies, and back at her handfast Household companions. "And let's get going ourselves."

CHAPTER TWO

CHOSŎN MINJUJUŬI INMIN KONGHWAGUK
(KOREA)
NOVEMBER 1ST
CHANGE YEAR 47/2045 AD

Fighting depraved cannibals ruled by evil sorcerers was something all their neighbors had an interest in. The Khökh-Khan of Mongolia was not the least of those.

Prince Dzhambul, son of Kha-Khan Qutughtu of the clan of the Borjigin—which made him a descendant of the great Temujin, not that half the world couldn't say that—reflected that being a Prince wasn't all that some people thought it was, particularly when your uncle disliked you and commanded the army in which you were serving. And, some said, or privately thought, he would be a better successor to the Kha-Khan than you would; the position was elective, within the line of Royal descent.

For example, if you're a prince in those boots you may get sent on a long-range scouting mission that may end up behind enemy lines, he thought.

It was snowing a little, hard granular flecks out of a low gray sky that made him blink when he turned his head northward and caught in his thin young-man's mustache and beard and made him glad he'd greased his face this morning. The ground was still mostly covered in dirty white and frozen hard, though it was early in the season for it, and he thought he smelled a change in the weather under the dry mealy scent of the snow. His horse snorted with resignation and turned a little under him, to get its nostrils out of the direction the snow was coming from.

He watched the top of the barren hill for the scout's signal, one booted foot cocked over the leather-sheathed arched wood of his saddle's pommel. He'd been up long enough that the stiffness of sleeping on cold ground wrapped in a cloak had worn off and he'd beaten all the bits of ice out of his wolf-fur lined coat before he put on his mail and ate a bowl of hot rice gruel, but it was still early morning.

Behind him there was a *wheep-wheep* of someone sharpening something, and the restless hollow clatter of unshod horse-hooves as stationary mounts shifted their weight, the creak of harness, the snap of a pennant on a lance, someone making a low-voiced invocation to *Sülde Tengri*, who was a war God but also the Ancestor, Genghis, and who dwelt in the *tugh* war banner:

"My Sülde who is without fear,
You who become the armor for my body,
Though it be threatened by ten thousand enemies—"

Mostly they kept a disciplined silence. Though he reflected wryly that if the wind were wrong the enemy might smell them coming, rank man-sweat and horse-sweat soaked into felt and cloth and leather; contrary to what foreigners thought, Mongols *did* wash when that was practical. In the field it wasn't and he hadn't noticed warriors of any other nation smelling much sweeter, including the Han who were always going on about their superior civilization.

Maybe that's why we keep beating them—we talk less, but we hit harder.

He waited with the stolid patience of a hunter and a herdsman, holding his helmet on his boot, though inwardly his stomach was clenching a bit at the thought of the weight of his decisions. This scouting mission wasn't a major operation, but there were still two hundred men depending on *him*, and the army needed the information they were gathering.

This little valley had grown maize in the year past, with some broken stalks still showing, and the remount herd were nosing at the ground, occasionally scraping with their hooves. They were down to three remounts per man, but the beasts were in good condition, since they'd looted enough grain to supplement the meager pasture since they crossed the Yalu. A huddled village of mud-and-stone shacks with one slightly better hovel for its supervisor stood about four long bowshots eastward, behind him.

The people had all fled before the Mongols arrived, and there had been nothing but a few chickens and the grain in pits, and the place was too filthy to use—and probably haunted by hungry ghosts and unclean spirits, anyway. Some of the remounts had sacks of the dried grain slung over their backs, half a rider's weight so as not to slow or tire them, others had reserve gear, mostly bundles of arrows. Scouting missions traveled light. They'd shoveled the rest of the corn out and thrown it into the cesspits or into the street and ridden the horses over it.

Beyond that, eastward, were low hills growing to mountains, mostly covered in scrub that might be forest someday; you could tell they'd been stripped bare of anything that would burn before the Change, and then soil had washed down in gullies. Dzhambul had never seen a country so bare of life, hardly even any small birds and scuttling marmots and the like, and it looked as if it had been even worse a generation ago. He thought the peasants were probably up there, watching and waiting for the armed men to leave.

Then there was the long hogback hill ahead of him, and a larger plain of farmland with more mountains westward beyond it, but far enough that they were on the edge of sight even from up there. Most of the plain was divided into rectangular enclosures by low baulks of earth, a sign it was planted in rice most years. Dzhambul hated campaigning in rice country, because it was so hard on the horses.

This country has too many mountains, he thought; on a map the flat places were like the veins on an old man's hand. *The rest is like a piece of paper you crumple and throw down.*

The signal came with a *blink* of light from a flame held before a hand-mirror, and he swung his foot down into the stirrup, took off his sheep-skin hat and put on his helmet, a steel bowl drawn up into a peak in the center with a horse-hair plume rising from that and falling down the back, and a neck-guard and hinged cheek-pieces of boiled leather covered in rows of small metal rings, salvaged stainless-steel washers of the highest quality. He tied the cheek-pieces together under his chin and gave the men a quick look. All was ready.

"The Ancestor is with us! Now! Forward!" he barked.

He stirred his horse into motion with thighs and balance, pulling his bow out of its case and an arrow from the quiver slung to the left side of his belt. Beside him rode his bannerman. The *tugh* battle standard had a spike on the end of the pole, with a curved U shape below it, points up, for the *Munkh Khukh Tengri*, the Eternal Blue Sky, and two horse tails dangling from it.

Which was far too grand for a command of only a few hundred horsemen. His uncle Toktamish had granted him that honor for the sake of their common blood—he was punctilious about the symbols of respect, if not the substance.

The *Miqačin* enemy—the word meant *man-eating ogre*, more or less—was still strung out in column on the other side of the shallow stream that ran from the north along the edge of the flat country. The Mongol force rounded the south side of the hill at the trot, spread out into a four-deep line and spurred into a pounding gallop towards them; it was much easier to hide here south of the Yalu than it was in most of the Mongol homeland, or even in the tributary parts of Manchuria he'd seen, but the mountains mostly just got in the way of large-scale campaigning.

The man-eaters were about his own numbers: he had two *zuun*—hundred-man squadrons—here with him, both at nearly full strength. The enemy was all mounted, too . . . and the *Miqačin* might eat men, worship evil spirits, and practice any number of other abominations, but they bred good horses. The enemy formation churned, and then turned to face his charge. It looked as though they expected him to barrel right over the stream—which had chunks of ice in it and a gravel bed—and go up the bank to smack into them; they had their swords out and/or spears leveled, there at the edge of the water. They didn't do as well at picking up Mongol plans as they once had; the shamans said it was because their evil spirits were weakened.

He grinned to himself: *That is going to spare my men and cost them*, and shouted—

"Flank turn right," to his bannerman. "Now!"

The horse tails went up, turned and swooped. The Mongol column broke right, turning their horses in the beasts' own length at the gallop; it was like a herd moving by itself, or a flock of birds, a rippling unison. He brought his bow up, locked his thumb-ring around the string and exhaled hard as he drew and the long bone siyah-ears on the ends of the stave levered against the horn and birchwood and sinew of the ten-strength bow—the draw-weight was two-thirds that of his own body on a scale, and he wasn't a small man.

The recoil pushed him back, in the always slightly surprising way it had when you were shooting well. Before the shaft struck a sleet of arrows was in the air, with others following it, arching up in a shallow curve and then down. Some came back, but most of the man-eaters had their bows cased and it took a moment to get them out—they weren't bad archers, but they were a bit slow. By the time they were all ready there were half a dozen empty saddles in Dzhambul's command, and ten times that many among them . . . and the Mongol force had simply galloped northward out of range.

"Cross left in column and deploy in line," he called.

The banner moved again. Dzhambul turned his horse and slowed to a trot, the column went through the stream in a froth of spray and ice, cold even through the sheep-grease rubbed on his face. Dzhambul reined aside to let the first *zuun* pass him, keeping his position in the middle of the line where everyone could see the commands, then turned to lead as they trotted towards the enemy and sped up to a gallop when he did. Everyone took their pace from him.

His stomach had settled completely; it always did in action. Waiting was hard, especially because you must show complete confidence, and afterwards he hated losing men and couldn't stop himself thinking about their wives and children and parents, but during a fight it was like dancing.

The banner moved, and they turned south and opened their formation up into the shape of a scythe-blade heavier on the right and charged, shooting as they came, forward over their horses' heads. Dzhambul shot three times himself, always picking that floating moment when all four of the animal's feet were off the ground. A black-fletched arrow went *whippt* past his face, and another *crack* into the tough larch-wood of the banner's pole. Then suddenly there were men in spiked helmets with snarls on their faces shockingly close. Snarls and scars, not just battle marks but sometimes an ear removed or a lip or the tip of a nose, those were standard punishments among the *Miqačin*. He cased his bow—one bending downward movement dropped it into the open mouth of the lacquered-leather shape—slapped his left hand onto the single grip of the small round shield hung to the outside of it, and swept out his saber as he came upright again.

Doing that fast at a gallop was a sport among his people, and he'd been good at it even as a boy.

"*UUUUUUUKHAI!*" the Mongols roared, a deep sound from the belly, like *Kargyraa* throat-singing but louder.

"*Juche! Juche!*" the man-eaters shouted back.

Their formation was loose, still disorganized from the losses they'd taken in the exchange of arrows. Maybe they'd lost officers, and the man-eaters never reacted well to that. The Mongol right swung around them, the outer part of the horn still using their bows and peppering their backs. Dzhambul put that out of his mind, since it seemed to be taking care of itself. An enemy swung at him and he swayed aside and to the left in the saddle, his point slamming up under the man's chin as he went past—you never had time for more than a stroke or two in this sort of melee.

A horse standing still in battle has a fool sitting on it, as the old saying went.

He twisted the curved sword without looking back, and punched at another *dao*-blade with his shield as a man-eater swung at his head. It banged off, hurting his left wrist, and he cut the man across the face—the thin bones there crunched under the edge and the other fell with a bubbling scream. Then one just too far away for him to use a saber on was drawing back a lance for an overarm thrust. Dzhambul set himself, but before the man could strike a Mongol right behind him shot him in the lower back, the arrow punching through his leather-and-metal armor to stand feather-deep, with the point coming out his belly.

The lancer dropped his weapon, shrieked like a woman in childbirth, and fell. The Mongol trooper grinned, and then whooped as he looked around. Mounted fights were like that, you were hammering away and suddenly one side or another was running. This time it was the enemy, scattering in all directions like drops of water skidding across greased leather in a high wind. The *zuun*-commanders were yelling for pursuit, and parties of his men went after the man-eaters, always three or four to one, and shooting rather than trying to close—you could point a bow backward over the rump of your horse, but it wasn't as easy as shooting forward. And getting into a long exchange of arrows with Mongols was not something other people usually did well.

Other troopers were carefully putting arrows into the *Miqačin* wounded on the ground from a safe distance; they were as dangerous as rabid dogs, and Mongols prided themselves on being a practical people. Still others rounded up the enemy horses, recovered arrows, and looted anything useful or valuable; one grimaced and held up a smoked human hand and forearm from a saddlebag before throwing it aside and wiping his hand. A few of the younger men gulped and looked queasy.

Fighting the man-eaters has advantages, Dzhambul thought. *Burning the Han out of the southern marches beyond the Gobi is a grisly business by comparison.*

It had to be done, the Kha-Khan was right about that; the farmers from the south had taken those lands once called Inner Mongolia from his people, the *Yeke Mongghol Ulus,* in the generations before the Time of the Change when they were strong. Turning it back into pasture for the clans was needful.

The Han had suffered far more in the Time of the Change than his folk, who even then had been mostly herdsmen who lived in *ger* among their pastures, not city dwellers or even farmers dependent on machines and the dikes along the great rivers. China was a wreck, seven or eight in ten of its inhabitants had died since the Change, maybe more. Whereas there were probably more Mongols now than fifty years ago, which wasn't something any other people he knew of could say. Even so, there were so *many* Han, and they wouldn't be weak and divided forever. They had to be pushed back as far as possible while it still *was* possible.

But fighting the man-eaters is a pleasure by comparison—harder, but a pleasure.

His hundred-commanders came up as he removed his helmet—wearing them for a long time always gave him a vile headache, for some reason—and ran his hand over his hair, feeling the stubble catch in the calluses of his palm. He also preferred the traditional style, shaven except for a roach above the brow and enough over the ears to fall in braids to his shoulders. The cold struck the sweat and seemed to make the iron band around his brow go away. He became conscious of the cut-off scream of a wounded horse put down, and the nasty stinks of a battle, like the latrine-field of a herding camp too long in one place, but just after you butchered a yak too.

Gansükh had a light axe thonged to his wrist, which he preferred to a saber, possibly because his name meant *Steel Axe*. He was wiping it as he spoke his report, a stocky cheerful man. Arban was lanky and as tall as Dzhambul's above-average five-foot-eight and never said a word when he didn't have to, possibly because *his* name meant *eloquent*.

Prompted by the sight, Dzhambul pulled a cloth out of his belt and cleaned his sword, checking for nicks. It was a gift from his father when he came of age, and a fine weapon of layer-forged alloy steel, broad and well-balanced, with a very slightly flared hatchet point.

"Very well done, Noyon," Gansükh said, and Arban nodded and grunted agreement as they both bowed.

Dzhambul's face was stone, but the sound of approval made him want to grin. Both the veteran *zuun* commanders were five or six years older than he, and while they deferred to his birth their professional respect was well worth having. Gansükh gave the details:

"We killed a hundred and thirty, maybe a hundred and forty of them before we called off the pursuit; we took a hundred and ten unwounded horses, another twenty worth taking along that we can eat if they don't recover, and the other loot."

The *Miqačin* made excellent swords and bows and fairly good armor, to much the same patterns as Mongols save for details. Their common people lived worse than any herdsman would treat a goat, and were used by their rulers quite literally like goats or sheep or possibly as Han peasants raised pigs, but they had some fine artisans somewhere, as good as the Han or the Uyghurs and better than the Russki. And some of them carried gold. It didn't make up for the fact that they had little livestock to raid, but it helped keep the men's spirits up.

"Losses?"

"Ten dead; a dozen wounded fit to ride but not fight. Four wounded who can't ride."

Dzhambul grunted a little. That meant the mercy-knife, and he never delegated that task, if a man wanted it from him. He was still relieved when Arban shook his head, meaning that they'd chosen to receive it from their own *zuun* commanders or from a kinsman or oath-brother. Or were unconscious.

"And—" Gansükh began, then stopped.

Their heads came up. The outer ring of scouts the Mongol force had automatically set up were raising a cry:

"*Yip-yip-yip*—"

That was the alarm call, and it was coming from the north. Dzhambul uncased his binoculars and looked that way. The snow had gotten a little heavier and there was no dust from the winter ground here, but he could see that it was a dozen riders and maybe six remounts on leading reins. And from the way they rode . . .

"Mongols," he said. "Mongols in a hurry." Then: "Ah. It is the *Günjüü-diin Khauks*, the Princess and her Hawks."

Arban groaned slightly; Gansükh muttered something like *"Merciful Bodhisattvas, it's Börte and her hens."*

Since he wasn't looking at them and it hadn't actually been said aloud, really, Dzhambul decided to let it pass. There was still a little frost in his tone as he said:

"I will greet my kinswoman. Get the men ready to move."

"The Noyon wishes," they both said, ducking their heads.

A few minutes later his sister Börte drew up her gray Uyghur horse, which had the foam of hard riding on its neck and chest; she preferred them for their speed, though Dzhambul thought they didn't have quite the stamina of steppe ponies. There was blood on her saber.

"What are you doing here?" he said roughly; this was a very dangerous place even by the standards of a campaign on foreign ground.

"Saving your life," she said and used the blade to point behind her before she cleaned and sheathed it; there was more blood on her face, but not hers. "More *Miqačin*. North up the valley. Half a tümen at least, and all mounted and coming this way . . . coming fast, by their standards. I think they're the screen for the retreat of their main force. We ran into their forward guard and couldn't break contact. There was a running fight before we turned on them when they didn't expect it."

He grunted, as if he'd been punched in the belly. It was very bad news, but much better to know than not.

He also suppressed an impulse to say: *Are you sure?* Several of her followers were wounded, and one was bent over the cantle of her saddle with her eyes closed and a hand clasped to the stub of an arrow in her lower belly. One look said she was a dead woman, just still breathing for a while; two of her companions helped her out of the saddle, and she made no sound though she bit her lip until it bled.

He and Börte were both twenty-five winters—they were twins, in fact—though she favored their mother more than he. She had been Russki, a Cossack woman from the Ussuri Hetmanate, and Börte was as tall as he was, longer-faced, and had eyes of an odd blue-gray; not altogether unknown among their people, but fairly rare.

She wore a fine shirt of light riveted mail over her *deel* coat and her gear had seen hard use. All Mongol girls learned to ride and shoot the bow and use sword and knife and wrestle, and it was a matter of pride that they would fight like she-demons against raiders or invaders on their home range, but it was considered rather eccentric for them to ride out to make war on foreign territory like this. Usually they stayed home to tend the herds and their families, which was one reason so many Mongol men could go to war when needed.

Börte had dutifully made the marriage their father wanted to a prominent chief's son up near Lake Höwsgöl in the far north of the *ulus*, but there had been no children and her husband had died on the Kazakh marches several years ago. Currently she spat on convention and went about with a group of friends who she called her Hawks, and he had to admit they were perfectly competent at light work like this even if it was a little embarrassing. Apparently, the Khan agreed, but then he'd always indulged her; some said he spoiled her.

"Thank you, sister," he said sincerely; time counted. "We'll talk later."

He shouted for his officers, turning his back to give Börte and her band what privacy he might. She knelt beside her wounded follower while he did, and out of the corner of his eye her brother saw her hold up the knife. Two of the Hawks held the injured woman's hands in theirs, not wincing at the white-knuckled grip, and another cradled her head. The dying warrior nodded.

"Yes . . . set me . . . free to run . . . with the Sky-Blue Wolves of Heaven," she said, carefully to avoid gasping. "I ask it . . . of my own will . . . and . . . make you clean . . . of it. I go to the wind and thunder . . . oh, Mother. . . ."

She clenched her teeth and turned her eyes to the clouds beyond which lay the Eternal Sky, and the steel flashed once.

The two officers came up with their chief subordinates. Both hissed slightly at the news.

"Split up?" Gansükh said.

It was the standard response. You fought when you had the advantage, and ran when you didn't, in the wars of the steppe and desert. The enemy was probably in a hurry. They'd almost certainly send a detachment after two hundred men fleeing in a body, but twenty separate parties was a problem without a solution for them if you didn't have much time. Numbers were only the illusion of safety here, not the reality.

"Yes. By squads."

Ten men was the basic Mongol unit. He forestalled the *zuun*-commander, who he could tell was *not* going to report to his regimental chief that he'd left the Kha-Khan's son in the hands of his sister and a bunch of wild girls.

"How many men in your hardest-hit squad? Not counting any too wounded to fight."

"Seven men, *Noyon*."

"I'll take them, then, and the Hawks. Three remounts each, from the best of the captured animals, and enough food for a week. We'll meet at the first of the agreed points."

They compared their maps, printed up in the army's mobile records *ger* from woodblocks before they started this mission, and copiously annotated since. They were in agreement, which was important. They all noted this location and the date to mark where they'd divide their forces.

"Go!" he said.

"Toktamish does not favor me," Dzhambul admitted reluctantly, and quietly, as they walked aside from the hillside camp.

It barely deserved that name; they were both gnawing at strips of dried horsemeat, only slightly softened by being stuck under the saddle. Even with the heavy soft snow that was falling a fire was out of the question, and they were in a globe of silence and privacy only a few paces from the sentries sitting up with the dirty-brown of their sheepskin cloaks gathering an extra layer of white and their bows beneath to keep them dry.

"Toktamish hates the children of our mother and wants us dead," Börte said. "But he hates you most of all, brother, because the common people and some of the *noyons* love you. When our father dies—"

"I will not begin a civil war," Dzhambul said. "Who sheds the blood of his own is a traitor to the people. Let our father live long, and the *kurultai* of noyons and chiefs will settle the succession among the blood of our grandfather."

He smiled at her. "Besides, remember the great prophecy of the *idugan* while this war was young. The dark magic of this land has been weakened. And the empire of Genghis Khan will be renewed. . . . What, you do not believe it?" he said, scandalized.

Börte's mouth twisted as if she had bitten into something sour.

"Of course I believe it," she said. "I was there. We all felt that the *Tengri* spoke through her. But I listened, where you did not."

"What?" he said.

She began to tick points off on her fingers. "She said the spirits the *Miqačin* worship and whose slaves they are could no longer bar the Yalu River against us, and she was right. But!"

Another finger. "She did not say that the *Miqačin* would not fight us with bow and saber and lance. And they are very many."

Another finger. "She did not say that their forts would fall without us having a proper siege train, and they have a lot of very strong forts."

Another finger. "She did not say we wouldn't have trouble with the Han, and the Manchus, and the Russki, at the same time we were fighting here. And we *are* fighting the Han, the Manchus, and the Russki. Oh, and we and the Kazakhs and Uyghurs are all raiding each other."

Another finger. "She said the Empire of our ancestor Temujin would be restored when the Son of Heaven and the White Tsar, the Courts of the North and South, were no more. But she did not say *how soon* it would be restored."

Then she clenched the fingers into a fist and shook it under his nose. "And she did not say you and I wouldn't be killed, you blockhead! By the *Miqačin*, or by Toktamish!"

He sighed. She wasn't necessarily wrong, but . . .

"First, we have to get back to the army."

CHAPTER THREE

"I tell her and I tell her," Heuradys said sotto voce as the Royal party walked towards the gangway at the side of the ship and the barge waiting below; the Hawaiians and Japanese had their own. "But does she listen? Nooooo. . . ."

"Enough, Herry," Órlaith said amiably but firmly; her knight was doing her job, after all. "The Powers gave House Artos a Sword to carry, not a notepad for writing orders or a megaphone for shouting them. We don't just command, we *lead*."

The knight nodded with a chuckle—probably at the thought of a supernaturally powerful order-pad or speaking trumpet—but she did silently push forward with her shield up to lead the way down the gangway, which was an arrangement like a long hinged staircase down to the water level. It wasn't even really paranoia; there had been more than one attempt at assassination lately, and from people none of them would have suspected.

Alan, Órlaith thought, and pushed aside the pain for a man who might not have really existed at all, though she'd felt his touch.

She'd thought it was more than diversion and sport. If they'd had more time together . . .

And one of the reasons enemies try that sort of thing is to kill your trust if they can't kill you, because nothing can be done without trust. Suspicion can be a prophecy too . . . a self-fulfilling one.

The boat at the bottom of the gangway was Hawaiian, with a crew that King Kalākaua had furnished, as he had for Empress Reiko. The Hawaiian monarch was proud but shrewd, and carefully courteous to both his new allies, looking ahead to a time after the war, when Hawai'i would be the entrepôt where the trade of continents met, to the benefit of his subjects and his realm, holding the balance between many and so being safer among larger, more populous realms.

So a King must think, if the job is to be done properly.

Montivallans wouldn't have been working stripped to the waist and the waists cinched with only a breechclout, but apart from that no single individual among the oarsmen would have looked out of place at home among a band of tall well-muscled young men, though as a group they ran more to brown skins and black hair than most parts of the High Kingdom. Heuradys made a slight *ooooh* sound of appreciation at the massed male hotness and one of them caught her eye and grinned and winked and gripped his oar so that the long muscles flexed on his arms and shoulders beneath smooth sweat-slicked skin. Órlaith was feeling too serious for that sort of byplay.

She nodded to their captain, an elegant youngster with a red flower tucked behind one ear and a wicked-looking long knife in his belt. From what little she'd seen of the ordinary folk here since her fleet arrived, Hawaiians tended to the casual and happy-go-lucky even by Mackenzie standards, but when they needed to they could work in a unison even a Boisean would approve of, and very hard indeed . . . and they went spear-hunting for shark here, for the sport of it. His face was grave with responsibility.

The boat captain waited by the tiller until the last of her party—the dozen boisterous tattooed McClintock caterans in their Great Kilts who

followed Diarmuid Tennart McClintock their sub-chiefly tacksman—
were shoved out of the way. The McClintocks were mountaineers from
the southern uplands beyond the ruins of Eugene, without even the slight
experience in boats a Mackenzie might get on the rivers of the Willamette low country. *Their* streams were rushing torrents good mainly for
trout, salmon in season and turning the wheel of a gristmill, but they
were agile as goats and adjusted quickly.

Two of them, a huge redhead with a beard down his plaid like a burst
mattress stuffed with ginger moss and a black-haired comrade nearly as
big, were taking turns carrying and guarding her personal banner, the
same Crowned Mountain and Sword as Montival's flag with the baton of
her status as Heir across it, flying from a ten-foot pole of polished mountain ashwood with a good practical spearhead atop it.

They looked fit to burst with pride, and their leatherwork and metal-
sewn leather vests and the hilts of the great two-handed *claidheamh-mòr*
slung over their backs had been lovingly polished to do the task justice;
they'd probably boast about it the rest of their lives, if they made it back
home to their native glens. She hadn't had the heart to tell them she'd
picked them for the honor because they were both, though immensely
strong and very brave, also "thick as three short planks set together" as
Diarmuid put it.

This way they wouldn't be expected to think quickly under unfamiliar
stress.

The Hawaiian officer called out sharply:

"Fend off!"

At his word the boatswain in the bows released the towrope, and the
longboat peeled away from the moving flank of the frigate that loomed
above it like a cliff topped with sails and masts fading upward to what
looked like infinity. The starboard oarsmen planted the tips of their long
tools against the metal-shod planks and shoved. In smooth unison they
slid them back into the oarlocks and poised as he turned the tiller and the
bow pointed towards the burning shore.

Everything rose and fell as they crested the long smooth curves of the waves, land only continuously in view from where the water turned green as the sand beneath shelved shallower. This close to the water you felt the sea's power more, the surge beneath them like the muscles of a blooded horse, the strong scent and the salt taste of spray on the lips.

The smoldering palm trees and thick-scattered bodies seemed oddly incongruous against the broad white beach, though it matched the harsh scents the breeze was carrying and the cries of the gathering gulls attracted by the bounty. That wind carried the blurred din of onset too, the dull clatter of blades on shields and armor, the ting and crash of steel on steel, and roaring voices muted with distance cut through with the occasional shrill shrieking. The fight was farther back from the water by now, long bowshot, though still visible as a line of black that glittered with edged metal now and then, and the bagpipers and drummers and horns-men were strutting forward to follow it.

Scores of boats and barges were turning shoreward now, the refilled ones of the first wave and more besides, up to the big specially-built types that had been carried knocked down in the holds of the ships from Montival and reassembled on Hilo to carry horses and field artillery. Cheers rose from all as her craft passed, weapons shaken in the air and her name on a thousand lips, along with nearly as many war cries and several languages. The feeling was heady . . . and heavy, as well.

It's not the first time I've gone into a fight. But it is the first time I've gone into one with so many depending on me.

As if sensing her thought, Heuradys added with another chuckle:

"I'd rather have my job than yours any day of the week and twice on Sunday, Orrey. Zeus father of Gods and men, why do people contend for thrones?"

The folk here in Hawai'i mostly used English with one another, though often in ways a Montivallan found strange. They remembered the older tongue of the canoe-folk who'd first settled these lands, though, preserving it for speaking to their Gods and for occasions of ceremony . . . and for things like this. Now they took up a chant in a call-and-response pattern with the helmsman, a deep musical chorus that helped with the hard skilled effort of swinging the oars.

The Sword of the Lady had given her their speech, as it did any tongue she needed:

Ia wa'a nui
That large canoe—
Ia wa'a kioloa
That long canoe—
Ia wa'a peleleu
That broad canoe—
A lele mamala
Let chips fly—
A manu a uka
The bird of the mountain—
A manu a kai
The bird of the sea—
'I'iwi polena
The red Honeycreeper—
A kau ka boku
The stars hang above—
A kau i ka malama
The daylight arrives—
A pae i kula
Bring the canoe ashore!
'Amama, ua noa
The taboo is lifted!

The last was a triumphant shout as the keel rutched on the sand. The oarsmen vaulted over the rails and ran the bow up higher and stood in the water to steady it; Órlaith ran to the bow herself and leapt down. She landed carefully with bent knees on the sand just beyond the highest riffle from the low waves and a slight grunt, but doing acrobatics in armor was one of the tests of knighthood and she could have done the same in a regular steel suit twenty pounds heavier than this. Her followers followed in a rush, shaking out behind her—or in Heuradys' case, to the right and nearly level—and standing alert.

Karl and Mathun and the other Mackenzies took their weapons out of the waxed-linen bags, tucked those away in their sporrans, strung the longbows in a practiced flex with the lower tip against the left boot and the thigh over the grip, and put arrows on the nock, their eyes scanning ceaselessly for threats.

One of her followers was Susan Mika, still in the leathers of the Crown Courier Corps, slight and wiry and dark, with her black hair in feathered braids and a band of white-edged black painted across her eyes. She gave a high shrill whoop and called out down the beach in Lakota:

"Wayáčhi yačhíŋ he?"

Another barge was bringing the party's mounts ashore, shuttled over from Hilo where they'd been enjoying a chance to get away from the cramped stalls of the transports that had brought them the long sea road from Astoria. Sir Droyn de Molalla was in charge of that, a dark handsome young man she'd knighted herself, and the third son of the Count of Molalla. He waved, and held up his shield. At this distance it was easier to recognize the arms, in his case an assegai and lion quartered with hers, than a face.

A quarter horse with a white-and-brown speckled rump threw its head up at Susan's cry, decided it liked the invitation to dance from its rider, and pulled its reins out of a groom's hand with a speed that left her yelping and wringing a burnt palm. By the time it reached the Royal party it was galloping with the jackrabbit acceleration of its breed, head plunging and braided mane flying.

Susan Mika—Susan Clever Raccoon—was running too, a stride that ended up with her grabbing the horn of her saddle, bounding into it, down on the other side, hitting the ground with both feet, doing a handstand in the saddle and flipping to stand on it and then dropping into it as her feet found the stirrups effortlessly as she circled back in spouts of wet sand.

Hurry up and wait, Órlaith thought, suppressing an impulse to snap at Susan for the display of brio. They couldn't move off the beach until those who'd be riding had gotten their horses.

War is full of urgency and then getting stalled.

"Show-off," Heuradys called as the Courier cantered up to them. "Is this a fight we're heading for, or a tinerant circus?"

Susan halted without needing to touch the reins, grinning as she slung her shete—the broad-pointed horse-fighter's chopper of the eastern plains—in its beaded sheath to the saddle, checked her bowcase and quiver, settled the two long knives she wore on her belt and the tomahawk through the loop at the small of her back, and reached forward to scratch the beast between the ears. The buffalo-hide shield slung over the bowcase was small and round, with a spread-winged Thunderbird symbol painted on it, and a small medicine bag and tuft of feathers.

"Hey, is it my fault if you *wašícu* have no natural talent for horses?" Susan said to the Associate. "Go get a bicycle, knight-girl, or one of those lumbering short-nosed elephants you manor-and-castle types try to *pass off* as horses."

"Is that the noble chivalric destrier you're slandering in your savage nomadic ignorance?"

"Noble?"

Susan glanced up at the sky as if in deep thought and put a finger on her chin before saying in measured tones:

"So *noble* is how Richard the Lionheart wannabes say *fat* and *slow*? Y'know, that explains a lot, it really does."

"Destriers are elegantly powerful and quick enough in the charge."

"So are elephants. *Or* destriers, as if there's a *difference* between a destrier and an elephant. Or maybe they're really just very skinny hippos?"

Then they pointed at each other and yelled:

"Bitch!"

In unison, and laughed.

Faramir Kovalevsky and his cousin Morfind Vogeler called to their horses as well, and swung up with equal skill to the backs of the dappled Arabs, if with a little less deliberate panache, reining in by Susan's side. They were both in the loose mottled light clothing and mail-lined hippo-hide jerkins that the Dúnedain of *Stath* Eryn Muir—the southernmost outpost of their scattered people, in what the old world had called Muir Woods—wore in the field, so that the crowned Tree and seven Stars were hard to see on their breasts. All three uncased their four-foot recurved horse-bows of horn and sinew and reached for arrows, guiding their mounts effortlessly with weight and knees, leaving the reins knotted on the saddlebow.

"Besides," Heuradys said, nodding to them. "Your tree-house-dwelling *wašícu* squeezes there are just as good at show-off trick-riding as you are."

"The three of us are *melethril* to each other," Morfind said loftily. "*Squeeze* is Common Speech, and just . . . so common, for one of noble blood, Lady Heuradys. And Faramir lived in a *flet* at Eryn Muir, but I was raised in my parents' perfectly nice stone hall east of there in the Valley of the Moon. Besides, *we're* not *wašícu*."

Her eyes were blue, though her hair was as black as Susan's; Faramir's were gray, and he had a mop of blond curls that peaked out a little from around the rim of the light helm he donned.

"You're not?" Heuradys said. "That's new."

"No, it isn't. You know perfectly well we're elf-friends," the young man named Kovalevsky clarified with sardonic helpfulness. "Folk of the West. Númenóreans, though our blood is sadly mingled with Common Men here in the Fifth Age."

Common, like you, went unspoken.

"I'd forgotten because there aren't any pointy-eared types around for you Dúnedain to hang with," Heuradys said. "Assuming they'd have anything to do with you, that is."

"Elves don't have pointy ears, or the *Histories* would say so, Lady," Morfind said.

The *Histories* were what Dúnedain Rangers called a series of hero-tales from before the Change that their founder Lady Astrid Larsson had been obsessed with from an implausibly early age. She was a martyred hero of the Prophet's War now, but her surviving Bearkiller brother Eric still referred to her as *Princess Leg-o-lamb* now and then, to the scandal of the younger generation and any visiting Rangers. You usually couldn't tell just how serious the Dúnedain were when they claimed that the stories were gospel true . . . *literally* gospel, as in divinely inspired by the Valar. Even with the Sword she couldn't be entirely sure, though she thought she felt ambiguity—what she often sensed, if irony was involved.

"The pointed ears are just a superstition," Morfind added, absently rubbing at the axe-scar that seamed her cheek; it still itched a little now and then, having been suffered less than a year ago. "The *Edhellen* are tall and noble-looking, and graceful as cats and handsome or beautiful, but otherwise outwardly like the race of Men, unless you have eyes to see into the Other Realm. So they look rather like us Folk of the West"—she pointed a finger at her own chest—"only *even more* noble and beautiful and graceful than we are."

Órlaith smiled at the byplay. There *was* a certain amount of inherent irony when Dúnedain Rangers and Associate nobles got into a mutual I-can-be-more-haughty-and-sneering-than-thou contest, though it was even more entertaining when they were serious about it rather than this teasing between friends. Growing up in the High King's family had taken her all over Montival, and exposed her to many different folk and their ways . . . and their myths about themselves.

It's good to have a Household of my own generation with me, she thought; Heuradys and Diarmuid were the oldest, and they had only a few years more than her. *If I had to be with nobody but my parents' generation, the Changelings, I'd run melancholy-mad in short order.*

Sir Droyn cantered over on a tall courser—the alternative breed for knightly combat, a bit lighter and longer-limbed than destriers proper, what they'd called a Warmblood or Irish Hunter in the ancient world. He led two more for her and Heuradys.

"Here comes Sir Wet Blanket de Propriety a l'outrance," Heuradys murmured.

Órlaith clucked disapprovingly; Droyn *was* far more conventional than either of them, but he'd been fiercely loyal and a fine fighter. And he'd sworn allegiance to her—his arms were quartered with hers, like Heuradys'—and come off on their adventure to south Westria with Reiko, when he could have stayed home as the third son of a wealthy Count and spent his days hunting and gambling and dancing at parties and riding in the tournament circuit and basking in the admiration and embraces of the local femininity.

He did look slightly baffled when Susan Mika called out, to a chorus of snickers:

"How's your *olifant* doing there, my lord?"

Olifant being *elephant* in the Old French with which Associate nobles peppered their conversation, particularly the ones more caught up in the mythos, much the way Mackenzies did with Gaelic. She was fairly sure that Droyn's own grandfather had actually been a leader of some sort of bandit gang before the Change, recruited by Norman Arminger in the early days of the Portland Protective Association. And married off to one of his Society for Creative Anachronism followers to give him a little polish, which had succeeded with his descendants if not with the old rogue himself, who'd at least died bravely leading his men in the Protector's War.

Nowadays the Counts of Molalla claimed, via well-subsidized troubadours and heralds, to be descended from a long line of African kings, including several Órlaith knew for a fact had never come within six thousand miles or several thousand years of one another—that was a very big continent and as old as anywhere—and from French aristocrats through Droyn's grandmother. Who'd been something called a *dental hygienist* when she wasn't *playing* at being a noblewoman . . . though admittedly she'd done the real thing quite well, diving into her Society persona and never coming out again.

Grandmother Juniper says a lot of them did that, Órlaith thought. *As a way of going mad and surviving at the same time.*

"This is my courser Roland, Lady Susan," he replied gravely, giving her credit in north-realm terms for being the daughter of a prominent Lakota chief. "He's in fine fettle and ready for deeds of honor!"

A sixteen-hand roan with a blond mane whickered as he caught Órlaith's scent, and Droyn grinned as he looped its reins to the high pommel and released the animal. It trotted over and paused, and Órlaith took a hopping skip, put her hand on the leather, sprang into the high-cantled saddle men-at-arms used and braced her feet in the long forward-canted knight's stirrups.

"Back to work again, eh, Wardancer?" she said, and slapped its neck; coursers were less specialized than destriers, but about as big. "You must be deadly bored."

Vaulting onto your mount in full armor and shield was *another* of the tests of knighthood; Heuradys did it moments later with her tall black mare. Sometimes Órlaith sympathized with men meeting that particular challenge; getting it just right was even more important for them, and doing it wrong was apparently very painful indeed, and a source of much merriment to the other squires when a bunch of candidates were practicing, along with expressions of false sympathy and offers of ice packs.

The three horse-archers spread out before them, and those on foot formed to either side and behind her and her two full-armored companions. The Mackenzies and McClintocks paced along effortlessly with the slow trot of their mounted companions. Not even clan warriors could keep up with a galloping horse . . . but a horse couldn't gallop for very long, and they could maintain a swinging lope like this from dawn to dusk. A light-riding Crown Courier like Susan with a string of four or five remounts on a leading-rein or changes at substations and nothing but open grassland to cross could leave them behind for a good long time, but not a rider on a single burdened horse, not for long. That was why infantry could run cavalry to death, over a week or two, and why armies usually left a trail of horses foundered or dead in their wake.

Besides moving faster, a warhorse gave you a better view. She could see troops landing now up and down a mile of the beach, rallying, and heading off where couriers and officers directed.

Just north a regiment of foot from the Theo-Democratic Republic of New Deseret was forming up, men in three-quarter armor fitting their knock-down pikes together and raising them in blocks to their full sixteen-foot height, and light troops in half-armor in thinner formations between with crossbows. The banner borne before them was of golden bees on black, and a beehive shone on every breastplate. A battery of horse-drawn field-catapults, twelve-pounders, wheeled up and trotted along behind them as they double-timed forward with feet hitting the ground in earthquake unison, the glittering foot-long heads of the pikes rising and falling rhythmically.

They raised a cheer and a shout of:

"Princess Órlaith! Long live Princess Órlaith!"

House Artos had saved Deseret in the Prophet's War, led them to victory over those who'd laid their land waste, and brought much-needed aid in its aftermath, food and cloth to feed and warm the hungry and seed-grain and stock and tools to rebuild ruined farms and towns. The folk there remembered it still, being a breed much given to solid virtues like hard work, gratitude and keeping their oaths. Órlaith admired and liked them on the whole, but found them even duller than other Christians.

She saluted with gauntleted fist to breastplate at the loyal cry, and they burst into an earth-shaking chorus:

"The morning breaks, the shadows flee;
Lo, Zion's standard is unfurled!
The dawning of a brighter day—
The dawning of a brighter day—
Majestic rises on the world!"

A field hospital was in the process of setting up on the beach with gear and staff from the expeditionary force's hospital ships and was already treating a steady flow of wounded brought in by stretcher-bearers and the first field ambulances. A difference of minutes in treatment could mean the difference between life and death, or saving and losing a limb. One of her less agreeable duties later would be to tour it and talk to the hurt. Her parents had both sworn that it genuinely helped them.

The headquarters table was just inland beyond that, with a canvas windbreak already up, ranks of mounted messengers, and a skeletal launch rack for lofting observation gliders half-assembled and growing fast; Boiseans were very good at things like that, with the folk from the city-state of Corvallis their only real rivals for the title of best field engineers in the High Kingdom. In the interim, a heliograph snapped out Morse to the ships offshore and took it in return, getting the viewpoint from their kite-borne lookouts.

That efficiency was appropriate, because the land commander of the expeditionary force was General-President Frederick Thurston, a tall handsome middle-aged man with a light-brown complexion and loosely-curled black hair worn short in the way his folk favored. His staff—which included two of his children of about Órlaith's age, Alice, in light-cavalry leather and mail shirt, and Lawrence in the same heavy-infantry armor as his father—and a clutch of other contingent-commanders were grouped around him and messengers came and went. Reiko and Kalākaua arrived just as she did, though they were on foot.

Captain Edain of the High King's—

High Queen's, she reminded herself; her father's enormous absence still caught her now and then, like a root tripping you in a darkened forest.

—Archers was there, giving her a salute followed by a bow and smile and dryly amused look; her father's old right-hand man and Guard-Captain had spent several months earlier this year trying to chase her down in the wilds of Westria—what had once been California—and express the High Queen's extreme displeasure that she'd gone haring off with Reiko to find the Grasscutter.

Despite the fact that she did pretty much the same on the Quest of the Sunrise Lands when she was younger than I, and Grandmother Sandra raged about it spectacularly. I was right and she was wrong and I get to sing the "I was right" song. Though I won't . . . not aloud, at least. And maybe I'll rage likewise, when I'm her age.

Heuradys' brother Lord Diomede d'Ath, heir to Barony Ath and Captain-General of the Associate men-at-arms for the expeditionary force was there too; he had black hair and pale blue eyes like their birth-mother Lady Delia, the theoretical Countess de Stafford and actual Châtelaine of Ath, a serious-looking man in his late thirties. He nodded and gave her a grave fist-to-chest, one knight to another.

Certain things had to be said, and said publicly, for reasons both personal and political—if there was any difference, in the world her birth had handed her. Órlaith returned Fred Thurston's salute.

"General Thurston"—rather than *Mr. President*, since he was here in a military capacity, in the service of the High Kingdom—"please let me console you on the death of your nephew, Captain Alan Thurston. We know the enemy in this war, as it was in the Prophet's War, can twist men's minds. Your nephew fought valiantly against that infection, and killed himself rather than let himself be forced to harm me. That was truly death in battle, fighting a brave and lonely fight for the High Kingdom against overwhelming odds. Surely he feasts among the *einherjar* in Odhinn's hall tonight."

That had the benefit of being substantially and generally true, though the reality was complex enough it would have taken hours to cover it all; for instance, it wasn't at all clear if *the enemy* who'd crept into Alan's mind was the same one who'd been behind the Prophet in their own country a generation ago and was the same to the Kim dynasty in Korea now. There were hints it was some new Power, equally malign.

She didn't make any reference to Alan briefly being her lover either, though of course Fred Thurston had known about it, and wouldn't have been human if he hadn't hoped something on the order of a marriage alliance might come of that between the Thurstons and House Artos. The more so because he'd been a Quest-companion and longtime friend of her father, a comrade and valued commander in the Prophet's War.

He probably wasn't too deeply or directly grieved for Alan's personal sake; the young man was the posthumous son of his usurping parricide of an elder brother, and had been raised deep in the country. Alan's mother had been given a good ranch after the war in a very remote area, and then strongly advised to stay there for the rest of her life. He'd visited to show he didn't bear the children a grudge—his sister-in-law *had* switched sides in a public, spectacular and very helpful way, albeit for her own reasons—but not enough for a personal bond. The wounds of *civil* war healed slowly, even with the best will in the world.

"Thank you, Your Highness," the elder Thurston said.

He sighed. "Though at times I think it might be better for the family if Jokin' Joe had won the last election and we could retire to our ranch."

Most of those present smiled, though a few of the foreigners or Montivallans who hadn't been much outside their own member-realms before this war looked puzzled. The United States of Boise was rather old-fashioned, and had free and fair democratic elections for President every seven years, though nobody not named *Thurston* had ever won one.

In the latest the main challenger to Fred Thurston had been a young man who'd officially changed his name to Jokin' Joe the Jokey Jokester, and campaigned as head and sole member of the Gibbering Lunatic Party, wearing a large red nose, floppy shoes, and a fright wig, along with a fake carnation in his lapel that shot water into the faces of the unwary.

His speeches had consisted mostly of things like reading the Boisean constitution backward ostensibly as a prayer for electoral aid from Satan, a proposal to substitute royalties from the Big Rock Candy Mountain mines for all other taxes, and promises to decree that all the railroads in the Republic run downhill both ways to reduce the cost of horse-feed.

Punctuated by fist-waving screams of: *"I'm the most serious alternative you've got!"* and *"We need honest government—elect someone who admits that he's an absolute clown!"*

She reflected that you couldn't say Boiseans had *absolutely* no sense of humor; he'd gotten fully ten percent of the vote, after all.

Then Thurston cleared his throat and spoke with flat sincerity:

"Thank you also for the timely information about the enemy counter-attack. That let us contain it much more quickly, and it saved lives."

Órlaith nodded and touched the hilt of the Sword of the Lady to show where the credit was due. Thurston had already glanced that way; he'd been one of her father's commanders at the Horse Heaven Hills and the long march to the Church Universal and Triumphant's capital of Corwin, and he knew what the Sword meant from firsthand experience, as much as anyone not of House Artos could.

She swung down from the saddle and examined the map, with Heuradys at her side and Diarmuid taking a keen interest too, though both were silent.

Órlaith looked at the commander's map carefully; she'd been taught to read the like from an early age. And then she blinked. For her, suddenly the symbols on it were *alive*, they were moving . . . and she could see them as if she were in truth in the sky above, as if in a glider or balloon. Knowledge slid through her mind, the summation of what *all* her folk facing the enemy knew.

Lord and Lady, but that feels strange, like empty rooms in my head suddenly furnished! And no wonder Da had a reputation as a tricky demon of a commander! Though to be sure, many of those he fought were actual *demons.*

"What are their numbers?" she asked, more for time to think than information.

"About like ours when all three armies are deployed, we think, or a bit more—say twenty thousand. Archers, spearmen and swordsmen. Very little in the way of cavalry, though, just mounts for some officers, and no field catapults to speak of since the Navy very efficiently sank them all."

Kalākaua hissed in dismay. "I'd have trouble matching that with a month to mobilize!" he said. "And that would be everyone in the islands who could carry a spear or draw a bow, from the big kids who think they're grown to the graybeards who babble about TV and airplanes and computers!"

Reiko nodded politely. "It is very fortunate that the *bakachon*—"

Chon was a very impolite word for Koreans, but older and not quite as packed with murderous loathing as *jinnikukaburi. Baka* meant something like *imbecile* or *moron.* There was no precise equivalent in modern Montivallan English for the compound, but a whisper at the back of her mind translated it as *dumb gooks*.

"—did not come this far before you had powerful allies, Your Majesty."

Kalākaua nodded agreement, but he still wasn't happy about it. His people had suffered from Korean piracy when they sailed abroad anywhere near northeast Asia, but not from longshore raids or direct confrontations before this . . . and pirates were, after all, fairly common everywhere and were never very nice people to their victims.

"Or perhaps they have come this far *because* of the arrival of . . . allied . . . forces," he said dryly.

Reiko's Imperial Guard commander, Egawa Noboru, was one-handed and scar-faced from a lifetime fighting the same enemy, and he stirred slightly and scowled, his armor clattering. His sovereign made a very small gesture with her folded *tessen*, the steel war-fan she carried and used for verbal emphasis . . . and sometimes for slitting throats . . . and he bowed.

"My apologies for my humiliating lack of manners, *Heika*," he said in a voice like a bucketful of gravel being stirred with a spear-butt. "I will try to be more self-controlled."

"You owe the apology to our honored ally, King Kalākaua, my *bushi*," she said with iron in her voice, and he made a bow to the Hawaiian.

"Very sorry," he said.

Then she continued in slow careful English, a language Egawa understood reasonably well but couldn't speak beyond curses and mangled clichés.

"If . . . when . . . they had disposed of us, they would next have come for you, Your Majesty. We have protected the outside world from this evil with my people's blood and their lives for two generations; not by our choice, but that is what we have done. And they are not an enemy who are merely greedy for land or plunder or dominion. What kingdom, what people, has not tried to seize what they could at some time? Certainly, we Nihonjin have, now and then. But the *bakachon*, they are wicked and the tools of wickedness, the enemies of all humanity. Ultimately their masters seek not to rule or even to plunder, but to destroy for its own sake."

Kalākaua looked at the smoke of his devastated land, visibly thought of the reports he'd received of how the invaders had acted, which he hadn't wanted to believe until the Nihonjin had confirmed them, sighed and nodded.

"We had peace and I wanted more, there's so much to do," he said. "But I won't let the wish father the thought; it takes two to make peace, but only one to make war. You're right, Your Majesty. This was a fight that was coming anyway, and it could have come in a way that was far worse. *We'll eat you last* isn't a very convincing argument for staying out of it."

Órlaith looked at the map and listened to the thoughts that were not hers, but flowed into her mind as if they were. Decision firmed.

"They're swinging back on our right like a door on a pivot"—her hand traced a line on the map—"and then they're going to hit us here when we reinforce success on the other side."

Her gauntleted finger moved back over to the closer, left-hand side of the line of little metal markers placed on the paper.

Thurston frowned. "That's not a winning gambit," he said. "Not if they have any idea of our capacities and not unless I . . . we . . . were idiots. If they had more cavalry, maybe, but they can't pull it off; I'd just refuse the flank and commit some of my reserve . . . even if you *hadn't* told me they were going to do it. I wish *we* had more cavalry, come to that, but we do have some and it gives us superior tactical mobility."

"They do not think in such a way, General," Reiko put in. "We have noticed many times, the *jinnikukaburi* are . . . are crev . . . clever . . . but in a way that is"—

she appealed to Órlaith, who supplied the words

—"is *abstract* and *alien*."

Órlaith nodded. "And remember, General, that to the enemy's leaders human beings are vermin, their own troops included. They genuinely don't care about losses in the way we do."

Thurston's mouth twisted wryly. "Yes, I noticed that in the Prophet's War."

"They're trying to bleed us to weaken us for the future, rather than beat us here," Órlaith said. "If they can, they'll try and make us kill every one of their soldiers, so they can hurt us as badly as they can in the process."

"It's a butcher's way to operate, but I see your point," Thurston said.

Órlaith noticed the Nihonjin blinking as they tried to follow the argument; their own tradition was that fighting to the death was the only honorable path for a warrior, and it hadn't occurred to them that there was anything odd about it. That attitude had probably been heavily reinforced by two generations when their only enemy would simply torture, kill and eat you . . . not necessarily in that order . . . if you fell into their hands.

Órlaith looked at the map again. "We're going to need a bigger army, for the rest of this war. It's going to take longer and cost more than we thought."

She thought she caught a virtually subliminal murmur from Heuradys: *Astonishing!* That's *never happened before!*

"Probably, Your Highness, but today we fight with what we have. What do you recommend?"

"I'm not going to second-guess your strictly military judgment, General, but there's something . . . else involved here. The enemy's leaders—"

"The *kangshinmu*, the sorcerer-lords," Reiko put in.

"Yes, the *kanghsinmu* will be concentrated here, where they try to drive in our flank. If we can remove those, the ordinary soldiers may not fight to the death. Though they've probably been taught we'd treat them the way they would us if they won."

Thurston nodded. "What do you suggest, Your Highness?"

Órlaith glanced at Reiko and got a nod. "We have certain assets we need to apply," she began.

An instant's ringing silence fell. Everyone knew what she bore, and stories had circulated widely about the Grasscutter, growing in the telling. But stories were one thing, and the living reality another. It made most people profoundly uncomfortable, which was an attitude she sympathized with.

"Her Majesty of Dai-Nippon and I will lead a reinforcement *there*."

She tapped her finger on the left end of the allied line.

"Her Imperial Guard, the High King's . . . Queen's Archers and the Protector's Guard, the Association men-at-arms, and . . . some light horse as well. I think the Lakota contingent would do nicely."

CHAPTER FOUR

PORTLAND PROTECTIVE ASSOCIATION
(FORMERLY NORTHERN OREGON)
HIGH KINGDOM OF MONTIVAL
(FORMERLY WESTERN NORTH AMERICA)
DECEMBER 20TH
CHANGE YEAR 46/2044 AD

"*It's absolutely bloody freezing out there! And it's* still *raining!*" Philippa Arminger Mackenzie—née Balwyn-Abercrombie—said.

In fact, Pip almost *snarled.*

This was the sort of weather her ancestors had known and loathed and through the centuries had conquered colonies to avoid . . . or before that, gone on Crusades; a Balwyn had gone over the walls of Jerusalem in 1099 behind Godfrey de Bouillon, wading ankle-deep in blood on his way to the loot with the Pope's blessing on it all.

She herself had grown up in Townsville, where sugarcane grew in the steam-press heat, and gigantic saltwater crocs occasionally ambled out of the marshes on the edge of town looking for something tasty to eat. She hadn't quite believed her mother's stories about the sustained dreariness of which England was capable. Though she had been willing to abscond from Townsville and go adventuring on her own ship northward to frustrate her father's plans to send her to Winchester in the hopes of picking up a Windsor sprig to decorate the bloodline of the newly and recently hereditary Colonels of Townsville.

And I ended up snagging a Prince on my own, somewhere with weather just like *England! God's sense of the ironic . . . Granted, Johnnie makes up for a lot, but . . .*

"Bugger me, Johnnie, is the cold always so murderous? I can see now why there's no brass monkeys on your family crest. Is it always like this here? I haven't seen the sun for five minutes since we docked, and then it looked embarrassed, as if you'd walked in on it while it was bathing."

Prince John Arminger Mackenzie, heir to the Lord Protectorship of the PPA, next heir to the High Kingdom of Montival after his elder sister Órlaith, listened to her and winced slightly. He sat across from her as he sipped at his hot tea and tuned his lute. This car in the Royal train was comprised of sets of chairs set opposite each other in groups, across a low table that held a tea service and cups. The railcar was heated by a little airtight metal stove with a glass window that let you see the cheery flicker of the burning apple-wood that scented the air, there were some quite splendid rugs on the floor, and the walls and ceiling were carved and in-laid woods, some of which must have been imported from her part of the world.

My previous, decently warm part of the world.

"Well, this *is* winter," John said. "And it's fairly typical for this time of year. We call it the Black Months. At least it's typical this far north, and west of the Cascades. It's drier and sunnier here than it is on the coast."

"Ha!"

He continued doggedly. "And drier still east of the mountains. And warmer farther south, of course. Summer is sunny and warm here and it doesn't rain much. In South Westria it's as hot as the islands of the Ceram Sea. In the Mojave Desert for example, I went there recently—"

With the Empress of Japan, of all people, she thought. Though from the description that hadn't been an affair with a starring role for John and she got the impression that this Reiko had frankly terrified him.

"—but that's hot and *dry.*"

He didn't laugh at her reaction to the weather—which was wisdom—but Deor Godulfson and Thora Garwood, who were sharing his side of the railway coach, did. And still worse, they did it indulgently.

"Be happy, Princess Pip of the Flowering Frangipani. It's not snowing, not yet," Deor said.

He was a wiry black-haired, gray-eyed man with a musician's long supple fingers, a *scop* as his people called it, a wandering bard. Pip gave the minstrel and the swordswoman a look of loathing, wondering why she'd never realized how much they resembled a pair of laughing hyenas before; though objectively, they looked like the two battered thirty-something adventurers she'd known, and liked, and fought and fared widely beside for months now.

Deor and John had been playing a round of improvised tunes—jamming was the technical name for it—on John's mandolin and Deor's harp, a pleasant tinkling buzz that occasionally gave way to what she recognized as jazz. Uncle Pete liked that sound.

"You could be first rate, if only you didn't waste time on being a Prince," Deor said.

John snorted. "And why don't you stay home and make music then, my friend, rather than roaming the whole wide world?"

"I needed things to make songs *about*. And now and then I must make *seidb*, to rescue Princes from ill-wreaking trolls, or swing a sword. Our time on Baru Denpasar certainly gave me materials I'll be years working up!"

I'm extremely nervous about meeting the Queen Mum and it's making me irritable, so maybe I'd better shut my cakehole, she thought. *Let's not take it out on the other kiddies, Pip, old girl. Buck up! You've fought pirates and storms and kept a crew of pretty rugged desperados well in line, and then dealt with what looked like bloody evil magic . . . well, no, what* actually *was bloody evil magic in Baru Denpasar. I don't know what else to call it, even if it is too much like those pre-Blackout books Uncle Pete used to love so much, with barbarian swordsmen and busty wenches and such. And, well, being a little bit preggers is upsetting the balance of my . . . what did they call them before the Blackout . . . humors? No, hormones.*

Another reason for her envy? Thora's impressive and lanky height was tricked out in Bearkiller formal garb, which started with that little blue mark between the brows that was some sort of warrior-caste thing. But the clothes were a very sensible combination of knee boots, loose pants of dark maroon wool, linen shirt and fur-lined leather jacket of soft brown doeskin with a bear's-head badge on it; all super premium quality, with touches like gold buttons on the coat and a silver Thor's-Hammer pendant, and she carried her sword—a basket-hilted backsword—resting easily between her knees.

It all made Pip feel like a very gaudy Christmas-tree decoration in her new Associate court garb, overdressed and under-armed. You had to adjust your whole way of moving, and Pip wasn't used to feeling gauche. Or adjusting anything she did for anyone.

That's Princess *Philippa Arminger Mackenzie, now,* she reminded herself. *Daddy will love it, almost as much as if I had gone to Winchester and snagged the giggling chinless third cousin of the King-Emperor. Mummy would have laughed herself silly over a gin and tonic and said I was a true Balwyn and always landed on my feet . . . in stolen shoes. Uncle Pete and Auntie Fifi* will *laugh themselves silly when they read the letters I sent back with the* Silver Surfer, *and so will King Birmo . . . and then he'll wring everything he can out of the connection for Darwin and Capricornia, the evil old scrote.*

The outfit she wore (and several others in the helpfully-provided luggage) had been scrounged from the very accommodating Mayor and Corporation of the Free and Loyal Chartered City of Astoria and cut and sewn and refitted by frantic day-and-night relays from the Seamstress' Guild, which she'd endured with as much good humor as she could; at least it was partly made out of the gorgeous fabrics the suitably grateful Raja of Baru Denpasar had pressed on her. They called them cotte-hardies. They had full skirts and fitted bodices and they were surprisingly comfortable.

Astoria had been impressive. As big as Darwin, if colder, a gray city massively fortified against a hilly forested shore green and gray, and a gray sea and river bustling with shipping from all around the world, and riverboat and barge and rail traffic from the Columbia Valley and ringing with workshops and small factories, sawmills and shipyards and ropeworks—though also quaint, with all the half-timbered new buildings, which she supposed were practical in this climate. And the medieval-ish clothes, which ditto. Crowds had turned out to cheer John as soon as word got out that the lost Prince was back from heroics to rival his father's and safe on the frigate *Stormrider*, almost as soon as the families of the crew had arrived on the quay amid laughter and tears.

Pip knew ships and cargo; she had successfully captained a trading schooner herself. Her father was heir to a realm whose capital was a busy seaport second only to Darwin and Hobart, and her mother had been a seaborne merchant-adventurer. She was the friend of King Birmo of Darwin and the unofficial niece of her mother's friends Pete and Fifi Holder . . . who were currently heads of the Darwin and East Indies Trading Company, having worked their way up with her mother as very successful salvagers-cum-buccaneers.

They'd cheered her as well, since apparently the rumors about the exotic foreign bride were considered romantic in the extreme—the seamstresses had been very competent, but inclined to twitter and gush and sigh over John's dreaminess, since the *Troubadour Prince* was a major heartthrob here, with girls putting his lithographed picture cut out of magazines with names like *Tournaments Illuminated* on bedroom walls and mooning over him.

John playing and singing at some lady's knee in a castle solar dressed in slightly disheveled finery, John alone under a tree in loose shirt and tight hose dreaming and composing, John in armor at tournaments with some lady's favor tucked into his breastplate, John kneeling before an altar and looking soulful . . .

All rather amusing . . . in a way, though in another way one is inclined to roll one's eyes and possibly chunder up lunch. Which I couldn't eat anyway because my stomach was clenched too tight and now I'm starving.

The two bureaucrats from the Lord Chancellor's office had been oddly dressed—rather like a subdued form of the clothes you saw on playing cards, with a robed and tonsured monk as number three—but they'd also been as workmanlike in their way as the seamstresses in kirtles and wimples had been in theirs, and had extracted everything in jig time.

The news that she was expecting had produced a mild panic combined with exultation, whereupon they'd brought in a nun-doctor who had confirmed that yes, she had a bun in the oven though it was early days yet and everything was going fine, if God and His Mother were kind. Thora had privately snagged the medical sister on the way out, but nobody else had noticed since they were focused on her and John and apparently the local medical profession was very strong on patient confidentiality, possibly as a sort of penumbral spillover from attitudes towards the confessional.

Sometimes the report-takers had been inclined to choke on the exotic details of what had happened in Baru Denpasar off in the Ceram Sea, where the good . . . or rather bad . . . ship *Hastur* docked with the Pallid Mask as captain, and *Carcosa* rose in pink-and-white abomination on the shore like a tumor with the brooding presence of the King in Yellow looming above it trying to shape the world according to hellish dreams older than time. But Deor and Thora and John had backed her up on that from their varying perspectives, and unlike her they had plenty of local credibility.

And anyway, here in Montival they seemed to have more experience with evil sorcerer-lords and malignant otherworldliness than was common in Oz, where it was mostly rumors about foreign lands or things the Aborigines got up to in the lands they'd taken back. It did produce a temptation to run for some remote outback station and never ever *ever* leave again, but with her current run of luck she'd get sidetracked into the Dreamtime and have to live on witchetty grubs and honey ants for the rest of eternity, squatting over a fire on her hams while the grubs roasted on twigs.

You could tell from the questions that they already knew a good deal about Oz here, more than she'd known about Montival. There *was* a trickle of trade and apparently John's maternal grandmamma had had a thing about collecting intelligence and it had stuck, locally, and the ones taking her story down were specialists.

The density of traffic on the Columbia and the way the network of heliograph stations had flashed the news before them had been even more impressive. Mirrors and sunlight were used back home too, but they had a backup system here of limelight—quicklime burning in a hydrogen-oxygen flame—for when it was dim or dark . . . which seemed to be a lot of the time.

The railways here were well kept up and equipped with things like the hippomotive—eight big horses on treadmills driving geared wheels—pulling this Royal train, which with relays kept them going at over twenty miles an hour. That was very fast indeed for overland travel; the only other way to do it was along a route with relays of *riding* horses at the stops.

Which means pounding your arse to sausage.

The Royal train was *much* more comfortable than that. Despite her complaints it was actually quite warm inside . . . if you thought sixty degrees Fahrenheit was a good indoor temperature; there were excellent incandescent mantle lanterns and even a hot-water shower in the rear car, and the food had been a welcome relief from shipborne rations when she wasn't too wrought-up to eat.

Even more impressive than that, however, was the extent of the softly green-and-brown tilled land and cow-and-sheep dotted pasture and leafless but flourishing-looking orchards and vineyards surrounding manor houses and villages outside the windows, in the intervals between conifer-forested hills. It was the ultimate source of all wealth, after all, of which all others were at seventh and last merely symbols.

Montival held, or at least claimed and held in part, the western third of this continent from Baja to Alaska, which made it a bit smaller than Australia. Unlike Australia it wasn't a rim of habitability clinging to the edges around an empty desert heart, and it hadn't permanently split up into dozens of squabbling statelets either. John's father had brought the local successor-states together a generation ago, and while there was supposedly plenty of ruin and wilderness here they did have nearly five million people—at least twice what Oz did. This great river and the valleys running into it were the heart of things, evidently.

And those castles . . . my God! Talk about picture books!

This subunit of Montival here was the Portland Protective Association, where Associates were the top-drawer and built castles and manors,
and the rest were the common herd. Apparently Associate *ladies* didn't
wear swords on public occasions, though she'd already heard there were
exceptions; she just didn't feel familiar enough with the local customs to
be one of them yet. She'd barely managed to hang on to her cane, a yard
of black super-hard Ireng wood with grooved gold heads on both ends;
which she privately called *Bash 'em* and *Thrash 'em.*

Fortunately Associate ladies all carried a knife much like their
menfolk—again, some sort of warrior-caste thing—and the one she'd
been given was a solid poniard with a ten-inch, double-edged blade of
watered steel kept very sharp and a jeweled but practical hilt, which kept
her from feeling entirely naked, although her mother's twin kukri-knives
would have been better.

Deor had hung up his coat and was comfortable in his long tunic of
fine Merino twill dyed deep green, and embroidered with crimson and
gold thread at hem and neck; an arm-ring of worked gold showed clearly
around the sleeve, and his black breeks were cross-gartered below the
knee above elegantly buckled shoes. There were silver-and-turquoise
plaques on the belt that held his seax and Saxon-style broadsword, currently hung with his coat, and a silver-and-gold valknut on a chain around
his neck, showing his allegiance to Woden, who was apparently Lord of
poetry and music, as well as running a celestial retirement home for old
soldiers complete with booze, bints and roast pork.

"You're too bloody right, Pip!" the big man beside her said. "This
makes Dunedin down in South Island look like fuckin' Tahiti. And it
bloody *snows* in sodding Dunedin, regular as clockwork, nearly once
every year."

Toa was *very* big—a full foot on her five-six—and very broad and
very brown, including his stiff roach of hair drawn back through a bone
ring, his eyes and his skin. It made a striking contrast to her gray-eyed,

tawny-haired cat-build; Uncle Pete had once said she was a perfect Hyborian, whatever the hell that meant.

Usually Toa didn't wear much but two feathers thrust into his topknot, a broad belt of patterned flax to hold his loincloth and knives, and a sort of short string apron before and behind. Almost all the rest of him was covered with a swirling pattern of tattoos, including his thick-featured face, contrasting with the scars he'd picked up in an adventurous forty-odd years. Perforce he'd left his broad-bladed seven-foot spear on the baggage rack above their heads, but he got to keep his personal ironmongery.

Pip smiled thinly. He hadn't objected to wearing more than a breechclout in *this* climate, but his comments had been memorable when they'd offered him a getup like John's—she'd taken a very quick lesson in the local terminology, courtesy of the Guild of Seamstresses—of skintight particolored hose, puffy-sleeved Robin Hood shirt with a drawstring neck, high-collared jerkin and a houppelande coat with wide dagged sleeves and a chaperon hat with a liripipe. Particularly at the sight of the shoes with upturned toes topped with silver bells; he was in a plainer version of Thora's clothes now.

John looks scrumptious in that outfit, I admit, even with the jerkin and coat hiding his delectable bum.

"It snows five or six times a year this far north," Deor laughed. "Much more than we have down in Mist Hills barony in Westria, where I come from; we see the white feathers once every few years."

California, Pip thought.

Mist Hills was an odd little survivor's colony tucked away just far enough north of the Bay that good luck and good leadership had brought it through the Change, and like many of those everywhere it had been founded by the extremely eccentric—it had been a time of madness, which gave the mad an advantage. She'd always thought of herself as an Anglo-Saxon with Norman antecedents, but Deor's folk (a word they were extremely fond of) took the *Saxon* part very literally indeed, looking down on people like Harold Godwinson and Alfred the Great as mere deracinated cosmopolitan modernists.

North of where San Francisco used to be. They've got bad Biter . . . Eater . . . infestations there but my God, think of the salvage! Pete and Fifi would piss themselves at the thought of it.

"There is rain there in winter, but sun and fine spring-like days too, much of the time. Just enough frost now and then that we can grow good apples, and every other goodly fruit, as well as have fine vineyards. This is cold compared to where I was born . . . but Thora and I have seen Norrheim—"

"Where?"

"What they called northernmost Maine in the old world."

Pip remembered maps and blenched at the latitude.

"Why's it called that now? Apart from being very . . . northern."

It turned out to be a bunch of Odin-worshippers washing down the moose-meat and potatoes with mead and ale.

"And we've been to England . . . and Iceland . . . and we spent a winter on the Trondheimsfjorden once. And it's mild here compared to those."

"Hela's realm is mild compared to Norrheim in February, and the Icelanders eat rotten shark and mutton they call *wind-cured* because there isn't anything else, but Norway was fun," Thora said affectionately. "Once your body temperature dropped eight degrees and you learned to cross-country ski and you grew fur like a polar bear. I learned why the sagas have so much feasting on roast pork—you need the fuel!"

Thora and Deor had been mates in the Australian sense of the term since they were younger than her current twenty years, and as close to the other meaning as was allowed by the fact that they both preferred the company of men in bed; Deor's lover, Ruan Chu Mackenzie, had temporarily parted company with them, off to someplace a little south to tell his family he'd be moving out. Together they'd literally been around the world; it made her recent adventures seem . . .

Well, not tame. But smaller-scale, and they were there for that as well.

Pip was reluctantly resigned to the fact that Thora was pregnant too, and from the same source—it had happened before John and she met.

The thirsty bastard. Well, it makes us a good match; it's not as if shagging wasn't a hobby of mine too.

She'd ruthlessly detached him, without much resistance, and suspected Thora had gotten precisely what she wanted out of it, and *all* she wanted.

Still, I'm glad we all agreed to pretend it's not so.

Thora went on complacently: "Now, Larsdalen, where I grew up down in the Willamette in the Bearkiller Outfit's territory, is a perfect compromise—yes, we get the Black Months and nice crisp weather perfect for a good muddy boar-hunt and enough snow to be interesting. The summers are lovely and warm, but not too hot. Still"—she glanced at Deor and smiled—"Mist Hills will do. Good place to raise kids. And horses, on that land your elder brother gave us."

"There are much warmer spots close to my home," Deor said, taking mercy on her. "I'm sure Órlaith will give you and John an estate from the Crown lands in Napa to winter on, with olive trees and orange groves. There's even eucalyptus trees. Some Associates have already settled there, along with Mackenzies and Corvallans and folk from Deseret and Boise."

"That sounds . . . nice," Pip said, a little grudgingly.

It did. Rather like, say, the Republic of Goorangoola in the Hunter Valley, which she'd visited with a friend from Rockhampton Grammar School for Girls in her teens.

None of them except she and John seemed upset at the prospect of meeting his mother, High Queen Mathilda Arminger Mackenzie. Objectively, Pip knew that New Mum wasn't going to start screaming "Off with their heads!" though apparently John's granddad on that side had been very given to that sort of thing, being a tyrant's tyrant whose name still made people shudder. His grandmother Sandra had been if anything worse than her ghastly spouse, being considerably smarter as witnessed by the fact that he perished by the sword only ten years after the Change, while she died old, rich, powerful and universally honored and respected . . . or feared, as if there was a difference . . . and in bed of natural causes. And that people still glanced both ways and checked behind the curtains when they mentioned her name.

Objectively I know it's going to be socially stressful at most. My emotions aren't as convinced.

Then the train turned a long curve and Castle Todenangst showed ahead, rearing on its great mound with a few villages huddled about at discreet distances, and a road thronged with traffic even in the winter wet leading up to a massive gatehouse that was a fortress in itself. That helped to snap it all into scale for her; the people and wagons were like ants under the cyclopean bulk.

"*Bloody* hell!" Pip blurted.

It wasn't just that it was huge. She'd seen a few bigger buildings, but only as empty ruins of the ancient world, and this had been built *since* and was very much in use.

It was the fact that it *had* been built since the Change, a building the size of a town, that *was* a town as well as a fortress-palace; a great crenelated wall studded with machicolated towers topped with witch-hat roofs, and above that the towering curtain wall of the inner keep . . .

I'm thinking the word towering *a lot,* her mind gibbered.

. . . eighty feet and looking like more because it crowned a shaved-down hill and with more towers yet in its circuit, and above it all the two *real* towers . . .

There's that word again.

. . . that made the others seem small—one of shining black tipped with gold, and the other gleaming silver. Banners flew from the roofs and from poles above tower and gate, and edged steel glittered wetly on the battlements. She could imagine the catapults and crossbowmen crouching behind the narrow slit windows. . . .

"*Hardout fa!*" Toa exclaimed obscurely; occasionally he reminded you he hadn't grown up in the former Queensland, though the time he'd spent there had rubbed off on his accent.

Then he continued with a quotation: "Towers and battlements, tall as hills, founded upon a mighty mountain-throne above immeasurable pits; great courts and dungeons, eyeless prisons sheer as cliffs, and gaping gates of steel and adamant."

At the surprised glances he went on: "Pip's mum lent me the book."

John sighed. "I think that was exactly what my mother's father had in mind; hence the Lidless Eye as the Arminger arms. And the name of the castle."

Pip didn't speak any German, which was more or less a dead language in the modern world; the Change had hit very hard there. She did have enough to know that Castle Todenangst meant *Fortress of Death-anguish*.

John went on: "I never knew him, of course. . . . He and my other grandfather killed each other in single combat when *my* parents were still about ten. But my grandmother Sandra told me once he picked out the location and had this place planned even before the Change."

With a grin that made her heart turn over: "It's concrete and cargo containers underneath. The black marble sheathing on the Dark Tower and the white on the Silver Tower mostly came from some banks in Seattle. Granddad Norman laired there in the Enormous Black Phallic Thing . . . where else? And he was indeed a gigantic dick, to use an old-fashioned term, but it's full of bureaucrats now, and parts of my grandmother Sandra's art collection."

"She collected?" Pip said; it seemed an unlikely occupation for Madame Tyrant.

"Yes, she . . ." John began.

"Plundered," Thora cut in.

"Looted," Deor supplied.

"Stole," they said in slightly overlapping tones.

John cleared his throat. "Not stole, exactly. The owners were mostly already dead from the Change. Sometimes her expeditions had to fight the people who *ate* the previous owners. She was a fanatic about it, though, and *carried off* everything she could grab for decades."

"The thing *is* bloody huge, though," she said. "How could anyone have built this right after the Blackout . . . I mean, the Change?"

An embarrassed silence fell; embarrassed on the part of John, she thought, and more in the nature of tactful from Deor and Thora.

"My grandfather Norman . . . really wasn't a very nice man," John said at last. "Great, terrible, a genius with a deep vision, a devil in battle and a fine swordsman personally and cunning to a fault, but . . . not very *nice*."

Or in translation, Pip thought, *Norman was a murderous lunatic and built this with hordes of starving slaves dying under the whip and his architect probably sweated blood while he was making his reports and cried and grabbed a bottle and got totally legless afterwards. Oz was lucky, comparatively speaking.*

And Darwin luckiest of all.

King Birmo just sort of talked people into helping themselves. And Mummy and Fifi and Pete got rich helping him do it.

Although, she would admit, the kukri blades her mother had bequeathed her did some fast talking in those days too.

The big State capitals like Sydney and Melbourne, and the areas within a couple of day's walk of them, had died hard and gruesomely, but it was over quickly except for the degenerate gangs of Biters who haunted them to this day. Most of the outback and the smaller centers like her home in Townsville had pulled through without much strain, protected by sheer distance.

Townsville, home to a huge army base, and the center of the cattle industry, had *skated* through. Food and discipline, the magic totems to ward off any apocalypse.

And some places, Tasmania or the South Island of New Zealand, for example, hadn't even gone particularly hungry, not having big cities to drain off the fruits of their agricultural hinterlands anymore, so that even drastically reduced production was more than enough.

There were more sheep than people in the outback of Oz. And more kangaroos than both combined. It was good eating meat of the roo, as long as you spiced it up and didn't dry the steaks out. Between the old farmers and the tribes, there had been plenty of lore to draw on about how to live well on bush tucker.

You just had to develop a taste for grubs and roots, was all.

Unless you were Lady Julianne Balwyn, of course.

My mother was on an airplane over the Great Barrier Reef when the Blackout hit! She survived the crash, the overland trek, a dustup with a gang of "bikers" and not once did she ever ever eat a bloody witchetty grub.

Pip glowed quietly with pride at the thought that her mother would approve of all that she'd achieved. . . .

Lady Jules had been on the Reef partly as a tourist, but really as an extended vacation from England after a series of unfortunate financial misunderstandings between the authorities and her father.

We Balwyns can survive anything!

She mentioned the airplane, though not the fraud, and Thora grinned.

"So was Johnnie's spear-side grandfather Mike Havel, the first Bear Lord of my folk, the Outfit," she said. "He was piloting a small flying machine over the Bitterroot Mountains. That was a thousand miles away; we Bearkillers have epics about their trek west."

One look at the walls of Todenangst told you they'd gone through a much rougher patch here after the Change than in her homeland. Trumpets blared as they passed through the thickness of the outer wall; it was a dedicated railway entrance, but when they rolled into the tunnel-darkness, if you squinted a bit you could see where massive steel slabs hung ready to slam down, probably stronger than the walls themselves and doubtless with various forms of lethal ingenuity of the boiling-oil and red-hot sand variety ready to shower on anyone trapped between them.

"Home. And back to living over the shop," John said.

That surprised a chuckle out of her, and reminded her of why she'd fallen for him in the first place—besides the broad shoulders and narrow waist and long legs and flat stomach and dreamy brownish-hazel eyes and lovely shoulder-length brown hair and regular features and beautiful singing voice and very, very sensitive hands.

Pip found herself taking a deep breath and relaxing. Granted, it wasn't quite the relaxation you'd expect before meeting friendly in-laws, and more the feeling she'd had on the quarterdeck of the *Silver Surfer* as they came coasting into catapult range of a proa full of unfriendly buggers waving blowguns and kris-knives, but at least she felt her self-control snapping back.

The train came out of the tunnel, up an incline that had the horses laboring and the gearing of the hippomotive whining on a deeper note, and rumbled to a stop. John rose, and she saw him consider slinging on his lute, then decide not to be the Troubadour Prince just now, leaving it for the staff to bring, and extended an arm to her instead.

"My Princess?" he said, after a brief kiss.

Pip laid her hand on his, and touched the jeweled fillet and net that bound her wimple to make sure it was still on straight. The people in Astoria had offered to find her a lady's maid, or what they called a lady-in-waiting—in fact, they'd been politely at daggers-drawn with one another over the privilege.

And I can see that a wardrobe like this means you need help. But . . .

She'd equally politely declined and hinted mendaciously that Sovereign Mum-in-Law had reserved the choice, sensing that the post was an important bit of patronage, and one in which she'd need someone she could trust. Which she couldn't from her present state of utter ignorance and clueless baffled alien strangerhood.

The wimple covered most of her tawny sun-streaked hair except for an artfully arranged fringe at the front, and enclosed the sides of her head and her throat, and fell down her back in a narrowing tail to almost waist-length. She'd thought it was silk at first, and it was . . . but very, very fine white silk lace rather than cloth, in a pattern of minute ovals with a narrow band of red and black embroidery along the edge. Like the rest of the clothing it at least had the advantage of keeping out drafts.

"How do I look?" she muttered to John.

He grinned. "Almost as dashing as I do," he said, giving his sword-belt a hitch. "And together . . . we'll knock their hose right off their legs!"

"That stuff does flatter a man's nethers," she admitted.

His knit hose were skintight, and showed off his long legs to perfection, leanly muscled but not thick. She'd been told that his looks favored his mother's side of the family, and that he strongly resembled his grandfather Norman except that his face was longer. If so, Granddad must have been a handsome devil . . . in more senses of the word than one.

The door of the railroad car opened, sliding sideways on internal tracks, and a deafeningly loud *Tarr-ta-ta-ta-rah!* of trumpets just outside followed by multiple echoes made her blink and John sigh. The two-score of trumpeters on either side of the strip of red carpet were blowing long instruments with flags hanging from them, all very much in the playing-card style, as were their heraldic tabards.

The train had evidently gone under the outer donjon of the immense castle, with its barracks and workshops and armories and granaries and bakeries and whatnot built against the inside of the curtain wall, and right into the inner court. They stepped down, and there was a massive *chunk* as lines of guardsmen in black plate-armor slammed the butts of nine-foot glaives—like spears except with a head the shape of a long butcher knife with a curved hook on the rear—down on the flagstone paving.

A great arched roof supported by slender pillars on the outer side covered the spot where tracks stopped; a huge rain-swept open court flanked it on that side, paved with varicolored stone and spotted with clipped topiaries, leafless trees or trained cedars, and planters and great pots that probably had colorful flowers in season.

On the western and eastern sides of the court were the bases of the Silver and Dark Towers, each surrounded by three-quarter circles of stairs leading up to massive doors, and a series of great buildings with point-arched windows and doors and engaged columns and statues in niches. There was a smell of cold wet stone, wet wool from the crowds, and the faint tang of a piped biogas system; all the windows lit as they stepped down, and exterior globes on cast-iron stands that gripped them with the mouths of hawks or dragons; there must be some sort of clockwork ignition system, since nobody was running around with a Firestarter on the end of a pole. The yellow lights gleamed through the thin streams of rain, catching in wavering patches on edged metal or gilding or bright tile and brighter clothes.

It would be bloody inky here without those on an overcast night, she thought; she'd been in cities without lighting systems, and it was like being inside a closet with the added joy of running into hard eye-pokey things and stepping in wet, smelly disgusting things. *Hurrah for technology.*

The buildings included a cathedral—her mind filled in *Flamboyant Gothic,* courtesy of Rockhampton Grammar School for Girls and its art-history courses and her parents' libraries in the town house and the country place. Then she noted it was an enlarged version of the Sainte-Chapelle in Paris, a fond pre-Change teenage memory of her mother's who had collected equally pre-Change picture books that included several studies of it. The walls were a slender tracery of uprights dividing far larger vertical panels of stained glass and a giant rose window at one end, glowing like a jewel box in rainbow shapes right now with the interior lighting.

Though I think the solid parts of the walls are reinforced concrete covered in stucco and glazed tile. Doesn't really matter, I suppose. Very nice!

She blinked again, doing a quick cost estimate on the great church structure; even allowing for the ease of salvage back then, and how much cement and rebar must have been lying around . . .

"How did you do the stained glass?" she murmured to John.

"In pieces over the years, as the workshops built up," he said. "The last of it was finished in time for my confirmation, when I was about twelve."

That *was* impressive, not least the determination involved. Either they were very religious here, or just very persistent, or both. An archbishop and a full train—including incense-swinging acolytes—were standing under the overhang at the tall doors covered in low-relief bronze, singing and generally projecting blessings at her. They'd probably be closer if it weren't raining.

John had warned her they'd probably have to have another ceremony there to mark the marriage and give the panjandrums of the Portland Protective Association a chance to attend, though nobody would dispute the one they'd had was ecclesiastically correct. Pip was an Anglican Rite Catholic, of course, and they were Roman Rite there, but both styles worked for the same boss off in the hills of Umbria these days.

And after what we saw in Baru Denpasar . . . and off in that weird evil whatever-it-was Deor took us through to get to Johnnie's indubitably separated . . . soul, I suppose . . . I'm going to treat it all a bit more seriously. In the world as it is, a girl needs help from On High. The other side certainly seems to get it Down Low from their spiritual patrons! Though there's all the manky mind-enslavement and degradation and living-death eternal suffering botheration they go through too.

If the weather had been better the greeting would probably have been in the courtyard, for the maximum audience—there were at least a couple of thousand people there anyway, braving the drizzle and the gathering darkness. More, those with higher rank or pull, lined the arched way to the semicircular steps at the base of the Silver Tower, kept back by the glaivesmen, and well-disciplined enough that the men-at-arms didn't need to put the shafts level and push.

Pip blinked again; as they passed all the men except the guards went to one knee—the right—and uncovered and bowed their heads, and the women sank into deep almost-kneeling skirt-spreading curtseys with eyes downcast.

I suppose I could get used to this, she thought, and almost burst out laughing when she imagined trying to get the inhabitants of Darwin to perform in such a fashion. You were likely to get a pie chucked at your head.

It certainly wasn't much like home. Even in staid Townsville ordinary people tended to be aggressively self-assertive, and in freewheeling Darwin . . . Jeez. It didn't bear thinking about.

But I'm not absolutely sure I want to get used to it. It's amazing how easygoing Johnnie is, if he grew up with this! It makes the sunny self-confidence more understandable, but it's reassuring he didn't turn out spoiled and arrogant.

John seemed to pick up on the thought; he was good at that.

"Don't worry," he said, hardly moving his lips at all and keeping up an occasional nod to either side. "This is much more formal than usual."

They went up the steps between more of the motionless black-armored guards, looking disturbingly mechanical with their visors down and their shields blazoned with the creepy flame-wreathed Lidless Eye. This set had their longswords sloped over one shoulder, and as the couple went by they snapped them up before their faces in salute as they passed and then back to the slope, in a rippling motion as regular as if done by gears.

High Queen Mathilda Arminger Mackenzie stood waiting for her within a great room that spanned the entire ground floor of the Silver Tower, under an embroidered canopy with a clutch of ladies-in-waiting in the background, and officials lay and ecclesiastical. She glittered darkly in her cotte-hardie, but the face was ordinary until you saw the eyes in the wimple-framed face; middle-aged, slightly stout, a little darker than John and with the marks of recent grief and care.

John went to one knee and kissed the extended hand—which was incongruously roughened and bore old scars and nicks.

"My mother, my Queen, and my liege," he said. "I have returned; forgive the prodigal, as Our Lord said in the parable."

"Rise, my beloved son, in whom We are well-pleased," Mathilda said warmly despite the formal language, and gave him an embrace and kiss on both cheeks. "No forgiveness is necessary on this happy, happy day!"

Then she covertly tweaked his ear sharply, prompting a well-stifled yelp and twitch.

"And that's for running off with your sister and scaring me half to *death!*" she added in a non-carrying tone. "And getting yourself blown to God-knows-where and menaced by demons and evil magicians! There are some family traditions it's better to let drop!"

Cheers broke out in the huge room and echoed off the carved plaster of the groin-arched ceiling high above. There was a subdued *fumph!* of flash-powder as photographers for magazines and newspapers did their business, providing material for the mezzotints and woodblocks that would grace posters and newssheets and papers and magazines all over Montival.

Pip sank into the deep curtsey that she'd been given a quick course in—not much different from the one they used in Winchester, at that; left leg forward, right back, heels in line, toes out, sink down with the torso upright, then incline forward as you used both hands to extend the skirt until you were almost touching the rear knee to the ground. Then she did the hand-kiss thing, which required a bit of juggling.

Thank God for Rockhampton Grammar.

"And rise, my newest daughter!" the High Queen said warmly, giving her a kiss on both cheeks too; she wore some mild flowery scent. "Greetings and welcome to the High Kingdom, and twice welcome to the House of Artos, Princess Philippa."

Stone the crows and bugger the ducks, I am a Princess now!

More cheers, and then a quick address to the crowd: ". . . I ask your pardon, Gentles, as a mother who feared for her son that this evening be private and not an affair of State . . ." followed by cheers that made the roof ring.

Despite the plea, a little more bullock poop followed before they could get going, and Pip quickly filed the names—it was a useful talent and she'd worked hard on it.

There was a working elevator enclosed in a framework of gilded brass with accordion-pleat doors drawn aside by pages, and they all paced over to it between crimson ropes looped on stands and more guardsmen, through a cheering, bowing-and-curtseying (and photograph-taking) mob. It was the first she'd ever ridden in and it took a bit of an effort to be blasé as they lifted smoothly upward; it wasn't crowded with the seven of them—the five who'd arrived, the High Queen, and a quiet but extremely clever-looking woman about a decade younger who was evidently her confidential secretary, or amanuensis as they said here, and stayed resolutely in the background but missed nothing and had a notepad ready to take dictation.

The cage went up smoothly; at her glance Thora pointed down: "Convicts in a giant hamster-wheel in the dungeons. Usually there's music."

"I had the carillon disconnected for the occasion, Mistress Garwood," Mathilda said dryly.

Apart from Toa and Pip, everyone here seemed to be old acquaintances at least.

And Queen Mum is stuck with me. I hope . . . think, actually . . . she's more than smart enough to realize that getting off on the right foot is her best option.

John held up his hands defensively as the High Queen turned to him. "I couldn't help it, Mother! You know Órlaith can talk anyone into doing anything!"

Mathilda chuckled grimly and nodded.

"Well, she's her father's daughter . . . and you're not so bad at it either. All's well, John. And apparently, you're presenting me with my first grandchild, too, for which I will forgive you a good deal."

"Umm . . . yes, we are, Your Highness," Pip said.

"Though it's a minor miracle it didn't happen earlier, and without the sacrament."

Pip choked back a nervous laugh. Apparently, the Queen Mum had no illusions about her darling boy, and that remark was . . .

Too right, she thought. *We didn't know we were serious when the impregnation came along. I hadn't noticed myself, Deor just picked up on it with that spooky thing he does.*

"It . . ." she began.

"*Don't* tell me it 'just sort of happened,' child," Mathilda said.

Pip clenched her teeth; she hadn't intended to be *quite* that inane about it, but that was the gist of anything she could have said.

"I have five of my own, one not weaned yet, and I'm fully aware of *how it happens.* And in close company, style me Mathilda, I think. Or Mattie, if you like. Perhaps it's a little soon for *Mother,* though I hope that'll seem natural in time."

"Pip, then . . . since we're family . . . Mattie. Whether we like it or not. . . ."

"So we'd better like it, shouldn't we?"

Pip snorted, and met a raised brow that echoed the sentiment exactly. She liked this woman already . . . and the more so because she recognized exactly how she'd been manipulated into it, and how she'd been shoved slightly off-balance at the same time.

Then the High Queen gave Thora a fleeting glance that convinced Pip she was entirely aware of their arrangement about the unacknowledged second . . .

First, really. Month farther along than I am. Fertile little bastard, my Johnnie!

. . . pregnancy and very willing to keep it confidential.

The elevator went high enough that when it opened the windows at the ends of the cruciform corridors dividing the tower were actual *windows* rather than arrow-slits, though widely spaced; no practical siege tower or ladder could reach anything this high, even a first-class modern steel one driven by hydraulic rams. The guard-captain here was in half-armor, with a livery badge pinned to the front of his roll-edged chaperon hat, a blond good-looking man in his thirties who saluted and bowed smoothly. His second-in-command looked almost identical, except that he was shorter, darker and had slanted eyes.

"Ah, Lioncel," Mathilda said to him. "Glad to see you back from the wilds of the Palouse. How's my lord Count your father? And your good lady and the children?"

"My father's still the pattern of knighthood and a bit of a fashion plate, Your Majesty," he said. "But champing to be off overseas and most displeased that you won't let him go. Azalaïs and the children are busy preparing Castle Campscapell for the Twelve Nights."

"And you, Huon. My goodness, you look more like Odard all the time."

They were presented as Viscount Lioncel de Stafford of Campscapell and heir to the County of that name, and to the Barony of Forest Grove; his second in command was Baron Huon Liu de Gervais.

God, these names! It's like a historical novel. . . . Wait a minute, the names are mostly from actual historical novels. Though that was their parents and grandparents; I suppose to them it's just their names. And what they're wearing. . . . It's not costume anymore, to them it's just their clothes.

Lioncel added: "An honor to make your acquaintance, Your High-ness," to Pip, with Huon murmuring the same.

For a moment she blanked, her mind not translating *Your Highness* into *me*, and was panic-stricken at how exactly to respond. Then she copied John's friendly nod to him and his second. Their attitude to John was respectful, but . . .

But they saw him growing up as a spotty adolescent and don't subconsciously re-ally regard him as an adult, she thought. *Hmmmm. And he notices it.*

"The Lord Chancellor, the Grand Marshal and my lady mother and the others await you in the Lesser Presence Hall, Your Majesty," Lioncel said to Mathilda; Huon walked ahead to open the door and bow them in.

The ceiling of the corridors was high, fifteen or sixteen feet and cov-ered in ancient-looking carved wood coffering, and the walls were smooth pearl-gray marble flecked with green. Glass doors at the end of one corridor led onto a broad balcony that must have spectacular views in good weather, but they were closed now and streaked with rain, be-yond which was blackness like a velvet curtain.

Above their heads were bronze light-standards with softly hissing gaslights in frosted-glass globes, and there were niches between the widely-spaced doors along all four corridors. Those held an eye-catching assortment of art, pictures or small statues or things less describable. At first she was too tight-wound to more than let her eyes flick over them and note that they'd make this a fantastic place to loot . . .

Pardon me, salvage.

. . . but gradually they began to sink in as they passed. Darwin and Townsville held a good many treasures garnered from the lost cities by salvagers like her mother and friends, but nothing approaching this.

"Good God, that looks as if it was really as old as it looks," Pip said, halting almost involuntarily before one for a moment.

It held a Madonna and Child done in an almost-Byzantine style, in egg tempura on wood with a gold-leaf background, but softer in outline, the play of light and dark colors revealing the figures underneath the heavy drapery in rounded three-dimensional life, with an inviting warmth that felt somehow compassionate. Swatches of precious fabric and jewels had been incorporated into the work, and it glittered softly.

"It was done about seven hundred and fifty years ago, in Sienna in Tuscany, by Duccio di Buoninsegna," Mathilda said.

"How did it end up here?" Pip said, unable to keep a little awe out of her tone, and then added: "Mattie."

"My mother Lady Sandra sent an expedition to Hearst Castle . . . that was a wealthy man's palace in California before the Change, what's Westria now . . . to salvage the artwork there, a few years after the Change. More than one expedition, actually, and she said to me once that she regretted not doing more, and earlier. And she swept up more from museums and galleries in the dead cities, and in abandoned mansions . . . paintings, books, statues, tapestries, the ceiling up above us here. . . . There are still warehouses full of it in Portland and the Crown castles, not counting what she gave out as gifts to nobles and the Church and the guilds. . . . I suppose she *should* have concentrated on saving people alone. But these things matter too."

She gently touched the wall below another niche, this one a statuette of a warrior in a fantastic rayed feather headdress and jade earplugs, carrying a decorated shield.

"These things *are* people," Pip said, carried away by the grandeur of it all.

Everyone looked at her. Curious. She blushed, but she was sure of this. It was something her mother had taught her, and something she had long felt.

"People come and go. We will all of us go back to the dust sooner or later. But this"—she waved a hand to take in the magnificent collection—"this is the legacy of the human race. It cannot perish from the earth."

Her skin dimpled with gooseflesh and she saw a smile tug at the corners of Mattie's lips. Blushing, she hurried on.

"It was why my mother, my uncle and aunt, why they took Royal

Warrants of Salvage into the fallen cities. Not just for fortune and glory, but because it was the right thing to do."

Mattie's smile broke like a new dawn on her face.

"Oh, Sandra would have loved you. You're going to do just fine here."

She turned and waved her hand at another piece.

"This is Mayan—from Campeche, originally, and about twelve hundred years old. The jade in the next is a Guanyin, the Han Goddess of Mercy . . . not that Mother wasn't a great patron of our modern artists and makers, too."

CHAPTER FIVE

PORTLAND PROTECTIVE ASSOCIATION
(FORMERLY NORTHERN OREGON)
HIGH KINGDOM OF MONTIVAL
(FORMERLY WESTERN NORTH AMERICA)
DECEMBER 20TH
CHANGE YEAR 46/2044 AD

T wo more of the armored guards stood outside the panels of the door to the private apartments, saluting as Baron Huon bowed them through. Pip blinked again when they stepped in, past an antechamber, and into the dining room; it wasn't nearly as grand as she'd expected.

Well, grand enough, but not huge. And I'm used to open-plan buildings in hot countries, so I underestimated the size. Still, not overpowering.

There was an oval mahogany table with a snowy linen cloth set for twelve under a chandelier, and the walls covered in tapestries and lined with side tables—neither were ancient, but very well done, the tapestries showing elongated lords and ladies flying their hawks in a rolling countryside of hills and flower-starred fields. The cloth gave the room a warmer feel, as well.

Dinner started with introductions, including an array of John's siblings: a redheaded fifteen-year-old boy named Faolán, in a kilt and plaid; a ten-year-old girl called Vuissance crying with happiness in a dress called a kirtle with only a band around her loose black locks as she threw herself against John and hugged him and was hugged in return; and a sleepy baby in a nurse's arms with that who-are-these-people-what-is-this-place-what-the-devil-am-I-doing-here look that they had at that age.

"God, Johnnie, you got to have actual adventures like Mother and Da!" the boy said, torn between happiness and envy, and giving her a covert appreciative glance after he kissed her hand; he was old enough for that. "*And* brought home a beautiful princess—it's like those *chansons de geste* you like so much!"

John shuddered and gave him a brotherly push on the side of the head that was nearly a clout.

"I got to be lost, terrified, nearly eaten by a giant enchanted crocodile, have a burning siege tower collapse on me, nearly be assassinated by headhunters with bones through their noses, be captured by demonolaters, and subjected to nameless frights by eldritch abominations, squib," he said.

Then a smile at Pip. "But the beautiful princess was worth it all! And the epic I compose will live forever!"

The younger ones were packed off after kisses and embraces, and Faolán got to sit at the foot of the table for educational purposes, under a binding oath of shut-up-ed-ness, which he obeyed in an obvious bid not to be remembered and excluded.

Pip filed names and faces. That was a trader's trick she had learned at her uncle's knee. The non-immediate-family members were more immediately important, and there were five of them. One was in a much longer version of a kilt called an arisaid, with a plaid pinned over a loose shirt of embroidered linen, wearing a silver headband around hair gone white that had obviously been fire-red once and bearing something that she realized was a triple moon—waxing, full and waning. Faded, very keen green eyes marked a face she was so at home in that the wrinkles looked like an expression in themselves.

"I'm your new grandma, Pip," she said, with an impish grin that made Pip feel they were of an age for a moment, sharing a secret at school. "Juniper Mackenzie, but call me Juniper—or anything you want, to be sure."

She had an accent, more or less Irish, which Pip had met before at home from a few elderly survivors, and a hint of something else.

"How about Mac?"

The old woman threw back her head and laughed, a rich, silvery sound that recalled cathedral bells peeling.

"Oh, yes." She chuckled when at last she had herself back under control. "You will indeed be fine here. Mac it is, then. So mote it be."

Pip tilted her head, slightly unsettled.

Mac had not been anywhere near Mattie when she'd said . . .

The old witch, or wiccan or whatever the Hell she was gave Deor a long considering look.

"I see you've been putting my teaching to very good use, young man."

"I have, Lady Juniper, and I thank you for it once again. It saved more than my life."

"And I thank *you*, Deor Woden's-man. You saved my grandchild . . . and my great-grandchild, the thought! I won't forget it."

"My grandmother, and former Chieftain of the Clan Mackenzie," John explained. "The Witch-Queen."

"Oh, not that again!" Juniper said, rolling her eyes.

"Now retired, which means she has the power but doesn't have to do the routine work down there in the Mackenzie *dúthchas* anymore."

"Nonsense, Maude's the Chief of the Name now, I just give her advice when she asks," Juniper said stoutly. "There's such a thing as knowing when to step aside."

John smiled. "And Aunt Maude . . . and the *Oneach Mór* . . . that's a sort of parliament, Pip . . . disregard your advice so *often*, Grandmother."

"The which is why I give it so *seldom*, Johnnie-me-lad."

There was an elderly cleric in a plain black-and-white Benedictine monk's robe, introduced as Father Ignatius, and also as Lord Chancellor— of the High Kingdom, not the Association—which accounted for the gold chain of office on his chest. Watching him stand and move told a story too.

This was a fighting man, and a very good one, Pip thought, and knew from Toa's thoughtful grunt behind her he'd sensed the same thing.

More surprising was a sixtyish woman, tall and blade-straight, with hair cut in a pageboy bob that must have been mostly pale blond once, and the coldest gray eyes Pip had ever seen, though they warmed just a little at the sight of John. She was in a darker, plainer version of John's hose and jerkin and houppelande coat with dagged sleeves, and also had a chain of office and the little golden spurs on her heels. Nobody was wearing weapons except for the apparently-ceremonial jeweled daggers, but you could tell *this* one usually had a sword at her side.

"Baroness Tiphaine d'Ath, Grand Marshal of the High Queen's Host," John said, as he made the introductions.

"Chief of the Montivallan General Staff, to put it without the folderol," she said coolly. Pip realized with a jolt she must have been at least a teenager at the time of the Change.

She bowed and kissed Pip's hand. "Welcome to Montival, Princess Philippa."

With her was a very feminine woman in exquisite Associate garb involving a good deal of lace that made you want to examine it in detail; she was about a decade younger than Tiphaine, but could have passed for forty and was still stunning in a matronly way.

"Don't be old-fashioned, Tiph," she said, and poked the Marshal in the ribs with her fan.

"Lady Delia, Countess de Stafford and Châtelaine of Barony Ath," John continued, as Pip got the kiss-on-both-cheeks greeting and a waft of some indefinable scent that smelled as if it had started as lavender and lilac before squads had labored over it.

Châtelaine . . . does that mean what I think it means? Pip thought, looked at the two of them, and decided: *Too bloody right it does. They have that look like Uncle Pete and Aunt Fifi, been together forever and worn grooves in the world doing it.*

"Nobody told me this was a matriarchy," Pip said, looking around.

That got a general laugh; except for Delia, who giggled and managed to bring it off despite a buxom middle age.

"Oh, this one's going to run you ragged, John," she said, tapping him on the cheek with the fan. "But you'll enjoy the process."

John laughed again. "Very likely, Delly."

"It's not a matriarchy, Pip," Mathilda said. "It just looks that way."

"It is so a matriarchy, Mattie," Juniper Mackenzie said. "And all the better for it! We just didn't intend for it to work out that way; but human-kind proposes and the Powers dispose. Even you Associates have had a Lady Protector and not a *Lord* Protector for thirty-six of the past forty-six years, between Sandra and you, and that despite all the plate-armored machismo."

"Women just survive better," d'Ath said, and at Mathilda's swift re-proving look: "I miss him too, Mattie, but it's true."

Juniper sighed. "It was the same with his father. Ah, a beautiful man he was, body and spirit both, and Rudi was so like him. My lovely Sun-born boy, with a spirit like the morning light."

"I'm just a monk," Ignatius said dryly. "Like mules, we don't count in the pedigrees of the Great Houses."

Pip snorted. She'd never been religious, but she liked this bloke right off the bat, she decided. He seemed . . .

Cheeky.

A pang of homesickness followed immediately upon the realization that Uncle Pete would probably pick him out and whisk him away from the informal formalities for some serious drinking and yarn spinning at the first opportunity.

"Are you implying the nobility are horses, or just some particular part of a horse?" d'Ath said.

Everyone chuckled at that. "You're a monk of the Order of the Shield of Saint Benedict, my Lord Chancellor," she went on. "Who are sover-eigns in Mount Angel and have chapter houses all over the realm. I re-member fighting your Brothers during the Lord Protector's wars; you weren't the most numerous enemies we had but you were trouble enough."

"Ah, but then you were in schism from Holy Mother Church," Igna-tius said urbanely.

"Personally I was just faking it because Norman wanted his own Pope and that lunatic he picked burned people alive if he thought they were heretics," she replied. "Until Sandra . . . solved that problem, after the Protector's War when Rudi's dad put Norman out of the picture."

Pip's head was spinning like a willy-willy with the effort of keeping up.

Juniper Mackenzie gave d'Ath a look that went with a raised eyebrow. "You were close to Sandra, as I recall."

"I was her finest assassin, Lady Juniper, as you well know," d'Ath said calmly, and left it at that; Delia winced slightly.

My, what a lot of history they have here! Pip thought. *And history is mostly about people killing each other.*

A squire with a white baton cleared his throat. Pip put her hand on John's again and he led her to the table; Mathilda sat at the head, with her son and new daughter-in-law to the right, and everyone followed in a ripple of precedence.

Pages in their early teens served the meal, which arrived via a dumb-waiter shaft in the wall behind a carved screen; with the previous exchange in mind Pip noted that the majority were page *boys*, but not all by any means.

Page didn't mean servant, exactly, not in the sense she thought of the word. John had said it was a sort of chrysalis stage before you burst out as a squire, which in turn was the stage before knight, and all the upper-class sprigs went through it; girls became maidens-in-waiting if they had a different career path in mind, one that didn't involve plentiful sweat and bruising and a focus on sharp pointy things. Both were rather like going to boarding school, and as with the classic British hellholes one of the purposes was to drum a little humility into the spawn of the upper orders. Along with building social contacts and networks of patronage.

Ignatius led the Catholics in crossing themselves and saying their grace:

"Bless us, O Lord, and these, Thy gifts, which we are about to receive from Thy bounty. Through Christ Jesus, our Lord. Amen."

"Amen," Pip said.

Then to herself: *Well, here's an assortment,* glancing out of the corners of her eyes and listing them mentally:

Baroness d'Ath and her Châtelaine put aside a crumb of bread dipped in wine and murmured:

"Holy Hestia, Hearth-guardian, to whom we offer first and last on every day, glorious is your portion and your right, for without You mortals hold no feast."

Deor and Thora Hammer-signed their plates and invoked someone called *All-giving Nerthus*; Juniper Mackenzie's equivalent, which her grandson Faolán echoed, began with a pentagram and ended with: *Their hands helping Earth to bring forth life.*

The memory of weeks of naval slumgullion and sea-biscuit was recent enough that the meal itself was very welcome.

They started with caviar on rye-toast points, which she'd read about but never had before and could see would be an easily-acquired taste, accompanied by a chilled Chardonnay, dry and flinty, that had her exclaiming slightly as she sipped her pregnancy-dictated half glass. One of the things her mother had taught her was how to appreciate wine—Townsville didn't have vineyards, but plenty came up from the southern parts of Oz and over from New Zealand by ship.

The Kiwi plonk is always better, she grudgingly admitted.

"Ours," Delia said proudly. "From the demesne vines of Montinore Manor; that's the home-estate of Barony Ath."

"I just drink it; my Châtelaine manages the estates," d'Ath said. "Farming was never my strong point."

A clear seafood broth with scallions and small chunks of lobster followed and then a winter spinach salad with chopped toasted walnuts, pomegranate seeds, a little feta cheese and dried cranberries topped with cored and thin-sliced pears that were firm but ripe, dressed with herb-infused olive oil and apple vinegar, and accompanied by a Chenin Blanc that had hints of pear, honeysuckle, quince, and apple, and perhaps a little ginger.

"And here I was expecting to rip with my teeth at great joints of meat laid on bread trenchers," Pip said appreciatively as she broke and buttered a warm crusty roll. "And tear chickens apart with my hands and quaff from tankards."

That got another laugh. "About some things my mother put her foot down, even with Father," Mathilda said. "Actual medieval food wasn't like that either, really . . . though they did use the bread trenchers. And eat with their fingers and share cups, but there was an elaborate etiquette about it. Some of the noble Houses do that, but usually only on special occasions."

The main course was slices of marinated roast boar haunch covered in a tangy dark gravy with a fruity taste and flanked by steamed halved Brussels sprouts topped with lemon butter sprinkled with chopped hazel-nuts, honey-glazed carrots, and cubes of potato grilled with rosemary and garlic-infused oil, and with it a glass of Pinot Noir. She rolled it over her tongue and tasted overtones of sage, cedar, coffee, and tobacco.

"All right, there are compensations for the weather here," she said mock-grudgingly, and got a chuckle.

"This pig died happy!" Toa said . . . happily, taking a second helping from the attentive page, who was covertly fascinated with his tattoos.

D'Ath suddenly grinned at him, though she seemed a bit dour in general; Pip revised her initial ice-woman estimate, and even more favorably. She tended to approve of people who approved of her mother's old friend-retainer-bodyguard-right-hand-man.

"No, Master Toa, it didn't die happy. It died squealing and trying to run up my spear and kill *me*, all five hundred pounds of it."

She pointed with her knife at what Pip had assumed were ivory orna-ments on the side of the serving plate where the slices lay in a neat fan on a bed of parsley. At a second glance the *ornaments* turned out to be tusks, curved and pointed and easily as long as the dagger at her waist, remind-ing her of the ones warrior tribesmen in New Guinea wore through their noses or made into necklaces.

Then the noblewoman indicated one of the tapestries, which showed a beast built like a battering ram on legs, with huge shoulders, flashing tusks, and . . .

Vicious piggy little red eyes, Pip thought. *Rubies there but the reality is just bloody, I suppose.*

. . . lunging at hunters with broad-bladed spears that had cross guards below the steel as hounds jumped about being understandably hysterical. Pip suddenly realized that the cross guard was entirely practical, with something that strong and that size—five hundred pounds was a small pony—and that determined to take you with them to Hog Heaven, doubtless to be the *object* of the hunts there.

Toa's eyes lit up and his smile smoldered. "If it died trying to gut you, mate, it died happy."

Lady Delia's eyes rolled up. "Don't encourage her! You're too old for boar hunting now, darling! Your bruises from *this* beast are still that disgusting yellow and green color!"

"I'm too old for *duels,* and for tournaments, except as a judge," d'Ath said. "And I'm not allowed to duel as Marshal, anyway. Hunting I can still do; allow me *some* outdoor pleasures, sweetie."

"Fighting with massive murderous pigs in deep cold mud is a pleasure?" Delia asked with a sigh.

"Sounds bloody awesome," Toa said around a mouthful of pork. "A lot more fun than fighting with murderous blokes any day of the week."

"Yes," d'Ath said succinctly. "And I don't do it alone."

"There's hawking," Delia said. "We can do that together."

"And we do, as often as I can tolerate watching a bird have all the fun of killing something edible," d'Ath said.

She turned to Toa: "If you'd like, you can have a taste of it in a little while. After all the"—her voice held an exaggerated disgust, and she winked at her partner, who gave her a pout—"parties and ceremonies and the Christmas revels."

"Too easy. I'm there!" Toa said with an enormous, alarming grin showing white tombstone teeth.

"If you weren't Grand Marshal, some duelist *would* have killed you long ago, Tiph," Mathilda said.

"Dueling is barbaric," Juniper said. "You should ban it."

"Rebellions are even more barbaric," Mathilda said to her, with the air of someone treading a familiar measure, and turned back to d'Ath:

"Did Rudi and I save you from murderous relatives out for revenge just so a *pig* could kill you?"

"Probably," d'Ath said tranquilly. "Not that there's all that much difference between Count Stavarov and a wild boar and his relatives are mostly pigs except the ones who are weasels."

Toa laughed appreciatively, even though he had no idea who they were talking about. There were more than enough Stavarov types in Townsville or Darwin to get the joke. Unsure whether she was supposed to be scandalized, Pip simply smirked.

"Or a tiger will get me, or I'll break my neck falling off a horse jumping a log. I'm older now than I ever expected to be . . . ever expected since the Change . . . and the children are pretty much grown."

"Well, *I'd* miss you, I assure you!" Lady Delia said tartly.

Then she looked at the dessert tray, sighed, patted her midriff and shook her head.

Ignatius cleared his throat; he'd restricted himself to water and soup and bread, and he ignored the plates of little fruit-tarts with dabs of whipped cream, gleaming glazed confections of blueberries, dried candied apple and peach, and toasted hazelnuts and walnuts on clove-and-nutmeg infused yellow custard inside pastry shells. D'Ath loaded a plate with them and began methodically eating them and stirring rich cream and sugar into her Hawaiian coffee.

Delia looked at her and murmured: "Brute! *Skinny* brute!"

"Mud-wrestling with giant pigs works it off," d'Ath said, and they smiled at each other.

"Your adventures in the Ceram Sea are intriguing, and disturbing, Prince John," Ignatius said, ignoring the byplay.

"They were *even more* disturbing at the time," John said fervently.

Pip nodded as she tried one of the tarts and sipped the Hawaiian coffee, which was excellent—it was sold in Darwin, though the Papuan product was much cheaper—and sampled a small glass of a clear pear brandy whose label showed a volcano and the legend *Hood River Ducal Reserve*; there was a whole peeled pear in the bottle.

"More than you think," Ignatius said. "There is the question of how Alan Thurston—"

Pip felt herself sit bolt upright, and the others of her party did likewise. They'd met a man . . . or possibly the quasi-material projection of a man—of that name in the domain outside time and space where Deor had led them, into the world of a mad God's dream.

"—ended up with a knife emblazoned with the Yellow Seal . . . on Crown Princess Órlaith's ship off Pearl Harbor. Young Thurston killed himself with it, by the way, rather than injure the Crown Princess . . . which some mental pressure was evidently trying to force him to do. And then the knife . . . went away."

"Wait a minute, he was in Hawai'i?" John said. "But we saw him in Baru Denpasar!"

"John," Deor said. "We saw him, yes, but not in Baru Denpasar. Where we saw him was when our spirits walked—and where yours was taken as captive by the King in Yellow after the battle. Our bodies were there in the Raja's guesthouse, but the rest of us was . . . elsewhere. And there the essence of Alan Thurston, the real man, was held captive with you. When we freed you, with his aid, we freed him as well."

He sighed. "It's a pity to hear he died—I liked him."

"So did I," John said soberly. "But apparently he died well, fighting for his own soul."

"Which is as much as a man can do," Deor said.

He signed the Hammer; Pip felt herself crossing herself again, which was a new habit for her when it wasn't obligatory.

Ignatius and Mathilda did likewise, and the monk continued: "Yes, I do not think that could be classified as suicide, though I shall pray for him, and it would be a charitable act to have masses said for his soul."

He glanced at Mathilda, who nodded and made a gesture to her amanuensis, who made a note on her pad. The monk went on:

"When your reports all mentioned such a person in this very unpleasant Otherworld from which you rescued the Prince it was . . . alarming."

"Saint Michael by my side," John said, halfway between reverential prayer and reverential curse and a factual description of what had happened there at the end.

He crossed himself. Pip did the same again, Thora and Deor drew the Hammer, Juniper Mackenzie the pentagram, and Toa muttered something in Maori.

"Precisely," the cleric said, with an iron in his tone that reminded you that his was a warrior order. "There was a link there, one that spanned both time and space . . . very large spans of both."

Mathilda's amanuensis leaned forward and murmured in her ear, and handed her a slip of paper. She read it and nodded.

"I've had searchers looking into some things—in the libraries here," she said. "Alan's mother took a book from the Silver Tower collection just after the Prophet's War, when she . . . went to her ranch. Part of a bundle, a gift from my mother the Lady Regent. It was called *The King in Yellow*."

CHAPTER SIX

PORTLAND PROTECTIVE ASSOCIATION
(FORMERLY NORTHERN OREGON)
HIGH KINGDOM OF MONTIVAL
(FORMERLY WESTERN NORTH AMERICA)
DECEMBER 20TH
CHANGE YEAR 46/2044 AD

Pip started; she and John shared a glance, with each other and with Deor and Thora, and Toa cursed under his breath again.

Mathilda looked at the note and frowned. "It's listed in the archive as a book of fanciful tales by a man called Chambers, who wrote a century before the Change," she said. "There are three other copies. But the head librarian, Lady Bruissende de Chehalis . . . she was a junior there at the time . . . handled the records when the gift bundle was made up and she says . . . and wrote at the time . . . that it was a *play*. And bound in strange gray leather, not like a pre-Change book at all or like the written record describing the binding. Her notes list it as having the figure of a masked man in yellow robes on the cover, and no author's name at all."

Silence fell. The four adventurers looked at one another again. John spoke:

"When we were . . . wherever we were . . . we heard a play of that name mentioned. Reading it always led to madness and death, and the King in Yellow mentioned in it . . . and the Pallid Mask, and Carcosa . . . they were there in Baru Denpasar. In the waking world, not in Shadow."

Ignatius kissed his crucifix and murmured a Latin prayer. "I think, Your Majesty, that we should ban this play . . . or the book of tales that can apparently *turn into* the play that's mentioned in the tales. . . ."

"Turn into . . . mentioned in . . . my head hurts," John said under his breath.

Pip nodded in sympathy; that was far too self-recursive for comfort and gave a queasy feeling of unreality to *everything.*

As if the world is spinning in circles and might disappear up its own arse with a wet plopping sound at any moment.

Mathilda frowned. "I don't think we *can* ban it, under the Great Charter," she said. "The Cardinal-Archbishop can certainly put it on the *Index Librorum Prohibitorum* here in the Association territories, and I'll ask him to—and urge him to—write to the Holy Father in Badia that the Church as a whole do the same, and we'll forward our reports on the matter to them, and to friendly governments generally. And the head of your Order can do the same in Mount Angel. But the other member-realms of the High Kingdom . . . I certainly can't do that on my own authority as High Queen under the Great Charter."

"Mackenzies don't hold with banning books of any sort," Juniper said. "And raising a great stink about it will arouse curiosity, so it will."

"Yes, Lady Juniper," Ignatius said. "That is a real risk. But I think this is more than a book . . . or a play. Or at least it is in the world that the Change has given us."

Deor had been lost in thought. "I think. . . . You know of that insect in the southern deserts, the one that digs a pit that is *just* too steep to climb out of?"

"Ant-lions," Pip supplied. "We've . . . they've got them in Australia too. It's the larvae that do it. Manky little things, if you imagine yourself the size of the ant that's scrabbling to get out of the pit and knowing what's down at the bottom."

Deor nodded. "We had them in Mist Hills too; sometimes I lay and watched them on summer afternoons, as a boy. And I think that this book . . . this play . . . this *thing*, is like that. It is a digging through the wall of the world, or perhaps in the floor of the world would be a better way to put it. It lies in wait for human-kind. . . ."

"For men's souls," Ignatius said.

Deor made a gesture of assent. "And if one falls into the trap . . . through ill-luck or a . . . an attunement of the self . . . then you become just such a trap for others. So it spreads and grows, in growing circles of madness and chaos, where all things become mingled . . . good and ill, life and death themselves. It is a Power of black evil, but not the same one behind our other foes. We have seen good takes many forms; why not the other?"

Mathilda frowned. "But the book of tales with the same name?" she said.

"That was written before the Change, when the walls between the worlds were thicker, stronger, when things were . . . flatter," Deor said. "It was a reaching-through by the King, but into the most gossamer and elusive of things, a mind. He placed images into an imagination already attuned to the strange. Now, the walls thin, they grow weak, and the . . . the trap . . . becomes more itself. And seeks to warp all around it, to absorb all and become all."

John leaned an elbow on the table and put his palm to his forehead. "That makes an unpleasant amount of sense after what we went through."

Juniper Mackenzie looked at Deor, her head tilted to one side. "It's a joy of a teacher's life when her pupils surpass her," she said. "I would be wishing that the occasion itself was a happier one."

"We have to live in a world where such things are," Mathilda said.

With a bitter smile: "I thought that when Rudi first drew the Sword of the Lady, on Nantucket. I didn't know the half of it then. Now we need miracles."

Ignatius smiled at her. "Remember, my daughter, that miracles don't do the work for us. They open a possibility in the world, no more."

Mathilda nodded assent and turned to her son: "Órlaith won a victory in Hawai'i . . . you know that?"

He nodded, and Pip did too; the news had been all over Astoria, just in via a naval courier, an odd-looking vessel of pre-Blackout . . .

Pre-Change, she reminded herself.

. . . pre-Change materials unearthly light and strong, a catamaran with sails of a fine hemp weave that mimicked some of the properties of the ancient sails and included a balloon spinnaker that she wouldn't have believed possible if she hadn't seen it. She wouldn't have believed the speed, either, if she hadn't seen similar vessels working the Gulf north of Darwin, and off Cairns and Townsville. Mostly they were toys for the rich, but they had their uses for commercial or government or military couriers, where the cargo was information and speed was all-important.

"Good for her, and Montival, and God speed the right," John added.

"Amen," his mother said. "But she says they're going to need substantial reinforcements to tackle Korea itself. The war's going to be bigger and cost more and take longer than we thought."

Lady d'Ath chuckled like light bones and feathers rustling in a box. "Oh, and that's *such* a surprise, since it's *never* happened before in all the history of wars. Which is to say, all of history."

Delia sighed. "I wish they'd never come up with that stupid *Lady Death* nickname, darling," she complained. "Honestly, sometimes I think you're trying to live up to it. At least you haven't taken to cradling a Persian cat and giving evil laughs, the way Sandra did when they called her the Spider of the Silver Tower."

John put his hands up in that don't-blame-me gesture he'd used in the elevator again; Pip hadn't seen it before then, but she realized she'd be seeing it again, as long as her mother-in-law lived.

"I *have* to go, Mother," he said. "I'm a knight, I'm the right age, I'm of House Artos, I can't *not* go, the nobility here in our PPA fiefs would never respect me again if I didn't."

"No, you must," Mathilda said, obviously unwillingly, and obviously too smart and too conscientious to let her emotions matter. "Whatever other weaknesses the Associates have, tolerating shirking in battle isn't one of them. I think that's why my father accepted Mike Havel's challenge to single combat, back when I was a child—because the lion eyes he'd created and trained himself were on him, and he couldn't do otherwise."

Watch out for this one, Pip, the new Princess told herself. *Watch yourself around her, always. She's the most ruthless sort of all—driven by duty.*

"That's precisely right," Thora Garwood said. "And the Bear Lord knew it and was counting on it."

Then the High Queen smiled, a slightly evil expression. "But you won't be going anytime soon, John. If it's going to need more mobilization, which will take some time . . ."

She glanced at the Grand Marshal.

"Oh, it will, Mattie. The victory will help keep people enthusiastic . . . but there's the logistics. We've got hulls building on every slipway from Vancouver Island to Newport and new yards just coming up, but that takes time; fitting out and working up and training crew. And it would be better if we waited until after the winter wheat harvest is in, too, and threshed and a lot of it baked into field biscuit; we're already salting down and smoking and canning a lot of meat and fish and drying vegetables and whatnot, and shipping remounts and equipment and fodder pellets and the like across the ocean. That will give more time for troop-training . . . especially large-scale maneuvers . . . and accumulating weapons and gear, as well. Say . . . September."

"Which means there's no reason Órlaith shouldn't come back in the interim," Mathilda said.

D'Ath's thin pale brows went up. "Is there a reason she *should?* Admiral Naysmith and General Thurston are both good, but unity and continuity of command are important. Especially as other heads of state are involved. They need someone they won't be too insulted to take orders from."

"Yes, there is a reason, and it's political. I intend to abdicate as High Queen in her favor, and we need to hold the ceremony at Lost Lake. Preferably a crowning at Dun na Síochána too."

John gave her a stricken look, and there was a rustle as everyone else looked at her too.

She chuckled: "I said *as High Queen,* boy. I'm only High Queen by marriage to your father; Órlaith inherits automatically anyway when she turns twenty-six, which isn't that far off. I'm Lady Protector of the Association by right of birth, so you needn't look as if I was going to expect you to do that one just yet."

"But you're a fine High Queen, Mattie!" Delia said. "And you were Rudi's right hand and other half, ever since the war! Well, since the Prophet's War, I suppose we should say it that way now."

"I can help my daughter, too," Mathilda said. "She'll be abroad at first anyway. But we need a High Queen who's not an Associate on the throne now; the Association is just too disliked and feared in many quarters, and that would get in the way of prosecuting the war—someone would be sure to say it was a plot, and people will always believe the worst of those they fear. And a High Queen who's not a Catholic and who wears a kilt and sounds like a Mackenzie doesn't hurt either, though it pains me to say it. Unlike the Association, Mackenzies are popular nearly everywhere because they're not a threat."

"Well, I like that!" Juniper said. "And the fact that we don't go about attacking people has nothing to do with it?"

"That's a matter of perspective, Juniper. But it's a *fact* that we need to keep the houppelandes and coats-of-arms in the background as much as we can."

She steepled her fingers and rested her chin on the tips. "I'm reasonably popular but I'm also Norman Arminger's daughter and I'm an Associate. And now you're back, John, with a bride, and you're very much an Associate . . . and young and newly married with an heir on the way."

"I don't. . . . Wait a minute. Mother, that's why you had me come here to Todenangst, rather than the capital, isn't it? To avoid reminding people that I *might*, God forbid it, become High King if Órlaith falls without an heir?"

"See, you *can* think when you try, boy. If you became High King you might reign for forty or fifty years and pass the throne on to children and grandchildren who were Catholics and Associates too."

"Mother, if there's one thing I want less than being Lord Protector of the PPA, it's being High King of Montival!"

"Yes, and *I* believe you. If only because you're lazy and you know how much *work* it is."

John made a gargling sound and she smiled and patted him on the shoulder before going on, all seriousness once more:

"Too many won't believe it. Too much of the realm remembers the old wars, and we can't afford to make it look as if the Association has won by birth now what it couldn't take by sword and lance then. I pray for Órlaith's life every day as a mother, but also as a monarch. I don't know if the High Kingdom could stand an Associate monarch by right of birth."

"Ah," d'Ath said. "You always were better at the politics, Mattie. And with a war on, the Association will bulk larger anyway, our nobility are fighters, when they're not drinking and hunting and fornicating. And *I'm* an Associate too, and in wartime the Grand Marshal actually gives people orders a lot; it's a nice quiet behind-the-scenes planning job in peacetime."

Mathilda sighed. "I only wish . . . God and His Mother and Saint Michael protect her, but we have to think of the Kingdom . . . if only *Órlaith* could leave an heir of her body coming before she went back to war. . . ."

D'Ath raised a brow. "Your Majesty, it just doesn't work that way. The foam-born Cyprian knows I've tried. . . ."

"Tiph!" Lady Delia said indignantly in a half-screech, before dissolving into giggles.

Even Mathilda laughed this time, though a little reluctantly; only Ignatius cleared his throat and looked away.

"Yes, this is wisdom," he said then.

He rose for a moment and bowed deeply.

"My most profound respect, Your Majesty. Yes, this is a good plan and best for the Kingdom. As Lady Juniper said, it is a joy to a teacher to see a pupil excel."

Mathilda's smile was fond, but with an underlying hardness.

"Father Ignatius, I had my mother to teach me politics as well; I learned much from you, but I think of you as the one who trained my conscience as much as my wits. Take credit, if you will, for making me someone who doesn't convince themselves that keeping power in their own hands is always their duty."

He smiled. "And that tempts me to the sin of pride as well, my daughter. Though if I know the Crown Princess, *she* won't like your inspiration a bit."

Mathilda nodded decisively, and spoke to her secretary: "Lady Bricet, draft a report for the Crown Princess incorporating our information from Prince John and his companions, and summoning her home for . . . call it consultation. I'll read and annotate your first draft tonight."

"And we can tell her she needs to get a grip on the second wave troops," d'Ath said. "That'll actually be useful, because it's true and she'll know it."

Mathilda signed agreement with the comment:

"Be polite, Bricet, but make it plain I will brook no disobedience . . . and yes, another to Empress Reiko, inviting her to *consult* too. Lady d'Ath, have your office draft a report for forwarding to the Crown Princess with the same dispatches, outlining your plans for further mobilization— emphasize that Órlaith's needed for that, too. My Lord Chancellor, I'll want one from your office as well for Órlaith's eyes, outlining the costs of what we're doing. And the three of us will consult the next few days over the necessary moves with the Congress of Realms and then fill her in on the politics."

She was silent for a moment, then went on thoughtfully: "We can use this to push as many as possible of the Realms on the *King in Yellow* matter too. Make it plain that it's not a matter of banning a book because we Catholics find it blasphemous, but that it's an active threat to human life and the Realm in wartime."

Juniper sighed. "I'll add my voice to that. Reluctantly."

"Wooosh," Pip murmured under her breath.

John cocked an eye at her. *Told you,* it seemed to say; but she didn't know if he saw *quite* how formidable his mother was. He didn't have her perspective. . . .

The High Queen's brown eyes turned on her. "And Pip, I'm giving you into Lady Delia's hands. She's been my Mistress of Ceremonies for . . . great God, Delia, is it a quarter century now?"

"And a bit, Mattie."

"Well, Pip, she *is* Mistress of Ceremonies, and this right here is a very ceremonial part of the world. And Delia's one of our arbiters of fashion."

"Not so much anymore, Mattie. That's a younger woman's position and I'm a matron now, not a reigning beauty."

"But you've still got your finger on the pulse of it. Also she's the mother of four, all of whom turned out very well, and you're going to need someone to fill in for your mother about that and I'm going to be too busy . . . I understand your own mother has passed on?"

"Yes . . . Mattie."

There was no need to add that Lady Julianne Balwyn-Abercrombie had had about as much maternal instinct as a hungry dingo, or possibly a salt-water crocodile, which was part of the explanation of why she hadn't married until late in life and why Pip was that rare modern phenomenon, an only child. They'd gotten on splendidly, but only after Pip was able to walk, talk and control her own bodily functions. Until then she'd been in the hands of servants.

"Lady Delia will be very useful to you in that respect too, then . . . and there's nobody in the realm better informed on the decisions you'll have to make in establishing your own Household, now that John's not a bachelor anymore . . . and of course we'll need an affirmation ceremony to placate all those people who have their noses out of joint they didn't get to attend the wedding of the generation."

John smiled with relief. "I'm glad you're not worried about their rage at not having their prize heifers . . . pardon me, their beloved daughters . . . married off to the prize bull . . . pardon me, me."

Everyone laughed at that except d'Ath; even Ignatius chuckled.

The Chancellor spoke: "Call it an equality of dissatisfaction, Your Highness."

"Just so," Mathilda added. "None of them get the prize, but none of them are enraged to see a rival get it either; that was giving me night-mares. And as a matter of principle, I'm not eager to encourage arranged marriages. And her personal qualities aside—I trust you on that, John, and frankly you're the one who has to live with her, and vice versa—Pip's perfect for the future Lord Protector's consort. Catholic, granddaughter of a sovereign with another as a patron, excellent blood on her mother's side too, that even gives us a link with the King-Emperors in Greater Britain, young, healthy, intelligent . . ."

"*Mooooooo*," Pip said, imitating a heifer.

She kept her own expression deadpan, but this time even d'Ath laughed. When it had died down, Mathilda finished briskly:

"Órlaith belongs to the whole High Kingdom, but Pip's going to be the Lord Protector's lady eventually, and it's the Association you need to know first, from the ground up. Delia is perfect for that."

"I'll be glad of the advice, Mathilda," Pip said, very carefully. "And I'm looking forward to working with you, Lady Delia."

Delia and the High Queen both looked at her with knowing smiles.

"Meaning you'll listen to advice, which is worth its weight in gold, and then make your own decisions," Delia said in a pleased tone. "Good for you, my girl!"

"Your mother's quite something," Pip said thoughtfully as she combed out her hair.

They'd both switched into lounging robes of thin fine wool, green for her and dark blue for him. The heating system kept the place at the locally comfortable sixty degrees or a little more, and there was a psy-chologically cheering fire crackling in the hearth. The bedroom rug did its best to imitate an Impressionist version of a flowering meadow in spring over pretty but chilly tile, and the walls were mostly oak paneling, which helped to make you forget you were in a piece of monolithic cast concrete.

John had been a bit startled when they were shown to a suite that was not the one he'd used as the . . .

Bachelor Pad of the Dreamboat, and probably Tomcat, Troubadour Prince, Pip thought with a slight smile.

More of Mathilda's tact, or possibly Lady Delia's. I think I'm going to like her, and she'll certainly be very, very useful. And do not be in the least fooled by Delia's bouncy-beauty-fashionista thing. It may have had some truth when she was eighteen and setting her cap for the dashing young knight. Now there's a very experienced mind there and this is her environment, not yours.

John's valet-cum-bodyguard Messer Evrouin had come on ahead posthaste from Astoria and had been on hand to help him out of his court dress, assure him that his gear had been moved up here, set out the nibbles and drinkables, and discreetly fade out. Somehow a set of clothes in her size had mysteriously appeared as well, complete with riding and hunting outfits that for some reason closely resembled what (male) samurai wore: short kimono and broad *hakama* trousers like a divided skirt.

"Darling?" John asked as she chuckled.

"It's . . . just that I'm having trouble convincing the underneath-part of my mind that I'm not *traveling* anymore. I've *arrived.* Time to mentally unpack."

For a while, at least. But I'll be popping out the heir long before Johnnie goes off to war . . . from the way they were talking about bringing Órlaith home and waiting until after the next harvest is here, roughly September . . . and we'll see if I have more maternal instinct than Mummy did. I doubt it, somehow.

This suite was obviously designed for a couple, with changing rooms flanking the bedroom with its four-poster, a bath arrangement of which she thoroughly approved—large sunken marble tubs were a Balwyn weakness, and the shower setup with its multiple nozzles and sliding walls of cast glass etched in designs of waterfowl and reeds had *definite* possibilities. There were sitting and reception rooms and two generously sized study-libraries, and a balcony the size of a small room itself, made of cast aluminum terminating in eagles with interlinked wings, which would be very pleasant when it wasn't cold and, as now, pitch-black outside except for the lights of the castle-town and the fainter glow of nearby villages.

Just the place for an alfresco tea or whatever.

Speaking tubes and bellpulls would fetch anything you wanted.

It's a bit like a luxury hotel. Possibly because a lot of the features were looted from luxury hotels and spas, she thought.

Of course, Todenangst had been built before modern crafts were up to the job and salvage was cheap here, because several of the large pre-Change cities like Seattle and Vancouver and Eugene were actually under government control and could be outright and systematically mined, rather than be the target of hit-and-run raids from a distance by small bands of adventurers, the way it was back in Oz.

Then she looked at the walls; there were a couple of actual pre-Raphaelite paintings including *The Prioress' Tale* and *Veronica Veronese*, which John had said he'd gotten for his sixteenth birthday because it was about musical composition; the rich greens and velvety textures were incomparably different from even the best pre-Change photograph.

And a clunky-looking chair on a pedestal in a corner incredibly enough was a genuine William Morris, with his panel *The Arming of a Knight* on the seat-back; nobody would be putting their bum on that ancient English oak anytime soon. And not just because it looked magnificently uncomfortable in that wonderfully arrogant damn-your-eyes Victorian British way that expected you to sacrifice your buttocks gladly in the cause of Art with no insolent back talk to your betters.

Make that like living in a luxury hotel crossed with a museum.

"Unpack and start acting as if this was home? I know what you mean," he said. "Though we were always traveling when I was younger—as my father liked to say, if your government's going to culminate in a person, people have to get to see him sometimes. Saint Christopher, but we got dragged everywhere! In tents, a lot of the time, and to places where they'd lost the habit of washing."

"You won't have to tour that much?"

"No, thank God. And here in the Protectorate, we have the City palace in Portland, and manors and hunting lodges. And sometimes Mother keeps over-mighty nobles under control by visiting them."

Pip raised a brow. "That works how?"

"Expense. It's an honor to get a Royal visitation—no matter how much of the Court follows along and how ruinous it is to put on the fiestas and feasts and tiger-hunts and tournaments and whatnot. None of them can resist trying to out-splendorific their rivals; and then Mother sends in accountants to make sure they don't try to up the squeeze on their vassals."

Pip laughed. "That's . . . diabolical!" she said. "I like your mother."

"I think she likes you." He said more seriously: "I'd have defied her if she didn't, Pip. But frankly I'm glad I don't have to live up to that resolution after all."

Pip laid down the hairbrush and smiled, looking at him out of the corners of her eyes.

"And now that we're not traveling in cramped, uncomfortable, no-privacy ships anymore . . . is this the honeymoon?"

John rose and made a sweeping bow that ended with him sweeping the robe off and tossing it aside.

"My lady . . . shall we essay the experiment?"

CHAPTER SEVEN

Susan Mika and her companions waved and kept their bows conspicuously cased as they rode up to the Lakota warband, conscious that they'd been observed for minutes and that several dozen had arrows on the strings of *their* bows, though nobody was actually pointing one at them or drawing. They kept their horses to a trot because of the footing; creepers and grass and the general vivid green of the vegetation here covered a multitude of sins once you were off the beach, not least holes left by two generations of abandoned ancient houses falling down or burning down and being torn to bits by the rampant tropical vegetation or salvagers or both.

The speed also helped them look nonthreatening. Montival's endlessly varied local customs and dress and ways of life had produced a wide variety of military skills for this army. But it also meant that a lot of the participants looked like weird foreigners to one another, particularly to the jumpy, disoriented and overwhelming majority for whom this was their first trip away from home and their first battle.

Apart from being short—a grandmother had called her *vertically challenged*, which she supposed was an oldster's joke—Susan personally looked the way Lakota were traditionally supposed to look, and which not all did. That despite the fact that one of her grandmothers had been called Fox Woman for the color of her hair, and a grandfather had been an exchange student named *Ulagan Chinua*, which was Mongol for *Red Wolf*, studying range management at SDSU before the Change. Individuals had moved around a lot in those years as the needs of survival dictated, and paired with the people to hand.

She didn't dress in the full Lakota regalia most of the time, though she did braid her hair and wear a couple of feathers she felt entitled to for her deeds. And she felt a little ambiguous about finally talking with the Lakota contingent of the Montivallan expeditionary force, which was another reason why she had kept her horse to a fast rocking trot getting here, not the flat-out gallop she would have used normally.

On the one hand she was proud of her folk, their power and famous deeds. And that the *Očhéthi Šakówiŋ*, the Seven Council Fires, were the lords of the *makol*, the high plains and the Black Hills that marked the easternmost march of the High Kingdom. There were times when she missed the prairies bitterly, when things like the memory of the buffalo hunt and the Sun Dance festivals made her want to cry, and even the frigid stinging blizzards of winter could bring a sigh. And it would be nice to hang out with people who spoke her own language, literally and metaphorically. Though their everyday tongue was their own version of English, they remembered the other too, especially the prominent families like hers, and everyone learned it or at least took some lessons along with reading and writing and math and so forth in the schools that accompanied their herding camps.

And dropping in might mean a chance to score some buffalo-hump jerky. Oh, that taste of home, just like Mom used to make!

On the other hand, there was the little matter of why she'd *left* home, with a fair number of people wanting her dead. Which led into why her uncle had used his influence with the High King to get her a post in the Crown Courier Corps that put her under the protection of the Crown of

Montival everywhere she went, and why she didn't ever intend to go back unless it was briefly and on official business.

It's not as if I'm running from shooting someone in the back from ambush. He did hit me first and he outweighed me by fifty pounds. What was I supposed to do? Not pull a knife and just try to punch him back? Yeah, I called him an asshole before he hit me, but then, he was an asshole, and what business of it was his in the first place?

The problem was that some people, who were idiots but still there they were, thought he'd had a good reason for that, and she'd never really gotten to tell her side of the story. That was another reason her uncle had advised a quick departure; not letting it develop into a feud.

And Unk did have a point; the guy may have been an asshole, but he's a very dead asshole, and seeing me all the time was going to remind his friends, if he had any, and certainly his relatives of that.

Winter camps could get very boring up on the *makol*, plenty of time for brooding, and the Lakota had a very decentralized form of government by consensus. It was a chief's job to keep divisions under control and he couldn't look as if he was giving her a break because she was his niece, or some people would just stop listening to him.

On the good side, they were all a long way from home here—a very long way, she knew, looking around. This open area—she'd seen a faded, flaking sign, obviously at least fifty years old, reading *Pu'uloa Beach Park*—was surrounded by what had probably been housing before the Change; you could still see the remains of building pads here and there, or where the roads had been before the Hawaiians levered them up to remelt the asphalt and use it elsewhere, a familiar form of salvage. Smashed-up concrete made a good material for a rammed earth wall, too.

Modern houses had been scattered through it, mostly of light construction with palm roofs. Each had been surrounded by a large garden and usually an orchard of orange trees and lemons and mangos and breadfruit and bananas, some of the fences still incongruously gay with masses of flowers on bush violet or bougainvillea.

The houses had all been burned by the invaders, which given some of the things she'd seen might be a mercy to anyone passing by. The enemy apparently liked to get humorously structural with body-parts. Some of them had been very small body parts, and there had been a lot of grilled bone split for the marrow; goats, pigs, cattle and people all mixed, all adding to the scorched-rotten stink heavy in the warm perfumed air. There must have been a fair number of livestock around, too, or the rampant tropical growth would have been even more rampant.

The three of them drew up before the Lakota standard, which was a dark red flag with seven white tipis set base-to-base in the center to make a circle. Faramir and Morfind got some curious looks, since there weren't many Ranger *Staths* as far east as the Lakota country yet.

"*Théhaŋ waŋčhíŋyaŋke šni,*" Susan Mika said, raising her hand; it was literally accurate, if you took "long time, no see" as "several years."

"Backatcha, Susie," the Lakota commander Ivan *Mat'o Gi* replied, returning the gesture.

He was also an Oglála, an older cousin of hers, and fortunately a rather sympathetic one; a couple of his *akicita* were giving her hard looks, though not the especially honored one who bore the Eagle Staff beside him, like a shepherd's crook wrapped in otter skin with feathers along the outside. Most of the band were Húŋkpapȟa or Sihásapa or whatever and hadn't known her from a prairie dog until the ones who *did* know her realized she was here and the gossip mill got going.

"Still living it up, I see," he continued, looking at her companions.

She didn't reply to that; as far as she was concerned, she considered Morfind and Faramir as *settling down* rather than *living it up*. She wasn't nineteen and fancy-free anymore.

"Mae Govannen, *blotáhunka Mat'o Gi,*" the two Dúnedain Rangers said, giving him the Dúnedain salute, right hand to heart combined with a slight bow, and getting a nod and:

"Hiya, pleased to meet 'cha," in return.

Susan hid a smile—in Eryn Muir she'd been the exotic outlander girlfriend, and now it was their turn. Though she had to admit the Dúnedain Rangers were more open-minded than her own folk, possibly because they lived scattered all over among outsiders rather than in a single shared place that was a world in itself.

The Ranger cousins were slightly mispronouncing the word for *war-leader* and the man's name—Brown Bear—despite her coaching, but would get props for trying and coming close. He usually went by *Ivan*, anyway, and as kids they'd all called him Big Nose, since it was a truly commanding beak that had only grown as he approached thirty.

But good enough. My Sindarin is still lousy too, and I've had a lot more practice.

"Not that we don't appreciate the rest, but we were just getting stuck in and we didn't come here to *watch* a battle," Ivan said to her, lounging at ease in his light saddle like someone who'd grown up that way, which of course he had. "So, what does Golden Eagle Woman want us to do now?"

Lakota generally referred to the Crown Princess by that name; the Golden Eagle was her totem by Mackenzie custom, and she'd gotten the same protector's call when she spent time up on the *makol*. It helped that the *waŋblí* was a symbol of warrior power and courage among the Lakota, and they'd been impressed with her along those lines even as a teenager.

"Well, first she wants to double check your horses are good and recovered," she said.

And ran her eye over them, with the benefit of an experience that started as a toddler and had been refined even more as a Crown Courier, riding two hundred miles a day at times.

"Look fine to me," she added.

"Yeah, though they could have used some more free grazing and exercise than we got over on that other island," Ivan said. "Being shut up in those floating wooden boxes is even harder on horses than people . . . unless sailors count as people, which I doubt. But basically we're okay, though I'd like some more remounts."

She grinned at him. "Since when were there *ever* enough horses? I mean, even counting the ones we hadn't stolen yet?"

He laughed at the reference to their national sport and looked at the sleek dappled gray Arabs the two Dúnedain were on.

"Are those ones your friends 'r riding as good as they look? They sure are pretty."

"*Better* than they look. Fast, real staying power, especially in hot weather, scary smart, and they turn even sharper than a quarter horse."

"Nice to know," he said, like a horse-breeder making notes. "So, action? Getting sort of boring."

Susan swung her arm to the northwest.

"If you're good on the horses, the Crown Princess wants you to cautiously develop the enemy's position there."

"Translation?"

"They're pushing ahead there, or will be. In a big column. Shoot 'em up and slow 'em down and make 'em spread into line."

"That's what I *thought* you said, but it pays to be sure. *Wašícu* sure do like to talk fancy," Ivan said.

"But don't get tangled up. She's got someone else in mind for the heavy lifting. The Japanese will be along, and some Portlander knights."

"Well, the crawdads have their uses," Ivan said, using the eastern slang for Association heavy cavalry. "Ramming their heads into walls, for one. When they don't have 'em somewhere else."

"And the enemy shoot back pretty well, so be careful."

"Yeah, we noticed. Their bows look funny but there's nothing wrong with the performance. Okay, tell Golden Eagle the Guardians of the Eastern Gate are on it."

He swung his helmet on, a steel cap topped by buffalo horns and fur with a long tail of pelt that fell down his back, and turned to his command, several hundred wild youngsters, grinning faces painted with red and black and white for war. Here and there a few gray-streaked braids with more of the feathers of accomplishment in them showed veterans . . . who'd been wild youngsters themselves in the Prophet's War where they got the varicolored scalps sewn to the outer seams of their leggings or dangling from lances.

They were mostly in short-sleeved shirts of light riveted mail or leather jerkins sewn with steel scales or washers, with round shields of buffalo-hide taken from the neck-humps of bulls and faced with sheet metal from ancient autos, armed with bow and shete, knife and toma-hawk and now and then a rawhide-bound stone-headed war club, which was nicely traditional. And on a yard-long shaft of springy laminated horn it also cracked skulls just as effectively as any alternative.

"*Hoka hey, Lakota!*" Ivan shouted, and waved his shield; it had a buffalo head on it facing out, divided into four quarters and painted white, yellow, black and red.

"Let's go! It's a good day for those shits over there to die! We'll sting 'em and slow them down and skip when they try to punch back."

The warriors all started forward, and broke into a canter within a few paces in fluid unison. Their yelping war cries split the air with a shrill menace. Susan and her companions joined them; her instructions were to observe, but she *definitely* intended to do some shooting. For the sake of the thing, and because she already had a lot of grudges piled up against these people from the High King's death, and then the expedition to South Westria where they'd come uncomfortably close to killing *her* several times, not to mention her friends. And now from doing all this nasty stuff here in Hawai'i; they managed to give her more reasons to kill them every time they met, personal and principled together.

And I'll go along because what I see, Orrey knows, what with the Sword. Which is sorta creepy, but way useful.

She reached over her shoulder to her quiver and checked the shafts there and the bow in the case by her knee. Her bowstave wasn't very thick; the general rule was that the draw on a war bow should be about two-thirds to three-quarters your body weight, and she was five-foot-one and built in a way she thought of as *whipcord* or *graceful* and unkind people called *skinny like a rattlesnake*. But nobody had ever complained about her accuracy, on foot or on the back of a *šúŋkawakȟáŋ*.

"C'mon, Big Magical Dog, we've got work to do," she said, and leaned forward slightly; the horse took the hint and speeded up. "Forward the Lakota and the Dúnedain!"

The terrain they were heading into was flattish and open and had been cleared of pre-Change ruins except for an occasional snag; mostly it was covered in well-grazed grass and low shrubs, though there were blue-green hills on the edge of sight ahead that looked as if they were densely wooded. Here and there were coconut palms, whose feather-duster shape she was still getting used to. Patches of younger trees had the pruned look that meant they were coppiced regularly for small wood or more likely for charcoal and planted amid stretches of ruin too stubborn for anything else, to get some use out of otherwise useless ground while the patient roots ground brick and concrete back into soil.

She'd seen the technique often enough in Montival with very different types of tree. It was usually the sign of a large settlement nearby or of some sort of smelting industry, or both.

"You know," she said to her companions, and waved around. "If it weren't all fucked up, this would be even prettier than the country around Hilo. And the weather's great—like the air was kissing you. Like you guys' home down in Westria, but not as dry."

"Well, yes, *meleth e-guilen*, but right now you can tell it's a battle," Morfind said from her right.

"Most of the songs leave the . . . the *mess* out," Faramir said grimly from her left.

Neither of them said more; one of the many things Susan liked about both of them was that they weren't chatterers. They left that to her, mostly.

"Yup, messy," she said, as she clapped her light helmet on and fastened the chin-cup. "Like I said, seriously fucked up. It's worse somehow *because* it's so pretty otherwise. I like the flowers. Like home in the springtime, only I think it's all year-round here."

They were close enough that the snarling brabble punctuated by shrieks and scrap-metal-on-cement sounds, which went with a big fight, was fairly loud, but still blurred by distance into a seamless whole.

It was astonishing how far thirty thousand yelling voices carried, but then, that was more people than most cities had. Battles were even more densely packed than cities, too; the line ahead was less than a mile long west to east from one end to another.

She could see the low black string that marked where the armies made contact, and the sparkling ripple that was its movements. Bolts and cast-steel roundshot and napalm shells from the Montivallan field-catapults firing over their own troops' heads made flickering streaks or lines of black smoke in the distance amid the ratcheting clatter of the cocking pumps and the *TUNG!* of release.

Occasional dead bodies littered the fields as they rode north over the ground where the fight had gone; mostly Koreans in their spiked helmets, but a fair scattering of Montivallans too, since the stretcher-parties took only the wounded until the post-battle cleanup.

Here and there a dead horse lay, which she admitted in strict privacy bothered her too. Lakota were mostly nomad herders, who raised cattle and sheep and horses and managed the buffalo herds that had returned since the Change, and they couldn't afford to be sentimental about animals . . . even less than most people could, in the modern world. They all calmed theirs down when they began to roll their eyes and snort at the smells and noises, even though if you thought about it from their own point of view the beasts were totally right to convey:

You absolutely sure you're absolutely sure about this, boss?

But you couldn't depend on horses for your life and live with them from colt-hood on without feeling *something* for them; they weren't machines, after all. They had a spirit, like people.

"The horses cannot choose to stay at home," Faramir said, which proved they'd gotten to the point of thinking alike.

"Neither can humans, most of the time," Morfind answered.

"Yeah, but at least we have some idea of what's going on," Susan said. "Of course, that makes things worse too, sometimes."

Arrows bristled from the ground, with clusters where a flight had come down before the lines shifted, and there were bent javelins, broken pikes, bits and pieces of gear such as water bottles, little pools of blood that attracted some of the swarms of flies from the bodies when a hungry kite or gull landed and disturbed them with its flapping wings—they went to work on the faces first, since those didn't have armor. That was why the Montivallan dead were all rolled onto their stomachs with a jacket or shield or whatever laid over their heads by the medical squads that had checked they were goners.

Charred patches still smoldering showed where napalm shells had landed, and added burnt meat and a chemical reek to the stink.

Not all the bodies looked much like bodies anymore. The results when a catapult bolt designed to punch through a foot of hardwood hit living people wasn't very pleasant at all, and when roundshot struck human beings at close range the target *splashed.*

They passed the Japanese contingent double-timing forward, their lamellar armor clattering and the long blades of their *higo-yari* spears rising and falling; sunlight gleamed from the almost liquidly intense brightness of their lacquered armor, red and black and yellow, protection and boast at the same time. There was a leashed eagerness to them that Susan could sense, even though their faces had a stone restraint; this was an enemy they'd fought all their lives, usually at a disadvantage, and they were looking forward to the boot being on the other foot and risk be damned.

Empress Reiko rode at their head, with a few mounted commanders and standard-bearers. Susan cast a critical eye; the *Nihonjin* leaders were competent in the saddle, but . . .

Not bad . . . for farmers. That about sums it up, she thought, which confirmed her earlier experiences.

When they got close enough to see individual banners, beehives and honeybees made it clear that the far left of the Montivallan infantry line was the Deseret regiment that had passed them on the beach.

Three blocks of pikemen with crossbowmen between held the end of the line, with a fourth phalanx in reserve; evenly-spaced ridges of dead about fifty yards behind showed that the Koreans had fallen into the trap of trying to push into what looked like holes between the blocks of pikes and get at their flanks, not knowing how fast the rear files in a good formation could turn ninety degrees and ram right into you like a wall of high-speed points, flanking you in turn like the steel jaws of a bear trap.

Right now the long shafts of the first four ranks of pikes were leveled, held so that they all extended to the same length, and the long heads of spring steel were locked into the shields of the Koreans where they formed an overlapping wall.

"*Push of pike*," Morfind murmured.

The phrase was technical and evocative too, because this was like a giant lethal football scrum, a grunting heaving snarling shoving match of armored bodies with braced booted feet churning at the dirt. Dust hovered over them as the hobnails ripped up the grass, adding an odd mineral tang of volcanic soil to the stink of sweat loaded with rage and fear, and blood and wastes from the dead and wounded.

Behind them the fourth line had their weapons held overarm, snapping forward in punching two-armed stabs aimed at men's faces, hard enough to smash all the way through to the spine if they hit. Farther back still was a forest of pikes held upright by the rear ranks, rattling together occasionally or making sharper sounds and swaying when an arrow struck them, or bobbing when a man stepped forward to replace a casualty. The Koreans jabbed back when they could with their shorter weapons, or hacked at the heads of the pikes with swords; now and then one would try to crawl forward beneath the points, which usually ended badly. Mostly they took the pike-points on their shields, keeping them as an overlapping wall, and now and then the whole formation would heave a few steps back or forward in rippling panting unison.

Occasionally a chant would break out, shatteringly loud until there wasn't enough breath and it died back down into massed grunting and cursing:

"*Juche! Juche!*" from the enemy, or something like: "*Jug-ida! Meogda!*"

And from the Deseret soldiers a huge crashing bellow, resonant and blurred from being shouted out behind lowered visors:

"*COME, YE SAINTS! COME, YE SAINTS! COME, YE SAINTS!*"

The half-armored crossbowmen—and women, unlike the pike forma-tion with their sixteen-foot weapons—were shooting in a kneeling-standing two-deep line in the intervals between the pike-blocks, well back from the close-quarter action: leveling their weapons and firing, then pumping the cocking-levers built into the forestocks, taking another thick stubby pile-headed bolt from the cases at their belts and clipping it into the groove ahead of the bent string and repeating the process. It was more like labor in a water-powered linen mill than what Susan thought of as fighting, with a lot of extra danger thrown in, but it certainly *worked*.

Many of the bodies behind the line had bolts in them, rather than the bigger wounds the heads of the pikes made; the vanes that guided the bolts were mostly cut from pre-Change credit cards, though thin var-nished leather was increasingly used as the plastic aged and crumbled.

The noise—which included the near-continuous heavy *tung!* of cross-bow prods made from salvaged leaf springs releasing, a tooth-grating sound not quite in synch—was too loud to hear their noncoms' com-mands, but they'd be chanting, or screaming:

First rank, take aim . . . fire! . . . reload in nine times: reload! . . . second rank, take aim . . . fire! . . . reload in nine times: reload! . . .

Or if the line went forward: *Company will fire by advancing ranks. . . .*

Arrows came flicking and whistling back from the rear ranks of the Korean formation; not an overwhelming mass, but a steady whickering flow arching across the sky, enough to give a continuous rattling chorus of *bang!* sounds as they deflected or shattered on the plates of the heavy infantry's armor, or a shriek or curse as they went home in flesh. They weren't running out of shafts yet, though with their fleet sunk they wouldn't be getting any more, either. Arrows went fast in a battle, and they were bulky if not heavy to lug around.

"You know," Susan said to her companions, "I went through Deseret a lot as a Courier. Nicest people you'd want to meet, I mean, mostly—you get the odd hard look or cold shoulder for being a *gentile*, or some guy who's absolutely a no-go tries to get into your pants, or you run into one who's bound and determined you're going to hear about Joseph Smith and the angels and the golden plates and the Lost Tribes, which is how I found out I was really Jewish."

The two Dúnedain chuckled indulgently at the odd beliefs some isolated folk had. Susan went on:

"But nine times in ten they're real friendly—after a while I had families in all the towns I touched who treated me like little sis, home-cooked meals and all. Mostly they don't drink, they don't brawl, they hardly even cuss or cheat. But put them on a battlefield . . ."

"They are doing well," Faramir agreed. "I wouldn't want to be taking what they're dishing out."

The Lakota column, or mass or band, swung wider westward to avoid the field ambulances and stretcher-parties and pack-mules bringing up more bolts and the trickle of walking wounded helping one another towards the nearest field hospital. This wasn't Susan's first fight by any means, but it was her first big set-piece battle. Montival's last major war had petered out in guerilla skirmishes about the time she was born, or a few years earlier depending on how serious you considered the final scuffles with holdouts hiding in caves in the Bitterroots living on camas and the odd gopher and what they could rustle and steal and harder and harder to tell from plain old-fashioned bandits.

But she'd grown up on the descriptions of the storm-and-thunder parts of the Prophet's War as told around the fires, and one of the things the oldsters all agreed with was that in a mounted skirmish you could be killed anytime, but in set battles things were dangerous only for about half bowshot on either side of the line of contact. Beyond that it was only mildly risky.

An extended line of light cavalry guarded the flank; they were on quarter horses too, and equipped much like the Lakota, with a few differences such as wearing chaps instead of leggings and high-heeled boots instead of the simpler moccasin-like gear her folk preferred. Their guidon-flags had a bucking horse on them, or spiky rancher's brand-signs. That meant they were from the territories of the Pendleton Round-Up, with its capital at the little city of that name: ranchers and their retainers from the arid lands south of the Columbia bend and around the Blue Mountains, east of the better-known Central Oregon Ranchers' Organization with its center at Bend.

A lot of them had volunteered, and were anxious to demonstrate their loyalty. For reasons of chance and if-they're-against-it-I'm-for-it local squabbles and the dynastic foibles of their ruling Bossmen they'd been on the wrong, losing side during most of the Prophet's War a generation ago. The second wave from back home would probably include a lot of riders from the Crown Province of Nakamtu, what had been the core territories of the Church Universal and Triumphant and before that Montana, for the same reason. The distance from the coast was the only reason they weren't here already.

A few genial shouts of:

"Well, if it ain't the Injuns come to rescue the cavalry!" rang out.

They were answered by elevated Lakota middle fingers and cries of:

"Every damn time, cowfuckerboys!" or "Get off that poor mangy dog and get a horse, why can't you?"

To which some wit replied: "'Cause you Sioux horse-thieves stole them all."

"While you were riding them! And you never noticed!"

An officer came galloping up to Ivan Brown Bear, flanked by a signaler with a brass trumpet slung across her chest and holding a light lance flying a pennant of dark blue with a yellow brand shaped like deep *U* whose left arm was drawn out at the top to make a 7, and whose right merged into a capital *P*. The man wore a breastplate of overlapping steel-rimmed lacquered bull-hide segments, and had a scabbed-over cut on a red sweating cheek that he rubbed at absently with the back of one of his rawhide gauntlets. He also had a long blond beard braided into a fork and the skull of a cougar minus the lower jaw mounted on his light sallet helm, snarling endlessly. His high-horn saddle was liberally adorned with tooled leather and silver accents and rested on one of the colorful patterned blankets for which his realm was famous.

The broken-off stub of an arrow stood in it, too.

The man was in his thirties. The signaler was around Susan's age, had freckles, and looked enough like him to be close kin and probably was. She gave the Dúnedain and the Lakota woman a curious look and a nod. Both their horses were sweating, and had flecks of foam on their necks and chests, evidence of hard work; their round metal-faced shields had the same brand symbol as the banner. Ranchers throughout the interior of Montival used them much like an Association knight's coat of arms.

Coat of arms you burn into a cow's ass, Susan thought to herself; she considered the habit absurd.

"Hi, Ivan, finally come out to do some work, right?" the stockman-officer said with a smile that showed gaps in his teeth. "Late to the dance, as usual."

They leaned over in the saddle to slap the palms of their hands and then the backs of their fists together, two rangy tough-looking men with the weathered appearance of a life spent in the saddle, and both in their prime.

The Lakota leader grinned back. "Thought I'd check whether you were asleep or just jacking off behind a bush, Red Bull," he said and pointed at the other man's face. "But say, *wašícu*, look out! You've got a dead pussycat biting on your head!"

"That's *Cap'n* Red Bull Anderson *sir* to you, you idle bastard," the rancher replied. "And I kilt this catamount my own self! With a kitchen knife! When I was six! And *asleep*."

Then seriously: "What's up?"

"Golden Eagle Woman says the savages are going to hit this flank with a column," Ivan said. "So we Lakota are going out to completely fuck up their day."

"Yeah, we got a runner with that news 'bout the enemy a little whiles ago and didn't like it one damn bit—not enough of us to stop a big column. Ain't been nothin' but a few pokes and slaps at us so far, they're all afoot and we cut 'em up bad, but Lordy they're mean as *snakes*, this bunch! Can't say I enjoy fightin' 'em all that much, lost some good boys, but *killing* them's just a pleasure, it purely is."

"You don't fucking say," Ivan replied. "Okay, so we're going out to *develop the position*."

"What?"

"Shoot 'em up, make 'em spread out."

"Then why in seven hells didn't you say so?"

Ivan chuckled and said: "Expect the Japanese and some Portland crawdads along in a bit, so don't get in the way—the crawdads, they're not much on looking where they're going once they drop their visors and swing those barge poles down."

"God give you good shootin'," Anderson said. "We'll switch to our remounts while you do, and thank you kindly for the chance."

"Don't take too long. Remember, blanket first, *then* the saddle, and both of them go *on the top side of the horse*."

"Dang, who'd a thunkit? Thanks for that there deep Injun wisdom, good luck, and kill a few extra for me."

"Same to you, and glad to oblige."

The rancher and his signaler galloped off. The Lakota moved forward at a faster trot, over ground littered with the byproducts of what Anderson had called *pushing* and *slapping*. That included a fair scatter of enemy bodies with arrows sticking in them that bore the distinctive Pendleton fletching, made from the iridescent blue-green tailfeathers of the black-billed magpie. All of the enemy dead had been archers, judging by the gear and by the dead quarter horses with arrows in them littered here and there. The Round-Up fighters had removed their own fallen, including the dead.

The Lakota didn't gallop yet. You did that only when you were within bowshot of the enemy; a horse could keep up a gallop only about as long as a man could run flat-out, so you didn't waste it. When you needed the speed, you needed it to be there and you needed it *bad*.

Susan leaned down to her left as they cantered past one clump of bodies, hooking her right heel around the horn of her saddle, using one hand to keep the arrows from falling out of her quiver. With the other she scooped an enemy bow off the ground and flicked herself back into the saddle with a flex of leg and torso, foot finding stirrup as she examined the Korean weapon.

It was about the same four foot in length as hers, and likewise made of a sandwich with wood in the center, horn on the belly and sinew on the back, but it was much rounder in section, rather than flat strips. The grip was merely a stiffer section wrapped in hide strips, instead of a rigid hardwood grip with a shelf cut in so that you shot through the centerline of the bow. And the ends were rigid forward-canted levers of hardwood tipped with bone, with a notched string-bridge to hold the cord off them. She tried a draw, and found it too heavy for her as she expected, but the pull was quite smooth.

It was covered in fine leather. . . .

A closer inspection of the leather covering and the bone tips of the levers made her shudder and hold it out between thumb and forefinger; also the string-bridges were made from human teeth. Morfind leaned in, looked, and grimaced.

"*Yrch,*" she said, as Susan threw it away and wiped her hands on her doeskin breeches.

In the *Histories,* that word meant *orcs,* though from her recent immersion in Dúnedain society what exactly orcs were or had been in the first Three Ages was something you could chew the fat about endlessly around the fire on winter evenings, which at least beat the crap out of horse genealogies and buffalo-hunt anecdotes on the boring scale.

Though maybe that's because I haven't been listening to it all my life.

In MSS, Modern Spoken Sindarin, *yrch* just meant *the enemy*—especially enemies who ate human flesh or did other things that were . . .

Well, orc-like, I suppose?

. . . like working for evil sorcerers.

"*Yrch?* You said it, girlfriend!" Susan said fervently.

It certainly fit the bill pretty precisely here, or close enough for government work.

"*No dirweg, birillath!*" Faramir said quietly: *Watch out, ladies!*

Susan let out a long breath. She and her companions pulled their shields off the hooks on their bowcases and slung them over their backs with their leather straps, then set arrows on their strings. She opened the steel-lined leather case that held her binoculars too, which she had a lot of practice doing one-handed, and stood a little in the stirrups with bent knees as she leveled them—you had to compensate for the up-and-down motion of your horse or the magnification flicked your vision all over the landscape.

The enemy column was coming towards them at a uniform pounding trot to a hammer of drums, successive blocks ten men across and twenty deep one after another, driving forward like a steel fist. They had banners with them too, a flag with a central red panel with a white circle around a five-pointed red star, bordered above and below by narrow white stripes and broader blue ones. That was innocuous enough, but the human skulls with the red-painted teeth of dogs or wolves added on top of the poles rather spoiled the effect.

So did the skulls bobbing on the sides of the horse-litter in the center of the formation. She couldn't see much of the person sitting cross-legged in it; the intervening cavalry was in the way. But she thought she'd seen that baggy costume of many colors and strips of cloth before, and the fringed mask, and the tall three-peaked crown of gold filigree. Two more in similar but simpler costume capered on either side, waving open fans and carved wands.

"Uh-oh," she said. "Take a look there!"

She handed the glasses to Faramir, who did and then passed them to his cousin Morfind, moving their horses around each other as easily as they would have their own bodies.

"One of the *kangshinmu*," Susan said.

Órlaith had told her—knowledge courtesy of the Sword of the Lady—that originally the word had just meant *shaman possessed by a spirit*, part of the traditional beliefs of Korea and no more good or evil than anyone else's faith. Only after the Change had it come to mean possessed by a *particular* spirit, as the Prophet of the Church Universal and Triumphant and his magi had been taken over and twisted by the same entity back home. Only in Korea, they'd won.

"*Morgul,*" Faramir called grimly over the drumming hoofbeats: black magic. "*Tego ven i Melain am mand!*"

Susan most certainly didn't mind the thought of the Valar keeping them safe, but . . .

"*Tunkasila, le iyahpe ya yo!*" she murmured as she recased the binoculars, just in case Grandfather needed reminding; and there did seem for a moment to be a strong hand on her back, though she couldn't have sworn it wasn't her own mind.

CHAPTER EIGHT

"*H*oka *hey!*" Ivan screamed, and the rest of his band echoed it hundreds-fold.

The Lakota burst into a gallop and swerved in towards the head of the enemy column, stretching out as they did so, then angling for the corner in unison like a flock of birds. The warriors leaned forward along the necks of their horses, faces close to the manes, as arrows began to wicker out at them.

Hitting moving targets was *hard*. The square corner of an infantry block was where it was hardest for the people in it to shoot back.

Susan leaned forward and rose in her turn, the movement rippling down the formation like a wave as they all aimed at the corner-point of the enemy formation, drew and loosed, which would give three or four arrows for every enemy soldier under the lash. She was timing it to the floating motionless moment the horse had all its hooves airborne; she shot at a banner-bearer, ducked again . . .

. . . and the Korean ranks went by in a blur of motion and the nerve-wracking *whupt* of arrows driving by in return, and then they were swinging wide and angling in towards the next block. There was more return fire this time, since the enemy had more warning.

A man ahead of her pitched sideways off his horse with a black-fletched arrow through his neck, an O-mouthed expression of shocked surprise on his face she suspected she'd be seeing for a long time, then hit the ground and bounced. Another leapt free as his horse was hit in the hock of its left fore, and tumbled to the ground in a crackle of breaking legs. He struck the ground rolling, came upright and ran; one of his comrades swung in and extended a hand and he bounced up behind his rescuer.

Something banged into Susan's back just as she started to straighten up to shoot again, painfully hard and right over the kidneys, below the part the shield on her back covered.

"OOooooh!SHIT!" she said.

The arrow wobbled off her bow and she got a mouthful of Big Magical Dog's mane and a painful bump on the nose as the upward motion of his neck met the downward plunge of her face.

She pulled in a breath—the stab of raw fear she dealt with by ignoring it, the way you did—and felt around with her right hand.

It scratched on a few broken links in the mail lining of her jacket, protruding through the ripped surface of the leather.

Glancing blow, she thought. *But two inches lower, and that arrow would have skewered me all the way across.*

Light mail wouldn't stop a hard-driven bodkin at close range . . . and she'd seen people dying with an arrow through the kidney. It always killed, but never as quickly as the victim *wanted* to go by then.

"Fuck you, you evil dickweeds!" she wheezed.

The groping hand also met an arrow standing in her shield which she hadn't even noticed when it hit. She screamed wordless rage and stood in the stirrups, shooting six times as fast as she could into the mass of Koreans whirling by, not trying to aim anymore except into the formation.

Ivan Brown Bear gave a wild whoop and peeled left, right between the third and fourth of the enemy blocks. That meant they were shooting at the Lakota from both sides . . . but mostly over them, and their formations wavered as they stopped and turned and tried to bear on the racing mass of horse-archers. The Lakota leaned forward into their horse's necks, and the enemy's arrows mostly went into *each other*.

Susan gave a wild whoop of her own, waving her bow over her head and yipping derision at the enemy as they rode free out the other side; her companions joined with a few choice Sindarin insults of their own:

"Hû úgaun!"

Which was Morfind's contribution: *cowardly dog*.

Faramir was a bit more imaginative, as much as you could be in a language that wasn't yet very strong on scatology, obscenity or blasphemy.

"Thiach uanui a naneth gín gen hamma!"

Which meant: *You're stupid and your mother still dresses you!*

The Lakota poured out the other side of the enemy formation and turned south again, which kept their left sides towards the foe—perfect for horseback shooting, and monstrously inconvenient for them to shoot back, which they couldn't do at all without halting and turning themselves to put their bow-hands towards their targets. That cut down on the number of arrows coming back at them, and return fire was the main difference between this and hunting stampeding buffalo on the *makol*—the risk of being pounded into mush if you fell or your horse stumbled was about the same.

Drum and trumpet sounds from behind them made the first troop of the enemy halt; the others double-timed out to either side, moving from column into line . . . which had been the point of the exercise. Ivan brought them wheeling down the line of the enemy's front just as they were forming up. Streams of arrows sleeted out as the Lakota emptied their quivers in a ripple that spun men around and dropped them limp and sent them stumbling and screaming and clutching at the wood and iron in their bodies. In one spot a dozen fell in a single instant.

"Hoka hey!" Ivan screamed again.

In the same moment he sheathed his bow, swept out his shete and put up his shield, and turned his horse into the gap in the Korean formation, where there were no spearmen left standing with shields and spears to shelter the archers. His band followed him with the instinctive savage unison of wolves avalanching onto a wounded buffalo. It was a maneuver that had broken infantry more than once in the Prophet's War. And before that during the post-Change wars with the Square Staters to the east, when the Seven Council Fires were seeing how much of their ancient range they could take back, pushing until the farmers got too thick on the ground and they had to start worrying about the Prophet's growing strength to the west.

Susan and her companions followed suit—she felt a flush of savage irritation, but there wasn't any choice, not when the alternative was trying to turn around into a dense stream of galloping horsemen waving edged metal or leveling the light lances some carried.

Even well-trained horses usually wouldn't ram right into what looked like solid obstacles to their limited sight; their inbred fear for their legs forbade. They *would* shoulder people aside, hard, if they'd been accustomed to it and they had no room to stop. Their own fear of falling when they were traveling at speed made them ready to do it, to get something out of their way before it tripped them. A shoulder-to-shoulder line of men with sharp pointy things was too much to ask of them, but a straggling clump was another thing altogether. The Koreans were being a little slow in rallying, and it was going to . . .

Thump!

Big Magical Dog's left shoulder hit a man trying to aim at her; he pitched backward, fell, and screamed briefly as the Lakota onrush rode over him. The horse stumbled, and Susan gathered him up with knees and balance. To her right Morfind had cased her bow and had her bush-sword in her hand—about two feet of what looked like a kukri that had been straightened out and lightened a little. She drove the point into the face of a Korean who was trying to hack at the hocks of a horse in front of her, and then freed it by letting the motion of her mount swing her arm back and yank it out of the bone where it had lodged. That let her make an upward sweep like a polo-player, right into a wrist holding a sword, and both went flying in a spray of red.

This is going to cost them, Susan thought.

Galloping horses moved at better than thirty miles an hour, and nobody was slowing down—which meant that a couple of hundred tons of flesh moving at speed had rammed into the opening in the Korean ranks, wedging it further with their bulk and close-quarter killing. The Lakota were screaming like files on stone as they drove steel home with that momentum behind them. She could see Brown Bear up ahead, whirling a head-breaker—a long-hafted club with a stone head shaped like a small football—around his head and striking down to the right and left while he shouted out an earthy war cry that translated roughly as: *beat 'em so bad you can fuck 'em up the ass!*

They were almost through and the noise was like a waterfall in the mountains next to the ear, but sharp as well as blurry. Even so Morfind's scream of:

"Natho Faramir!" cut through: *Save Faramir!*

Big Magical Dog repaid all her patient training in that moment as she slugged herself back against the cantle of her saddle, tucked the toes of her boots under her mount's elbows and snatched at the reins with her free hand. He reared up and stopped in little more than his own length by crow-hopping forward on his haunches, using his own weight thrown backward against the momentum of the gallop. It was something that would have been difficult if they were all alone on a patch of nice firm dirt. Surrounded by running horses and slashing hostiles, on ground littered by bodies, it was an astonishing feat of athleticism.

Thanks for trusting me, Big Magical Dog! flashed through her mind.

Faramir's Arab had an empty saddle; it was dancing in a circle, lashing out with its hind hooves every few seconds and squealing. Faramir was on the ground, with an arrow in his left shoulder and a Korean standing over him with an upraised sword. He didn't wait for it to descend; instead he lashed a foot upward beneath the skirt of the soldier's steel-studded leather coat, which was split like a horseman's before and behind. The Dúnedain's steel-toed boot rammed home. The Korean was probably wearing a cup and if he was it would reduce the damage, but Faramir was a very strong young man.

He also had a long knife in his right hand, even if his left wasn't much use right now. He stabbed as the Korean jackknifed forward, then pulled the bleeding body over his. Several arrows and two swords struck it as more of the enemy crowded in to try to finish him off. It could only be seconds before something serious hit him.

"Aöa ye!" Susan shouted, and shifted her balance again.

That was a command: *bit*.

Big Magical Dog did exactly that, rearing and lashing out with both forefeet, snorting and eyes rolling. Susan felt her body flex with the movement, and something like an interior *click!* snapping her teeth together as the steel-shod hooves struck with nine hundred pounds of quarter horse behind them. The enemy who'd been raising a spear in both hands to stab down at Faramir was flung like a rag doll launched from a catapult, knocking down his comrade on the other side.

Morfind was there now. In unison they bent low as Faramir struggled out from under the body, his face and chest and hair a mass of blood; he'd lost his helmet somehow. Susan ran her left hand under his armpit, and he reached up and grabbed her belt with reassuring strength. It was different on the other side; the head of the arrow was through his jerkin there, and his teeth showed in a grin of pain as Morfind lifted with the same underarm grip.

But there was no time to be gentle. Susan grunted with effort and levered herself back into the saddle, using the thrust of her foot against the stirrup as much as she could. That put him on his own feet, but suspended between the two riders.

Her companion did the same, and their horses broke for the clear space behind the enemy formation in the wake of the Lakota warband, bounding off their haunches. They weren't quite the last out, but it was uncomfortably close, and Faramir was giving gasps of pain every time his feet struck the ground between them.

Judging from the empty saddles, the band had lost more riders in the thirty seconds or so it took to burst through the ruptured Korean line than in all the rest of the engagement, but the enemy were reeling. Faramir's horse came trotting up behind them, and Susan took a quick look around. They were out of bow-range of the Korean force, which was busy trying to repair its formation anyway, but they were also *behind* it, and the Lakota weren't stopping.

"Can you get back in the saddle, sweetheart?" she asked.

"Don't . . . have much . . . choice, eh?" Faramir said between clenched teeth.

Susan caught the reins of his horse, and Morfind bent over to grab the back of his belt, where the tomahawk-loop was. Faramir scrambled up, and she thought with a stab of alarm that he was starting to look a little gray—possibly shock was setting in. They kept their speed down to a canter; all three horses were panting like bellows, and had foam spattering on their necks and chests . . . and on the riders. The Lakota slowed down too as soon as they were out of bowshot of the enemy, and hooked around to get in front of them again . . . but now the Imperial Guard of Dai-Nippon were deploying there, and the shaken Koreans didn't show any great eagerness to rush them.

Beyond the Japanese a forest of lances moved, the heads and pennants blazing in the air, as high as the heads of pikes—twelve feet of their own length, and then the height of the tall horses the knights rode. Their armor glittered too, eye-hurting bright where it was *white*—bare and polished—or merely vivid on the colors of shield and horse-trappings and plumes. Susan looked back towards the enemy as they cantered towards the spot where the High Kingdom's banner marked Órlaith. . . .

Something struck her. It wasn't physical, but it was real none the same, and it struck her mind. She had just enough time to realize it was something the *kangshinmu* were doing before—

Where am I? she thought. A voice seemed to whisper: **I . . . see . . . you.**

Part of her knew. She was in her trailer, sprawled in the recliner; and nearly filling it, flesh bulging against her jeans and tank top. Both her feet were in the pressure-bandages that kept the compresses against the sores that wouldn't heal. She had a can of beer in one hand, and the VR goggles in the other, and she wanted to pop a few more before she put the headset on, to make the illusion better . . .

Fire!

She bit back a scream as for an instant she seemed to *burn*. Then she was back in the saddle, with Faramir making choked-off sounds and pawing at the arrow in his shoulder. Morfind was . . .

Her face looks as if she's not here! Same thing's happening to her that happened to me!

That gave her a hint, and Susan leaned across and poked the end of her bow sharply into the other woman's ribs, getting a violent start.

"I saw . . . I saw . . ." she gasped, then fell silent.

Morfind's pale blue eyes were wide; they went wider as she looked past Susan's shoulder, raising a trembling hand to point.

Susan turned to follow her finger. Órlaith and Reiko had both ridden out in front of their formations. And they had both drawn the weapons that hung by their sides, Órlaith holding hers up with the point towards the sky, Reiko slanting hers forward. From among the Korean ranks there was a thrashing, and then the *kangshinmu* and his acolytes staggered forward, walking as if they were being dragged unwilling.

Then the center of the three, the sorcerer-lord, screamed. It was a sound of such agony that Susan shivered even at a distance too great to see expressions. He tore off his three-horned crown and screamed again, and *light* broke from his eyes and nose and open mouth. Light that started as a sullen red, and swiftly grew brighter and brighter . . .

Then the man was gone. His acolytes went mad, one rolling and tearing at his face with his hands, the other stabbing himself in the face and chest and gut, over and over again, the knife driving in like a hydraulic machine's pistons.

"Tennō Heika banzai!"

The Japanese raised their war shout—*To the Sacred Majesty, ten thousand years!*—and charged, their spears leveled. Behind them the Association's oliphants screamed, and there was a shout:

"Haro, Portland! Holy Mary for Portland!"

"I wish we had the Jewel and the Mirror here, too," Reiko said. "I could better serve my people and our common cause if I did."

They handed the reins of their horses over to grooms and dismounted.

Órlaith chuckled. "I think we have other things to attend to, before there's a second Quest."

Reiko gave her a half-admonishing smile. The Imperial Regalia of Japan comprised three great treasures; *Kusanagi no Tsurugi,* the Grasscutter Sword, the mirror *Yata no Kagami,* and the jewel *Yasakani no Magatama.* The Sword for strength, the Jewel for abundance and the Mirror for Truth.

Before the Change they had long been hidden away in the great shrines, for their ancientry and their symbolism. All three had been given by *Amaterasu-ōmikami* herself to Her grandson when he was sent down to the earth of Japan, to father the line of the Yamato dynasty in a dark predawn past, and all three had been kept secret in the most sacred shrines, brought out only in strictest privacy for an Imperial investiture— the Sword had been so secret that it had never become known after the Pacific War of the past century that it had been stolen!

"Your Sword . . . it is more *compact,*" Reiko said. "It fulfills the three functions in itself. And besides, of our three treasures the Mirror is still missing."

Órlaith frowned, and spoke slowly and seriously. "I think . . . Reiko, I think that it will come to you. How unlikely was it that the Grasscutter would be found, and come back to your hand? Yet it did."

She touched the hilt of the Sword of the Lady. "I think that if this were cast into the deepest depth of the sea . . . that somehow a great squid would catch it, and the squid be eaten by a cachalot, and then the Sword would be cast out of the whale in a lump of ambergris and be brought to my heir as a gift by a fisher who caught it in her nets."

Reiko started to speak, then stopped for a moment before she continued:

"Something . . . something like that was in the history of the Grasscutter Sword that I saw in dreams . . . in visions . . . before we came to the lost castle. A fatedness."

Órlaith stripped off her gauntlets. The hands beneath felt a little sore; she hadn't taken any actual *wounds*, but she had the full set of nicks, bruises, scrapings and wrenchings that went with a fight, when you used every part of your body and the joints in particular to an unrestrained ten-tenths of capacity against those doing likewise with life and death as a prize.

Men-at-arms were usually extremely fit, until their youth caught up with them—her father had just begun complaining now and then about stiffness and old injuries before he died in his forties.

Not far away, Susan Mika and Morfind Vogeler knelt to either side of Faramir Kovalevsky. Their hobbled horses were nearby, and Faramir was lying on a saddle blanket, with his head and shoulders propped up against a saddle laid in the dirt. He'd been stripped to the waist, and a set of bandages immobilized his left shoulder and arm; they were stained yellow and smelled strongly of a spicy-medicinal ointment. His eyes were closed, but fluttered open and looked at Órlaith a little blankly.

"I say well done to you, and very well done, my faithful friends," Órlaith said, smiling down at them. "I've congratulated Brown Bear and his folk, but you helped with it—the timing was perfect, luring out the enemy shamans. They were mad with rage against you . . . and that left them more vulnerable."

"Yes," Reiko said, and nodded to them. "Because of your very great trouble and taking pains, my Guard's fight is less hard, fewer have died than might be. *Osoreirimasu.* Very great thanks."

Morfind and Susan bowed their heads.

Then Susan spoke: "I'm worried about Faramir, Your Highness. He's been logy ever since he got hit—I don't think it's just shock. He's been hurt before."

Órlaith went down on one knee. She felt Faramir's brow, and then laid fingers very gently on his injured shoulder. He stirred and made a throaty, inarticulate sound. His pale skin didn't have the taut sheen of health that it usually did; it wasn't exactly flushed with fever, but there wasn't something quite right either. Presumably he'd been dosed with morphine. . . .

Reiko picked something up; the bloodstained stub of an arrow, scored along its length with marks where a field surgeon's arrow-spoon had been used—an instrument that slid along the shaft and encased the head. Arrows were often barbed, even if subtly in the narrow punch-heads used to penetrate armor, and the heads might be weakly attached so that they would remain in a wound if you just pulled on the shaft. Both were true in this case.

Reiko flicked it aside with a grimace. "Sometimes the *jinnikukaburi* weapons are poisoned or just filthy. Sometimes there is no infection, but the one injured simply . . . declines."

Morfind had lost her brother to this enemy not long after the High King died, in the same fight that had scarred her face; her expression went blank. Susan's eyes appealed.

Órlaith frowned, touching the hilt of the Sword of the Lady. Trying to remember . . .

"Yes. My father was wounded on the Quest, by an arrow shot by a Cutter magus—and he very nearly died. It wasn't poison or wound-fever, not as they usually are."

She sighed and laid her hand on the hilt. More than her body ached now. Holding the Sword in your hand in battle gave you pains that went as deep as the soul. You were pushing that part of your very *self* as hard as your body.

But when she drew the feeling was . . .

Gentler, she thought.

Everyone around her still stiffened or gasped; the world *flexed* when the Sword of the Lady was unsheathed, as if beneath the weight of something that was too powerful for the fabric of reality—for the story of things that made up the world. Or *almost* too powerful. She reversed the grip with a quick snapping flex of the wrist, so that the blade lay along her forearm. It felt like a longsword to the hand, but a little lighter than a steel weapon of the same dimensions.

But when Da bore it, it was an inch longer in the blade and a quarter-pound heavier, I remember that, she thought with a slight shiver. *Then it was as if it had been designed to his hand, now as if to mine. As if the world could be amended, quietly, so that we scarcely notice, like a letter re-drafted and stuck back in the file.*

She held it very carefully as she lowered it to rest on Faramir's body for a moment, with the pommel between his brows. The Sword wouldn't cut her, or her near kin; in fact she could bounce it off her skin like the edge of a wooden ruler. To anyone else, someone not of House Artos, the edges were sharp enough to part a drifting hair . . . and they were indestructible, unlike steel. Órlaith had had to unlearn some of her long training in the arts of the blade, to use one that could not be damaged, was utterly rigid, and had so little friction that blood ran off it as if it were greased and left not even dampness.

The sensation that followed when the Sword touched Faramir was indescribable; the nearest she could come, even to herself, was like a bent muscle relaxing, or a blockage that flowed again as it should, the feeling you got when you drowsed into sleep after a long hard day and a bath and your body felt warm and contented under a duvet.

Faramir's gray eyes fluttered open. "The hands of the King are the hands of a healer," he said softly in the speech of his folk. "And so the rightful King shall be known."

Órlaith smiled, lifted the blade, and sheathed it with a *shing* and *click* of metal on metal . . . or what sounded like that.

His eyes drifted closed again and he sighed and slept. "Is he healed?" Susan Mika said anxiously, and added: "Your Highness," because others were present.

"No," Órlaith said. "But he's healing. I think . . . I strongly suspect . . . that something was preventing that. It's been, ummm, removed. The enemy paid special attention to him. It's an honor, of a sort."

The looks on their faces made her slightly uncomfortable; so did those on those observing from a distance. She restrained an impulse to snarl. Reiko looked almost amused, as they walked away to have their armor off—you could do that yourself, but it was much easier with assistance—and said in *Nihongo*:

"I am sorry, my oath-sister, but to see you wince as another layer of myth and legend wraps around you . . . it amuses me."

"I admit you're worse off that way," Órlaith said dryly.

"Órlaith, my friend, we have fought all day; we have wielded powers that are not of this earth. We have seen to our other duties and succored our people. Now I have another suggestion."

"What's that?"

Reiko smiled: in fact, she grinned and held up her *tessen* war-fan to mark off points.

"That we wash and dress in comfortable clothes and then have a dinner my cook prepares—he has been weeping with frustration that I have not allowed him to make a *kaiseki-ryōri* and Hawai'i has all the ingredients—and listen to my court ladies play, and drink sake, of which they have an excellent brand here, and recite sad poetry until we weep and witty poetry until we weep with laughter and get gloriously but not too drunk and watch the moon rise and then bid each other farewell and go off to our beds and sleep."

Órlaith laughed. "Even better if there were a comely young man of a madly romantic variety waiting for each of us, but the food and poetry and drink and sleep sound more than good enough. *Ikou!* Let's go!"

CHAPTER NINE

I am never going to eat pork again, Dzhambul thought.

Which was a pity, because he was rather fond of the way the Han did it. Especially pork ribs with sweet and sour sauce the way it was served at a little place in Ulaanbaatar run by a man named Hua, in what was left of a pre-Change building mostly disassembled for its metal. They served good rice wine there too.

He wasn't an overly sensitive man—Mongols rarely were, and he'd ridden on his first raid and killed his first man when he was sixteen, and seen towns burn before he was twenty—but watching, and worse still smelling, what the *Miqačin* were doing around their fire . . .

The child can't have been more than six, he thought.

Dzhambul closed his eyes for a moment and wished he was home; Hua's place would do, carousing with some fellow-officers and joy girls, but even better his mother's *ger* at one of the clan's herding camps, waking and wolfing down a handful of dumplings before heading out on a hunt on a crisp fall day.

He couldn't order an attack just because what he saw them doing disgusted him; rather, he could, but he couldn't order it without having his command rightly lose all respect for him. Luckily, he had a perfectly good tactical reason for what he was about to do, which was a nice change from duty nagging him into something he disliked. He turned and crawled snake-fashion, pushing himself along on his belly down his own back trail with slow cautious movements, bringing each foot up, testing that the toehold was secure and wouldn't produce a clattering of loose rock.

It wasn't snowing anymore, and it was a little warmer—not so warm that ice melted, but warm enough that body heat or a fire melted it quickly. It was very dark indeed, though, with the moon down, and fortunately the cooked-meat smell faded quickly, leaving only the cold dirt and his own rankness, also controlled by the weather.

The loudest sounds were his own breathing, and the rustle and chink of his clothing and mail shirt. He crawled over a low crest and down the other side a little without running into the man-eater picket he was sure was out here somewhere.

Something hard and cold touched him behind the ear.

I must still be night-blinded from looking at the fire, he thought.

"Urt Khan Khutushü amidardag," he said aloud—which meant *Long Live Khan Qutughtu.*

That was not only impeccably loyal, it was also full of sounds that the man-eaters found hard to pronounce, which was why it was the password for tonight.

"Advance, Noyon," the darkness said softly.

In a woman's voice, and showed itself as a blackness against blackness as the knife was withdrawn. He thought she bent and slid it into a boot top, but it was difficult to be sure. He *was* sure that there was another of the Hawks not far away, ready to slip away and raise the alarm if enemies took out one sentry. That was the way the Kha-Khan's army worked, and the Hawks had learned from their fathers and brothers . . . and from Börte, who'd learned everywhere.

He rose and walked—very carefully—in her wake. They were in a region of bare ridges, with only an occasional pocket of flatter soil, running between steep mountains that horses couldn't travel. Gansükh and

Börte were waiting for him, shapes in darkness, crouching on their heels. One of them passed him a skin of *airag*, fermented mare's milk, and he couldn't even tell if it was his sister or not. He took a single mouthful and passed it back; they didn't have much left.

The *zuun* commander had been there with the seven-man squad when the scouting force split apart to dodge the *Miqačin* pursuit, looking stubborn. It hadn't been worth the trouble to argue, and he did have to go with *someone*; this was the largest single group of those that had made up Dzhambul's command, since it included the Hawks. Gansükh's stolid broad face had said as plainly as words that he wasn't going to show up back with Noyon Toktamish's army to find that Prince Dzhambul had been among those who didn't return alive.

Even if Toktamish would not be grieved. Especially if Toktamish would not be grieved; he would need a scapegoat, doubly so if he were under suspicion. Who better than Gansükh to take the blame and provide a severed head to point to? Which Gansükh knows full well, so I cannot even really blame him *for sticking to me like a burr to a horse's tail—this way he can at least die trying to see that I get back.*

"There are thirty of them," he said softly, as they leaned their heads together. "Infantry—no horses."

He closed his eyes—it made little difference—and thought. Then he went on:

"This is probably part of a screening force strung across our path. There will be horsemen somewhere nearby to take up the pursuit if they give the alarm. There are just enough of them to be very risky for a single squad to tackle."

Both the others grunted thoughtfully. Then Gansükh cursed quietly but eloquently, ending with:

"—*jüjigchin khüü!* We can't get by them undetected unless we abandon the horses."

Dzhambul and his sister both snorted. They might as well take turns slitting one another's throats as do that, with the unlucky last one to kill himself.

Or herself, he thought mordantly.

Gansükh continued. "And if we fight them, we have to kill them all and do it quickly and without much noise. Even so it will not be long until the rest knew we have passed."

That made thirty against nineteen; man-eater infantry were fairly well equipped, but the enemy's cavalry were their elite. In a Mongol army, of course, everyone except some specialists was mounted, and even the siege engineers and such rode to where they did their jobs. It was still long odds, except for the advantage of surprise.

Börte said it for him. "We can't just fight and beat them—that'll have their reaction force on our track before sunrise. We have to *eliminate* them."

Dzhambul grunted agreement, and thought again, calling up the ground in his mind. Always the ground, for a start. Neither of the others wasted any more words while he did.

"We'll do it this way," he began.

Mongols were tough and hardy, and many of them were willing to tell anyone willing to listen all about just how hardy and tough they were. Dzhambul had heard a tümen-commander boasting (or possibly complaining) about how being a Mongol made you too mean and tough and hardy to even get drunk, while he slurped down bowls of mao-tai in a tavern south of the Gobi near the ruins of Hohhot. That had trailed off into mumbles just before he passed out with his face in a puddle of his own sour vomit and started to snore.

Dzhambul himself had been raised mostly on the steppe, in a *ger* winter and summer, and often enough sleeping out under the Eternal Blue Sky, learning to ride and shoot, herd and hunt and fight as his ancestors had, though more bookish schooling hadn't been neglected either. The Khan didn't believe in coddling his offspring and possible successor, though that wasn't certain. Anyone descended from Dzhambul's great-grandfather, Kha-Khan Tömörbaatar the Unifier, could be elected by the *kurultai* of notables . . . and between youth, vigor, multiple wives and plentiful concubines, his great-grandfather had left a *lot* of descendants.

But hardy and tough or not, Dzhambul was tired of being cold and hungry, and it was a very cold midnight right now.

He was also tired of crawling through the dark with *Miqačin* around, trying not to clatter as he carried his weight on toes and knees and elbows, ignoring the way it made muscles stiff with cold ache and crack. The arrows in his belt-quiver were muffled by rags, and his bow and saber were slung across his back, but moving silently in armor was just *hard*. Even in a chain shirt, more flexible and less likely to clank than lamellae on a leather backing. He was also cold in a bone-chilled way that made you tired and restless at the same time, and hungry in a way that eating mostly dried lean horsemeat for a week turned into an almost insane longing for something like *tsötsgii*—separated cream—poured over fried millet.

Something with *fat*, eaten in a nice warm *ger* with double-felt walls and a glowing fire under the smoke hole. And plenty of *airag*, and a big bowl of boiled mutton, and some meat dumplings fried in fat too, and everyone chatting and laughing and children chasing each other around. . . .

He pushed the thought out of his mind. Not being tortured and eaten and killed was very good motivation to remember practice and hunts and previous scouting and raiding expeditions, but he'd had too much of it lately. He was doing it well—at least as well as the others, Gansükh and his seven men who were moving forward on his flanks—but it had a nasty feeling of conscious effort, not the mindless ease that let you focus on something else.

There.

There was someone ahead. He might not be able to see it beyond a suggestion, but he was sure that someone had stood and turned around, facing him.

The glow of the man-eater campfire was in that direction, though they'd at least had the wit to put it in a hollow, rather than setting up a beacon that could be seen for miles. But even with the wind from the south at his back he could smell something warm and close. Man-stink, but subtly different from his own. People smelled differently depending on their diet; grain-fed Han had a milder smell than Mongols who lived on meat and dairy, for instance, more acrid, sharper but less rank.

I hoped they wouldn't have sentries out but I didn't expect *it*, he thought. *But I could be pretty sure they wouldn't have as many as we would.*

And reached up to take the hilt of the slender, slightly curved Uyghur knife he'd been holding in his teeth while he brought a foot forward and braced it solidly. The metallic taste was strong in his mouth, and the buttery tang of stale lanolin from the swatch of raw sheepskin he used to keep his weapons rust-free. Now he could hear breathing . . . steady normal breathing, not the slow cautious way he was letting his breath in and out through an open mouth.

The man ahead stirred, and a rock clicked against a rock. A few seconds later Dzhambul was close and his outstretched hand closed on a boot; a crude moccasin-like boot, at that.

That told him where the man's head would be. He grabbed hard, jerked the foot out from under the man-eater and lunged up, and by luck his left hand closed on a man's neck just below the angle of the jaw as he toppled. It was an awkward place to grab a man, but there was frantic strength in his grip, and his spring had all his weight behind it, over a hundred and ninety pounds with all his gear. The man-eater went over backward, trying to shout, but it came out as a gurgle, more like a strangled yelp than anything but with words in it.

They grappled in the dark, and the *Miqačin* was strong and knew what he was doing and fought like a python with hands, even though Dzhambul sank his knee into the man's belly. That hurt his knee too, because his enemy was wearing a stiffened leather breastplate studded with steel nailheads, but it knocked some of the breath out of the man beneath him in a puff of rotten-meat stink.

His hands clamped at Dzhambul's face, thumbs groping for his eyes, while he tucked his chin into his chest. As he did the Mongol bit down savagely on one hand and stabbed hard and fast. The first was turned on the man's metal-studded leather cuirass and nearly gashed his own left hand, the second struck a spark on a stone, but the third rammed home into the armpit of the arm that ended in the thumb trying to gouge out his eye, and coming far too close to succeeding.

He shoved to drive the point in with all the power of his thick shoulder and arm, felt it stop as the point skidded on bone and then suddenly jam in blade-deep, and jerked the hilt back and forth. Blood coughed out, thick on the hand he had on the man's throat, a spray on his face that made him spit. It was unpleasantly like cutting the throat of a wounded deer, a parody of the act.

We are herders, we are hunters, went through some distant corner of his mind as the death-stink told him his enemy was gone; so did the limpness. *Why do we fight to rebuild the empire of a man eight hundred years dead?*

"Kyung-joon?" a voice called from ahead, as he blinked away stinging pain and the eye throbbed.

Put such thoughts aside. Evil spirits ride the night here. Do not give them entry. If we weren't fighting here, we'd be stealing each other's horses and sheep and fighting over that instead back home.

He thought that *Kyung-joon* was a name, but that was about the limit of his Korean; there wasn't even the usual soldier's incentive to learn *surrender* or *hands up*, since they generally didn't surrender and couldn't be trusted if they did. He had to improvise now, but the time was about right and a plan with no allowance for mishap wasn't a plan at all, it was a suicide pact.

He filled his chest and belly and made a sound; it was a low deep warbling that was something like a night bird, though not one from this country . . . if there were any here. It had three advantages: it carried very well, it wasn't easy to mistake for anything else, if you knew it, and it was extremely difficult to place, seeming to come from everywhere and nowhere. Then he crawled past the body, and up onto the low ridge overlooking the enemy outpost.

"Kyung-joon, neo mwohaneungeoya, babo ya?" a voice said from those grouped around the fire, in a sharp commanding tone with a question in it.

With his eyes just above the crest line Dzhambul could see a helmeted figure standing before the low red glow, looking up towards him—but standing next to a fire and looking into darkness was a fool's game, you might as well have your eyes closed.

But he'll think of that—the sentry was well away from the fire, and looking away from it, he thought. *Except that now there's no time for him to come to his senses.*

An earsplitting scream came from beyond the higher ground on the other, northern side of the man-eater camp. It was precisely the sound a sentry might make if someone rammed a thin blade into their kidney from behind, almost certainly because that was precisely what had happened.

You're being hit from two directions at once, Dzhambul thought towards the Miqačin commander. *You don't know which is important . . . you can't decide . . . be paralyzed. . . .*

Somewhere nearby Gansükh was being quietly, obscenely thankful that the *hens* had pulled it off.

If Börte is ever the Kha-Khan's sister, this man is doing his prospects at court no good at all, but at least he's no lickspittle, Dzhambul thought as he pulled his bow off his back and reached for an arrow from the quiver at his belt. *Or he may change his mind tonight, if we aren't all killed.*

The enemy commander in the helmet whirled and swept out his sword, looking northward to where his second sentry had evidently just died. If he wasn't very stupid, he'd be realizing he was in a situation where he had few choices, all bad, and it was entirely his own fault.

In his shoes, Dzhambul would have had *half* his force out as sentries, and spent his own time moving between them at unpredictable intervals.

"*Mong-go!*" the man-eater commander yelped—the Miqačin word for Mongols.

Whichever bad choice he'd picked didn't matter, because an arrow came whispering out of the night, right from the direction he was looking. They were close enough for Dzhambul to hear the solid crunching *thuck* sound as the arrow hit him square in the face, penetrated all the way through and went *tink* on the inside of his helmet at the rear. He wasn't close enough to see the fletching on the shaft, but he'd have bet his best horse back home that it was Börte's; she used stork feathers, where he preferred eagle or vulture.

She would be more or less where he'd lain while scouting the enemy camp, and that was only seventy-five or eighty *delem* from the fire—*delem* were what they'd called meters in the old days, about one long stride—which was pretty close range. Borte's bow drew at two-thirds of her body's weight, much less than his, but she was just as accurate, or better if you listened to her.

The enemy officer fell backward, head and shoulders in the fire; the embers flared up as he twitched and his heels drummed on the frozen ground.

All the enemy were on their feet, even the ones who'd been sleeping off their meal of abominations. Some of them even had arrows on the string, for all the good that would do them, trying to shoot into impenetrable blackness. The right move would have been to draw their swords and charge the direction of the shot; it wouldn't save them at his point, but they'd inflict far more damage and crucially slow their targets down. Though doing that would be very hard without someone to give the order; his sister had picked her target well.

And probably nobody had told the man-eater troops why they were here. In a Mongol force they'd have been thoroughly briefed on what the high command intended and thought, which made for flexibility.

"Now," he whispered.

And as if hearing the command another ten bows began to snap along with Börte's. The arrows were invisible until they caught the firelight near their targets, and then they were the merest flicker. He'd had experience with being shot at in the dark, and it was nerve-wracking, with only the very briefest of whispers to warn you of what was coming in, which made your mind multiply the arrows and think you were being bombarded from everywhere.

Some of the man-eaters drew their own bows and then hesitated, or shot blindly; half a dozen did charge the northern ridge with blade or spear in hand, and died quickly as all the archers concentrated on them, which was why a uniform rush would have been better. A lone hero was nothing but an arrow-riddled corpse in the making.

"The hens . . . the Hawks . . . can shoot, at least," Gansükh said grudgingly from his position a little farther down the line.

The fall of the last of their men attacking northward was the signal for all the surviving *Miqačin* to stop cowering, turn and bolt south. They crowded together, an unconscious seeking of reassurance in numbers. That made them better targets and several fell silent or shrieking with arrows in their backs and legs, but some had picked up shields that they wore slung on their backs, square ones that covered them from the back of the head to the calves, and those did provide a fair amount of protection. A new sound rang, the hard *thock* of shafts punching into wood and leather. For a moment he could see their faces, gaping eyes and mouths, and then they were only silhouettes against the dying fire.

"*Sumnuud!*" Dzhambul shouted.

He came up on one knee and drew with the full stretch of his arms, for the long heavy war-shaft with the plum-needle head. *Sumnuud* meant—

"*Arrows!*"

The man-eaters screamed again as the Mongols shot, more arrows coming from nowhere. Dzhambul drew and loosed four times; at this range and from his bow the heavy pile-headed arrows made nothing of armor. The last one in front of him swung a polearm of some sort at him, a gleam of steel before a flash of eyes and teeth. He reached back and up over his left shoulder, swept out his sword and parried with a shower of sparks as his blade struck the metal wire wrapped around the wooden shaft below the cutting head.

The hard shock jarred his wrist painfully. Before the *Miqačin* could draw back for another blow something glittered behind him and he toppled backward with a scream. Before he hit the ground Börte struck again, this time with the long thin dagger in her left hand rather than the saber she'd used to slash across his hamstrings.

"You keep bad company, brother," she said, panting.

"Then let's be gone, sister," he replied, sheathing his blade and running the bow back into the case slung across his back.

From across the hollow he heard a high shriek—very hawk-like, in fact, shouting triumphantly:

The Sky-Blue Wolves are in the fold!

And a thunder of hooves, as the two Hawks who'd been left with the mounts brought them forward at the gallop despite the darkness and the uncertain footing. The flood of horses poured down the slope opposite, a moving carpet of darkness in the night. They parted around the *Miqačin* campfire, red catching on tossing manes and rolling eyes, trampling the fallen under-hoof, and as they went smaller figures ran by them and caught the pommels, bouncing into the saddles and lying forward along the horse's necks.

"What do you say about Börte's Hens now, hundred-captain Gansükh?" his sister shouted through the darkness and chaos.

"That the Hawks ride like leopards, Princess!" the man called back, and you could hear the grin in his voice.

Dzhambul whistled sharply; his mount veered towards him, stumbled on something—a rock, a man, who knew?—recovered and half-reared above him. He leapt, grabbed the saddle and swung up, clamping it with his knees and then sliding down into the leather embrace, yelling like the boy who'd played this game amid the ruins on the outskirts of Ulaanbaatar.

A scatter of man-eaters were ahead of them down the slope, running towards the narrow dirt road that cut into the side of the hill. Dzhambul whistled signals, and the Mongols fell into a column of twos, which was all that the track would take. There wasn't time to be afraid, but he could feel the loom of the hillside to the right, ever steeper, and the slope to the left was a chasm now that went . . . somewhere, but he couldn't see it.

That was what he'd been waiting for. He leaned forward, and the horse—who had spent as much of his life being ridden as Dzhambul had spent in the saddle—lengthened its pace, albeit with a snort of disbelief at the risks he was making it take. The man-eater running ahead of him gave a weak breathless scream as he tried to run faster, and then a much louder one as Dzhambul freed his left foot from the stirrup and kicked out. The scream fell as the *Miqačin* arched out into emptiness for ten *delem* and then struck the stony slope, presumably bouncing and rolling down it, though it was mainly the clatter of rock that told him so.

Behind him two more of the man-eaters threw themselves down and covered their heads with their arms. They screamed too . . . briefly.

"Thank you, *Ataya Tengri*, who gives me a horse to ride with my thighs, who walls away servants of dark Erlik-Khan who seek to destroy me," he murmured, as he drew aside where the track flattened out.

The riders weren't making much noise, it was too dark to really see their faces, no talking, but he could feel their cheerfulness. The little engagement hadn't taken more than ten minutes, counting knifing the two sentries, and had been a demonstration of how surprise gave each one the strength of twenty.

Börte drew up beside him and so did Gansükh, when they reached a lower spot where the ground opened up.

"My apologies, Princess," the *zuun*-commander said. "That worked perfectly! The Ancestor could not have done it better when he was a youngster hunted by his enemies!"

Then he stopped, not seeing their faces but able to tell that their helmeted heads were turned towards him.

"What?" he said. "What?"

"Hundred-commander," Börte said. "What direction are we moving?"

"Why, south . . . oh."

"Oh," Börte said, loading much meaning into the little sound, including but not limited to *you idiot.*

That's a little unfair, Dzhambul thought. *Gansükh is excellent at tactics. Strategy is not his strong point, though. And we're all short of sleep and food. That makes your mind stiff, focused on what is right in front of you.*

"We've been dodging the traps the enemy lay," he said aloud instead. "But they're still keeping us from breaking through northward."

Gansükh had a frown in his voice when he spoke. "Yes, Noyon. That means they are devoting a good deal of manpower to this . . . to *us*, specifically, not to other bands from our force."

"*Kangshinmu*," Börte said.

Dzhambul and Gansükh both stiffened at the name of the enemy's sorcerer-lords.

"They can still feel us, I think, even if they are weakened. I do not know why they are concentrating on my brother and me, but they are."

"We are doing our people a service by distracting this many troops," Dzhambul said. "Though I wish we had a shaman with us."

"I wish we had ten shamans and five *tümens* of the Kha-Khan's *Kheshig* guard," Gansükh said.

"Why not wish for twenty *tümens*, while you're at it?" Börte asked.

"Not enough grazing here for the horses of two hundred thousand men," Gansükh said, his voice matter-of-fact.

They all chuckled at the joke; which would be heartening for their followers.

Dzhambul thought for a moment. "If they're trying to herd us south, to break contact we should *go* south—fast, instead of trying to loop back every time they push at us," he said. "Once we have lost them, we have options. They cannot have big armies everywhere and they cannot put screens across the whole country—or even the parts of it that are not mountains."

His eyes sought his sister, but it was too dark. . . . Still Gansükh's head swung towards him as he said, "So, the extra part of our mission . . ."

Börte nodded. "We are heading that way after all, without even trying."

He called up the map of the territory in his mind. "We will head for this Pusan place."

CHAPTER TEN

PORTLAND PROTECTIVE ASSOCIATION
(FORMERLY WESTERN OREGON)
HIGH KINGDOM OF MONTIVAL
(FORMERLY WESTERN NORTH AMERICA)
JANUARY 22ND
CHANGE YEAR 47/2045 AD

Órlaith forced herself not to snarl. Being called back was doing that. The fact that Tiphaine d'Ath was smiling at her didn't help; it was a thin, knowing smile of the type her elders gave her when they were educating her inexperience.

You have to put up with it, she thought. *I am . . . or was . . . inexperienced.*

It was even more irritating that the Grand Marshal would *know* that she was thinking that. Being around someone who'd known you from babyhood was like that, especially if they'd spent a lot of time teaching you. Tiphaine d'Ath had been one of her instructors in the sword and the arts of war, from how to sneak through the dark on your own to how to move heavy cavalry units at speed over rough country.

Remember, you like Tiph. She's not what most people would call likeable, but you do like her—you always have.

"Frustrating not to be able to charge in with the Sword and settle it all with one big decisive battle, isn't it?" the Grand Marshal said. "Your Highness."

They were in a tower of the great fort that guarded Astoria and the

Columbia mouth, built at the southern end of the pre-Change bridge and incorporated into the outer defensive wall of the city. It had been erected by the first Lord Protector, then mostly handed over to the Chartered City for its militia headquarters after the Protector's War during Lady Sandra's reign as Regent for Mathilda, then to the Royal Navy after the founding of Montival. All three forces still used it and others were present on a smaller scale.

This room right under the steep witches-hat tile roof looked out northwest over the tidal estuary of the Columbia, and the docks and shipyards beyond. The wind found crevices, and carried the silt-salt smell of where the river met the sea, a hint of green spice from the forests, and always the woodsmoke and forge-smoke of the town.

It was an unusually clear day for this time of year, with blue sky and fleecy clouds, but chill. The gray-green water of the estuary was beaten into low endless ruffles of whitecaps by the onshore breeze, over which ships beat tediously, tacking back and forth into the wind to make enough westing and run free into the ocean, up and down the coast. The glass windows between the crenellations—they could be quickly removed and replaced by heavy shutters—gave plenty of light, but it was cold enough that she was glad of her tight green Montero coat of fine wool and good drawers under her kilt.

"My father did like that decisive-battle approach, Lady d'Ath," Órlaith said; there were aids and staff officers present, which imposed a certain degree of formality. "To get things over with as fast as possible."

"Like shit he did," Tiphaine said, ignoring a few shocked gasps from her underlings. "The Prophet's War lasted *years*, and for a lot of that we were avoiding battle because they'd have beaten the crap out of us. They did, a couple of times."

Órlaith looked at the tables and map-easels. She'd assimilated the information they contained very quickly . . . but then, she bore the Sword. Having the numbers at your fingertips was no substitute for judgment, though, and she knew she was feeling annoyed, which made considered thought harder.

"I think we've covered the logistics and planning?" she said. "It's not too complex; *more troops are better* versus *how many can we ship, equip and feed?*"

"And strategy is need-to-know," d'Ath agreed, and made a gesture.

Her subordinates gathered up the files they'd been presenting from and filed out down the curving stairwell in obedient silence save for the sound of boots on pavement and the occasional click of a metal sword-chape on stone. There was a rap of glaive-butts as the sentries below saluted the officers, and then a distant murmur of voices as they began discussing what they'd just seen—a castle was as gossipy as a village.

That left Heuradys standing behind Órlaith's chair with her left hand on the hilt of her longsword and her right resting on her belt, but the Crown Princess more or less had to have an attendant . . . and Heuradys was Lady d'Ath's adoptive daughter, after all.

When the other subordinates were gone the Grand Marshal went on: "Even the Quest of the Sunrise Lands lasted nearly two years. And while your daddy was off traveling across the continent, getting Iowa on our side and doing derring-do among the moose-eaters of Maine . . . pardon me, Norrheim . . . and fighting Moorish pirates and Bekwa and getting your enchanted snickersnee there, and *finally* returning . . . the rest of us were fighting all the time, defensive battles, raids, guerilla operations, retreating, standing sieges, hanging on by our fingernails, so he'd have something to come back *to* when he arrived to save the day."

"Which he did, at the big decisive battle of the Horse Heaven Hills."

D'Ath grinned, always a little shocking. She'd gotten gaunter in the face over the last decade; you'd always been able to see the skull beneath it, and now it was more obvious, though it was a handsome skull.

"By which point the Prophet's men were within spitting distance of the sea and cutting us in two, after having started east of the Rockies. I was there, Princess, as Grand Constable of the Association, while you were a fetus. I saw Rudi fight an entire campaign over months to *set up* the Battle of the Horse Heaven Hills, incidentally that was a *really* nice piece of work . . . and while he and your mother and Sandra and Juniper and Ignatius did the politics and alliances . . . which was just as good, in a field

I don't follow as well . . . and then we had years more effort to root out Corwin and the Church Universal and Triumphant's diehards hiding in the hills . . . there are still probably a few of them up there, living on camas roots and sleeping with bears. It was only really *over* about the time you were learning to walk."

That's all true, Órlaith thought; now she fought not to sigh.

Heuradys did sigh, very slightly, but then she'd probably been listening to the Wise Strategist even more than Órlaith had over the years.

"By the Lord and Lady, Tiph, all right, it's going to be a long war. I said so myself, didn't I? But you're handling all this"—she gestured to the piles of reports—"perfectly competently on your own. I didn't have to come back to be told what I already know, or to watch you do staff work I know you'll handle as well as anyone could. It's *weeks* across the Pacific even in a fast lightly-laden ship."

"I can do the administration, yes," Tiphane said. "But you need to get a grip on the troops you're going to be commanding in the field—let them see you, get a feel for them, take them through some large-scale maneuvers. Naysmith and Thurston are handling things in Japan, at the Omura Bay camp, well enough, aren't they?"

"Yes . . . I put Reiko in charge of selecting deployment areas there."

At Tiphane's raised brow she continued: "I know, she's a foreigner, those are Montivallan troops, and I wouldn't have done it if I didn't have perfect confidence in her."

D'Ath's eyes narrowed. "She's hoping we'll bleed the enemy for her while her farmers get their harvest in."

"Yes, that's true. And it's fair enough from their point of view. But the Nihonjin have a lot of experience defending their settlements. What I *could* be doing there that nobody else can is helping get our intelligence in order. The Japanese have a lot on the enemy, but it's all tactical. And we know far too little about the Asian mainland. I've got the languages . . . any languages I need . . . and with the Sword I can make interrogations a lot easier."

"True, but your mother also wants you back for political reasons, which she'll explain. And she wants Empress Reiko here, for at least a while, too. *Don't* whine at me, Your Highness! Wars are political! I'm a technician of the sharp end, but I work for people like your mother . . . and you. I'm the point, you people are the hilt, and that's where the sword is steered from."

"Mother has far more experience with the politics, too."

Tiphaine grinned, and this time there was an edge of gloating anticipation in it. "She has some surprises for you . . . and no, I'm *not* going to talk about it. You'll get briefed at Todenangst, before you go down to Dun na Síochána to address the Congress of Realms and have *such fun* in endless meetings."

"Ah, the joy of it," Órlaith said hollowly, and Heuradys snickered very quietly.

She'll just have to stand quietly a lot. I'll have to listen *and* think *about what a lot of intensely parochial and sometimes deeply stupid people say, at great length.*

"You'll also be taking Johnnie back with you. And probably his new bride."

Órlaith's eyebrows went up. "Your son's doing a fine job commanding the Association contingent," she pointed out. "He handled the charge at Pearl Harbor perfectly . . . and the rally afterwards, which is harder. You know as well as I do how hard it is to get men-at-arms to admit that chasing people needs horse-archers, light cavalry."

There was a slight flicker of softening in the hard sardonicism of d'Ath's face; her relationship with Diomede d'Ath wasn't biological—the heir to Ath was adopted—but close enough for all that, starting with holding Delia's hands during the birth.

"I'm glad to hear you confirm the reports. But we'll be sending a lot more of the ironheads"—

which was her private term for the Association's warrior nobility

—"with the second wave. Diomede's only the heir to a barony."

"But he's going to be a tenant *in capite* when he inherits," Heuradys pointed out unexpectedly; that meant d'Ath was held directly from the Lords Protector in the chain of vassalage. "And his brother is heir to Count de Dad, pardon me, Count Campscapell."

"That still isn't going to make Counts happy about obeying a baron," Tiphaine said. "And House Ath are . . . eccentric."

"They obey you, and you're a Baron and . . . more eccentric than any of us kids. For that matter, Lioncel and Diomede are both Catholics, unlike the rest of us."

"I don't count; I'm a freak of nature," Tiphaine said, and then gave a momentary death's-head smile. "Also, Diomede doesn't scare them and I do—I killed a lot of their daddies or grand-daddies in Lady Sandra's purges after the Protector's War. No, sliding John into the chain of command is a good idea."

"And Mother probably wants him to get some field command experience," Órlaith said thoughtfully. "He did fine on our trip to South Westria after Reiko's sword, but that was all small-scale. But will we be able to pry him loose from this new bride of his?"

D'Ath sat, and so did Órlaith; Heuradys remained standing at parade rest, which happened to be the best position for a quick draw-and-strike with a longsword.

"That's not quite the problem," the Grand Marshal said. "It's more a matter of what she'll do."

"I thought she was pregnant?"

"She is. Somewhere between three and four months, so that she'll be well recovered by the time you sail for the fall campaign."

"Ah, not the excessively maternal type."

"No more than I am. Sorry, Herry."

"Why apologize for the truth?" Heuradys said.

Órlaith went on: "What's she like, then?"

"She reminds me a little of me at that age."

"Murderous? Ambitious?" Heuradys said. "Murderously ambitious?"

D'Ath leaned over and poked her in the jerkin. "Mannerless whelp. But yes, to a certain extent. She keeps herself close. Delia likes her, but . . ."

"Mom likes most people," Heuradys said.

"Unlike me, but I like her too . . . respect her, rather."

Órlaith frowned. Who John married wasn't really her business, not on a personal level, but it *would* affect things that *were* her concern all her life.

"I'll have to make an occasion to have a chat," she said.

"You can look her over and make your own judgment," d'Ath agreed.

"And vice versa, Mom," Heuradys said.

"That too," Órlaith agreed. "It's a two-way process."

Well, aren't you the big girl! Pip thought, settling herself into the comfortable armchair and looking at Órlaith where she stood at her ease. *And now we get a chance to chat; the welcoming banquet was just a bit formal.*

Her new sister-in-law and prospective High Queen was a full five inches taller than her own very respectable five-six and moved with an unconscious gliding dancer's gracefulness and stood with a tensile readiness that said . . .

Oh, bloody dangerous, this one! Her heels never touch the ground hard when she walks, even. And Miss Henchwoman behind her is another of the same. Delia's daughter . . . looks a little like her . . . a little like her very theoretical husband the Count via that turkey-baster people gossip about. . . .

Órlaith gave an impression of being almost slender, until you looked closer, or at things like the way her forearms flowed into her hands without much of an indent at the wrists. The kilt she wore—the pleated knee-length skirt-like philabeg, not the enormous blanket-like Great Kilt—and the plaid pinned at the shoulder with a gold-and-rubies broach done in swirling Celtic knotwork, the loose drawstring linen shirt and knit knee-hose and buckled shoes . . . it all looked indecently comfortable, even compared to the maternity kirtle she was wearing herself.

But a bit drafty, outside, even with a coat. Surprising people took the style up in a cold damp place like this . . . on the other hand, think of Skye, think of Lewis, think of bloody Caithness, think of a place even bleaker and colder than bleak, cold and dank merry sodding England.

She had an excuse for taking the chair, since she was definitely starting to have more symptoms of her condition. Lady Delia had cheerfully told her they were entirely normal and would get worse, along with slightly swollen legs and intense sleepiness at odd moments.

And gigantic, very sensitive tits, and rolfing unpredictably though that's dying down at last, thank God, and peeing at unbelievably frequent intervals. And I must admit, it would all be more difficult in Townsville's climate. I cannot imagine Mummy doing this at all, even once. It's . . . so . . . inelegant. But then, chopping people up with kukri knives was messy too, and she did that quite a bit.

The room was medium-sized, part of a suite for the heir to Montival that covered two floors of the Silver Tower, with its own interior staircases and ingenious arrangements that let the exterior access be quickly cut off, and speaking-tubes extending upward and down. A pine-scented fire crackled in the hearth and spat occasional sparks against a screen, and what appeared to be a large painting of leaves and branches occupied most of one wall; if you looked closely you could see disturbing-looking faces peering out of it. Below it was a low rectangular table, with two six-inch statuettes on it—a blue-robed woman who was not the Virgin Mary . . . or maybe in a way was . . . and a man with the head and antlers of an elk, caught in the middle of an ecstatic dance.

There were a few other things on the table: a dagger, a chalice, a book bound in glossy brown leather, what looked like a wand . . .

Because it is a wand, stupid!

. . . and a little censer that held a stub of incense that gave the air a slight tang under the smells of furniture-wax and books and the fire and the gaslights.

"My aunt Fiorbhinn—aunt on my father's side, his younger half-sister Fiorbhinn Loring Mackenzie—did that," Órlaith said, nodding her head towards the painting behind the altar.

Juniper Mackenzie's second husband had been English, and of the Loring family, who were of Norman blood . . . though of a much more dutiful and law-abiding and usually rather poorer variety than the Balwyns, of whom they were distant cousins.

"Fiorbhinn's the mystic in the family in that generation. And an artist and a *filí*, the Mackenzies say. Which is as pretentious as *troubadour* in its way, but there you are."

"You're *not* a Mackenzie yourself?" Pip asked. "I thought you were. There's the kilt, and you talk that way."

Although not as strongly as Juniper does, and in a slightly different way.

"Well, I am more or less, but I didn't grow up there full-time the way my father did—I and my sibs pretty well got to choose what we'd call ourselves."

"Johnnie says you moved about a lot."

"Ah, with his trademark whinge, I've no doubt. Actually he enjoyed it—what child doesn't like camping out a bit and seeing strange sights?"

Pip snorted; she had an instinctive urge to spring to his defense, but John did have a tendency to act put-upon at times.

Though after meeting his family, I understand it better. Talk about your strong personalities! Aloud she went on:

"And *filí* means, precisely? Some sort of musician? Or magician? Or both?"

"Both; a sacred bard, more or less; pretty much what Deor's folk mean by *scop*."

"Deor's . . . well, I suppose he *is* a magician, of sorts. Which turned out to be damned useful. Just not the pointy-hat, throwing-fireballs sort."

"Fiorbhinn's very like that; of course, she and Deor both studied with Grandma Juniper. You may have noticed how his Mist Hills people are about the ancient Saxons . . . as far as they're concerned they *are* the ancient Saxons . . . and the way the Associates are always dropping in bits of Old French into things—" Órlaith said.

"Bother and bugger, have I! It's like going swimming with the Lady of the Lake! And then Richard the Lionheart stops by for tea . . . with the Count of Campscapell, no doubt."

That was a bit snide; there was a legend that Richard had loved men, which was not necessarily true. The Count of Campscapell most definitely *was* that way, in a very manly-muscular, battle-scars and butch finery sort of manner. Associate garb actually leant itself to that, with its macho peacockery of tight hose and padded crotches.

"Mackenzies are like that about things Celtic—a broad term from which they grab bits and serve them up blended like an Irish stew. Grandmother Juniper says it used to bother her. . . ."

"It wasn't her idea? Because she's *quite* Celtic."

"She comes by it honestly; Highlander on her father's side a long ways back and a mother who grew up speaking Erse on Achill Island in Ireland. Things were . . . looser here then, the Change had jellified everything and it took a while to firm up in new shapes."

Órlaith touched her kilt and plaid. "These started with a warehouse full of blankets they salvaged and then they took it up as a uniform, more or less. But she eventually learned to . . . *go with the flow,* as she puts it. Fiorbhinn, now, she wears a *filí's* robe, the idea for which she got out of a book . . . what did Juniper call it . . . a D&D player's manual . . . when she was a little girl."

Pip blinked, calling up a memory. "Oh, that game they used to play?"

It had been a game about the sort of thing her mother and Pete and Fifi had actually done as salvagers under Royal Warrant in reality, minus the eldritch elements . . . which seemed to have crept in too by the time Pip took the *Silver Surfer* north from Darwin.

Though I did eventually send her home with a really fabulous cargo . . . wish I could have seen Pete and Fifi's faces when they saw it and read: For your trouble! I'm off to marry a handsome Prince. . . .

"Is she as spooky as your grandmother Juniper?"

Órlaith grinned. "*As* spooky? That's a judgment call; I've seen Grandmother do some very spooky things indeed. I'd be after saying Fiorbhinn's more showy about it."

The rest of the walls were mostly in polished-wood bookshelves crowded with volumes both pre- and post-Change . . .

I've managed to stop saying Blackout *to myself,* Pip thought. *Next thing you know I'll be able to say* vassal *without wanting to slap a knee and roll about laughing.*

. . . and maps and folios and very elegant versions of filing cabinets, all looking as if they'd been well-used. Armchairs and a desk with a typewriter and tables with more documents and books heaped on them made up most of the rest of the furniture. The *invitation* from the newly-arrived Crown Princess to drop by for refreshments and chitchat had been a politely worded summons, and it pointedly *hadn't* included the Crown Princess' brother John.

As she watched, Órlaith unbuckled her sword belt . . .

Make that the "belt of the capital T, capital S, The Sword," Pip thought, uneasily eyeing the . . . Yes, yes, it's a bloody enchanted sword! And Empress Reiko has one too! It's The Castle of the Magical Swords!

Looking at the Sword of the Lady, you couldn't tell, there wasn't any glow or humming of magical tunes . . . but somehow you most assuredly *could* tell.

God, how Uncle Pete would love this! I hope I get a chance to tell Aunt Fifi what her native Oregon is like these days!

Heuradys d'Ath took it, carefully holding the arrangement of heavy tooled black leather and stainless-steel buckles and fittings so that no part of the weapon or its sheath touched her; the henchwoman looked like a nine-tenths version of Órlaith below the neck, except that she was in hose and houppelande, and above it you could see the resemblance to Delia de Stafford and the Count of Campscapell, whom she'd briefly met.

And there's a certain family likeness to Tiphaine, too, but that's biologically imposs— No, wait. It's really in the way she moves and some of her expressions. Training and early exposure, I suppose. Though I'm pretty sure she's straight. And my oath, I bet she'd be fast in a fight.

D'Ath spoke to Toa. "Want to go into the next room and have a beer and hash over the hunt Mom Two told me about? She says you're not going to leave a boar alive in the Columbia Valley if this keeps up. We can exchange lies and brags."

"You're a hunter like yer Mum?" Toa said.

D'Ath grinned. "*Oh,* yes. I've been hunting demon-possessed Korean cannibals just lately, but boar are more fun and more tasty."

"How do you know about the way the Korean cannibals taste?" Toa asked politely, and snorted at her *touché* gesture.

"We've got tiger here, as well, if you like something a bit more bitey."

"Got 'em in Townsville and around Darwin too—and lions in the drier parts, and cheetahs and giraffes and elephants and every bloody thing. I blame Werribee Open Range Zoo."

"I must go there someday!" Heuradys replied; then added seriously: "You can relax. There's no other way into this chamber besides the door. Except through several feet of concrete and steel."

Toa snorted. "You hope, right?"

"This overgrown termite farm of a castle is lousy with secret passages and hidden chambers, like a bad *chanson* with masked villains popping out from behind the tapestries every third verse and brandishing daggers, but there aren't any *here*."

Toa glanced at Pip, leaning on his broad-bladed spear, and she nodded; everything in here did look very solid. The two walked out through the far door, which had a pointed arch carved in low relief with acanthus leaves. It was left open, but the distances made anyone overhearing them unlikely unless they shouted.

"You may have heard what the Sword can do," Órlaith said as she settled down across the low stone-slab table with its wrought-bronze legs. "It's out of range now."

"I've heard that it lets you tell when someone's telling porkies?" Pip asked. "And now I'm free to fabricate? Liberated to lie? Empowered to equivocate?"

"Yes," Órlaith said, and grinned. "Porkies . . . I like that. When you're wearing the Sword . . ."

"You mean when *you're* wearing the sword. I notice that your, ah, knight there didn't touch it."

"It probably wouldn't harm her. But we did have a case of someone trying to steal it, when I was a girl. There were people who didn't really believe in it, back then."

"And?"

"The guards rushed in when they heard the screaming; they said afterwards he used it."

"Used it on them?"

"On himself. You wouldn't think a man could cut off three of his own limbs, even with *that* sword . . . it's got an indestructible edge like a glass razor, by the way . . . but apparently he managed to manage it, so you might say. Since then we've been cautious. The guards are to keep fools away from it, not to guard it from them. You might say the alternate name is *Foolkiller Sword*."

I should think! There's *a fool who came a gutser and no mistake.*

"But if you're one of my blood . . . my mother and my sibs . . . if you touch or wear the Sword, you can tell if someone is *trying* to deceive you. Though if they really believe they can walk on water, you'll hear the sincerity, not the insanity. Someone . . ."

Her mouth twisted. "Someone who had his mind tampered with got quite close to me lately. I couldn't tell because *he didn't know*."

"What happened?"

"I nearly died . . . and he did. He died well, at the end, but he's still dead."

Alan Thurston, Pip thought with a chill. *Who I met thousands of miles away . . . if distance applies to the place we were.*

Órlaith shook herself and continued more lightly: "And irony and jokes can be sort of ambiguous."

"But not a direct question?" Pip said. And to herself:

Good grief, what a bonus for a merchant!

"Then there's nothing anyone can do but tell the truth as they know it or lapse into a telling silence. My father warned me before I . . . inherited it . . . that you had to be careful about using it. He left it on the stand as much as he could."

"You suffered some disillusionments?" Pip guessed.

When you think about it, absolutely knowing *when people were trying to put one over on you could make human relationships a bit difficult.*

"Some, but fewer than you might think; folk here in Montival have known about the Sword since before I was born, and that my parents would wear it when they were giving judgment or the like. The flatterers and would-be corrupt placemen betook themselves elsewhere."

Probably the Court with the lowest arse-kisser quota in human history! she thought, her mind racing through the implications. Órlaith went on:

"There were some disappointed hopes. For example I learned that Herry"—she nodded to the doorway, and Pip realized she meant the knight, Heuradys—"really does love me like a sister . . . like an impulse-ridden *younger* sister who's occasionally not fit to be let out without a keeper. And here I thought she was exaggerating. Or hoped so."

Pip snorted. "Sounds bloody useful. What was your father warning you about?"

"That it's an invitation to be a bad *bachlach* of a bully nobody feels safe around," Órlaith said. "And to feel righteous about it, which is worse, and to go sour on the human race in general. One of the few times I saw my da really lose his temper was when a man jumped off a castle tower rather than face him carrying the Sword; what angered him was that others laughed about it."

I'd be tempted to laugh, too, I suppose . . . if I didn't know or didn't like the man. On the other hand, if he was a decent sort who'd just made one mistake . . . or was afraid of being asked about something really private . . .

Órlaith nodded, following her thought: "If you can't fib or even shade things to someone as powerful as a monarch, you have no defenses at all."

"Ah. And people couldn't hide what they felt about you which would— Goodness, that would be . . . what was the word . . . a negative feedback cycle!"

There was a collation on the table between them: actual tea and coffee over spirit lamps, finger food and a bottle of wine in a cooler. Pip poured herself a glass, and one for Órlaith when she got a nod. Suddenly she felt quite hungry, which was a switch for today, and she slid several of the oysters arrayed on a bed of crushed ice into her mouth—they were small and had an intense, almost coppery flavor that all at once tasted ambrosial—took a bite of the brown bread that went with them, and loaded a plate with some of the spiced liverwurst on rye, deviled eggs, and bits of this and that.

"I noticed you were off your feed a bit at that banquet—the boredom at official functions here is paralyzing, but the food's good," Órlaith said as Pip leaned back and began to daintily shovel it in.

"This preggers thing does very odd things to my appetite," Pip said. "I suppose I'm not supposed to call you *Your Highness* in private?"

"Órlaith will do, or Orrey if you prefer," Órlaith said; the name was actually pronounced *Ooor-lah*, more or less. "Since we're sisters. Not that I want you pulling my hair, or bursting into tears and shouting you hate me before you run out of the room, which Vuissance did once."

Then she sighed. "I envy you the baby . . . just a wee bit, you understand."

"You can have the chundering twice a day," Pip said with a shudder. "Though that's dying down, thank God."

Órlaith did a little friendly nibbling to keep her company—unlike Pip she'd done the banquet full justice—and sipped at her wine, politely waiting for the hormonally-stoked hunger pangs to be satisfied.

"So, you'll understand one of the advantages of the Sword is that you can sum someone up faster and more reliably," she said when Pip progressed to the cherry-tarts and miniature apple-cinnamon pastries with clotted cream and hazelnuts. "Like getting a running commentary on what they say and what they mean, and triangulating from there."

Pip felt a prickle of alarm. "You have a summation of me, Órlaith?"

Another of those grins; friendly enough, but with a hard edge.

"Yes. I'm thinking you're a ruthless bitch of the purest water, and that you weren't a pirate before you got trapped in that Baru Denpasar place . . . not *quite*."

Pip felt herself bristle, and fought it down. "I was in a slightly edgy line of work," she observed. "And I didn't end up slightly dead, either."

Órlaith laughed. "You're talking to Norman Arminger's granddaughter here, Pip. You've been here for weeks, you must know what that means."

Pip put her head to one side. "You don't seem to be as upset about that as Johnnie. He wallows in it slightly, now and then."

Órlaith shrugged. "Johnnie's a Catholic. Guilt comes naturally to him," she said. "I'm a witch, and we don't."

Pip chuckled; she could see the point. It had never taken with her, but then she was the descendant of a long line of titled scoundrels on her mother's side, and Scots colonial adventurers . . . or plunderers . . . on her father's, and she was Anglican Rite.

"And Norman is dead. He was a bad man who did much evil and would have been and done worse if he'd lived. But if he'd never been, or died in the Change, this"—she rotated her wineglass in a slow circle—"would be ruins and bones. And Mike Havel, my other grandfather, was a hero . . . but also a very hard man. Honorable, but hard, a bad man to cross and a bad enemy to have, as many found out to their loss and cost and often enough the cost was their lives. Norman Arminger among them! This world we've been given is not for those who can't be hard and use a hard hand, at need."

"John's a fighter too," Pip said. "I saw that the hour we first met, when I sailed the *Silver Surfer* out to rescue the *Tarshish Queen* from the Pallid Mask's men, in the harbor at Baru Denpasar."

"Ah, but that's not *quite* the same thing, is it now? I don't doubt Johnnie was brave as a lion—before we got separated at Topanga, I saw him in action against the Eaters in San Francisco."

Biters, Pip thought; that was the Australian term.

"And in the desert countries south of that. And he's grown up, just a bit, while he was off on his adventures."

"There . . . really wasn't much choice, where he was . . . trapped," Pip said slowly. "If he hadn't stood fast, he'd have been dead, or mad, or a puppet of . . . the King in Yellow demon . . . god . . . whatever the bloody hell it was."

Órlaith nodded. "And glad I am to see that, and thankful for your role in it, for I love him dearly even if I ruffle him a bit at times. But speaking of choices, you got yourself before a priest with Johnnie with effortless ease, and he slippery as a greased pig about commitment since he started showing an interest in girls . . . which he did rather early. Many a one clutched hard at him, but he slipped free with a sad squeal, until you caught him."

"We're in love," Pip said, with a slight edge of frost. "You'll know that's true."

"Yes, it is. . . . Which is why we're having this nice friendly conversation, eh? He's not stupid in any way or form, our Johnnie, but around you he's like a steer in a slaughterhouse *just* after the man with the sledgehammer has done his business. Mind, I've seen him the same way before, but never struck so hard . . . and never to the point of the altar."

Pip sipped at the wine, keeping her voice under careful control. It was another of those delicious flinty whites.

"That's . . . interesting. So, you don't mind your little brother being hitched to a ruthless bitch?"

"To a *very intelligent* ruthless bitch who does love him . . . and has his interests, which are to say *her* interests, at heart?"

"Well, I'm glad you think I'm intelligent."

"You told the truth about your background . . . though with a few sins of omission, eh? *That* was intelligent. And you genuinely love Johnnie. That's pretty much what he needs, I think. And you did save his life . . . or his soul, at the same time. So I think that perhaps we'll be friends when we have the time, and that in the meantime we're going to be able to do useful work together, eh? For the family business you've married into."

"Right," Pip said. "And what particular work did you have in mind?"

"Why, the war west-over-sea, of course."

"Why not speak directly to John?"

"I will; he'll be appalled to learn he's to command the Association contingent. A great many ironclad men-at-arms and valorous, troublesome ironheaded noblemen."

Pip blinked. "Is he ready for that?" she said. "He's quite young. . . ."

"And you no older. But yes, he's been trained to it all his life, no less than I. And he'll have able help for the technical side of things; Diomede d'Ath, Heuradys' brother, will be his chief of staff."

"Will that be a problem?"

"With some it might be, but with Diomede . . . no. What he'll most need to do, and need the most help with, is to keep the nobles in order, and they mostly young men eager for accomplishment . . . glory and fame and honor. They'll snap at one another, and at John if he allows it. He'll need your help and advice, and you'll need to have all the feuds and alliances of the Associate Houses at your fingertips for that."

"Lady Delia will have all that in detail," Pip said. "And will be glad to fill me in, I'm a quick study . . . and you'll be there too, won't you?"

"Yes. But he's used to having me hector him to get off his arse and work, and to be sure in the past I've been a trifle . . . tactless about it, now and then. So there are times he just lets it roll off him, like hail off a turtle, so."

Big sister bullied him and stormed in and told him to shut down the music and stop the party and buckle down, Pip translated. *Perhaps with justification, perhaps without, but that stops now, big sister.*

"John's a very able man," Pip said carefully. "And he's a young man, but not a boy any longer."

Then her hand moved to her belly. "And he's going to be Lord Protector here."

And my daughter . . . or son, I suppose . . . is going to be Protector after him. Let everyone be very sure of that.

"And that's the very point!" Órlaith said. "He's a grown man with a baby on the way, and I can't tell him what to do anymore . . . well, no, I actually *can* tell him what to do, but as High Queen, not his sister. I have to back off on that now, or I'll put his back up and there'll be friction we can't afford. It's one of the drawbacks of monarchy that it's all tied up with who threw who's doll out the window in the nursery, I suppose. But since you come to it fresh, and you're John's partner in all things . . ."

Pip's eyes narrowed thoughtfully. "I'm sort of tied down," she pointed out, patting herself.

"Not after . . . say, the late summer."

"Are you encouraging me to neglect my maternal responsibilities?" Pip said . . . lightly.

"Pshaw. You're the partner of a Prince, nobody expects you to wash the baby's clouts yourself, or even nurse her, necessarily—up here in the north-realm wet-nurses are a common custom. And you're John's true partner now—the child sort of, ummm, symbolizes it. And fatherhood will be a duty nobody imposes on John but himself; I've noticed he's better at those."

Pip stopped, closed her mouth. *She's telling me she wants me to be John's active partner in whatever command he gets,* she thought.

"Well, and I wouldn't have pegged you as a temptress . . . Orrey."

Pip finished her wine and switched to the Hawaiian coffee. "Let's go into more detail. For example, Lady Delia loves children."

"And she's good at it, too, so—"

CHAPTER ELEVEN

LOST LAKE
CROWN FOREST DEMESNE
(FORMERLY NORTH-CENTRAL OREGON)
HIGH KINGDOM OF MONTIVAL
(FORMERLY WESTERN NORTH AMERICA)
JUNE 20TH
CHANGE YEAR 47/2045 AD
(PLACES OUT OF SPACE, AND TIME)

"Are you absolutely sure, Mother?" Órlaith Arminger Mackenzie asked.

"My darling, when have you known me to be unsure about a decision of State after I've announced it? I won't say I'm always *right*, but I don't open my mouth about it at all unless I'm at least *sure*."

It was the end of a clear warm day, the first day of summer, which meant it was still a bit chilly here in the forested uplands of the Low Cascades north of Mount Hood, chill, but not cold enough to make their breath smoke. The wind fluttered her shoulder-length hair beneath her Mackenzie bonnet, the bleaching of tropic suns fading to let the natural deep yellow with just a hint of fire show. It was much the same shade as red alder leaves turned in the fall, and there were plenty of those around now, still bright green against the darker shades of the Douglas fir and cedar, mountain hemlock and white pine.

To breathe that air was like drinking meltwater off a glacier, and it was full of the smells of pine and fir-sap, and the pungent beginnings of wood-smoke, but she was comfortable as it fluttered the edge of the plaid slung over her shoulder and the pleated knee-length kilt. It was all homelike, after Hawai'i and the southern oceans, and she'd be leaving soon.

Best to take a taste of home with me.

The sky was an aching blue, save for a band where the setting sun made crimson streaks westward across the little clearing and turned the great perfect cone of Mount Hood to gold and copper southward. A bald eagle went by in majesty not far overhead, and a pair of ravens larger than any she'd ever seen kept watch from a nearby branch.

And there were many other places in Montival as beautiful or perhaps even more so, according to an individual's tastes.

What a land of glories this kingdom of ours is, a land fit for heroes and Gods and giants!

But this was as close as anyone who wasn't of the line of the High Kings, or their handfasted mate, could come to Lost Lake now. Her father and mother had bound that place to themselves, to the blood they bore and mingled, to the land and the Powers that warded it, with the Sword of the Lady. Nobody had approached even this fringe of it since the Kingmaking, at the founding of Montival.

Guards weren't necessary to enforce that. Something about this place turned the mind and eye and foot aside unless the time and the person was right; it wasn't hostile, but these woods and waters were . . . other. You had to be some distance away before you could even find it on a map.

"For a war like this, far overseas, we need a High Queen regnant, the High King's heir, one who's sworn to the land," soon-to-be Queen Mother Mathilda Arminger said and nodded crisply.

And one who doesn't have an Associate's dagger, passed between them unspoken. Reluctantly, *I think she's right about that.*

Her round middle-aged face was lined with grief, olive-hued against the snowy white of a linen wimple bound with a chain of platinum and diamond and ruby, and her healthy but slightly stout form was wrapped in an ankle-length robe lined with ermine over a simple dagg-sleeved kirtle of fine cream-colored wool bound by a metal-link belt that bore a tooled-leather purse . . . and her Associate's dagger.

With a wry grin she continued. "Don't worry, daughter of mine, I won't dump all the administrative details on you right away! You'll be off west-over-sea with your friends again as soon as the grain's ground and baked, and I'll be finding the barrels of hardtack and the catapult-bolts and boxes of water-purification pills. *And* the money, and tearing my hair out when some small-town newspaper says something particularly stupid."

"I'd like to be able to stay longer, with you and the sibs—"

"No, you wouldn't, no matter how much you'll miss us while you're away," her mother said dryly, with a slight twist of the lips. "I remember being your age and having great tasks to do, my darling, and dreams burning like fire in the heart. The only *real* reason you came back at all was to get more troops, of which there's no shortage clamoring to join you."

Órlaith spread her hands in a rueful gesture. "It's been a long time since the Prophet's War."

Mathilda snorted. "Not just young idiots, either; plenty my age. And I had to take you by the ear to make you stay long enough for *this*."

"Half-true, Mother!" Órlaith said. "I've seen wonders and terrors and things beautiful and strange abroad, and made good friends, but there's nothing grander than this Montival of ours that you and Father built."

Mathilda shook her head. "We led the building, yes, but it was the fruit of many hands, and hearts, and minds"—she crossed herself—"and the will of God."

Órlaith signed the air with the Old Faith's pentagram in agreement: "The High King lives for the folk and the land, not they for him."

Her left hand was on the pommel of the Sword of the Lady. Her mother's hand touched hers, and for a single instant they were one and that one *was* the kingdom, its peoples and also its mountains and plains and waters and the life that thronged them. Her sorrow at Rudi Macken-zie's death was its sorrow too—

Ochone, Ochone! He is gone, his blood is spilled upon My breast, he who was Son and Lover and the Father to the land!

And so were things beyond the human kind: the slow hungry waking of a grizzly in its winter den, the flood of reindeer across a tundra, a lion lying up near the body of a scimitar-horned oryx it had brought down on the fringes of the southern desert, a bristlecone pine in the mountain scree that remembered Conquistadores in morion and breastplate as yesterday, and the long ages of the flint spearhead and hide robe before that, and the giant beasts of yet another age that the land still mourned.

"It's a burden," Mathilda sighed. "But you're ready to bear it. You . . . you are so like your father, you know that? Like him as he was when we were young together, on the Quest to Nantucket for the Sword."

Órlaith had faced battle and storm and the Powers that human-kind called evil in the course of her quarter-century of life. Even so she quailed a little at the thought of filling *those* shoes. Then she remembered her father . . . remembered him playing bear before the fire, whooping as his children tussled him to the ground in a squirming heap, or sharp-set and hungry, grinning as he rode up with the hounds belling around his horse's hooves at Timberline Lodge and smelled dinner after a long hunt in cold and mud and bent down to take the cup of mulled wine from her with a word of thanks, or laughing with her mother over the solemn absurdities of Court ceremony and the truly farcical ones of politics when the day was over.

"Da bore it," she said. "And I've never met a man who was . . . happier in his life, or more at home in his own skin."

Mathilda's smile was fond and sad at the same time. "He said to me once that if you didn't expect to make old bones, you should pack in as much as you could. He *lived*, while he lived, your father, every moment of every day."

Then she continued with a shrewd edge: "What we *don't* need when unity is essential is a High Queen who's an Associate. I've been uneasy about that since your . . ."

A swallow. "Since your father was killed. There are still places in Montival where monarchy feels a bit strange, and it's easier if it doesn't come with lords, barons, dukes, castles and cotte-hardies attached."

Órlaith nodded, since that was true enough as far as the politics were concerned. Though . . .

"No, they call their lords *ranchers* and *farmers* and *sheriffs* and *mayors* or *Presidents* or *The Faculty Senate*, instead, often enough. But you're right."

The High Queen took a deep breath and said: "The Realm needs *you*. Go then, my darling. Go!"

She squeezed Órlaith's hand one more time, kissed her forehead, turned and walked quickly to the Royal pavilion with the Crowned Mountain and Sword banner of Montival flying from its peak and two knights of the Protector's Guard flanking its entrance like motionless statues of black steel, kite-shields with the Lidless Eye on their arms and their longswords drawn and sloped across their shoulders. They snapped to attention, blade before face, then back to their eternal watchfulness.

There were plenty of other tents in many styles; little clumps of folk from wherever the heliograph net reached in the High Kingdom and there had been time to send envoys, here to the shelf of flatland where the trail paused before it wound down to the Lake. Here to witness as much of the ceremony as human eyes could see. That was their right, that they could take the word back to their homes. There would be a crowning eventually at the new capital, Dún na Síochána, but this was where the High King or Queen was truly bound to the kingdom.

She was used to living her life in public, under observation, and here it was true in spades. Some heads of member-states were present. She recognized Mike Jr., the current Bear Lord of Larsdalen and her father's half-brother, with the head of an actual bear on the helmet he carried tucked under one arm; the saffron-robed head of Chenrezi Monastery in the Valley of the Sun; her aunt Maude Loring Mackenzie, the Mackenzie of the Clan and her grandmother Juniper Mackenzie beside her in a white robe, leaning on the staff with the Triple Moon at its head.

More were delegates: grave bearded Mormon bishops of the Seventy from Deseret in long black coats and hats; a rabbi from Degania Dalet; ranchers in fringed buckskin jackets, with string ties and hats and belts bound with silver conchos and heavy-bladed shete-sabers at their waists, braids hanging to their shoulders; Lakota in fringed leather and elaborate headdresses, and envoys from other tribesfolk from the Yurok in Westria . . . what had once been California . . . to the *Deisleen kwáan* in the far north of what had once been British Columbia; the peacock splendor of Associate nobles; the deliberately old-fashioned rusticity of blue-jean bib overalls from the Free Cities of the Yakima league, or suit-and-tie on a Corvallan academic or merchant-prince; Christian clerics of half a dozen varieties; and more. . . .

The head of the High Queen's Archers spoke a word, and a semicircle of the kilted bowmen held their long yellow yew staves horizontally before them in both hands and spread out before the head of the trail. Her father's old friend and battle-comrade Edain Aylward Mackenzie commanded them, middle-aged but still strong as a weather-scarred boulder, and there was a quasi-uncle's affection under his careful professional respect. His son Karl grinned at her with a reckless youngster's smile until scowled into solemnity.

Órlaith took a moment to bow to Reiko, who was waiting in full armor beneath the Rising Sun banner of Dai Nippon and the red flag with the stylized sixteen-petal chrysanthemum that was the House *mon* of the Yamato dynasty, and received—for the last time—a bow of a nicely judged fractional degree less. After this day they'd both be sovereigns, and the bows would be equal. Montival's Nihonjin allies were a ceremonious folk, and Reiko was punctilious about it in public.

"Johnnie," she said to her younger brother. "Walk with me for a bit, to the head of the track. This is your trail too, you're allowed."

John favored her mother's family; he was an inch shorter than she, with dark-brown hair to his broad shoulders, and eyes were the changeable color that can be light honey-brown or green depending on the light, and very keen. She'd always thought he was quick of wit, but lazy about anything but his music and chasing girls. Though he was also a very passable swordsman. Possibly because there he'd been terrified into hard work by fear of disappointing their parents, and even more because it was popular with the Associate demoiselles; he'd earned the little golden spurs of knighthood they both wore.

Since he'd come back from his adventures in the Ceram Sea she took him far more seriously. Today he wore a Montero cap that sported a peacock's tail-feather, and green hunter's garb, with a short heavy falchion at his belt and a bow and quiver over his back.

"Mother's gotten over your bringing back a bride," Órlaith said teasingly.

In fact, she thinks Pip will rule him with a rod of iron and also that it's just what he needs.

John looked over his shoulder at Pip. She was in Associate garb—ladies' traveling garb of divided skirt and loose lap-over jacket—belted high over her gravid belly. She was wearing it as if it were a costume, and reacting to the chill with the horror natural to someone who'd been born and raised in Australia's northern sugarcane country. She was genuinely fond of John, though. When she spoke words of affection for him it had the subtle bronze tang of sincerity.

"Pip?" John said, with pride in his voice.

Órlaith could tell he was about to recite some of her manifold virtues and qualities, and not for the first time to her. He was more eloquent than most, which was his troubadour training, but otherwise babblingly repetitive, very much like any other besotted young man.

"As much a case of *her* bringing *me* here as the reverse!"

He went into a list of Pip's virtues which ended with her lineage and: ". . . which would have had grandfather Norman over the moon."

"Yes, it would have," Órlaith said, in a heavily patient tone which she thought he didn't catch.

It pleases Mother too, but not as much as Pip's character does. As she says, a Lord Protector of the Association or their consort can afford to be bad, but not weak, not and dominate that pack of wolves the way that's needful if you want to keep them on a leash. But Mother's parents . . . yes, they'd have been glowing at Pip's association with the House of Windsor. Not that that's much of a recommendation.

"But I attach more importance to the fact that she saved your life," Órlaith said. "And so does Mother—I could see that the sun rose in her eyes when you returned, and she's scarcely displeased by the prospect of grandchildren either. Everyone's descended from everyone, if you go back far enough, and every dynasty has to start *somewhere*. Even Reiko's!"

"Though hers is supposed to start with *Amaterasu-ōmikami* . . . and some of the things I've seen her do . . . I might believe it, if it weren't blasphemy."

Órlaith replied with malice aforethought—John was a sincere Catholic, though not a very good one as far as women were concerned:

"And *your* new children will descend from Odin through the Kings of Wessex, if the House of Windsor's official genealogy is to be believed. Both of them, philoprogenitive little brother of mine."

He had the grace to blush slightly. Complex personal dynamics had resulted in John getting Pip *and* his battle-comrade Thora Garwood pregnant during his late adventures, though not in that order and not intentionally in either case. Órlaith took a slight sly pleasure about twitting him over the matter; and it wasn't just a *personal* matter, it touched on the succession.

"That Odin thing is a historical fiction," he huffed.

"Except that Da *met* him," Órlaith pointed out dryly.

"In a dream! The legend about Pip's ancestors probably just means some Dark Age chief had a genealogy that ended with: *and who granddad's father was, only Odin knows.*"

"Probably," Órlaith said equably. "On the other hand, perhaps the Wanderer knew that his blood would be mingled with House Artos through Pip, eh? And that was one reason he helped Da when he lay wounded and near death in that cave? He's a tricksy one, Gangleri."

John snorted. "I'd say you pagans are all light-minded, if it wouldn't make my wastrel's head explode."

"*Former* wastrel. Pip will take care of that," Órlaith said, and grinned for a moment as he looked stricken, like a man who'd just had a truth revealed and wasn't sure about it.

"This is as far as I think I should go, Orrey," he said, turning his back on the lake and unconsciously relaxing a little once he had.

"You may have to go farther someday, Johnnie," she replied soberly, which was the point—it never hurt to remind people watching of the dynastic implications.

"God forbid!" he said sincerely.

She could tell that too, and it was one reason their father hadn't worn the Sword more than he must. There were reasons human beings had to rely on imperfect wit and intuition to tell how honest others were being.

He crossed himself. "That's for *your* kids."

"Which I haven't had yet. Until then you're the heir, and after you, Pip's little bundle of joy. Nice of you to choose Sandra for her name, if she is a girl, though." If a boy, John Michael was de rigueur. Norman was still out of the question; the memories of his rule hadn't faded enough.

The thought of children was starting to make her feel a certain wistful yearning, though she couldn't take the time right now—it was a different matter for men, of course, who could impregnate and run.

"God and all the *Saints* forbid," he said . . . sincerely again. "I've seen what the job did to Dad, and what it's doing to you. I'll be the High Queen's right hand, and wailing wall when you need it, and when Mother passes—in, say, another forty years or more if God grants—I'll be Lord Protector of the Association. That's all I want and more than I want, believe me."

"I do, Johnnie." She slapped the Sword. "I can't help it!"

"So I've no desire to walk this road again—"

He stopped for a moment, and looked up at the sky, and then at his watch—he had a pre-Change self-winding model strapped to his wrist.

"Wait a minute!" he said. "We've been walking for . . . We should have been at the Lake long ago!"

He shuddered; Órlaith made herself smile, but the same thought made the skin between her shoulder-blades crawl. She looked around: trees, blue sky, white-topped mountain . . . but this was *other*.

They hugged for a long moment; she took comfort from his warm solidity. Family was at the core of things, though friends and battle-comrades were close to it.

"Reiko will be nervous for me," Órlaith said.

Though she won't say so, of course, went unspoken. She'd thought she knew stoics, until she met the Nihonjin.

"Deor will help. I'll keep them all laughing, don't worry."

Órlaith turned, set herself and took a stride. She half-checked when she did; there was a feeling of presence, suddenly. Not just the looming awe of Lost Lake—in an older tongue, *E-e-kwahl-a-mat-yam-lshkt,* Lake at the Heart of Mountains. That had been there before, and it was growing, like a weightiness in the clear air.

What she felt was a person, unseen but *there.* And a feeling of overwhelming love, of safety and comfort walking beside her as she walked down, and then the way turned and the lake was there, like a blue eye looking up into the blue of Heaven. An osprey dove, struck the water in a spray of drops that the sunset turned into a necklace of rubies, and flogged its way back into the air with two feet of rainbow trout writhing in its talons.

"Well, as Dad always said, the job doesn't get easier if you wait," she said, took a deep breath and stepped out into the dying sunlight with her boots grating in the gravel.

A man faced her. "Órlaith?" he said softly.

Órlaith felt her eyes go wide, and her face milk-pale as blood drained from her. She staggered, and for an instant she felt her knees buckle as her pulse thundered and breath seized in paralyzed lungs and the world started to grow gray at the edges. He caught her by the forearms, and she clenched her hands hard on the corded swordsman's muscle of his.

The jewel-cut handsome face was achingly familiar, and the blue-green eyes, and the fall of gold-and-copper hair to his shoulders from beneath the Mackenzie bonnet. Those memories were graven on her soul. But . . .

"Dad?" she said. "Is that . . . you?" Then: "No. You're too young!"

"It's Rudi Mackenzie, I am, darling girl," he said. "Just . . . let's say I'm here on the same mission as I suspect brings you. The Kingmaking."

"But I saw you—" she began to say, then rammed to a halt.

No. I saw a man twenty years and more older than this die, in that skirmish down in Westria. This is Da as he was when I first remember him, only younger still.

This was the man who achieved the Quest to the Sunrise Lands, who fought the Prophet's War, and had a throne and a kingdom yet to make. Not yet the wise kindly land-father of the long peace he gave, when the littlest crofters might sow and know they could reap their own with none to put them in fear, and have his hand by their side to give just judgment against the powerful.

This is the warrior-king, the son of Bear and Raven, foretold at his Wiccaning to be his people's strength and the Lady's Sword. And foredoomed to die with blade in hand before his beard showed gray. Like Lug of the Long Spear come again, in glory and majesty and terror.

He grinned, and her heart felt as if it would tear itself loose with joy and hard sorrow mixed.

"Saw me die?" He laughed, the Clan's lilt strong in his voice but—now that she heard it from his youth—subtly different from the way Mackenzies spoke now. "My delight, I never thought myself immortal. Except in the sense that we all are, and I've had abundant proof of *that*."

"How?" she breathed. "How is this *happening*?"

"I haven't the faintest idea; and I have it on the best of authority that Those responsible don't explain it to us because they *can't*. How can a man explain all his mind to a little child, or a God to a man? But I suspect that here, from the time the Sword plunged into the earth with Matti your mother and myself your father holding it, all times are one. And the dead and the living and those yet unborn are none so different."

She cast herself against him and they embraced.

"I've missed you so much, Da. And Mother has been so—"

He made a shushing sound and laid a finger over her lips. "Arra, there are things *I* should not know. Let me find my own joys and griefs, child!

It's a comfort to hear you, though. I've a fair confidence I will be a good King, but it seems I'm none so bad a father, too."

She nodded vigorously and stood back, wiping at tears with the back of her hand.

"Come, walk with me," he said.

They linked hands; she remembered that from her earliest girlhood, slipping her tiny fingers into his and looking up at the tree-tall gentle strength that warded her days and made all the world safe and would forever more. Now hers were callused like his, the distinctive patterns left by blade-hilt and shield-grips. After a moment they came to the rock by the water; the Sword of the Lady stood in it, as if it had been planted there since the Ice retreated to the mountaintops and left the land free for human-kind.

She looked at it for a long moment, the form of a knight's longsword, a straight double-edged blade tapering to a needle point and guarded by the crescent moon, a double-lobed grip of black staghorn and white silver . . .

. . . and then up at him as her own blade-hand touched the moon-stone pommel at her side.

"I'm not going to say *how* again," she said, and heard a hint of an absurd indignation in her tone. "You're as bad as grandmother Juniper about answering questions with questions!"

"Sure, and I came by it honestly by inheritance from her," her father said.

His face held a delight that was different from hers, a joy in a promise of the future rather than a glimpse into a beloved lost past.

Then that face went serious: "I think that the Sword is now *here* forever. More, I think that it always *was* here . . . now, if that makes any sense at all; we drove it not just through rock, but through Time itself. And that this has become a place of awe and sacredness, the pivot about which Montival turns."

She nodded vigorously. "Nobody comes here except the High King or Queen and their handfasted," she said. "But you never told me much about . . . this."

"Because there are things that mean nothing until you live them," Rudi said. He grinned, and his voice took on a mock-solemn portentousness:

"Let me guess. You're facing a great challenge, the realm is in peril, and—"

She laughed, but there were tears in it. "Lord and *Lady*, Dad, but I've missed you! Johnnie and Vuissance and Faolán have too, but . . . I . . ."

I was coming to be not just your child, but your partner and your friend and strong support, one you could share your innermost thoughts with. And then you were taken away! We lost that half of you, your deep age, and the wisdom and the peace of it. You can never sit with your grandchildren and tell them your stories, and I can never be there to hear it.

Her father faced her and laid his hands on her shoulders, recalling her to duty.

"Now, this is what *I've* seen and done here—"

She frowned as he told her. "That's . . . strange. Those were ancestors, weren't they? *Our* ancestors."

"Yes. Some of our ancestors, here in this land of ours. From the very first of our blood, who came here when the Ice had barely left, the very first of human kind to dwell here, the first to leave their ghosts and their memories in the warp and weft of things.

"And I was led to see and do and know what a King must. What *you* will see . . . will be particularly tailored to yourself, I would say."

"Will I see Grandmother . . . I mean Grandmother Sandra? Grandmother Juniper's still . . ."

"And how would I know?" Rudi said. "That's *your* story, though I suspect you will. And perhaps your own children, or your heir at least. Come. Draw the Sword."

She drew the blade at her side, and gasped a little as her father reached and pulled the other Sword from the rock; it came free as easily as if that were the sheath. Light seemed to well about them as he reversed the blade and offered it to her. She took it reverently and he the hilt of hers.

"Quickly!" he said, and she sheathed the Sword he'd handed her.

They knelt on either side of the rock, and each touched a finger to the point, the red drops mingling.

"By the bond of blood," he said, and laid the point against the rock.

"By the bond of blood," she answered, and wrapped her hands around his.

Together, they thrust the blade forged beyond the world into the Heart of Montival. Órlaith felt a rushing, a sense of connection stronger than any yet. She *was* her mother weeping in private, with a picture of her father clutched to her breast; she *was* her grandmother standing alone beneath a great tree, with her staff held high and light playing across the Triple Moon. She *was* a farmer in bib overalls in one of the Free Cities of the Yakima League, laughing as he slung sixty-pound bags of threshed wheat into a wagon . . . and then falling silent for a moment, looking towards the distant ocean and thinking of a child gone to war west-over-sea.

And they were *her*, for that instant. Some knowingly, some in dreams, some only in a glance about themselves and a thought: *This is* home. *Here are my loves.*

They and million-fold others, human and nonhuman, spirits of place and things for which there were no words moving deep in the currents of Earth where the massive plates of the world floated on fire and ground against one another in a slow majesty that drove mountains into sky.

CHAPTER TWELVE

LOST LAKE

CROWN FOREST DEMESNE

(FORMERLY NORTH-CENTRAL OREGON)

HIGH KINGDOM OF MONTIVAL

(FORMERLY WESTERN NORTH AMERICA)

JUNE 20TH

CHANGE YEAR 47/2045 AD

There were four around the low table in the pavilion of the *Tennō Heika* of Dai-Nippon. Empress Reiko—though in Nihonjin the word had no gender and another altogether was used for an Imperial consort—her one-handed general Egawa Noboru, her hawk-faced Grand Steward Koyama Akira and Captain Ishikawa Goru, the captain who'd brought her and her father here to Montival. It seemed so long ago, though it was barely a year.

They finished their simple meal of miso, salmon and noodles, and sat silently in *seiza*—kneeling and resting on their heels—while the ladies-in-waiting rustled in to clear the table and pour warmed sake and light the brazier. One knelt by it, gently fanning the charcoal.

It was cool, and the air was pine-scented in a way slightly, subtly different from a mountain forest back home; even the canvas of the tent was alien, though she had hung a few block prints and calligraphy scrolls from home. One raised panel gave them a view of the sun-tinged snow-peak of Mount Hood, almost as pure a shape as Fuji.

Longing pierced her for the shores of Sado Island, but *giri*—duty—was master of all things, even *nihon*, human feeling.

Egawa sighed. "Majesty, I wish this war was over. I am uneasy with foreign troops on our soil, foreign ships in our waters."

Reiko carefully did not smile, but there was an irony in the way she moved her *tessen*; it was a steel war-fan, but she was in a woman's kimono tonight, if a very plain one—an *irotomesode* of dark blue with a narrow modern obi only six inches wide, and a white-and-yellow pattern of cranes and reeds below the waist. It was saved from informality by a full five of her dynastic *kamon*.

The motion of the fan said as plainly as words what she was thinking. For forty-odd years the only foreign troops and ships in Japanese waters had been *jinnikukaburi* raiders. Even their knowledge of the outside world had been very skimpy, and the Montivallans hadn't known that anyone survived in the Land of the Gods at all, except for ghouls—called Eaters here—haunting the vast endless stretches of scorched, earthquake-tumbled ruins. . . .

"Consider how the prospects were a year ago, General-san," she said. "When the only prospect we had of an end to the war was the enemy gnawing on the bones of the last Nihonjin."

Akira did chuckle. "I was entirely wrong to oppose your . . . journey south to find the Grasscutter with the Montivallan's Crown Princess, Majesty," he said. "And Egawa-sama was entirely right that it was worth discomfort . . . my discomfort, when I found you had gone without informing me . . . and facing their High Queen's disapproval."

"Which disapproval you shared, even though you could not say so," Egawa said dryly.

"Precisely. And Lord Egawa, you were correct both in terms of policy, and in exemplary vassal obedience."

They all glanced at where the Grasscutter in its sheath with the disturbing black lacquer that seemed to have points of starlike light drifting in it sat on the sword-stand.

It rested before the *kamidana*, the portable shrine that accompanied her now that they had a little to spare for the niceties. It held a beautifully worked miniature Torii, a gateway, and the other fixtures like the round mirror and the little dishes of rice and salt—save that they couldn't get any of the sacred sakaki leaves here. The mirror was supposed to hold *kami*-essence, but the Grasscutter itself was the greatest of all shintai, objects with incarnate spirits.

"But I was also right in my estimate of the importance of the alliance with Montival, General-sama—and now with Hawai'i and Capricornia," Akira said. "Now others will shed their blood for a change. Majesty, you brought *both* these aims to fruition."

Reiko nodded. "And while our samurai will fight, our ordinary people will tend their fields, harvest their rice, and bear their children. That is what we need above all. We need *time*. There are so few of us now! Barely a third of a million, where once we were a hundred million and more. We were millions upon millions even before Meiji, before the West came, before the era of the machines. We need generations of peace, so that we are millions once again. In numbers, as much as in the edge of the sword, is survival of kind."

Akira looked intensely thoughtful for a moment; he was very good at mental mathematics. "If we are spared more raids and do not need to call up our *ashigaru*-militia, with our present demographic profile . . . we should have a total of over a million within thirty to thirty-five years, Majesty. May you live ten thousand years, but thirty is by no means too much to expect."

It was a slightly daring joke, but she smiled very slightly in acknowledgment.

"Will the Montivallans be content with that degree of involvement on our part?" Egawa asked. "Sending only our full-time fighters, instead of mobilizing all our militia?"

Reiko nodded. "Yes. Crown Princess . . . soon to be High Queen . . . Órlaith and I have spoken much of this. They have taken the decision for this transfer of sovereignty for their own reasons, but it aids us."

They all nodded. A monarch abdicating in favor of an heir—

sometimes voluntarily, sometimes not, though it was always *portrayed* as a voluntary decision—was an old thing in their history. Former emperors had ended up in exile on Sado Island, the heartland of post-Change Japan, after the Jōkyū War eight centuries before, while the Kamakura shoguns put more pliable nephews on the throne. Nihonjin reverence for the Imperial institution hadn't always extended to the physical person occupying it.

"High Queen Mathilda was in favor of the alliance for reasons of policy, but she has never warmed to us, Majesty," Akira said.

"Understandably so, when indirectly we were the cause of bringing the *jinnikukaburi* to these shores, and so for the death of their High King, her husband," Reiko said. "Órlaith and I have come to a close understanding. She is a person of faultless honor; she understands the sacrifices we of Dai-Nippon have already made in the long war fought with the common enemy. And from policy, she wishes a strong and friendly Japan, to secure the Asian shores of the Pacific. She envisages a long-term cooperation."

"That is a sustainable policy, because it is in Montival's interests," Akira said shrewdly. "The coast of Asia is too far for them to easily intervene directly under modern conditions, and certainly not without a strong ally. There are other threats in the islands to the south of Taiwan, and in the long run they must be dealt with."

"Yes," Reiko said. Then to Egawa: "So General-san, the foreign troops and ships will be there only long enough to finally win this war—the war we have fought all our lives, and win us a peace with victory."

More nods at that; the reign-name she had chosen for herself was *Shohei*, Victorious Peace, and it was starting to look less of a pious hope and more a realistic goal.

Reiko permitted herself a slight smile and asked a rhetorical question: "And speaking of Taiwan . . . you led the survey expedition there several years ago, did you not, Captain Ishikawa?"

"*Hai, Heika,*" the sailor said with a respectful bow, his eyes cast down in modesty.

He was in his thirties, a decade older than her, more than that younger than the other two, with a cheerful round face that concealed a very sharp intelligence.

He'd found the great island mostly empty of human life, since it had been heavily populated and highly urbanized when the Change struck forty-eight years ago. In such cases, only great good luck or inspired leadership could preserve any civilized life; Japan had had both, and offshore islands like Sado which could be isolated from the inevitable famine and collapse of the megacities. Apparently, Taiwan hadn't been lucky that way, and only a few fugitive bands lived on in the eastern mountains, heirs to the ancient indigenes who'd lived there long before the Han colonists came.

"I have a pledge from the Crown Princess that when she comes to the throne Montival will recognize our rights there, and will ask . . . will strongly urge . . . the kings of Hawai'i and Capricornia to do likewise. Since there is no population there to speak of, we may over the generations make it not a possession but fully a part of our homeland."

"Excellent news, *Heika!*" Ishikawa said. "There is much good rice land, only thinly grown with scrub, and suitable for other crops as well—and less in the way of ruins."

Too much of the Home Island's best land was covered in crumbling concrete and rusting steel; and little bands of polluted survivors haunted those wildernesses of stone and metal, making them even more dangerous than fire and decay. In the long run the ruins would be valuable mines, but the *fundamental* source of all wealth, all power, was fields and the peasants who tilled them.

"And in the very long run, it will improve our strategic position."

Ishikawa probably expected fiefs on Taiwan, and possibly a viceroy's appointment to commence the settlement; she was inclined to give it to him, since he was very able and had shown unshakable loyalty when there was much risk of death and little chance of reward for it.

"With strong allies, we have every prospect of fulfilling my father's dreams," she said. "Now that the Grasscutter is ours once more. . . ."

They all looked that way again. She had drawn it on the beach at Topanga . . . and they had all seen what followed, too, as the burning wrath of the Sun Goddess had fallen on the enemy, blowing their ships to disaster. It had also blown *Prince John*'s ship halfway across the Pacific, with the surviving *jinnikukaburi* in pursuit, but that had turned out for the best as well, bringing Capricornia into the alliance, and returning him home with a glorious accomplishment and a suitable bride. On Hawai'i more recently Kusanagi and the Sword of the Lady had struck down the *kangshinmu*, the enemy sorcerer-lords.

"The Jewel we already possessed . . . though I think that now we must discover more, hmmm, immediate uses for it. As my father said, the Change opened once more doors in the walls of the world, doors that had been slowly closing for thousands of years, moment by moment, never enough at any one time to be noticed until what had been fact faded into myth. As it was in the time of legends, so it is once more in our day. Now a ruler is more than a general or administrator, more even than a symbol of the people and their link to their land. Now the ruler is the vessel of a spirit."

This time there was genuine fear in the gazes that flicked to the Grasscutter, though it was well-hidden, in the samurai tradition of keeping an iron rule over the self. All of them had reverenced the Grasscutter . . . done homage to the *idea* of it, as a symbol of ancient sacredness. Now they had seen it unleashed in war, the gift of the Immortal One Shining in Heaven, the ancient protector of the Land of the Gods. And they had seen Her will made manifest through it like a whip of air and fire, falling from infinity to rend the very substance of things.

And they had seen *Reiko* become the vessel of that One, of her Ancestress. Dancing with the Grasscutter Sword, and becoming the human form of Her power and Her wrath.

No, I do not think there is any risk of these three ever seeking to make a puppet of the Tennō, as happened in the time of the Sei-i Taishōgun, *the Barbarian-Subduing Generalissimos. Not when they know in their very bones that my descent from Her is*

*not a symbol, not a form of words, but a reality that lives and breathes . . . that beats
the very sea to madness, that burns men to drifting ash in an instant.*

"The Grasscutter is ours once more. Only the Mirror is still lost; and
that is a matter for our children. Though I suspect that in their day they
will need it as badly as we did *Kusanagi-no-Tsurugi* in ours. Power is needful to the realm, and prosperity . . . but wisdom has a power of its own."

Egawa preened very slightly, probably unconsciously, at the mention
of offspring. She had publicly told him she would take his youngest son
as Imperial Consort—a man she knew well, of course. A bit younger than
her, intelligent, healthy, handsome as an additional bonus, and she judged
not ambitious, or at least not excessively so. Being father-in-law to the
Majesty and grandfather to the next *Tennō* was a very great reward, but
Egawa had earned it . . . and could be trusted with it.

"Let us not count our wars before they're fought. Korea will be a
serious problem for a long time," she said.

Akira smiled, the peculiar smile a man made at another's misfortune,
before he added:

"But with the favor of the *kami, Heika*, it will be someone *else's* problem."

One of the ladies-in-waiting entered, sank gracefully to her knees,
into *seiza*, and then bent forward in the full *dogeza*, hands on the mats and
forehead pressed to the braided straw.

"Majesty, my most humble apologies, but she—"

The patter of light feet running came from outside. A girl-child of
between three and four burst in, grinning. Then she skidded to a stop and
plumped down in a creditable *seiza* herself and made a deep bow.

"*Heika!*" she said happily. "Look what I got!"

The girl was in zori sandals, divided-toe *tabi* and a colorful child's
kimono, but she was obviously of foreign blood, pale and with gingery
hair and greenish eyes. By now it was going on for a year since Reiko had
rescued her from the encysted horrors of the castle in the desert Valley
of Death. The hidden fortress had held the fragments of *Kusanagi-
no-Tsurugi*. The child was the great-granddaughter and last living descen-

dant of the man who had stolen it from Japan after the defeat Dai-Nippon had suffered in the great struggle of the last century, the Pacific War.

I took her from that place because I could not bear to leave a child in it, Reiko thought, making her face stern. *But I have kept Kiwako with me for my sake as well as hers. And to show that there had been atonement for the crimes of Cody Biltmore, and a lifting of the curse on his line.*

Kiwako meant *one born on a border,* and it was certainly appropriate; for her, it had been the border between the world of common life and the Otherword, and no healthy part of it, either.

Yet now she is much like a normal child—a clever and playful one and full of mischief. And even toilet-trained, at last.

"Look, *Heika!*"

By now she had as much command of *Nihongo* as a Japanese child of her age, and even a Sado accent of the type frequent at Court. The toy she held up was a set of propeller blades in a circle, made of a disk stamped from salvaged tin. It rested on the end of a spindle with a cord wrapped around it, in turn fastened to a handle. Kiwako pulled the string, and the disk lifted off, careening around the tent like a living thing, blurring like the wings of the little jeweled birds common on this continent.

Akira was smiling broadly; Ishikawa and Egawa laughed outright, the Imperial Guard commander snatching the thing out of the air with his good right hand. They were all family men, and the Guard commander's youngest daughter was about Kiwako's age. Her folk were mostly kindly with children, though firm; you didn't expect someone Kiwako's age to have perfect etiquette. Childhood was a time to learn.

"Soldier gave me," she said happily. "Looks like Egawa-sama!"

That almost certainly meant Edain Aylward Mackenzie, commander of the High Queen's Archers. He was a kindly man and absolutely trustworthy, but . . .

"Kiwako," Reiko said, and tapped her—very gently—on the head with the folded Tessen. "It is a good toy, but you should not run away from Lady Fumiko and wander alone among strangers! You have caused her bad feelings!"

Not to mention public shame for not fulfilling a duty.

Fumiko was a well-meaning childless widow in her thirties, but not particularly intelligent; if she'd been brighter, someone of her middle years would be doing more responsible work. Most of the day-to-day administration of Dai-Nippon was done by women of the warrior class, so that men could be spared for the unending war against the *jinnikukaburi*. The fact that your father was a samurai and that he and your husband had fallen bravely didn't mean you could learn to be competent at accounting or estate management or laying out drainage ditches or assessing tax levies, though.

Kiwako's face clouded and her lower lip pouted a little. She didn't like to make Reiko unhappy, but she also didn't like minding her minders.

"I'm sorry, *Heika*," she said, and leaned her head forward between her palms in a creditable childish copy of the dogeza.

"You should make apology to Lady Fumiko, Kiwako," Reiko said. "You hurt her feelings and made her sad."

The girl obediently faced her and bowed again. "I'm sorry, Fumiko-sama," she said contritely. "I'll be good."

Then with another grin: "It's a good toy! *Subarashii!*"

Fumiko smiled; it was hard to resist that enthusiasm, and Reiko knew the widow's lonely heart had long since warmed to the child. In a way it was a perfect match for both, and the loyal service of Fumiko and her kin deserved a little thought to find her a long-term place of honor at court.

"Did you eat your dinner?" Reiko asked.

Kiwako nodded; she didn't wake up weeping or growling or screaming much anymore, but she was still entranced by decent food. Reiko carefully didn't think about some of the things the child had probably eaten in the lost castle; body-lice were the least of it.

"*Okonomiyaki!*" the girl said. "And *anmitsu!*"

Which meant stuffed fried pancakes and sweet agar jelly with fruit. Reiko cocked an eyebrow at Fumiko, who nodded without looking back, which meant that Kiwako had been as mannerly as could be expected at her age.

She has made astonishing progress, Reiko thought, and opened her arms.

After the hug—delivered with surprising strength and a scent of clean well-washed little girl, very different from their first contact—she said:

"Now go play with your toy, but do not go out of Lady Fumiko's reach! I will come later and tell you another story."

"An *Inari*-fox story?"

The adults glanced at one another. It was impossible for a Nihonjin to look at Kiwako and *not* think the word *fox*. Reiko had taken advantage of that by directing her devotion to Inari, the great *kami* whose messengers were magical foxes. A physical protector, even the *Tennō*, could not always be there. *Inari ōkami* could, and with the eeriness of the child's origins everyone would remember it.

"A story of the nine-tailed golden fox who carries messages for *Inari*," she promised.

When Reiko looked up the three men had all schooled their faces, and had their eyes properly lowered, but she could sense their smiles and the approval behind them. That was nothing bad; she didn't want to be viewed as entirely a creature of power and awe. And they'd all been part of her education themselves, especially the two elders who'd been her father's right-hand men. It was good that they knew she too could handle children properly.

"We will be returning to Japan soon; the High Queen will follow with the additional troops and supplies when they are ready, and the final campaign will begin. I will see to settling Kiwako at the palace in the course of our stay in the homeland this summer."

The rather modest current palace had been the old Tokugawa governor's home on Sadogashima, and then a museum until the Change. Sometimes words were easier to preserve than things.

"My mother and sisters and Lady Fumiko will like her, I am sure," Reiko said, to a chorus of bows and murmurs of agreement.

They would; and however much a gaijin child stood out, by the time the campaign started up again in the fall it would be clear that Kiwako had the *Tennō Heika* as her patron. That wouldn't necessarily protect her completely from other children, but four or five was young enough that bullying wouldn't be a serious problem.

"All Japan owes that child a debt, Majesty, since she warned you of a blow from behind," Akira said, and the other two nodded.

Reiko inclined her head slightly; her Chancellor was also making a promise that he'd look out for her if there was a disaster in Korea and one of her sisters had to step into her place. It had been more of a reflexive scream of fear than a deliberate warning, but real enough for all that and quite possibly the reason she was here today. Reiko certainly wasn't going to take a child to Korea on campaign, but six months was a long time in the life of a toddler.

"All debts of honor must be paid," she said.

Her glance fell on the Grasscutter. "And when the campaign begins, we will pay many."

Another set of short sharp nods, but this time the subtleties of their expressions wouldn't have reassured a child.

Quite the contrary.

The reckoning with the tormentors of their people had been a long time coming, and it would mean a winter campaign in Korea's fabled frozen wastes, but all of them were looking forward to it.

CHAPTER THIRTEEN

CHOSŎN MINJUJUŬI INMIN KONGHWAGUK

(KOREA)

PUSAN

NOVEMBER 25TH

CHANGE YEAR 47/2045 AD

"**B**y the Eternal Blue Sky and the ninety-nine Tengri, what's *that?*" Dzhambul, Börte and Gansükh lay side-by-side on a hillside, binoculars leveled and watching ships out on the water, a novel sight to them all—he hadn't seen the ocean at all until after the Mongol armies crossed the Yalu, and not more than twice since. Pusan lay on the southeast corner of the Korean peninsula, far enough south that it was no more than a little chilly this evening, nothing like the deep cold farther back along their journey.

The sun was setting behind them, making this a good time for stealth—no risk of the light glinting off the lenses, to start with. They were most of the way up a mountain, on the crest of a cliff of pink granite and under the shade of sharp-smelling pine trees that had coated the rock with soft brown duff beneath them. Below the cliff were dense thickets of bamboo, and then a river-valley ran southward to the sea, its upper reaches in rice paddy and vegetable garden.

The remains of the pre-Change city were mostly out of sight to the left, the eastward side, but enough remained to make an enormous bulk of ruined leaning towers, scorched snags, and the cleared areas that showed where methodical salvaging was stripping out metal and glass and other goods.

"I've seen bigger," Gansükh said. "In China. But not much bigger, and never such heavy salvage."

Smelters and straggling slave barracks grimy with the smoke that misted around them showed where a good deal of it went, and there were timber yards and sawmills and shipbuilding slips too.

A huge modern-looking fortress stood a few miles away on a crest of the mountain. They'd seen troops marching to and from it, but it apparently hadn't occurred to the enemy they needed to patrol close to its walls. What attention they were paying seemed directed against the sea, as if the main threat lay there. The Mongols had been able to lay up for a day, and do some repairs to their gear and even bathe in a spring.

Perhaps they can hear my belly rumble in Pusan, Dzhambul thought ironically. *But at least we don't smell so bad.*

They had all lost weight, though occasionally they'd had time to hunt and usually Mongol troops could live off country where anyone else would starve, including the natives, not least because they would eat anything, except the natives. The problem was that there was hardly anything *to* hunt or forage here. The last place they'd had any luck at all was a strip of lusher territory that marked the division between the old North and South Kingdoms that had divided the peninsula back before the Change. The Northern dynasty had taken over the whole place in the aftermath of the Change, and kept itself going during the crash by systematically feeding most of the population to some of it, starting with the conquered southern part and going on from there.

There had been real forests there of ancient trees, not just the timber and fuel plantations they'd seen elsewhere. And thick-grassed meadows where deer grazed, and marshlands rich with birds and the pathways made by wild boar, enough to show that this peninsula wasn't barren by its nature. They'd gorged for a week, and smoke-dried some meat while dodging the patrols looking for them. But a few loads of jerky made from musk deer and *goral*—wild goats—didn't go very far among nearly twenty people moving fast and hard.

They'd been reduced to tapping a little blood from the veins of their horses, but that was an emergency measure . . . and the horses hadn't been feeding very well either. It was doubtful they'd be fit for much once they turned back north.

There wasn't even enough livestock to steal enough to eat. Dzhambul grimaced slightly, remembering lying up in some hills for a day with nothing to do but watch the man-eaters plow . . . using teams of fifteen naked men to each piece of equipment, and the outer one had come close enough to his scouting perch to see that the ones drawing the plow all had one eye, and to hear the thick tongueless gobbling they made, see the stunned brainless look on their faces. He'd heard reports of breeding pens where other types were raised, nice and fat. . . .

He shrugged that off. Who was keeping them company in the pot wouldn't matter to him or Börte or any of the others if the man-eaters caught them.

"What are the *Miqačin* doing out there on the water with all those big ships?" Gansükh said.

"I don't think they're *doing* anything at all," Börte said thoughtfully. "I think someone's doing it *to* them. That's a battle—a battle on the sea. Not all the ships are theirs!"

Dzhambul grunted and scratched with one finger under the edge of his helmet. Once she said it, he could see that it was true; it was just that it was all so unfamiliar, when the largest vessels he'd ever seen were boats on rivers. And nobody he'd heard of in this part of the world had a navy *except* the man-eaters, and the as-yet-unseen Japanese. The ships were maneuvering around one another like a slow stately dance, with tall shapes of sails above their decks. They were miles away, and small even with the binoculars, but being a couple of thousand feet up on the mountainside was an advantage.

As he watched one of the larger ones suddenly shot a series of flaming streaks—

"Fire-shells!" he said.

—and the target virtually exploded into flames; in seconds it was burning from front to back, red and yellow. Down there men would be screaming and probably throwing themselves into the water.

"Couldn't happen to a nicer set of fellows," Gansükh said with satisfaction, and Börte made a sound of agreement. "Whoever it is, may the Ancestor give strength to their arms!"

Dzhambul found himself nodding. Usually the thought of men, even enemy soldiers, roasting alive would give him no pleasure; you killed fighters on the other side *because* they were the enemy, and they tried to do the same to you because you were *their* enemy. It was necessary, but he'd never taken any great pleasure in it, only the transient rage of combat and the raw animal relief of realizing you'd come out the other side one more time. This enemy, though . . . after crossing their country, the nod was natural.

Another set of shells struck, invisible this time and therefore probably cast roundshot, and a . . .

"What are those tall things that carry the sails?" he asked.

"Sails . . ." Börte said. "It's a . . . *mast*, that's the word."

Mongol is a wonderful language for describing horses and grass, he thought. *But a bit short on matters concerning the sea.*

"One of them just fell over and the ship's burning even faster. As Gansükh said, a beautiful sight."

He scratched at his chin. "Who could it be, fighting the man-eaters?"

"The Han? There's a Han kingdom a bit south and west of here . . . a new one, founded by some warlord from the interior . . . what's it called . . . Yantai, I think," Gansükh said. "I've seen it on maps in the briefing reports. It's a peninsula with sea on three sides . . . perhaps they have ships?"

"Or it could be the Japanese," Börte said. "We don't know anything about Japan now except that there are people there and they fight the *Miqačin*."

"Everyone who's close to them fights the *Miqačin*, except the ones the man-eaters have eaten, Princess," Gansükh pointed out.

He frowned. "Didn't *we* invade Japan once?"

Börte snorted. "We invaded *everyone* at least once," she said. "Except the places that hadn't been discovered in the Ancestor's time. We invaded Japan, we invaded Europe and we invaded *Burma*. We even invaded *Java* once, merciful Bodhisattvas witness I speak the truth."

"Well, we didn't invade America," Dzhambul said. "Nobody knew about America then. Maybe those are Americans down there, fighting the *Miqačin!*"

Then he frowned thoughtfully as they all chuckled at the thought; Americans presumably existed in some form, but practically speaking they were more mythical than animal spirits, which at least some claimed to have seen with their own eyes.

The man-eater ships were pulling back into the old harbor, which was flanked by massive forts built of concrete and steel from the ruins. The stranger ships—whoever they were—sheered off when some monstrous engine there threw a boulder that must be larger than a horse, from the size of the waterspout when it struck.

"I think we should stay here in this general area for a while," he said. "There's grazing in that hollow we found. We'll slaughter the worst of the remounts, that bay who's favoring its left fore, and let the rest recover some condition before we swing west and back north."

Both the others sighed. They were all used to and fond of horsemeat, but they'd have to eat it raw, because they couldn't risk the smoke and light of a fire or the smell of cooking.

"The *Miqačin* are reinforcing here, Noyon," Gansükh pointed out.

"Yes, but they're doing that because of these strangers. They must fear a landing. The high command and the Khan need to know what's going on, and what's drawing troops away from the armies facing our main force. We're scouts; that is our task."

Gansükh sighed. "The Noyon wishes," he said.

Börte was silent, but her eyes glowed with curiosity as she looked down the tumbled, riven granite of the mountainside, watching the warriors from who-knew-where sailing up and down in their ships to blockade Pusan.

CHAPTER FOURTEEN

LOST LAKE

CROWN FOREST DEMESNE

(FORMERLY NORTH-CENTRAL OREGON)

HIGH KINGDOM OF MONTIVAL

(FORMERLY WESTERN NORTH AMERICA)

JUNE 20TH

CHANGE YEAR 47/2045 AD

(PLACES OUT OF SPACE, AND TIME)

H er father was gone when she opened her eyes and drew a long shuddering breath. Grief pierced her again, an odd overlay with the sense of loss she'd felt beneath everything else since he was killed.

But he's not gone. I felt him. I feel him now. He's part of this, part of Montival . . . or part of him is, somehow. And always will be. The tales will remember him for a long, long time, and the land and its spirits even longer.

She stood and held the blade of the Sword she bore across the palms of her hands, raising it high and turning to the four Quarters:

"By the North . . ." she began, calling the shapes of the Guardians and their protections, invoking their vigilance. "By the East . . . By the South . . . By the West!"

Then: "By Earth! By Sky!"

"I am the land's, and the land is mine," she said. "Its flesh has fed me, and I am its body; its water has given me life, and flows in my veins. As guardian to all its kindreds I shall be, and to that I pledge myself and the line of my blood so long as it shall last; until the seas rise and drown us, or the sky falls and crushes us; or the world's end."

A moment of singing silence.

"So mote it be," a voice replied, softly, from everywhere about her and nowhere.

Da is here. He's . . . everywhere in Montival, I think.

She could feel that now, like a shadow of a smile, like a hand on her shoulder, a warmth. . . .

Thinking that made her conscious of the cold. It had been a cool day before; now it was unambiguously cold. Órlaith looked down at herself. She'd been in kilt and plaid, and now she was in an unfamiliar outfit, stout laced boots, trousers, a padded jacket and gloves. Her hair was covered by a cap that had earflaps. It was all the sort of gear a hunter might wear, but nothing specific . . . and when she brought the jacket sleeve up the little details were off. The sewing thread used on the seams wasn't linen or even the rare imported luxury of long-staple cotton, and the stitching was very fine and even. The buttons were plastic—nothing unusual, that was a staple of the salvage trade, and they lasted very well in a dark place. But . . .

She put the strangeness out of her mind; her parents had told her stranger things than this about their own time at the Kingmaking, though mostly as hints or words spoken without thought in conversations about something else. She looked around. Snow stood on the boughs of the tall conifers that crowded to the rim of the lake, thick and clinging as a froth of whipped cream on the dark green and brown. The water was a purpling blue as the sun sank, and in the distance bands of crimson lay against the western sky. The same color flecked the clouds scattered in mare's-tails above and painted the cone of Mount Hood, and the image of mountain and clouds repeated itself in the mirror of the water, broken only for a moment when a trout leapt with a tiny audible *splash*, and re-forming as the ripples died. There were shapes moving in the clouds, like the patterns in the Sword's blade. A loon cried somewhere, its haunted call echoing through the quiet.

I'm out of my time. This is Lost Lake, but . . . and yes, you can still see something of the cabins that were here before the Change. It was just some bushes and mounds you had to look to see when I walked down, but now it's more recent. When . . . Da and Mother came here in winter, yes—but it wasn't winter when I talked with him, him as he was then. Does when *mean anything at all here, anymore? Anymore . . . but that's* time . . . *my head hurts. When this place became the Heart of Montival, did it change all the ways it ever* had *been?*

The cabins weren't intact, though, either. They'd burned sometime after the old world fell. Rain and snow, insects and clinging roots had returned ash to the soil, and reduced metal to rust and glass to fragments. Mounds of berry-bushes covered foundations and were well begun in the long toil of grinding them back into the earth, the canes standing in tangles through the knee-deep snow.

Órlaith shivered. She heard voices, and stepped behind a thicket of red cedar on the path. Two people came by on skis, and she recognized both of them.

Her mother and father dropped their packs, planted their skis upright, then walked to the water's edge hand in hand, looking about.

"As sure as the beat of my own heart that you should be here, *anamchara* mine," he said to her. "And that this is the rightful place."

Órlaith flushed, and turned and walked quietly upward.

I was there, she thought. *I was* there *right then. In a way I saw myself, for Mother was bearing me. But I mustn't say anything or show myself because I didn't the first time . . . thinking about this makes my head hurt. . . .*

The knowledge was strange enough to make her feel as if the earth was wobbling beneath her feet. These were not the woods she knew . . . and then they weren't woods at all, but a city park at night with a road through it. It was even one she recognized; in the center where the roadway parted stood the Elk, a statue of a noble animal on a pedestal . . . in the center of Portland, the Association capital where she'd spent years of her life. It was very dark, the gaslights weren't turned on. . . .

No, she thought with an eerie certainty. *They haven't been built yet; that happened just before my grandfather Norman Arminger was killed in the Protector's*

War—all of Portland was a vast building project then, streets ripped up and buildings torn down and things remade. This is after the Change, but not long after. Yes, those are autos in the streets, not salvaged yet, just pushed aside from where they stopped when the Change struck.

Somewhere distant a fire was burning, enough to outline the bronze antlers against the sky, despite the clouds that were just starting to let a little wet snow filter down. Órlaith set herself near a tree and let her senses fan out the way a hunter learned, letting her thoughts drift so that there was no filter between her and what eyes, ears, nose, skin, the very taste of the chill wet air told her. There was an odd heaviness to the overall feel of things, as if the world around her was a thing of gears and wires rather than a living being. . . .

Maybe this is more the way the world felt before the Change. It's so close in time that what started on that day hasn't gone so far yet. That door is open a crack, and swinging wider, but slowly, as Earth turns and swings about the sun. . . .

Voices in the distance, a scream, a shout, the clump of feet, the unmistakable hollow clop of shod hooves on pavement.

This is the start of the Association. The part nobody likes to talk about much with anyone who wasn't there, the years where the oldsters stop and change the subject when you come into the room, though in other parts of the realm they're not so shy about it. Am I in danger? Could I be in danger, before I'm born? I think . . . I think I had better act as if I was? Mother said she was in a bit of a fight, when she traveled to odd places after the Kingmaking, and Da said he had spears pointed at him.

She wasn't armed, except for a knife on her belt below the coat; she drew it for a moment and looked at it quickly, and found it was a good sturdy single-edged weapon-tool. About nine inches long, excellent steel and Parkerized gray except for the honed edge of the blade, with a clip point but no guard, and the fillets of the hilt were some odd rubbery pre-Change synthetic. And there was a cosh in her pocket, a flattened sausage of soft leather filled with something heavy, probably fine lead shot.

Her exploring fingers found something else pinned to the inside of her jacket, about a handspan below the neck. She opened the garment—struggling for a moment with the unfamiliar zipper fastening—and peered at it. Fingering the surface gave her more information in the murk, and memory did more because the image was quite familiar. It was a Saint's token—a figure of Mary as the blue-mantled Queen of Heaven, standing on a very glum-looking droop-eared Dragon of Sin. It was also the personal blazon of Lady Sandra Arminger, assumed when her husband proclaimed himself Lord Protector of the Portland Protective Association . . . and hanged the former mayor and Chief of Police outside his headquarters.

And a mark of her sense of humor; she stayed a private atheist as long as she could, long past this date, and she accumulated a fair catalogue of sins. Certainly all the ones the Christians call the Seven Deadly Sins . . . except maybe lust and gluttony . . . no, she was a glutton for her art collection, that's true . . .

As her eyes adjusted to the blackness she saw more differences from the city she'd known all her life. The skyline—she could see that more plainly than closer things because the distant fire backlit the outline— was different. Buildings above about ten stories weren't practical in the modern world, not for everyday use, and by the time she had memories that included such things almost all the ones within the circuit of the city walls had been torn down to that height. Or often demolished to ground level because they were impossibly stuffy and hard to light and heat properly and it was easier to build anew in brick or half-timbering or cement-stabilized rammed earth. A lot of the steel for Castle Todenangst had come from here, and even more had gone into the massive concrete of the city walls built along the line of the old Highway 405. . . .

Which won't be started until . . . this coming spring, I think. They may already be digging the foundations for Todenangst.

She shivered, and not just because of the cold. Even if it couldn't harm her, this was a bad place to be. It wasn't the worst place in the world in the era of the Change, far from it; the year was full of horrors like a blade across history's neck, the time when nine in ten of human kind had perished. That shadow had lain across the world all her life, only gradually growing lighter. But bad enough.

I wish I'd been walked into Dun Juniper. They were hungry and frightened there, but they had laughter and song too.

The city stank, and not in the usual way she was used to and that was one reason she preferred the countryside. As far as a city could be clean, Portland was a clean place in her day. It was well-policed by its Council of Guilds and Mayor and her mother's administrators, and had an excellent gravity-flow water and sewer system and many public baths and laundries that anyone could use. Enough that even the poorest could afford to wash themselves and their clothes once a week.

From her earliest visits she remembered aromas of stale horse-piss—the dung was carefully swept up and sent out by barge or rail for fertilizer—of woodsmoke trapped within the circuit of the walls, sweat from people and the wool and linen of their clothing. And while things like foundries and tanneries and soap-boiling shops had to stay outside the wall, the various trades added their tang—the divine savor of baking bread and pastries, the frying and spices of food-carts and restaurants and inns and homes, the scent of wood shavings and tanned leather from carpenters and harness-makers and cobblers, the scorched metal and burnt hoof from a farrier's shop shoeing horses, to the exotic oils and sweet scents of a *parfumerie* or the massed blossoms of a flower-seller who catered to the rich merchants and visiting nobles.

This smell was from the smoke of things not meant to burn, and the faint but unmistakable odor of death.

The clop of hooves came louder, and a clearer stink she recognized—old rot. She faded backward, into the parkland on the south side of the roadway, and went to one knee. The park was well-kept, or at least not a jungle of weeds, which surprised her until she stepped into a dried horse-apple, and realized it had probably been intensively grazed all summer.

She *did* remember her grandmother Sandra talking about the program she'd run for her husband, with agents and troops sweeping the lower Columbia Valley for horses and preserving and training and breeding them in guarded locations . . . and how difficult it had been to train people to ride, which was an odd thought when you came to it, since one of her first memories was her mother lifting her onto a pony. Apparently mounted combat had had to be reinvented from scratch, with only hints in books to go on.

People talk about Norman Arminger as the founder of the Association, but Sandra did as much of the work, behind the scenes, and more than half the thinking. Now, is that a good thing to say of her, or a bad one? I liked her . . . but the first I remember of her was as an old lady playing with her granddaughter or her cats. She'd . . . mellowed, but even then you got glimpses. . . .

Torchlight came down the road, heading eastward towards the river—towards the city's river-wall, in her day. Most of the docks and warehouses and dosshouses and shipyards for the riverboats and barges and deep-sea windjammers were on the eastern bank, since the great bridges made access easy and their landing-points could be covered by forts built into the wall itself.

The torches were on poles carried by raggedly-dressed men with wild hair and beards, their faces thin and with expressions that would have been terrified if they weren't too exhausted and too cold and nagged by dragging hunger. She knew her grandparents had seized trainloads and shiploads and elevators-full of wheat all up and down the river from here to the Snake in the immediate aftermath of the Change; it had been one of the first foundations of their power in a world of famine. They'd been quite sparing in handing out the bowls of gruel, though.

Behind them came the man on horseback, riding a good bay that would have done for a courser; he was in a rider's divided hauberk of good riveted mail that came down to his polished boots; his saddle was a rancher's type, though, not a knight's more massive affair. He had a conical helm with a noseguard and a leather flap at the rear covered in small plates on his head, and a broad-bladed sword and dagger at his waist. The teardrop shield on his left arm was similar enough to the modern type, and had the Lidless Eye emblazoned on it quartered with his own arms: *Argent, a fess Gules, in chief two greyhounds courant proper.*

It would have been outdated backwoods equipment for a heavy cavalryman in her day, but it was wealth here and now, and a badge of skills rare and deadly and valuable. So was the easy way he sat his horse, and the fact that he was merely cold and uncomfortable, not on the edge of starving.

Behind him came a long trail of light carts of half a dozen types, some what the ancient world had called trailers, others blazoned with odd slogans—what did "U-Haul" mean?—and all alike laden with corpses, illuminated by more torches on poles fastened to the carts. The bodies were long dead, some skeletons held together by scraps, some half-mummified. Órlaith's lips tightened. The motive power wasn't the precious horses, but gangs of thin dull-faced human beings.

She'd seen death often enough—walked over the battlefield in Pearl Harbor, and that had been worse than this. So had some parts of South Westria been, what had been Los Angeles in the ancient world, because the desert heat preserved bodies for a long time. She'd seen the fringes of the roads where they'd fled death when the water stopped coming out of their taps, fled it and met it in millionfold profusion.

But this was bad, not least because she disliked disrespect to the bodies of the dead. She'd punished a few cases of mutilation herself. Yes, the spirit had departed for self-judgment before the Guardians of the Western Gate, and the vessel would return to Earth the Mother who had furnished it from Her bounty, but even when you were rushed a certain degree of reverence was . . .

A sign of good character, she thought. *But then, there's abundant evidence here of bad character, isn't there? Though perhaps I should be less ready to sit in judgment. I was born to those born after the Change, and it's no accident that so many who lived through it are still slightly mad . . . the very mad ones didn't survive long enough to be old, and usually not long enough to breed.*

A line of armed men bearing spears made from poles and hastily ground-down knives of various sorts and bows and crossbows that she recognized as pre-Change hunting models flanked the train of carts, occasionally encouraging the men . . . mostly men . . . pulling them with a prod from the point or a blow from lengths of rubber hose filled with something granular and heavy, probably lead shot or wet sand. They made a heavy *smack* sound across a laborer's shoulders.

Rubber's not an expensive rarity here. It's still common as dirt.

They were wearing crude makeshift armor, too; helmets in the old style of the American army, like abbreviated sallets, and body-protection of cloth or leather jackets sewn with metal washers or scales or in a few cases of chunky sections cut from steel-belted radial tires. One of them walked beside the mounted man-at-arms; he wore better gear than average, scale-mail, and had a falchion . . .

No, they called it a machete, didn't they?

. . . at his belt, rather than just a knife.

The man on horseback's a knight, she thought.

He had the golden spurs and there were gold bosses on his sword-belt . . . probably added recently. Gold had been cheap this year, while food was treasure beyond price.

"Do we have to keep on at this so late, Sir Amauri?" the spearman said, scratching at a blond beard not quite as tangled as the laborers'. "It's cold and dark and I'm hungry. Uh, sorry, my lord de Grimmond, forgot about the promotion to baron and all that."

"No problem. This is the last load today."

The knight grinned; his features weren't obvious under the nasal, but Órlaith thought he was pale-skinned, hawk-nosed and had a neat black Van Dyke. From things she remembered he probably also had the old Norman style of haircut, shaven at the back to just before the line of the ears, rather than the bowl cut more common among Associates in modern times.

"And would you rather do this in *warm* weather, Bardol? Rot and bugs breed disease, we all saw that this summer . . . that's what these Halloween decorations back there died of, mostly: black plague, and typhus. Let's dump the stiffs and the Willamette crappies and bullheads can clean things up for us, and I hear the long-term plan is to plant trees on the suburbs once we've cleaned them up and salvaged what we can. Next year we'll be busy getting in the volunteer crop and doing some serious planting and starting the manors and more castles."

"I didn't join up to be a farmer, my lord. Standing guard on all the farmers and such we rounded up hasn't changed my mind, either. Or marching all the way to Walla Walla to fight those cons from the Big House, and then back."

"Neither did I," the knight said. "Even in the Society, I wasn't one of those people who got off on making things."

He slapped the sword. "But getting things working the way we want . . . that's going to be a lot of work too. And another epidemic is just what we *don't* need. I heard Lady Sandra say so herself."

The spearman shuddered ostentatiously at her name, and the knight crossed himself—intending it as a joke, but being more sincere than he intended—and the caravan moved on amid its cold oily stink, and the panting grunts of the men drawing the death-carts.

A lower-voiced, confidential-sounding comment from the knight floated back: "If I were you, Bardol, I'd get out of town as fast as I could. Now, Roehis and I have got a nice bit of a fief lined up out in the east near the Blue Mountains, and we could use some good vassals. . . ."

Órlaith grimaced slightly to herself when the last torches rolled away.

Why am I here? There must be a purpose to this.

She'd stayed by the tree, and her dark clothing melted in well. Being motionless in a dangerous situation . . . or while hunting, or both . . . was second nature to her; she stayed still until she moved, and then moved with no waste motion. Now she stayed in that relaxed tension, because someone was coming up behind her. Two someones, moving from tree to tree and doing it very well, their footsteps barely audible at all even to a trained ear.

They passed her quickly, flitting to the edge of the road and taking a knee behind some bushes. Órlaith blinked in surprise; even in the darkness she could tell they were too small for normal adults.

Young, she thought. *Girls, and in their early teens. Neither of them is going to be small when they grow up. If they do.*

They waited patiently behind a bush; the cold bit deeper, but neither moved. Perforce, neither did Órlaith; instead she used her time by seeing details as you did in the dark. Closing her eyes and then opening them for that moment when your pupils were at the largest, looking and then flicking the eyes away so that your brain filled in things that had been below the level the waking mind noticed.

She'd been right about the sex and age. One was taller and had a few tiny blond hairs escaping a dark knit pullover cap, worn balaclava style; the other a little shorter and less slender, and brunette, she thought. Both were in nondescript dark clothes, worn but not ragged. And both carried coils of rope bandolier-style over their shoulders, with blades and hatchets at their belts; one had a small crossbow as well.

They waited until the torches disappeared in the direction of the river, and she was fairly sure that one of them had been looking west all that time to give them all-around coverage. They waited a little more, while pedestrians or riders, bicyclists or rickshaws or pedicabs went by. The biggest interruption was a herd of cattle that must have been driven in from the eastern plains, plodding along and lowing discontentedly. When that was past, except for what it left on pavement, the two girls moved off in unison with no need for words, like one mind in two bodies.

However they had lived through the months since the Change, they hadn't been starving—the way they handled themselves bespoke fitness. They were sticking to the sides of the street, moving from doorway to doorway down the Avenue of the Immaculate Conception—probably still SW Main here, she couldn't remember when it had been modernized to honor the city's Patron—and that meant . . .

They're heading for the City Palace. I'm going to follow them. None of this is an accident.

Knowing where someone was going made it much easier to follow them. She waited until they were well ahead, then stood and strode out and turned down towards the west on the south side of the street; that would make it easier to keep track of them along the north side. They'd probably pick up on her, too, eventually. But she didn't *look* as if she was following anyone; she looked and moved like someone on an errand who knew where they were going. In fact, she'd look like a Gods-sent bit of good fortune to the clandestine pair, distracting people who saw her coming at a distance while they snuck along a little ahead of her.

And my, didn't my training include things I'd never imagined would be useful, but turned out to be, like how to sneak around a hostile city! Brigid the Forethoughtful bless my instructors and my parents!

As she walked past the old County Courthouse—five stories, stone-built in a severe Renaissance style nearly a century before the Change, and still in use nearly half a century from now—she saw lantern light at many of the windows, and smelled honest woodsmoke, though with an unfamiliar tang to it; after a second she realized it was sawn timber being burnt, from torn-down frame houses. Órlaith simply nodded to the squad of spearmen at the entrances, and they stiffened in unconscious response to her assumption of authority, a language of the body that she would have had to work hard *not* to show.

The building to her left was steel and glass and sheet metal and blue tile, looming huge; in her day the spot was occupied by a duplicate of the County Courthouse and both were exactly that—they housed courts, the Courts of Record, the Courts Baron and the Court of Star Chamber, along with some extremely comfortable guest suites that had locks on the outside and barred windows.

So it went down the tree-lined street for block after block, traces of the familiar amid eerie alien weirdness.

At the intersection where you had to turn right to get to the City Palace—which had originally been the Multnomah County Central Library—there was a four-way checkpoint of timber X-forms supporting coils of barbed wire, with a fire burning in a big metal bucket in the center, providing a little heat to those grouped around it and a bit more reddish, flickering light.

Besides killing their night vision any farther out, she thought.

It was manned by more infantry, all with shields and spears and a variety of crossbows. All young to youngish men, and all notably hard-looking.

"*Ay, chica!*" their leader said. "Where you goin'? It's after curfew."

Órlaith looked at him and replied in faultless Spanish: "Any particular reason you think you need to know, asshole?"

He bristled, and several spears were leveled. One of his followers laughed and grabbed his crotch.

"Because we're supposed to check!" the first man replied in the same language. "And we're"—he hesitated, probably mentally translating something—"we're *authorized* to hand out *summary punishment* for civilians breaking curfew!"

"Civilians? Take a look at this, *pendejo.*"

Órlaith smiled thinly and flipped back the collar of her coat as he raised a kerosene lantern. It was probably burning gasoline now, which was rather dangerous, and he turned the knob that elevated the wick to produce more light, which made it even more so, but the incandescent mantle functioned perfectly. He blanched as the brighter light fell on Sandra Arminger's token.

"Who's your lord? Baron Emiliano?"

"No, not that stuck-up *cabrón.* Eddie Liu's our boss. . . ."

Then he visibly halted and mentally shifted gears: "I mean, Lord Edward, Baron Liu de Gervais, is our good lord."

Órlaith maintained a sneer, though inwardly she was shivering. Those were names she knew; Eddie Liu had died in the run-up to the Protector's War, and Emiliano during it. Liu's son Odard had gone on the Quest of the Sunrise Lands with her parents, and died heroically; there was a *chanson* about it, which Johnnie had sung once. She remembered that because it had made Mother cry. His younger brother Huon was the current baron, and a friend of the family—her mother and father had been godparents to his children, and his sister's, a very close bond in Association territory.

"I'll tell Lady Sandra that you're on the job. Now get that fucking barbed wire out of my way before I throw you on it and use you as a bridge to walk on!"

Several of the men came forward to drag the X-forms out of her way. As she stalked through with all eyes on her—to *sotto voce* mutterings that included but were not limited to *whore, dyke* and *bitch*—she saw a slight flicker of movement out of the corner of her eye. The sort you'd see if someone came running, was boosted by a friend with their hands linked into a stirrup, dove over an eight-foot-high barricade, landed soft-footed and silently in a forward roll and stayed flat in a leopard-crouch.

That's the girls. They're using me as cover while they get through this.

While the first took a run herself, hit the brick wall, ran up it for ten feet and clamped her hands on a window-ledge, then brought her feet up and launched off in something like a cross between a forward twist and a somersault that landed her in a crouch.

I know that technique, Órlaith thought. *I've done it myself and it's not easy. I was taught it. Mother and Da were taught it, by—*

The girl using traceuse style ran to the other side of the enclosure as soon as her feet touched the ground, and then paused in a crouch. The one who'd been on the ground launched herself forward, the blond parkour type made another stirrup and threw her over the barrier; then she jumped directly at it, gripped the uprights of the timber X as if they were the handles on a vaulting horse and flipped in midair, ending up arching forward with her hands outstretched and knees nearly up to her chest, ready for another rolling landing.

Oh, my, they're good.

She didn't try to focus on it; all the bright light shone in her eyes would have made that futile, but your peripheral vision wasn't as easily hurt that way and experience filled in details.

Where are they going? she thought.

Certainly to the City Palace. But the hints she'd gotten about the visions you could expect at the Kingmaking were all to do with family, *her* family, House Artos. And crucial moments that led to the founding of the High Kingdom and its fate. Some within living memory, some very distant.

And my grandparents . . . Mother's parents . . . are almost certainly there now. But what are these two going to do? Assassinate them? Lord and Lady know plenty of people had good reason to want them dead! I really wouldn't like to rescue them . . . I mean, I suppose I would . . . I loved Grandmother Sandra and I wept when she died, but . . .

She went through the checkpoint with the same casually determined stride, and north along Horse Heaven Hills Avenue; named after the great victory of the Prophet's War, and formerly . . . in fact, *now* . . . SW 10th.

Nobody had turned this into the Palace District, not yet. There were more people about, and more light—from baskets of metal wire hung from the defunct electric light posts, with wood burning in them. There were also occasional bodies hanging, by their necks, left that way to inspire terror of the new overlords. Everyone she saw looked angry, or frightened, or preoccupied, or just stone-faced; she had to show the badge several more times, and the reaction got more polite, though no less impressed, as she got closer to the Palace.

The problem was that she'd lost track of the two extremely athletic girls.

And I don't dare stop, she thought. *But I'm pretty sure they're heading in the same direction. I have to get close to Norman and Sandra, because that's where they're going . . . for one reason or another.*

The City Palace—here still bearing PVBLIC LIBRARY BVILT BY MVLTNOMAH COVNTY ANNO DOMINI MCMXII chiseled into the white stone below the eaves above the third floor—was just the core here-and-now, a Georgian rectangle of white sandstone and red brick covering about an acre, with steps leading up to the three tall arched doorways in front, a second story of great arched windows illuminating the vast public spaces, a third story that in her day was the family apartments, and a flat roof with a stone balustrade all around that she knew as a pleasant gazebo and garden. Giant elms embowered the big building on three sides; some of them were even the very same trees she'd climbed in as a child, though there weren't any of the sky-bridges that connected it to the surrounding buildings.

The problem is . . .

Órlaith had just never bothered to learn the history of the City Palace in any detail. She certainly hadn't ever looked at the original floor plans.

Unlike Johnnie, who can recite it to you chapter and verse, and the date every single picture and statue was put in, and where it came from beforehand. I love art, but he's a maniac about it.

She'd lived here with her family from time to time, but it was going to be her brother's home eventually, once the throne of Montival and the subordinate one of the Lords Protector were separate again rather than united in a single couple . . . or a single widowed woman named Mathilda Arminger Mackenzie, until Órlaith had walked down that trail to Lost Lake and come unmoored in the history of her bloodline.

As a teenager she'd deliberately decided to avoid pinning the emotion of *home* on anything in Portland's domains and certainly not on the Palace or Todenangst; there had been hints of that in her father's attitude, though he'd been easy-going everywhere. Just a smidgen of discomfort around the places where his wife's parents had operated.

It hadn't hurt as much as making the same decision about Dun Juniper down in the Mackenzie Dùthchas, either. The plans for a palace in Dun na Síochána, the new capital on the ruins of Salem, had only recently come to fruit; her parents had always found better uses for the money, until the Congress of Realms virtually forced their hands. Not least because the delegates wanted the High Queen to have somewhere suitably fancy to stage the parties and balls and masques and ceremonies they'd be taking part in, and because everyone who wasn't an Associate resented the way the PPA's capital exerted influence well beyond the north-realm's borders just by being there, being so big with over sixty thousand people, and being a center of culture and the arts as well as a wealthy center of crafts, trade and government.

And it was the seat of the Archbishop-Cardinal who oversaw all Montival's Catholics, and Badia in Italy had made it clear he'd stay right there in Portland until the High Kingdom as a whole had a permanent capital.

Órlaith bared her teeth. Unfortunately that emotionally and even *politically* wise decision of hers meant she had no idea of how to get around inside the building as it was here—which would be instantly suspicious if she claimed to be an important retainer of Sandra Arminger. She *did* know that apart from some features like the grand black-granite staircase with its acid-etched flower designs and the domed skylight above it, and the bronze tree statue, the interior had been gutted thoroughly and rebuilt at some point. Lady Sandra had made the last alterations only about the time her daughter returned from the Quest of the Sunrise Lands and married Rudi Mackenzie-Artos-the-First.

Think, think, think. . . .

The street in front of the main entrance was brightly lit by gasoline lamps with reflective mirrors. The guards at the main entrance weren't the sort of scruffy irregulars she'd seen at checkpoints earlier. Their armor was better, long mail or scale hauberks and the nose-guarded helmets of the Norman era; her grandfather had been a professional historian studying it and his Society persona had let him further live out his fascination, before he branched out into warlording after the Change.

All their gear was dead-black, too, and the shields bore no arms but the Lidless Eye. This was the Protector's Guard at its birth; it had also been known as the Brute Squad then. The firelight glittered redly on the honed edges of their weapons, and they were alertly examining everyone who entered. That was only a trickle, because it was past dinnertime, though every window in the big building was brightly lit.

Then she noticed a tentative-looking party approaching from the north, and arguing with a civilian usher. They were clutching briefcases and in one instance a leather case big enough to hold maps for display on an easel, and they all looked as if they'd been traveling rough and outdoors recently. Órlaith took a deep breath, and walked over.

The Guard squad didn't ignore her, although they were focused on the argument too. The usher was a rabbity-looking young man a few years older than her; he had a jeweled knife at his belt, and was wearing tight pants that were probably the closest he could get to hose, a loose shirt and a jerkin.

"It's impossible for you to see—" he was saying.

"Wait a minute," Órlaith said, her voice firm but a little bored. "You people are here to do the report, aren't you?"

It has to be some report or other, with the documentation you're carrying.

"Yes, yes!" one of them said, a middle-aged woman in blue trousers— what they'd called jeans. "We've been working on the land survey and plans for the Walla Walla County for a *month* now, and the progress of the oxen and draft-horse plans and converting field equipment. Lady Sandra urgently needs these for the reorganization plan! It's key to getting agriculture started up again. That's the biggest wheat-producing area under control now that's within hauling distance of the river!"

Órlaith sighed—she recognized an obsessed bureaucrat who couldn't stop giving you details if her life depended on it—and showed her livery badge. The usher looked suspicious.

"I don't know you," he said.

"And I don't know you," Órlaith said. "But you do know *this*, don't you? There is a world outside town, and it's where the *food* comes from. Remember food?"

She tapped the badge and then turned away from him.

"Where have you people been?" she added to the party, who wilted under her glare. "You've been holding up everything! And I've been pounding my arse in a saddle going up the river looking for you! If God had meant us to do that, He'd have given us hooves of our own."

Another glance at the usher. "Have the Lord Protector and Lady Sandra retired for the evening yet?"

"Well, no, they're dining late, but—"

"Then Lady Sandra will want to see these people! They're overdue. Arranging the boundaries of fiefs and manors is *important!*"

The members of the survey team all nodded vigorously. More important, so did the commander of the door-guard and at least three of his subordinates, all with the golden spurs on their heels. Fiefs were just beginning to be handed out, and every single man-at-arms in the Association wanted one. The demand was still vigorous in her time—the nobility tended to big families—and dispensing land from the Crown's holdings was politically very delicate. It would be here too, with the added bonus that it was the way the Association had gotten food production going again.

She also remembered her grandmother saying how chaotic the whole thing had been for the first year or two, until *I got things in hand*.

Then a square-chinned blond woman in a green kirtle and white wimple slid through the door behind the usher and out into the night air.

"Is that the Walla Walla survey people, Bobbie?" she said to the usher. "Or should I say Dagobert?"

He flushed. "It's Dagobert now, BD," he snapped.

BD, Órlaith thought. *I know that name, Grandmother Juniper mentioned her . . . yes, she was one of Sandra's helpers, one who knew her and Norman in the Society before the Change. . . . She smuggled fugitives out of the Protectorate too, and had to flee for her own life later.*

"I spent *seven days* looking for them and I thought someone had killed them for their horses, but luckily I hadn't reported that yet," BD said. "Let them in."

"Oh, all right," Dagobert said and raised a wand of office, also familiar to Órlaith. "But if Lady Sandra isn't in a good mood, you'll answer for it, not me. Our Lord Protector's son and heir is well along now!"

"I'm aware of that," Órlaith said dryly. "I operate out of town mostly, but I do report to Lady Sandra directly. She doesn't hand these tokens out to the housemaids, you know."

And to herself: *That's my mother Sandra's carrying right now . . . she was born in January of the first full year of the Change, so it must be her seventh month. Yes, I bet Grandfather Norman was hoping for a son.*

BD gave her an odd look.

"I don't know you?" she said.

"And we'll both be happier if we keep it that way," Órlaith said neutrally and faded into the background of the delegation.

Fortunately there was a full baker's dozen of them, and five were women. She still stood out, but mainly because of her height and the way she moved. The Guard troops saluted, spear-butts to the floor or sword before the face, and the doors opened. Within was the bright light of dozens of incandescent-mantle lanterns, not as vivid as the similarly equipped gaslights of the future, but good enough. She could have read comfortably.

Órlaith felt an unclenching below her breastbone; it was totally irrational, since this was *more* dangerous. Hopefully this BD would assume she was another of Sandra's spies-agents-scouts-enforcers, and the survey party would assume she was part of Lady Sandra's apparatus too.

Sandra had been the head of the PPA's secret service right from the beginning, and she made a practice of employing women whenever she could. She'd also made a practice of never letting the left hand know what the right was doing.

In fact, she'd once told her granddaughter that as a girl she'd always wanted to be either Eleanor of Aquitaine, or Cardinal Richelieu, or both. Her warrants to her agents had often read:

"The bearer has done what has been done on my authority, and for the good of the State."

I'm walking into a place where my mother was born and where I spent years of my childhood, and it's also the den of a monster.

The black granite staircase was still there, and busier than she'd ever seen it. The second story was organized chaos—half mess hall, half barracks, and they had to stand aside as a chain of laborers came up with newly-made scale hauberks strung on carrying-poles through the arms, with helmets on the central pole, the whole looking like deflated scarecrows. The third floor was quieter, but mainly because the construction crews had knocked off for the day, though their materials and tools were still there.

"BD," Órlaith said.

"Yes?"

"I've gotten these people here and I've got better places to be," she said.

"You don't want the points?" BD said curiously. "Sandra's been getting impatient about these people. Impatient enough I don't mind interrupting the appetizers."

Órlaith shrugged. "You can accomplish anything if you don't care who gets the credit; take them on through."

She hesitated, then added: "It's better that Norman doesn't know my face, so don't mention me, if you don't mind."

BD's own cleared a little. If the survey party hadn't been treading on her heels Órlaith thought she might have argued, or at least asked questions. But they were and she nodded and led them forward.

Órlaith waited, quickly checked that nobody else was watching—the guards had their eyes on the surveyors—then ducked back into a room labeled *Collins Gallery*. She remembered it as an informal dining room-cum-study, where they had family meals or ones with relatives and friends, rather than the grander chambers downstairs, and then could comfortably sit around afterwards. Ironically for a place that had been a library until March seventeenth none of the books she remembered were here yet, unless there were some in the stacks of boxes, which mostly looked as if they were for oil-paintings. The rooms smelled of plaster and grout and dust.

What *was* here was a collection of Japanese *byōbu*, six-panel folding screens, some still in their improvised packing and labeled *Seattle Asian Art Museum*.

Most of which she recognized because she'd grown up with them; the one leaning against a stack of marble floor-tiles swaddled in padding had a *kinpaku* gold-leaf background, and a painting of a flock of crows coming in to rest. It was seventeenth century work, and it had stood in her City Palace bedroom here for most of her adolescence. Now she rolled behind it, lying curled up in her fortress of green-veined white stone and Nihonjin art, looking for a tiny scratch in the lacquer of the lower frame of the outermost panel. . . .

And it wasn't there now, because she would put it there herself, inadvertently, after her sixteenth birthday party.

The sounds from below died down, though they never entirely went away; there were a couple of hundred people in the building, counting the servants. Órlaith waited with trained patience. She'd been much more uncomfortable on hunts, in fact—once up to her ankles in a swamp in the far north, waiting for hours for a tiger turned man-eater and plaguing a Koyukon band . . . though what had shown up after her feet went numb had been a grizzly bear with a strong territorial sense and no fear of human-kind at all.

After a while the survey party and BD passed; the surveyors were chatting in relaxed tones and she was promising to find them quarters. Half an hour after that, the iron tramp and jingle of men in mail sounded, a small guard party. A voice she hadn't heard since her early teens sounded. Like a hand stroking warm velvet, with an undertone like a knife: Sandra Arminger, née Whittle, her mother's mother.

"Well, that was an interesting dinner, my love. Columbia caviar and probable yields of volunteer wheat, cream of potato and turning range steers into plow oxen. . . . That's a brilliant idea we should have thought of before given the horse shortage, we *must* reward the lady with something really nice, by the way . . . ennoblement and a pension at the least, possibly a fief. . . ."

"It's *that* important?"

"Oh, yes, darling. We're getting short of people now, we're going to need peasants, and having them *pull* things is so . . . so *wasteful*. And oxen can eat grass."

"If you say so."

"And then poached salmon with cattle numbers . . . grilled pork loin with capers and water supplies . . . and a jellied trifle with a garnish of optimum manorial acreage."

"It could have waited . . . darling! Are you all right?"

The last part was sharp with concern; it was a man's voice, deep, clipped-sounding—you could hear the beginning of the staccato North-realm accent in it, probably because so many in the next decade would imitate his patterns of speech that it became a habit with a life of its own, spreading down through the pyramid-shape of the Association's hierarchy.

Grandfather Norman, Órlaith thought, and swallowed. *Odd. He doesn't sound like a murderous tyrant . . . but none of human-kind are* all *one thing, are we?*

"Just a bit dizzy for a moment. This pregnancy thing is barbaric—we should divide, like bacteria, or do grafts and buds like plants."

"Let's get you to bed," Norman Arminger went on.

Sandra chuckled. "I'm afraid that's not going to be very entertaining for you, my dear. Tossing and turning and possible puking. Do feel free to go elsewhere."

"Damn entertainment and damn elsewhere," he said crisply. Then more softly: "You're the only one I like to *sleep* with, in the technical sense of the word, you know that."

"You charmer!"

The voices passed on, and the iron tramp of the guards. When the corridor lights were turned down a deeper silence fell. Órlaith crawled to the door of the Gallery and looked both ways. No actual guards except the pair outside the State Apartments on this level, but spearpoints caught the low light from the lanterns; the men-at-arms were lower down the stairs, where they could come at the run if someone called or blew a whistle. She waited again, and nodded to herself as she heard soft steps approaching. She would have had someone walking the corridors too, and at irregular intervals, unless it was specifically forbidden. The steps went by.

Time passed by; she grew conscious of thirst and hunger, and searched her coat's many pockets and in one she found jerky and a rectangular bar of chocolate with nuts in it wrapped in plastic, which was fascinating. The little luxury surprised her, though not enough to stop her eating it, though at the second bite she almost stopped at the unfamiliar taste.

She'd eaten chocolate fairly frequently most of her life, once a month or so . . . but this didn't taste much like what she was used to.

More sugary, for starters. Bland.

Of course, chocolate hadn't been such a luxury *before* the Change, but by the first winter of the Change she'd have thought it was mostly gone, scavenged by desperate, starving survivors.

No, wait a minute, I've got the clothes and gear that a real agent for Grandmother Sandra would have. Good boots, a really nice knife, a cosh . . . and chocolate in my pocket. The privileges of working for her.

"They'll be down here, Kat," a very soft voice said. "What used to be the Sheet Music Room."

"What do we do if they're not so impressed they want to give us a job—" someone, presumably Kat, replied.

"That's if *she's* not impressed," the not-Kat said. "Well, we try to run but we're probably dead. Look, we settled this, Kat, right? We need someone we can work for, someone *important*. She's our best bet."

It's her, Órlaith thought. *It's Tiphaine d'Ath . . . Colette Rutherton. That was the name her parents gave her. She was an acrobat before the Change! This is how she met Sandra and became her protégé, and then later her assassin and then a commander. The other must be Katrina Georges, her friend from the Girl Scouts who died in the Protector's War.*

The two girls ghosted by.

Grandmother Sandra kept Norman from killing Da while he was a hostage in the north-realm just before the Protector's War, but she used Tiphaine to watch over him at Montinore, Órlaith thought. And she used that to throw Da and her daughter Mathilda together, too. If Tiphaine doesn't become Sandra's henchwoman, I won't be born! Montival won't be born! The Prophet might win!

That was why she was here.

She waited to follow; and then waited a little more, letting her mind drift, not trying to suppress the strings of random thought that drifted through it, just *being*. That was rewarded when she heard quiet footsteps rutching down the corridor, the odd sound of rubber-soled footwear. And then something else, something infinitely more familiar. The soft hiss of a sword being drawn from a sheath of leather-bound wood greased with neat's-foot oil.

If Tiph and her companion are found fighting a guard, they'll be killed out of hand, Órlaith knew. *They'll just be assumed to be assassins. Fourteen-year-old girl assassins, but Grandfather Norman's mind always worked on the principle that when people caused a problem, no people meant no problem. Because death solves all problems.*

She swung to her feet noiselessly. *She said the Sheet Music Room . . . that's the State Apartments . . . out, turn left, turn right. . . .*

It was dark but not black outside, the lanterns turned down but still burning, and more light spilling up from the stairwell. There was a way to go; the building covered a full acre, and each floor had over forty thousand square feet of space. Órlaith used the space to keep her distance, flitting from one door—or pile of tile or sacks of cement or adhesive or tall piles of neatly bundled Isfahan rugs or sheet-wrapped furniture—to the next along the outer wall.

Wait a minute, she thought. *There will be guards at the door of the State Apartments! What are Tiph and Kat planning to do? Surely two fourteen-year-olds aren't going to tackle a pair of grown-ups in full armor?*

The officer doing the rounds was a tall brown-haired man with the back of his skull shaved, not in armor but in a set of black T-tunic and dark-blue cross-gartered hose and what the ancient world had called running shoes, with a longsword in his hand. He would have been very hard to see indeed, if it hadn't been for the gold-thread embroidery at the hem of the tunic, and around the neck and v-front. He pulled up himself at the sight of the pair standing at parade rest beside the door, and Órlaith ducked neatly sideways into a space that would have a door again when one was hung, but didn't yet.

They clanked to attention, bringing their shields up to their shoulders and their spears upright and thumping the butts on the floor. Those weren't pole-and knife specials, they were solid lengths of ashwood with ten inches of ground-down leaf-spring solidly mortised into it, double edges tapering to a wicked point, and the shaft wound with stainless-steel wire for a foot below the head.

"Nothing to report?" he began, sounding a little puzzled.

He was planning to catch them himself to get the credit, but now . . .

Then he stiffened. "I thought I saw someone unauthorized here."

He realized something. He realized what she just realized. Tiphaine and her friend went out a window and they're going around on the outside ledge to get into the State Apartments.

"Search this floor!" he barked at the guardsmen. "Quickly! Two intruders, both small! Look for open windows, check the sides of the building!"

Aha, Órlaith thought, following his mind.

She also plastered herself to the wall inside the door as the two men-at-arms clanked by, being as quiet as you could in a fifty-pound knee-length hauberk of scale mail, which wasn't very.

Probably they got inside in the first place by the elms on the other side of the building, they overhang with the ones across the street. Up, across, open a window. I'd break the branches, but if you were quite light and very agile you could do it. Then they crossed the third floor inside, that's how I saw them, and now they've gone out one of the windows again and they're going back into the State Apartments the same way, neatly bypassing the door guards. . . .

Órlaith sprinted as soon as the two guards had passed the doorway she was hiding in, running lightly on the balls of her feet. The knight ahead of her just had time to plunge through the door into the sitting room of the Apartments. He started a curse at the sight of the open window, with a cold wind blowing in and fluttering the draperies, and drew a breath before she caught up with him.

"M—" he began to shout; doubtless intended to be: *My Lord!*

The flat of the cosh took him behind the right ear. He'd chosen stealth over the protection of armor and helmet, and the bet wasn't paying off. For once the results were as neat as they were in a *chanson;* he simply collapsed limply after the flat *thwack* sound like a puppet with its strings cut. Unlike the way it worked in an adventure epic, he wouldn't spring up as if from a nap in a couple of hours. At the very least he'd feel the world's worst hangover, and there would probably be dizziness and headaches for some while.

He might well die, in fact, but Órlaith wasn't going to waste any regret on that. If you went to work carrying arms for a man like Norman Arminger, you'd already offered up your life to the Dark Mother of your own free will, and left your killer clean of it. And Órlaith hitting him was part of the sequence of events she was creating here . . . and which had created her. The two girls would be more than smart enough to keep their mouths shut and keep the credit for a silent takedown of the guard captain.

She dropped the cosh, and caught the knight's sword before it struck the floor, laying it quietly beside his unconscious body.

The sitting-room part of the State Apartments had already been redone in the style she remembered, save for a touch here and there. There was a big glass table supported on a cast-bronze dragon that always made you think it was going to bite your ankle while you were sitting at it, more conventional furniture carved in the Gothic style, and art that included a Botticelli crucifix of Christ, and a fourteenth-century Virgin and Child by Cecco di Pietro.

A sixth-century BC krater with a red-figure portrait of a bull looked familiar but out of place. Then she realized she was used to it in Montinore Manor's reception hall. Sandra had given it to Tiphaine d'Ath after the Protector's War in recognition of services that included removing several recalcitrant noblemen who didn't think the Lord Protector's widow was the right candidate as Regent for his only child.

Widows had run the Portland Protective Association for some time after that war, mostly. There had been a *lot* of widows.

Órlaith had laid the sword by the fallen man's hand; from his stertorous breathing and the way he was dribbling on the carpet he wouldn't be waking up for a while. Cat-footing over to the door to the bedchamber took only a moment as lamplight flared brighter behind it, and through the crack of the hinges she could see the two girls kneeling on the Khotanese rug with their hands linked behind their heads, and Norman Arminger standing before them naked save for a set of underdrawers of the type the ancient world had called tighty-whities for some reason, fury in his eyes and an entirely naked broadsword in his hand. He had a warrior's body, all flexible rolling muscle and ridged belly with a fuzz of dark-brown hair on his chest, and a hard square face marked by weariness and wariness both.

"No, Norman, don't kill them just yet, not on the rug anyway, the stains never come out," Sandra Arminger's voice came, amused and intrigued. "They could have shot one of us with that crossbow if that was what they came for. I want to get a story out of them first. And yes, if it's satisfactory, I think they might be amusing . . . and quite, quite useful."

"Useful murderous ninja moppets?" Arminger said, lowering the blade.

His own grim thin-lipped mouth relaxed; he was probably realizing he looked a little odd flourishing a broadsword over the heads of two unresisting near-children on their knees.

"Those are the *best* kind, darling! Nobody expects the golden-haired teenage ninja moppet!"

CHAPTER FIFTEEN

LOST LAKE
CROWN FOREST DEMESNE
(FORMERLY NORTH-CENTRAL OREGON)
HIGH KINGDOM OF MONTIVAL
(FORMERLY WESTERN NORTH AMERICA)
JUNE 20TH
CHANGE YEAR 47/2045 AD
(PLACES OUT OF SPACE, AND TIME)

"Cernunnos bless," Órlaith murmured as she looked around her. "Sure and this is the Cascades, and familiar as my own face in a mirror."

It was a soft summer's afternoon in a bee-murmurous meadow, the long light slanting through the tall western hemlock, Douglas fir and red cedar that surrounded it, the shade of small white clouds floating above, and the green slopes that drew vision up to the eternal snows at their peaks. She took a deep breath; mild warmth breathed with cedar resin and fir-sap and flower-scent. The meadow was flowers as much as it was grass, thick drifts of white Valerian, blue lupine, bright-red pokers of Indian paintbrush, purple elephant's ear and white-and-yellow pearly everlasting.

This was what a Persian carpet tried to imitate. But alive; Rufous hummingbirds and butterflies—monarchs and fritillaries and ruby tiger moths and more—were thick around the blossoms. Birds flew overhead, though less than she was accustomed to. That gave her an idea. She shut her eyes and *felt*.

"Yes," she murmured. "Like it was in Portland; the world feels closed, a bit, and . . . *flat*. But even more so."

She looked up again, and her eyes went wide. That ruler-straight cloud, with a metallic dot speeding at the front of it as it grew, like the arrow of a God.

"A contrail," she said; she knew the concept, and she'd seen pictures.

"But never the thing itself," she added. "And yes, there were wonders in this time too."

Looking down she saw she was in a Mackenzie kilt and knee-hose, and a loose green-dyed linen shirt, a *léine*. A sporran was slung from her belt, and a hunting knife, and a little *sgian dubh* with a hilt of black horn carved in knotwork was tucked into her right stocking. A six-foot yew longbow and quiver leaned against a nearby tree, and she slung the quiver and took up the weapon.

Then she heard a voice, a child's voice, a girl's, talking to herself . . . or perhaps praying, in the unguarded way of a youngster who thought herself alone.

Órlaith sank down in the shadow of a hemlock, sitting cross-legged, and listened:

"Gods of the Wild Ones, help me find my way home. I'm not scared but Gran'-Unc' will have to come and find me and he gets tired sometimes. I promised him I would be good, and Mom, and Dad, while I'm staying with him. And . . . I think I am a *little* scared. . . ."

Órlaith thought for a moment and reached into her sporran. The rest of her gear was what she took with her on a stroll in the woods near Dun Juniper, so there should be . . .

Wrapped in a dock leaf were two scones the size of her fist, honey-glazed and rich with hazelnuts and dried blueberries. It was *just* like what they made in the kitchens at the Dun, and left by the door in a basket each morning for travelers and hunters to take. The canteen at her belt was full of cold spring water cut with berry-juice and mint, and it included a cup of salvaged aluminum. She set both out on a coarse brown linen napkin also folded there, then took up another part of the contents. That was a set of panpipes, of the type Mackenzie shepherds kept to play to their flocks . . . and warn predators that their beasts were under human protection.

She began to play softly, letting the notes trickle through the meadow and the woods. The girl fell silent when she saw the source of the piping, then came into the clearing and looked around. There was relief and wariness both in her expression, and Órlaith stayed seated, so as not to loom above her. In the tight-knit world of the Clan Mackenzie's *dúthchas* where households lived in one another's pockets and youngsters were in and out of one another's houses all their growing years, a child would assume any adult to be helpful, but things were otherwise in other lands . . . and this was not exactly the dúthchas, not yet.

She was an eight-year-old, with a mane of flaming red hair the color of polished raw copper in braids starting to unravel from where a ribbon was missing, dressed in trousers of blue and a leaf-stained white shirt, with odd and rather grubby white-and-green shoes on her feet. A little knapsack was marked with a strangely manlike—or puppet-like—frog in a dagged collar like a jester, as if from a story. And there was the startling luxury of a watch on her wrist, its hands the limbs of a manlike mouse.

A watch made to measure for a child would be a rare thing and sign of great wealth. . . .

Though not in this time of marvels, perhaps. No, they were very common here.

Freckles marked a milk-white skin slightly sun-flushed and the eyes were leaf-green beneath a billed cap of the type still worn to play baseball.

"Oh!" she said, as Órlaith put the panpipes down and smiled. "I thought . . ."

Órlaith made a polite enquiring sound, and the child went on: "I thought you were the Piper . . . you know, the one at the Gates of Dawn, in the story."

"And would that be *The Wind in the Willows* you mean?" Órlaith asked.

And thought to herself, as the coloring and cast of features sank home:

I think I know who this is! Greetings, Grandmother!

A broad white smile with a gap in the upper row greeted that remark.

"Yeah! I've got that here!" and swung the little haversack down.

The book she flourished was a little battered with use and from the library markings originally bought secondhand, but obviously much-loved.

Órlaith nodded. "Ah, now I have that book as well, and my Da read from it to me when I was younger than you, and when I was younger still my grandma would tell me the stories in her own words. It's a fine tale, and I would go looking in the woods for Ratty and Mole and Toad of Toad Hall!"

And I tried to find the Super Man once, but let's leave that aside.

The girl flushed crimson. "I . . . well, I sort of did that. Went looking for Toad Hall. Just playing, you know? And I marked my trail, I really did! But then I couldn't find the marks. Mom and Dad made me promise I wouldn't be any trouble for Great Uncle Frank if I came to stay with him all by myself, but he'll be really worried."

"No need for worriment," Órlaith said. "I know these woods well, and I can put you on the path to . . . it would be a big cabin, no, of squared logs? On a stretch of open land farther down the slope, facing southward, and itself a little way above a small valley with farms in it, opening to the west towards Sutterdown. A cabin used by an older gentleman as his country place?"

She saw the girl's tension melt into relief at this proof she was someone who knew the neighborhood.

Órlaith felt a prickle of eeriness up her spine; she knew how things had been here in her grandmother's time because Juniper Mackenzie had told her the way of it herself, and how she'd been left the land and house years later in a totally unexpected gesture by the old man. The world-serpent was biting its tail with a vengeance.

What am I to do here, then? Just set you on the road to home? Is that why the

Sword brought me here? Surely your kinsman would come find you sooner or later—
you're not fifteen minutes' walk from the nemed *of Dun Juniper, and only another ten*
from home. A bit more for a child, but not much more.

The girl nodded, happier now, the more so when Órlaith went on:

"And so your name would be Mackenzie?"

"Yeah! You know Great-Unc' Frank?"

"Know of him, at least."

A broad smile rewarded her. "My name's Mackenzie, yes, miss."

"And your given name, would that be Juniper? For you have the look
of one who is kin to the spirit of the Junipers."

The girl laughed. "That's like the book! Juniper . . . that's a good
name!"

She cocked her head, taking in Órlaith's garb. "What's *your* name?
Does my Great-Unc' know you're on his land? You look sorta like a book
I have about Scotland."

"Órlaith is my name," she said. "And as chance would have it, in full
it's Órlaith Arminger Mackenzie. And yes, my people were Scots in my
father's mother's line, far back; as yours would be, from the name."

"Yup, my dad's folks too! Ooor-la," the girl echoed, getting the sound
perfect the first time. "That means . . . Golden One, doesn't it?"

Órlaith laughed. "Or Golden Princess. There's no hiding anything
from you!"

She poured the canteen's cup full. "I was just about to have a bit of a
snack and a drink of water."

Órlaith signed the food with the pentagram of the Old Faith, pressed
her palms together and murmured:

"Harvest Lord who dies for the ripened grain—
Corn Mother who births the fertile field—
Blessed be those who share this bounty;
And blessed be the mortals who toiled with You
Their hands helping Earth to bring forth life."

"Is that like saying Grace?" the girl asked. "It sounds pretty."

"It is much like saying Grace, yes," Órlaith said, remembering her grandmother's own hands holding hers, showing her the way of it.

She broke open one of the scones. It was fresh enough to steam very faintly, and the smell was tantalizing.

"Walking is hard work when you don't know your path. Share this with me, then, eh? And perhaps you've a bit of a thirst upon you as well. Travelers should help each other."

Young Juniper hesitated for a second, then:

"Thank you!"

That was said in mannerly wise, but she was obviously dry and hungry too. She gulped down the cup of water, and made an inarticulate sound as she bit into the other scone. Órlaith refilled the cup, touched a crumb to it and set it aside.

"And as for your kinsman Frank Mackenzie, he'll know I'm here when I bring you back to him, eh?"

"Thanks, Ooor-la!"

Then after inarticulate sounds of enjoyment: "This is good!"

After courteously swallowing first, and drinking from the cup again with obvious relief:

"Why did you do that? With the crumb."

"Why, that's a thank offering, part of saying Grace, you might say. To Lord Cernunnos and Lady Flidais."

"Who are they? Saints? Or like the Virgin Mary?"

"No, not saints, nor yet the Queen of Heaven in her blue mantle, though something like. You see, the Lord and the Lady . . . the great ones whose joining makes all that is . . . have many faces. And in the wild places of the earth, here in the forests, They are Cernunnos and Flidais. She of the white deer, and He the Horned Man, the Piper at dawn and twilight, that speaks the wildness in our souls and draws us beyond the fields we know."

Juniper's eyes went wide. "The . . . the Piper . . . like in *The Wind in the*

Willows? It's not just a story? It felt like . . . well, that part felt like . . . I always wished . . ."

"*Just a story?*" Órlaith said. "Why, girl, the world of human-kind is *made* of stories!"

"But . . ."

Her brows knotted, and Órlaith nodded. Children appreciated it when you took them seriously, and that was a weighty matter.

"I know what you mean. Yes, part of that story is what the man Grahame made from the stuff of his mind and heart; it's true, but not in the way your shoes are true."

Juniper giggled, and nodded and wiggled her feet to show she understood.

Clever, this one . . . sharp . . . but I knew that, Órlaith thought, and went on:

"But the Piper at the Gates of Dawn . . . when he spoke of that he touched something from outside his fancy, something deeper and truer. Something that is *more true* than shoes or scones. Do you see?"

"I . . . yeah, I think so. So there's the Lord and Lady, but they have many faces? Like masks?"

"Not quite. For the faces are true and real, not a false seeming like a mask. But behind them is another truth."

She dropped into Gaelic: "And would you be having this tongue, then?"

"I do! I do that! I talk it with my mother!" the youngster replied in Erse, abandoning what remained of her reserve as she chatted in what was obviously the tongue of home and love to her:

"Are you Irish yourself like her, then? It's from *Oileán Acla* she is, off the west coast of Ireland, where they speak the old tongue yet. I talked with *her* mom last Christmas, my grandma. I've never seen her, but we talked on the telephone, and she was so happy I could talk to her in Irish."

"No, I'm not from Erin myself, though full a many of my ancestors were. It's a beautiful language, a tongue of brave warriors and great poets and sweet song, and my father and his mother spoke it often with me. Yes, and sang the old songs to me too."

Juniper nodded, and then sang herself, the child's voice light but holding more than a hint of the purity and power it would as an adult:

"A bhean úd thíos,
Air bhruach an tsrutháin
Seothu leo, seothu leo . . ."

Órlaith laughed and took up the ancient lullaby:

"Do you understand my complaint?
Seothu leo, seothu leo
It's a year today since I was abducted from my horse
Seothu leo, seothu leo
It is I who was brought to the fort in the grassy hill . . ."

Then they joined in the chorus:

"Seoithin, seoithin, seoithin, seoithin,
Seo ul leo, seo ul leo.
Seoithin, seoithin, seoithin, seoithin,
Seo ul leo, seo ul leo."

Juniper looked at the bow beside Órlaith and reached out a hand and then looked for permission before picking it up and looking closely at it.

"Gosh, this is heavy! And it's so pretty!"

"It's a longbow of yew from these very mountains, and black walnut for the riser, and from the hand of a master-bowyer. It's just exactly what it is, and that makes for beauty."

In fact I'd swear it's Edain Aylward Mackenzie's work.

The girl's brows clouded. "Are you a hunter? I don't like hurting things."

"Nor do I, nor would I hunt on another's land without their leave and without need. But look you, child."

She pointed out into the meadow. "Our Lord the Sun pours down His power and His love to Earth the Mother, and from that joining the grass and the flowers arise, giving of themselves that those butterflies may live, and . . . yes!"

A dark-blue and orange bird swooped past, a moth in its beak, and vanished into the trees.

"So the bird takes what is needful to it. And the deer feed on the grass, and we upon the deer, and when the Huntsman comes for us in our turn we give back of our bodies to the Dark Mother, for Earth but lends them to us for a while."

Juniper was listening intently, her bright brows drawn down over slitted eyes. Órlaith felt her breath catch: this was what her grandmother had told *her*, the same words and not far from this very place.

What did the Wanderer say to Da? That Time is not an arrow; Time is a serpent. Fact becomes history, history becomes legend, legend becomes myth . . . and myth turns again to its beginning to create itself.

"And we too are part of the great turning of the Wheel. So if we take from need, and without wantonness we are like the wolf and the bobcat. With due respect to the creatures who give their life for us, and give honor to Cernunnos and Flidais who grant us of Their bounty, then this is right and fitting. Also, roast venison with onions and apples is a fine dish on a cold winter's night!"

Juniper's smile returned. "That sounds like a story!"

"It is, and a true story too," Órlaith said, which was true itself. "Shall I tell you a story?"

Juniper gave her gap-toothed grin. "Oh, *yeah!* I love 'em."

"Well, this is a story of the Lady Flidais, one of whose names was Sadhbh, when she was the deer maiden."

Órlaith sounded a few notes on the pipe and then sang:

"*Ní iarrfainn bó spré le Sadhbh Ní Bhruinnealla,
Ach Baile Inis Gé is cead éalú ar choinníní.*

Óra a Shadhbh, a Shadhbh Ní Bhruinnealla,
A chuisle is a stóirín, éalaigh is imigh liom."

"Now, there was a fair maiden named Sadhba, who was beloved of Fer Doiro, who was a Druid and a powerful magician of the *Tuatha Dé Danann,* the Men of the Green Mounds; but she would have none of him. In his anger at her scorn he by enchantment turned her into a deer—"

"What a jerk!" Juniper exclaimed.

"True, a jerk of the jerkiest jerking jerkdom. Now, when she had been a deer for three years—"

When she finished Juniper clapped and cheered, and then suddenly threw her arms around Órlaith and hugged her. Órlaith returned it, kissed her on the forehead, and said:

"Now come, and let's get you home to your kinsman, who'll be worried. Give me your hand, for it's steep just over here."

They walked down the girl's back trail, and Órlaith nodded at a particular spot. "Did you set out leaves there?"

"Yes. I read about how you could mark your own trail and not get lost. But they're gone!"

"No, disarranged. Maybe by your own foot, or a gust of wind, or a passing fox. To leave a marker, leave one that can't be easily moved. Like this."

She took a gray strip of bark from a hemlock and thrust it under a root. "See? Yet it looks natural enough."

"And I put a hair ribbon on a branch, but that was gone too."

Órlaith laughed. "Like those?" she said; the ribbons holding Juniper's fiery braids were sparkly with some odd kind of flecks. When the youngster nodded, she went on:

"Oh, the crows do love bright things, and they're thieves by nature, pirates of the winds. Likely your ribbon is the pride of a crow's nest now, and the envy of its flock!"

The sun was low when they came to a shoulder of land not far above the cabin that would one day be Dun Juniper; you could get glimpses of the patterned green and brown of crops in the valley-land to the west, when the trees were right. There was a circle of oaks here, plainly planted or transplanted by the hand of man, and they were already towering tall, with their branches touching far overhead.

Though not as much so as she remembered, and without the shaped boulder of the altar within.

And it feels . . . more free. Not so flat as most of this place . . . this time, rather.

Órlaith made the sign of the Horns, touching it to her heart and bowing. Juniper looked at her curiously.

"What's that?"

"Ah, that's the Horns. This is a place . . ." she thought before she went on, and decided on simple truth.

"This is a place of magic. And that magic is yours, for your kin planted these trees, did they not?"

"Yup. My great-uncle's granddad. I really like it here—I come and read stories and think and stuff."

Órlaith nodded. "And planted in a circle, and of the holy oak. So your kin brought into the woods something of human kind, a meeting-place between our world of common day and the Otherworlds. And by their toil and sweat, the joy and tears upon it, the songs they sang and the children they bore, and by their bones buried beneath the ground they made themselves part of the land's long story forever."

"Oh," Juniper said softly, and looked up into the rustling tops of the trees.

They walked on down the steep switchback trail; it was more overgrown than Órlaith remembered, to the big cabin that would one day be the kernel of a steading, a Dun, and a clan. That structure of great squared logs surrounded by a verandah stood strong in a broad stretch of nearly level meadow, thick grass and clumps of trees that included exotics like black walnut. There was a small stable, and rosebushes and a substantial neatly-tended kitchen garden showing lines of cabbage and carrot, tomato and strawberry beds and trellised beans in rich brown earth mulched with straw.

Smoke came from the stone chimney and a savory smell was in the air, but an elderly man in a plaid shirt and jeans was just setting out with a lantern and a walking stick, an almost equally elderly-looking gray-muzzled hound at his heels. His wrinkled face relaxed as he saw the child, who took off whooping and flew into his arms.

He hugged her and scolded at the same time: "You gave me a fright, girl! Didn't I tell you to be careful?"

Then he rose upright again, still holding her hand. "I'm very much obliged to you . . ."

"Órlaith Mackenzie," she said, shaking his offered hand; his eyes went over her bow and quiver without comment.

"Maybe we're relatives!" he said. "Frank Mackenzie; this is my place . . . our family's farm, once. They say my great-great grandfather claimed it because it reminded him of East Tennessee . . . forgetting why he didn't want to farm in East Tennessee anymore."

"We may well be kin, though it's a common enough name," Órlaith said with a smile. "I found this wee adventurous slip of a girl a bit unsure of her way, so I brought her back. I'm sorry for your worry."

"I was worried! You're welcome to say for dinner, Miss Mackenzie; just some venison stew and a salad, and biscuits. Though I am *proud* of my biscuits"

He cocked an eye at Juniper. "And some ice cream for dessert."

Órlaith laughed at the brightening of the child's face. "No, I wouldn't want to take ice cream from little Juniper's mouth," she said.

"Juniper?" he said.

"Órlaith said I could use that for a name because it suited me," the girl said.

"And thank you for your hospitality, but I have places to be and promises I must keep," Órlaith said. "Good fortune go with you, Mr. Mackenzie. That's a lively little girl you've got there, your niece—but better too much energy than too little, and too little fear than too much, eh?"

"Right! Thank you again, and drop by anytime."

"Órlaith means Golden Princess!" Juniper informed him. "You spell it
Ó-r-l-a-i-t-h but say it Ooorla."

"It does," Órlaith said. She bent to take a final embrace, and whispered
in her ear:

"Can you keep a secret?"

There was a quick nod.

"And the secret is that I *am* a princess of a far kingdom, with tall castles
and witches who cast spells, and shining knights and ships under sail, and
that you'll see it all yourself one day!"

The pair waved until she disappeared among the trees.

Órlaith walked up the trail, and it was the trail up from Lost Lake. The
Sword of the Lady hung at her side, and the fringe of her plaid brushed
the calf of her leg where it hung down behind her, and it was a chill
fall day.

"It's over," she said to herself. "Or . . . perhaps not."

There were tents and pavilions in the clearing, the sound of horses, a
trumpet blowing briefly . . . but they weren't the ones she remembered.
She didn't recognize any of the people at first glance either, and especially not the young woman walking down towards her . . . with the
Sword of the Lady at her side. She turned and waved to another woman
of her own age, one with long blond hair . . . and with Deor Godulfson's
harp slung over her back, or at least the unmistakable tooled-leather carrying case he used.

Órlaith retreated a few yards, until the others were out of sight. That
gave her more time to study the newcomer. About her own age and with
something familiar in her face, something of Órlaith or of her father and
mother and grandparents.

But differences, as well. She was shorter, about five-eight or nine to
Órlaith's five-eleven, and a bit broader in shoulder and hip. A little
broader in the face, too, with high cheekbones and a shorter nose; there
was a small scar on one cheek and a tiny continuation on the tip of her

nose, looking healed as if they'd been suffered several years ago. Her eyes were narrow and a little tilted, somewhere between gray and green, and the hair drawn back in a ponytail was very dark-brown, with reddish highlights that looked as if they'd been brought out by the sun.

She was dressed in a fashion not quite familiar either, with half boots and cross-gartered loose gray trousers and a knee-length tunic of gray-green with a little blue embroidery about the hems, and a forest-green cloak hanging off one shoulder held by a broach that was worked in the Crowned Mountain and Sword in silver and niello. A broad-brimmed hat with an osprey feather in its band hung down her back.

She's mine, Órlaith thought, and felt herself stagger a little; a few deep breaths cured that. *My blood and . . . whose? Going on down the years . . . our ancestors and our children's children, all one here . . .*

"Hello, and well-met," she said.

The other woman started and dropped into a fighter's crouch, her hands going to the hilts of sword and dagger in a fluent cross-draw motion. Then she froze, her eyes going wide, and stood.

"Mother?" she said, wonderingly. *"Mother?"*

Órlaith laughed and held up a hand. It was strange, to feel this sudden rush of overwhelming love for someone she'd never met.

"No," the stranger said. "You're—you're my mother when she became High Queen, aren't you? Oh . . . Mom . . ."

Grief marked her face. Órlaith shook her head. "We of House Artos are not a long-lived breed, my darling," she said.

They embraced. Órlaith drew back, her hands on the other's strong shoulders.

"And this is just a wee bit of a surprise to me too, you know," she said, and grinned. "To quote what my own father said to me in *just* these circumstances . . . let me guess, the realm's in danger and you face a great trial. . . ."

Laughter greeted that, though her daughter looked a little more grave by nature than she thought herself.

"Oh, Herry—Grand Constable d'Ath—*said* that you'd say that! You never said a *word* to me about it! And . . . if you're newly Queen, then you're off overseas to face—"

"Nor must you tell a word to me, child . . . except perhaps your name?"

"Darya . . . from my father's mother . . . Oh. . . ."

"Welcome Darya; welcome and farewell, fare ever well. Now listen. This is what we must do, and something of what you'll face. This is more than a ceremony. This is a rite, a mystery, that weaves our blood into the history of the land, through time and space, and we into it. . . ."

CHAPTER SIXTEEN

CHOSŎN MINJUJUŬI INMIN KONGHWAGUK
(KOREA)
NOVEMBER 25TH
CHANGE YEAR 47/2045 AD

"We can't force our way past those forts," Admiral Naysmith said, lowering her binoculars from their latest scan of Pusan. "And the landward approaches to the port are heavily fortified as well."

Órlaith nodded, feeling the long slow heel of the warship's hull as it moved across the wind hard enough to throw foam down its flanks. She could see one massive low-slung castle with a pagoda roof on its citadel from here, crowning a mountain blue with distance, and there were more of the grim-looking piles she couldn't. The morning breeze from the shore carried more than the usual city stinks; there was something cold and dry about it, though the temperature was no more than brisk by the standards of the Columbia Valley near the winter solstice. Something like a tomb.

"This is the warmest part of Korea," Reiko warned. "At this time of year, much of the rest of it is very cold. The northern parts are very, very cold."

And there was a hint of sour rot, though that might be the way her mind was interpreting what the Sword was telling her.

Usually I get a sense of the life of a land and the Powers that ward it when I first see it, she thought. *Japan was like that—as if every tree and rock were greeting us, as well as the people . . . I didn't think you could kneel and press your forehead to the ground and radiate dancing joy at the same time, but they did. And greeting Reiko even more, which was just and right, especially when she brought the Grasscutter back to the Land of the Gods; I could sense the* kami *themselves paying her homage. Her name will live forever in their histories as my da's will in ours, and in their songs and stories— Reiko the Great, who quested far for the great treasure, rescued her people and brought them strong aid to end the terror from the sea. But this place . . . it's not only darkened, it's dead, as if something had driven the very life and memories of the land downward into the core.*

"Crawling with troops, too, according to the Dúnedain Ranger and Yellowstone Scout parties we inserted ashore," General Thurston said thoughtfully.

The quarterdeck of the *Sea-Leopard* was an improvised conference room again, which was less trouble now that the ship wasn't doing anything more active than beating back and forth southwest of the harbor entrance and most of the Guard troops were on a separate transport.

"I didn't expect that we could force the harbor, General," Órlaith said. "But we did bottle up their remaining warships."

Reiko nodded. "According to the best intelligence my naval service has, this is all or nearly all of their remaining keels, after their losses in Hawai'i and today. No more than two or three ships of any size remain at large."

The Japanese naval commander Captain Ishikawa, and Egawa of the Imperial Guard—the standing army of Dai-Nippon—looked grimly satisfied in their businesslike but colorful Nihonjin armor.

"Look at the map," Órlaith said; there was one on an easel and she used a finger to trace a course. "We might keep Pusan under blockade and then send a landing force around to the other side of the peninsula . . . this Inchon place. Then they'd have to divide their forces and we'd be across their line of retreat and near their capital . . . did I say something funny, General?"

General Thurston bowed slightly, still smiling. "My apologies, Your

H— I mean, Your Majesty. It's just that the forces of the old American Republic did exactly that in a war here, and very nearly a full century ago. It was considered a brilliant move, and let them advance quickly to the Yalu—then things went south because the Chinese became involved."

Órlaith sighed. "No offense taken, General. My military education didn't emphasize the period in the century or two before the Change."

He nodded. "Only logical, Your Majesty. Neither did mine, formally. But my great-grandfather landed at Inchon, part of the Marine storming parties. Weapons have Changed back to the traditional forms, but the terrain is the same as it was in his day. I suspect the enemy would be waiting for something like that; they're much more likely to remember it than we are."

"I wish we had more information from the land side," Órlaith said. "Will they stand and fight, or withdraw northward? And we can't keep the horses on the transports indefinitely—if there's a bad storm, we could lose half of them, panicking in their stalls if nothing else."

"This is a stormy sea this time of year, Your Majesty," Ishikawa confirmed, with a bow.

Thurston had his helmet with its stiff transverse crest of red-, white- and blue-dyed horsehair under one arm. He ran his sword-hand over the short crisp mat of graying black curls on his head.

"Their fodder's more than half our shipping needs, too," he said. "Especially the destriers for the men-at-arms. The damned things eat their heads off and they need grain every day."

Her brother John shrugged easily; it clattered a little, since like her he was in half-armor, with plain dark padded arming doublet and breeks beneath it.

"They are *heavy* cavalry, General," he said.

"If I might add something?" Pip said from beside him.

She was in an Association lady's riding dress . . . which happened to be nearly identical to the *hakama* and short kimono that Reiko's samurai wore, an old joke of Delia de Stafford's from the days a generation ago when she'd been the Association's premier fashionista. Pip's were pinstriped and dark maroon respectively, with the Balwyn arms—a Wyvern—on the shoulders, two kukri-knives slung at the rear with the handles jutting out conveniently, a folding slingshot, and a black hat on her tawny locks she called a bowler; it was certainly very round.

She also had a document case slung over one shoulder, and now she pulled something out of it.

"If I might, General, Admiral, Your Majesty?" she said.

Pip was smiling as she said it, and the envelope was blazoned with the emblem of the Kingdom of Capricornia—a red flag with a stylized Desert Rose on it, seven white lobe-shaped petals around a black core, and the Southern Cross to the left.

"My mother's old friend King Birmo of Capricornia has a message for you."

"From that Aussie messenger boat that came in this morning?" Naysmith asked, and got a broad grin of agreement.

She handed it to Órlaith, who opened it—the seal was already broken—and pulled out the documents, turning her back to the shore to break the wind. The realm King Birmo ruled from Darwin was remote from her perspective, but fairly important. About as heavy a weight in the scales of power as one of Montival's more important constituent realms. Say to Boise, with the addition that Capricornia's capital, Darwin, was a major entrepôt and shipping center and was home base to a fairly considerable navy. That meant it could quickly mobilize a lot of liquid wealth from its rich trading companies and banks, without the slow process of hypothecating landed revenues that purely agrarian countries faced. In that respect it was comparable to Corvallis and its oceanic extension at Newport, but with a much bigger hinterland.

"Well, well, well!" Órlaith said, feeling her brows rise and a smile struggle to break free as she read. "Capricornia has declared war on Korea . . . and so have . . . it's quite a list . . . let's see, the Colonelcy of Townsville . . ."

"They'll have something useful. Wouldn't be surprised if Daddy showed up," Pip said. "You can ask him for my hand retrospectively, darling."

"The Royal Democracy of Cairns . . ."

"The democracy thing is a bit of a joke. The Joh dynasty is tyranny mitigated by gross incompetence. Nothing wrong with their troops, though."

"The Bloody Miracle of Bundaberg . . . that's the name of a *country?*"

"Don't ask. Just don't."

"The Republic of Goorangoola . . ."

"All four of them, and their little sheepdog too," Pip observed. "Though if what you need for the war effort is a really good Shiraz-Viognier blend that develops fruit and apricot overtones after a few years in the barrel, their contribution will drive you on to victory."

"Eden . . . *Eden?*"

"Really. Wonderful place for tuna sashimi."

"The Federated Abalone Cooperative of Mallaboota and Stationmasters' Association of Traralgon and Greater Gippsland . . ."

"More significant than Goorangoola . . . very good hard sheep's-milk cheese. . . ."

"The Republic of Tasmania . . ."

"Now, that *means* something."

"New Zealand . . ."

Toa grinned and thumped the butt of his great spear on the deck-planking. "Chur!" he said, obscurely. *"Tu meke!"*

"Major power, about a million people, but it'll take them a while to get stuck in," Pip observed.

Órlaith ran down the list. "We're getting thirty warships of various sizes, including five or so to match our frigates. And an expeditionary force of three or four thousand; they're calling it the Commonwealth Brigade."

Pip nodded. "We call Oz in general the Commonwealth."

"I hope we're not supposed to provide the supplies!" Thurston said. "I'm not aware of any operation that ever failed because someone used too many troops, but there are *plenty* that did because someone used so many he couldn't *feed* them. That happened to Napoleon, even. We're at the thin end here."

Órlaith started handing the papers to Naysmith and Thurston who read them and passed them on; their aides were making frantic notes.

"And they're sending supplies . . . in excess of what they'll need themselves, in fact . . . rice, wheat, milled sorghum, hardtack, salt pork, dried and tinned vegetables and fruit . . . and compressed fodder pellets. . . ."

"That will really help," Thurston said eagerly, scanning the papers for hard numbers. "Ah, *very* nice. I do like having a reserve for emergencies. Which there always are."

Naysmith nodded agreement. "We can switch our own carrying capacity to other items."

Órlaith nodded as well. "That will really help. . . . Oh, and Princess Philippa is now a Colonel in the Capricornian army, and a Major in Townsville's. . . ."

Órlaith raised an eyebrow, wondering why it wasn't a colonelcy in both. Townsville was ruled by Pip's grandfather with her father as the heir, already in charge of day-to-day administration.

"When it comes to Colonels, in Townsville there can be only one," Pip said. "The army goes straight from Major to Brigadier—*Colonel* is the ruler's title, my grandfather's and then my dad's when he goes. It might as well be King, but my grandfather is a stout Windsor loyalist. He was over the moon when they sent him a letter appointing him governor-general and representative of the Crown."

They exchanged a glance; from their discussions it had been that that made Pip's father decide to send her off around the world to see if she could snaffle off a Windsor prince.

Life's little ironies . . . she thought, and went on aloud: "And you're officially liaison between this Commonwealth Brigade and the naval contingent and our forces, I see."

"Well, someone has to do it, and I'm on hand, with links to both camps . . . and a baby in Montival's camp. . . ."

John was looking insufferably smug as his wife smiled; he'd been even more besotted since the birth of young Princess Sandra, and it had been a genuine wrench for him to leave. Órlaith didn't see the point, since babies at that larval stage mostly did nothing but eat, sleep and excrete, but presumably it was different when they were yours.

She met Pip's gray eyes and arched a brow; a slightly carnivorous smile replied. Princess Philippa Balwyn-Arminger had just acquired her very own power base in this war, and one which would give her weight in years to come as well.

Oh, that child was well-named, if she's anything like her mother!

"My Uncle Pete and Aunt Fifi . . . honorary relatives . . . are coming in person, since the Darwin and East Indies Trading Company is handling a lot of the shipping. One last hurrah . . . and probably sniffing for salvage contracts."

The admiral and the general looked at each other. Pip chuckled.

"Don't worry. The Darwin and East Indies Trading Company is a perfectly legitimate firm . . . which has also had strong ties to the King of Capricornia's intelligence services. They've done various errands for Birmo since before I was born. They're reserve officers in the Royal Capricornian Navy . . . and rogues, but honest rogues."

Pip's face was softer for a second, with the fond amusement of a young adult for an indulgently-loved elder member of the family. The elder members in this case were apparently slightly reformed corsairs, but what mattered was who'd dandled you on their knee and told you stories and given you dreams.

Órlaith put her hand on the hilt of the Sword. She didn't like the sensation of information being . . .

Ground up and reshaped, she thought. *Like grain going through a mill with buckets and conveyor-belts, or flax in a factory. But it's certainly a major time-saver.*

"Here's what we'll do," she said.

When she finished—adjutants were still scribbling—both the commanders were looking at her. Thurston had a reminiscent smile on his face, doubtless memories about her father from the Prophet's War. Naysmith blinked slowly; she was probably remembering things veterans had said about the same conflict. John and Pip were both grinning from ear to ear. Reiko gave one of her very, very slight smiles and nodded her head.

"How I wish we had the Mirror!" she said, but in her own language, which nobody here but her followers and Órlaith could understand. "If it could do that, we need to *use* it, not simply have it in a shrine."

Órlaith nodded her head and caught the eyes of the general and the admiral in turn. Thurston probably already had the information from past experience, but it wouldn't be tactful to single Naysmith out. The Royal Navy was a single force that answered to the Crown and it had been built up *since* the Prophet's War ended; when Montival needed an army beyond the Guard regiments, it had to be assembled for the purpose just as her father had to beat the Prophet Sethaz himself.

"Please, let me be clear, Admiral Naysmith, General Thurston. This"— she tapped that palm on the hilt—"does not make me infallible. It doesn't tell me where the enemy is, except through what *we* know. And it doesn't tell me anything at all about their intentions. I can still make mistakes; I just can't make them because I've forgotten a pertinent fact or terrain feature or without knowing the *probable* consequences of my actions."

Naysmith smiled. "I'd accept those limitations, Your Majesty," she said dryly. "If I could only get them."

"We'll need more scouting parties," Órlaith said. "And I'll be going ashore tomorrow after the first wave secures the perimeter."

Behind her Heuradys sighed slightly.

Dzhambul went forward on his belly like an eel, parted the hard thorny scrub ahead of him and peered through the gathering darkness. This slope had probably been forest at one time, since he came across large well-rotted stumps now and then, though right now it was covered in a six-foot fuzz of scrub with occasional rings of saplings. Most of the brush seemed determined to sink thorns right through his mail and padded jacket and into him, or to make him sneeze with its pungent herbal smells. The only thing he raised was his head, to look down the slope towards the road; there was another half bowshot of scrub, and then a steep falloff of tumbled rock that was almost but not quite a cliff, where the vegetation was much more sparse.

It was an excellent road, built by the ancients but carefully kept up— the man-eaters were good at things like that. A battalion's worth of spear-men was marching down it in the dimness right now from one of the mountain fortresses ringing Pusan, in an aura of dust and sweat and ran-cid oil and leather and metal, the scent of war. Behind them came supply carts pulled by oxen, and field-catapults drawn by six-horse teams, all plodding stolidly along. Every tenth man held up a torch tied to the end of his spear, which put them twelve feet above the surface of the road, and together with the three-quarters full moon gave more than enough light for marching on a road.

Much more interesting were the *other* three scouts who were looking down on the same sight just below him. One was holding up binoculars, except when he put them down and made signs with his fingers. The others would lean close to make sure they saw the movements in the dark, then one would write notes on a pad.

That must be some sort of language of signs, Dzhambul thought; he'd heard of such things. *How clever! And useful for work like this. I must remember that.*

All three of them were dressed well for night work, and they'd been very careful. At this level of scouting, luck and numbers helped, and one of Börte's Hawks had stumbled across their trail and fortunately not re-vealed herself.

One of the strangers, a slight girl in dark leathers with some fringes, might have been a Mongol as far as her looks went. The other two were more like Russians, or what the books and stories said Europeans and Americans and Australians looked like; Dzhambul found it less odd than most Mongols would, since his mother had been *Russki.* Their clothing was of the same cut and color, like a uniform—Mongols didn't wear them since their ordinary clothing was usually pretty much the same with mi-nor differences by taste and clan, and just as practical for war as it was for herding and hunting. But some of their neighbors did.

The Han love uniforms for some reason. So do the man-eaters.

The Russki-looking two wore loose trousers and coats of mottled fabrics, with knee-boots and jerkins of tough-looking rough-finished leather. The tunics were probably mail-lined from the way they draped, and they had light flare-necked helmets to hand, covered in the same multihued cloth. He thought one of them had that extremely odd yellow hair like sun-bleached grass, and the other a long scar on his . . .

. . . no, *her* face.

Sex was sometimes surprisingly difficult to tell in circumstances like these, but the way she was lying made the shape of her backside apparent, and his judgment in such matters had gotten much better after a month around Börte and her Hawks.

It had been a bit startling to realize that he'd thought he was seeing people's faces and bodies, when in reality all he was doing was looking at their clothes and filling in details from memory without bothering to really *notice* things. That made the old stories about women passing themselves off as men more believable.

Probably easier still among people where women don't wear pants, he thought.

All of them had swords and knives and bows, with odd little differences of detail like wearing their quivers over their backs rather than at the rear of their belts. It all looked efficient enough. They also all carried light hatchet-like axes through a loop at the small of the back, which was interesting.

I'll bet those are throwing axes, he thought. *Hmmm.*

They kept on taking notes and observing the man-eater column. Dzhambul began working his way back, which was even more difficult than the other way, especially if you had to be very quiet. After a hundred yards or so he came to a slightly broader place where he could turn on his belly and go headfirst until he was out of hearing distance of the strangers.

Gansükh met him there, also on his belly, and Börte was another shape in the darkness.

"You found them?"

"Yes, and they were looking at the *Miqačin* like scouts sizing up an enemy. Doing it fairly well, too. And the enemy of my enemy . . ."

"May be a friend, or at least a useful tool," Börte said clinically.

"Let you and him fight, and I'll take the loot," Gansükh added, grinning.

Dzhambul nodded. You couldn't afford to be too picky, when you were fighting enemies who outnumbered you—and the *Miqačin* did, by a considerable margin. Or at least they outnumbered the forces his people could spare from all the other military problems they had, which wasn't quite the same thing but had about the same effect. Nobody loved the man-eaters, but then again, not many of their neighbors liked the Mongols and their program of taking back anything that had ever been theirs, either. Particularly when all the territory they lived on had been under Mongol rule at one time or another; half the earth shared that history.

An ally or two would be nice. We're effectively allied with the Japanese, even though we have no contact with them and know nothing except that some of them are still alive and still fighting. These other strangers seem stronger than that. We need to know more.

"Let's go have a talk with them under favorable circumstances," he said.

The strangers had left their horses more than a mile off, in a little ravine they'd blocked with brush, hobbled . . . and trained too well to make much noise. The Mongols waited until the foreigners came, with silence and craft enough that they'd have been undetectable to anyone who hadn't known the destination. They started to pull the branches loose—two of them, with the other waiting with an arrow on the string. He and Börte and her second-in-command, and who he considered something of a harridan despite her extremely inappropriate name, "Odval," which meant Chrysanthemum Flower, stepped forward. They were all three unarmed and unhelmed, with their hands up.

Gansükh had been very unwilling to let Dzhambul do this in person, but he himself spoke no language except Mongol, apart from just enough of *Hànyŭ* and several other tongues to say *how much* and *hands up* and *show me your money/food/horse/soldiers*. Dzhambul had carefully refrained from saying that the *zuun*-commander was also extremely unsuited to a diplomatic negotiation because his basic attitude towards all foreigners could be summed up as:

Who dares to approach the Kha-Khan's man, except crawling on his belly begging for mercy?

He brought Börte and one of her Hawks because no women bore arms among the man-eaters, except for (stories said) the inner guard of their ruler's harem. Their hair was done in traditional women's style, with a number of braids woven with colored wool and bound with a headband, which made it more obvious.

"Sain uu. Bid amar amgalan irlee. Mongol kheleer yaridag uu?"

That was safe enough. *Hello, we come in peace* and *do you speak Mongol?*

The Russki-looking woman, who he now saw had a very creditable battle scar on her face that had probably been made by an axe, had been on watch. She whipped up her bow and began to draw—using a curious three-fingered grip, rather than the normal thumb-ring—and Dzhambul threw up one hand and barked:

"Gölög bolokhgüi!"

The rest of the party didn't shoot, but they made enough noise letting the weight off their bowstrings that it was obvious to anyone with keen senses that only his restraint had kept them all from looking like a target at a *Naadam* festival. They spoke among themselves in some liquid-sounding language, and Dzhambul repeated what he'd said in *Hànyŭ*, *Uyghur tili*, Russki and several other languages, though leaving out the *don't shoot* part.

The scarred woman lowered her bow and took some of the draw off, but he knew from the way she handled it that she could shoot very quickly. The other two kept their hands on their hilts, their faces hard and wary, but he thought that the man, who did indeed have that not-quite-human-looking sun-colored hair, grasped a word or two of one of them.

"Mongol?" he said, pointing at Dzhambul and his companions.

He didn't pronounce the word the way the Mongols did, but eventually Dzhambul grasped it and nodded eagerly, pointing to his sister and her retainer and then out into the night—there was no harm in driving home the point that the strangers were outnumbered.

All three were young, now that he had a closer look at their faces; younger than him, in fact. The man pointed to his scarred companion; they didn't really look like Russians, having unnaturally narrow faces and rather large noses.

"Dúnedain," he said. Then at the other girl, and: "Lakota."

Then he indicated them all. "Montival."

Ah, Dzhambul thought, nodding and smiling. *Different clans, same kingdom.*

He called the others down; they cased their arrows and helped tear down the barricade of branches, and Gansükh came to stand beside him.

After a moment the . . . Lakota . . . woman spoke: *"Bi mongol hel zhaahan medne."*

It took several repetitions before he penetrated the atrocious accent enough for the sense of it, that she spoke a *little bit* of Mongol, to come through. Dzhambul smiled broadly; it was rare for outsiders to have any at all. They spoke to each other, slowly and carefully and trying until some meaning came through.

He turned to his companions. "Did you catch any of that?"

"Not a word that she said, Noyon," Gansükh said.

"A word here and there," Börte replied, and Odval just shook her head.

"Well, she seems to be saying that her grandfather was named *Ulagan Chinua*"—which meant Red Wolf —"and was one of us, trapped over there by the Change, and that they *are* Americans . . . or at least from that continent . . . and they're fighting the man-eaters."

"He's saying that yes, they are Mongols, and they're fighting the Koreans, and they want to meet our leaders," Susan Mika said. "I can't be absolutely sure, but I'm pretty confident. But we're not going to get much out of him with just me. He speaks Chinese and something called Uyghur and Russian—maybe one of the Associates from House Stavarov could talk to him?"

"You forget who we're working for," Faramir said with a smile. "And won't this be a treat for her?"

CHAPTER SEVENTEEN

CHOSŎN MINJUJUŬI INMIN KONGHWAGUK
(KOREA)
NOVEMBER 26TH
CHANGE YEAR 47/2045 AD

"*Halt! Who goes there?*"

The three Montivallans leading them reined in, and Dzhambul's party did the same behind them with a ripple of instinctive coordination. A hilltop ahead of them suddenly had about fifty riders on it; they'd come up over the crest, and they all had arrows on the strings of their bows.

"Dúnedain Rangers and a party of envoys!" the man called Faramir shouted back.

Dzhambul thought it was an extremely odd-sounding name, but there were more important matters at hand. Fifty sharp points leveled at him, for instance, with lots of springy horn and sinew ready to drive them home.

One of them came cantering down.

"Yeah, you're Dúnedain," he said, as he pulled up. "What's the password?"

"Hood Hang Glider," Faramir said. "Countersign?"

"Horse Heaven Hills," the man replied, and then examined the Mongols.

"Who are these fellas?"

"Mongols."

"Jebus!" he replied obscurely. "Genghis Khan rides again!" After a long careful glance: "Tough-looking bastards. *And* tough-looking bitches."

Dzhambul picked the words *Genghis Khan* out of the indecipherable English stream and felt a rush of pride; even across the ocean, they remembered the Ancestor. Susan Mika translated the rest, and there were nods and grins when he passed the words along.

The Mongols did the same careful examination in return; the riders were well-mounted, and each was equipped with a mail shirt and the odd low-domed flare-necked helmet and armed with sword and bow; the one who'd come down to look them over had a saddle decorated with silver studs, a projecting horn at the front and a braided-leather lariat slung over the bowcase in front of his left knee, with a round shield over his back.

Hearing English actually spoken was strange. It sounded so odd and staccato and clipped. . . .

"That cavalry screen looked alert," Gansükh said a little grudgingly as they swung back into a trot.

The Montivallan horse-archers on the rise above lowered their bows as their leader returned.

"Yes, they were very alert," Dzhambul nodded. "Which is a good sign."

They'd been doing what cavalry screens were supposed to, establishing a cordon; he'd picked out one or two hidden stationary observers, too, and was fairly sure that there were others.

"I'd like to see them shoot, though. Their bows aren't exactly the same as ours. That riser with the cutout looks clever, and their arrows are stiffer-splined because of it."

"Yes, but they don't have ears at the ends," Börte said, referring to the stiff rigid outer parts of a Mongol bowstave that acted as levers. "You can see that the string lies along the curve of the bow right up to the nock. It must come off as the stave pulls through and bends back. I wonder how well that works."

Dzhambul shrugged. If there was one thing Mongols could talk about endlessly, it was archery and its gear. He'd like to see them shoot too, but he was willing to bet they were fairly good at it.

"They *ride* well," she said.

"True," Dzhambul said. "And that usually goes with shooting well."

As they passed on at a slow trot-canter-trot one of the cavalry pickets came down the fairly steep part of hillside they'd been watching from at a flat gallop, not bothering to go around to the gentler northwestern slope. He sped off across the low ground ahead, without breaking pace and bow in hand, the reins knotted on the neck of his horse and leaving them behind quickly.

Off to announce us, Dzhambul thought.

The saddle the Montivallan cavalry used was only slightly odd-looking; they also let their stirrup leathers out a bit longer than was steppe custom, with the knee bent but not sharply. It seemed to work. The Mongols' eyes followed the man. They could all have done the same easily enough, but . . .

"I don't think they're farmers at all," Dzhambul said. "Not the ones we're seeing here, at least. I think they're herders, plainsmen. They ride like folk born in the saddle, not just well but as if it was as natural to them as walking."

Dust was hanging over the bit of coastal plain ahead of them, and the sun was setting behind them; that meant they couldn't see much, except that the *amount* of dust argued for a *lot* of movement. They could hear the edge of the growling racket an army made, too; voices shouting, since war meant raising your voice a lot, boots, hooves, hammers pounding in tent pegs, hammers on anvils as someone set up a field-forge.

"They shoe their horses," Börte noted.

The *other* thing their people talked about, even more than archery, was horses; only the state of the grazing and weather came close—though there was ample justification for that, since a *tumer dzud*, a combination of a brief thaw and intense cold could kill half the livestock in the country and mean hunger for all.

The two men nodded, having seen the steel shoes on every mount.

There were advantages both ways, though Mongols mostly left their horses without. That was fine on the grass of the steppe or the sand of the Gobi, and if it went unshod a horse's hooves were naturally tougher. Though there was no disputing that shod hooves held up better on rock or gravel or in soft wet dirt or on pavement.

They'd had several mounts go lame on their flight south, which was why they'd eaten a lot of horsemeat, mostly raw.

Then again, for shoeing you had to drag a lot of weight around in the form of farriers, their anvils and fuel and tools, and the shoes themselves, since horseshoes needed to be renewed frequently and it needed a skilled hand to put one on, or take it off for that matter. Dzhambul had learned a little of the craft years ago, just in case.

There were also odd metallic ratcheting sounds from the camp ahead . . . and the smell of massed smoke and sweat and crap that accompanied armies like an invisible flag. Lights flickered through it, since it was just late enough for fires to show, and the odd blink of metal catching the falling sun.

"Those look awkward," Börte said, as they and their escorts passed a block of men on foot, marching along carrying giant spears sixteen feet long.

Then the three Mongols watched silently as a trumpet sounded. The great weapons the infantry were carrying swung down to present a line of points four deep and then back upright without a lost pace in the block of men. Apparently, they spent much time in practice. . . .

"Or possibly not so awkward as I thought," Dzhambul said, and Gansükh grunted thoughtfully. "Even if that was put on for our benefit."

The two Dúnedain and the Lakota woman were watching the Mongols watch the pikemen. Dzhambul was fairly certain that Susan Mika didn't speak Mongol better than she'd let on, but that wasn't the same as being *absolutely* certain.

"Perhaps you're right," Börte said. "I wouldn't want to charge them if they had an unbroken front."

Noise and dust grew as they penetrated deeper into the newcomer's perimeter, but there was little confusion. But . . .

There are so many different styles of gear and clothing!

He thought he recognized the Japanese samurai from descriptions in rumors and old books, but the others! Much of what he saw was so strange that the eye of the mind slipped off it, and he had to deliberately focus. All the Mongols were maintaining a good stone face; his people had that reputation among strangers, while in reality they were mostly cheerful and talkative . . . under ordinary circumstances and among their own.

There were a lot of soldiers coming ashore, and a fair number with their boots already on the rocky beach in the pale light of a winter dawn. The sun rising out over the sea backlit the spiky forest of . . .

Masts, he thought. *That's the word.*

. . . and many boats propelled by oars, which looked more familiar from those he'd seen on rivers, and lakes like *Dalai Eej.* Others were more broad and stubby, like floating boxes, and were carrying catapults and horses. Those got keenest attention from all his party; the beasts ranged from those not unlike the steppe ponies or Börte's Uyghur horse, to monsters taller than most men at the shoulder, long-legged muscular beasts like the vision of a horse in the mind of one of the *Tengri.*

"Those things probably have trouble turning quickly and I'd say they don't have much endurance," Gansükh said critically. "And look, they're feeding them *grain,* as if they were human beings, or at least Han peasants. How can you keep an army moving if you have to carry along grain for the mounts? Though feeding on the enemy's stocks is all right, of course, if you're careful not to founder the animals."

Mongol ponies had strong guts, but they could bloat themselves to death if allowed to eat too much rich food like oats or millet. Horses were like children confronted with honeycomb that way.

"Yes, but they could probably knock a horse-shaped hole in a fortress wall in a charge," Börte said. "And they'd be fast enough with some time to get going. Imagine one ramming into your horse shoulder-to-shoulder at speed."

"They'd bowl you over like a rabbit," Gansükh said immediately, estimating the weights and then adding in the suit of steel armor the riders wore. "Then trample you into mutton fat. Best not be where they want to run, then. Stand off and pepper them."

Some of the riders were covered in articulated steel plates from head to toe, and carried lances twice the height of a tall man. Many others were armed more normally to Mongol eyes, and the foot soldiers were obviously not the sort of peasant rabble he was accustomed to in that role.

Field engineers had marked out a fortified camp and other troops were either standing guard or had stacked their wildly varied arms to dig under the specialists' supervision. Piled up beside them were other materials; angle-iron posts, coils of barbed wire, which might be salvage or made post-Change, and baulks of timber with steel spikes driven through them to create barriers. The troops were swinging picks and using shovels to throw the dirt from the ditch on the inside, where still more pounded it flat in layers. Watchtowers of prefabricated wood with sheet-metal exteriors were going up too.

It looked as if it had all started that morning and was about half-finished, and the Montivallans hadn't landed in strength more than a day or two before that. Dzhambul pursed his lips and looked at his sister, who replied with a similar expression and a nod. The Mongol armies had good engineers, some their own, trained in schools in Ulan Bator and on the job, some hired Han or Russki experts, but they were both impressed. Of course, an army composed almost entirely of mounted archers had less need for field fortifications than one with a lot of infantry and wheeled supply trains like this, but it was still impressive. He also mentally increased the size of the Montivallan army overall; he'd been calculating on the area needed for cavalry and their remounts, and you could get a lot more footmen into the same space.

"Forts," Börte said.

"Yes," Dzhambul replied.

Korea had a *lot* of forts. Relative to the size of the place, it had even more than the Chinese states to the south of Mongolia, past the ruins of the old Great Wall, and that was saying something. It had a lot of very *big* forts, combined with much more mountainous terrain than China. If the men from across the eastern sea were as good as this at digging in, they were probably good at siege-work generally. Which left the question of why they were here, and how determined they were. No matter how good your gear or training, laying siege to forts and walled cities was slow work, expensive in treasure and in blood.

"Funny-looking bastards," Gansükh said as the Mongol party went through various checkpoints, in a tone of queasy disgust. "Their skins are almost leprous, as if they grew up in caves."

"That's not fair. They can't help the, ah, the *odd* way they look," Börte said. "Though I admit, even my mother wasn't *that* ghostly."

The oddness *was* more than the clothes. Most of the strangers had the odd bleached blood-pinkish tone that the two Dúnedain, whatever that meant, shared, and even odder beaky elongated faces. And they were elongated in body too; Dzhambul was used to being taller than most, and now found himself no more than average. Though others were perfectly normal in appearance, and some were a very dark brown that made them look like overdone bread, nearly as odd-looking as the pink ones.

The gateway to the camp was made by overlapping two stretches of the earthen wall they were building, so that you had to take a ninety-degree turn to get inside. There were gates, set up on wheels so that they could be rolled aside.

I'd hate to have to attack these gates; you'd have enemies shooting at you from both sides, Dzhambul thought. *That's really very clever. These people take war seriously and think about it.*

Inside the growing earthen wall, tents were going up beside a rectangular grid of streets, along with horse-lines and vehicle-parks full of wagons or parts of wagons being knocked together. Field kitchens and hearths were being lit, and there was a smell of unfamiliar cooking as soldiers formed lines with empty bowls ready. The grilling meat was unmistakable, but there were strange spices—Mongols didn't usually use many at all besides salt—and odd yeasty odors. And someone was boiling rice not far away, which he at least recognized.

There was an inner core of guards; archers on foot, with bows of an absolutely unfamiliar make that were taller than they were. They wore pleated skirts, knee-length and all of the same checked pattern, some had savage-looking designs painted on their faces, and in this contingent nearly as many were women as men.

Börte smiled slightly. "I think I like them already," she said, and Gansükh sighed inaudibly and rolled his eyes.

One of their officers, a scar-faced man in middle years, held up a hand imperiously. The trio of Montivallan scouts swung down from the saddle, and Dzhambul followed suit . . . although putting himself on the ground among so many folk who were so unreasonably tall and mostly armored to boot was a little disconcerting, like running back in time to a child-hood memory of toddling around among adults.

The three exchanged words with the guard officer; the short one who looked a little like a Mongol raised her voice and slapped the hilt of her sword. The man shrugged and spread his hands, and darted the Mongols a look.

"I'd bet he wanted to disarm us," Gansükh said.

Nobody objected when they kept their sabers and daggers, though they tactfully left shield and bow with their horses, which made the quivers slung at their belts merely symbolic.

"As the Kha-Khan's *Kheshig* guards would, with unknown strangers in a hostile land," Börte said.

Gansükh gave her a baffled look as if to ask what that had to do with anything. Of course no stranger would be allowed armed before the Khan, and of course the Khan's men should go where they pleased as they pleased whatever damned foreigners wanted.

No, the Tengri *did not make him of the leather from which diplomats are sewn,*

Dzhambul thought affectionately—he'd come to like the blunt-spoken officer a good deal. *Fortunately, he does not have to try.*

He took a deep breath and threw his shoulders back. He *did* have to try, and the fortunes of his people in this war might well depend on his success. A lane was cleared for him at a word of command; he and Gansükh and Börte were ushered forward and the rest kept back. He could see Gansükh start to object, then shrug—they were eighteen among an army of thousands, and if the outlanders wanted to kill him, they could.

The last circle of guards were in plate armor, but of a type that came only to the thighs; he could pick out the details, because large and very bright lamps had been lit, mounted on poles. Their flared helmets had visors, smooth curves with a long narrow slit across the eyes like a window into a cave as they turned to follow him. The hair tried to start up on the back of his neck, and he forced it down again, scolding himself for being childish.

They stood with the butts of their weapons planted between their boots, seven-foot shafts with a long angular cutting blade on the top like a giant slanted straight razor that in turn topped by a foot of spike and backed by a cruel-looking hook. The three Mongol leaders gave them a considering look; with a strong skilled man behind it that thing could be very dangerous to a horseman at close range, and the armor would make it very, *very* difficult to use a sword downward to any effect. It was probably good protection against arrows from a distance, too.

"These bastards are dangerous," Gansükh murmured. "And not just because they're rich and have good weapons. They've had wars since the Change where they come from."

"Like us?" Dzhambul said, making himself smile.

Gansükh shook his head doggedly. "But they've had different *kinds* of wars. I know how to fight the Han and the Uyghurs and Kazakhs and the man-eaters. I wouldn't know how to fight these people, but I have this feeling that we wouldn't be nearly as much of a surprise to them as they would be to us and it would be a bad time while we learned."

He is thinking in terms of fighting them, but the same thought gives me hope, because it shows they can fight the man-eaters. I'm not afraid of them killing us, I'm more afraid of failure to get their help, he thought. *I don't suppose they're going to turn around and go away because of anything I say or do, but* Tengri *witness, what a gift an alliance would be to the Kha-Khan my father, and to all the Mongol people!*

The fact that he hadn't suspected there was anything to *win* until just now made the thought of failure worse, not better.

"If it's any comfort, they're a lot farther from home than we are, Gansükh," Börte said. "I think it must be a strain for them to fight here . . . and that going to where we live would be even worse for them. Like us trying fight a war in the Kirghiz marches."

Gansükh grunted again. "Well, you have a point, Princess. We're a people of the steppe, and from the look of all the ships, they're a sea people."

He paused a moment, then went on: "But from the look of their cavalry, they know about steppes too. And we *did* fight the Kirghiz in the Ancestor's time, yes, and went beyond to sack Moscow."

He's no fool, Dzhambul thought. *And he can think of new things, if he must.*

The guards with the spear-axe-hook things all had the stylized head of an animal on their breastplates in orange paint; from the chisel teeth, he thought it was meant to be a beaver.

The foreign commanders were grouped around a table and easels with maps on them, itself shielded from the wind by fabric screens on poles. He recognized the Japanese from descriptions, but saw with surprise that their self-evident ruler was a young woman. You could tell the bubble of deference through your skin if you'd grown up with courts, and it was even less likely that she'd be a general or something of that order, considering that the armed followers with her were all men and included a scarred middle-aged obvious commander with a curved blade in place of his left hand.

So. A monarch, or someone else of very high hereditary rank.

A moment later he saw that the foreign leader . . .

The Mon-ti-vallan *leader,* he reminded himself, mentally pronouncing it for practice sake; if he spelled it out in his head he could see that it said something about mountains and valleys.

. . . was also female and about his own age. It took a moment or two to be sure of her sex, longer than it had with the Japanese woman.

Because she was towering, easily three inches taller than he, and wearing trousers tucked into boots and a long padded jacket with leather laces here and there that was obviously intended to be worn under armor, with the expected smells of old cold sweat and oil. Her braided hair was grain-yellow with hints of a fire color, and her eyes were bright blue; the face was blade-thin, and at first glance harshly ugly, a cruel eagle-like caricature of a human being. Then he saw it was regular and quite handsome, even beautiful in a strange way, simply so in a manner very different from what he was used to. Even his own mother had been normally stocky and snub-nosed, though pale and taller than average.

Their eyes met, and he felt a slight shock. They stayed locked for a moment and then he looked down, feeling slightly winded.

Crossed belts of tooled leather at her waist held the things you'd expect, a dagger and pouches . . . and a long straight double-edged sword. Apart from the alien form and the superlative workmanship—the pommel was some sort of strange jewel the size of a chukar's egg that almost seemed to glow on its own in the lamplight—there was something about it that made his eyes prickle. If you looked into the moon-colored jewel, distances seemed to open. Each beyond the other, deeper and deeper. And deeper, like the patterns you saw in the clouds, and deeper, until a tune hummed in your head. . . .

He wrenched his vison away. Then his eyes flicked back to the Japanese ruler. *Her* sword was a katana, a form he knew about even if he hadn't seen it often. The sheath was lacquered black . . . but there were specks of golden light in it, and they were *moving*. Like golden stars in the deepness of a night sky, but in motion. He had the same prickling feeling from looking at it. Or not, though it was similar and similarly uncanny; it was *hotter*, somehow. Threatening, but in an impersonal way.

Like watching an idugan *working a summoning,* he thought, his eyes going wide. He pulled his eyes away from that, too.

All three of the Mongols bowed; Gansükh adjusted his to be deeper than the two children of the Khan, though the degree made him scowl.

No, not born to ride a diplomat's saddle, Dzhambul thought.

Then Dzhambul spoke in slow Russian, as he remembered it from his mother. She had taught her children off and on, if only to have someone she could speak to in her own tongue, but she had died when he and Börte were in their mid-teens and he hadn't had much occasion to use it since.

"Does anyone here speak this language?"

"I do," the Montivallan leader said.

Then she shifted into his own:

"But wouldn't you rather that we spoke Mongol? We are closer to your home than to mine . . . or to Russia, for that matter."

All three of them simply stared for a moment, astonished; he felt his own mind slip and gibber, Gansükh swore under his breath, and if you knew her well you could tell Börte only just managed to smother a startled laugh. The Montivallan Queen spoke Mongol. She spoke *very good* Mongol, without any accent that he could detect.

Dzhambul drew a breath. When he spoke it was proudly. These people had great power at their backs, but so did he . . . even if it was a little farther *behind* his back right now, while they could rest their shoulders against their backing.

"I am Prince Dzhambul son of Qutughtu, Qutughtu Kha-Khan of all the *Yeke Mongghol Ulus;* of the clan of the Borjigin, descendant of the Ancestor, Temujin, Genghis Khan, who was by the blessing of the *Tengri* ruler of all that lay beneath the Eternal Blue Sky. This is my sister, the Princess Börte; and our trusted commander Gansükh son of Tömörbaatar."

The yellow-haired woman smiled and inclined her head rather than bowing; which was fair enough, she was a sovereign and he wasn't. And a sovereign with a large army around her, a fleet behind her, and the ruler of Japan beside her.

"And I am Órlaith Arminger Mackenzie, High Queen of Montival and all its realms, heir of House Artos, and my totem is the Golden Eagle. This is my ally, the *Tennō Heika* of Dai-Nippon, the Empress of Victorious Peace. It appears we have a common enemy, Prince Dzhambul."

She must have seen his surprise that she demanded no proof. Dropping her left palm to the hilt of the strange sword she said:

"I know you're speaking the truth. Except that your officer . . . who I have no doubt is a strong axe against your enemies and a true iron hero, and well-trusted . . ."

Those were plays on Gansükh's name, and that of his father Tömör-baatar. Dzhambul blinked again. It was one thing to know a language, and another to be able to easily and diplomatically jest in it.

". . . is not your *supreme* commander, is he? As you . . . perhaps . . . meant to imply."

"Commander of a hundred," Dzhambul corrected himself. "We were on a scouting mission and became separated from our forces. Our main army is . . . to the north."

This time she grinned . . . and was that the shadow of a wink?

"Quite a few miles to the north, eh?"

He was startled into a nod, and she returned the gesture and went on:

"Come, let's talk. Briefly for now, then at length tomorrow. I can tell that you've been doing some hard traveling, descendant of the Universal Khan."

"Well," Dzhambul said considerably later, as the Mongol leaders sat around a fire.

It will not do to say that the Montivallan Queen is like a heroine from an ancient tale, he thought. *I must be more practical.*

The rest of the Mongol party was grilling mutton and organ meat from the sheep they'd been given on skewers, toasting barley, and drinking from skins of *airag*, which the late Red Wolf had evidently taught his adopted people to make, and with which the Lakota contingent in this army was plentifully supplied. The Montivallans had politely furnished food, fuel and fodder and plenty of space to let the Mongols talk among themselves.

Most of the troop settled for stolidly stuffing themselves to bursting, after week upon week of stinted rations of raw horsemeat, and then falling deeply asleep in relief . . . after week upon week of rest snatched while standing guard. Mongols learned to take what was available when it was, because soon enough it wouldn't be, whether in war or riding herd in a blizzard.

Though after a while giggles and other sounds from convenient shadowed places showed other priorities for some.

"The Montivallan Queen is like a heroine from an ancient tale," Börte said.

Stoic discipline kept Dzhambul from laughing out loud—that and a desire not to offend his sister, and the thought of explaining that he was laughing at himself. Instead the three leaders stared blankly into the blaze for several minutes before Dzhambul went on:

"Well, well."

Gansükh shivered, something that Dzhambul sympathized with profoundly.

"Ancient tale? Ancient tale with magical powers! Ten thousand devil-spirits! How are we going to deal with people we can't *lie* to?" he said plaintively.

Börte laughed, but there was a quaver in it. "I suppose we'll have to tell the truth," she said.

At Gansükh's threatened explosion she went on: "Or we can simply refuse to discuss some matters."

He snorted. "Princess, refusing to answer a question is also an answer! Not as good as the full details, but still very good! We can't even hide what *we* believe of what they tell *us!*"

Dzhambul made a chopping gesture. "You are both right. And we will not quarrel with each other!"

After a moment they both bowed their heads. He took a skewer from the fire and bit into the meat, clearing his mind and enjoying the crispy taste of the fat at the edge of the lump. He had been hungry for a long time, and he could feel the meat and juices giving him back strength; it was cold enough that the morsel steamed as he fastened his teeth in it. Roasting was a bit wasteful, but he really preferred the taste to boiled mutton.

"We certainly found something worth being away from the main army for so long," he said after he swallowed. "Even my uncle won't be able to complain."

All three of them laughed at the understatement. The three leaders were passing a skin after they ate, but slowly; not that you could really get drunk on fermented mare's milk without a lot of time and effort, since the alcohol content was below two parts in a hundred, usually well below. Even rice wine was like vodka by comparison. The main reason to ferment the stuff was to make it more digestible, since raw mare's milk was a laxative for most people, and to improve the keeping qualities. This was a good skin, dry and slightly tart. Red Wolf had taught his hosts well; they made *ger* of the Mongol style to live in too, apparently, and their country was much like the homeland north of the Gobi.

"Toktamish will most certainly complain," Börte said. "He'd complain about it if we brought the *Ancestor* back to fight with us, unless he could get all the credit for it! Toktamish cares about the glory of Toktamish and nothing else. And he will complain about the strangers' . . . powers . . . as well. Claiming that they league with evil spirits, in order to discredit you and me, brother."

Dzhambul wondered about the . . . powers . . . himself. He wasn't a superstitious man, not being the type who couldn't piss behind a bush without a prayer or a gesture of aversion. Though of course he believed in the *Tengri* and the Bodhisattvas—the Buddhist side of his people's inherited religion had been less prominent since the Change—and performed the rites and sacrifices. He certainly believed in the powers of the *Miqačin*. They were *evil* powers, of course. And *idugan* were in touch with things beyond the world of common day as well. Neither helped him much with this.

Gansükh coughed slightly, took another pull, wiped his mouth with the back of his hand and elaborately looked up at the stars.

"This is good *airag*," he said. "By the way, did you notice that the foreign khatun didn't just speak Mongol, she spoke perfect Sükhbaatar dialect, like someone from court? Like you, Noyon, and your sister the Princess."

That was a gentle reminder that he couldn't get involved with the disputes of the Royal family, especially not when he was a minor officer in an army commanded by the Kha-Khan's brother but containing two of his children, with no love lost between the two branches. He *could* be diplomatic, at home among his own folk and in the world he knew.

Dzhambul and Börte looked at each other. "That's a very acute observation," he said neutrally. "But then, we've seen that you are an intelligent and energetic officer, Zuun-Commander Gansükh, and impeccably loyal."

Which translated as: *yes, we'll look after you*. That would be comforting . . . assuming that the brother and sister could look after themselves. Gansükh was a hard-charging young officer, and probably dreamed of commanding a tümen or more someday. Sharing danger and hardship with the heir would be a straight path to rank, if the heir actually *was* the heir. Dzhambul certainly didn't grudge him a dream of success, since he *was* able and wanted to shine while helping the Mongols to victory and glory.

He glanced at his sister again, and she smiled thinly and nodded. It had occurred to her earlier than it did to him, but if they could produce an alliance with these Montivallans against the man-eaters it would certainly help the realm . . . and it would *almost* certainly help the children of their mother against their uncle Toktamish. If Toktamish gladly accepted the results it would show that he had the good of the Khanate first in his mind. If he didn't . . .

Well, that would clarify some of my choices. May my father live long!

One of the disadvantages of being the child of a man with many wives with separate households was that you didn't see your father much; he'd often envied ordinary men, whose sires were not remote and godlike figures who swept in and departed with no more than a nerve-racking interview. It had probably made him closer to his mother and certainly had given him and Börte a tight bond. And it let him see the man more objectively; he was a competent ruler, if no new Ancestor, and had kept the clans and regions in harmony with one another.

After a spell of silence he took another skewer of meat and blew on it.

"We've stumbled across something new and uncanny," he said after another mouthful. "But we can't let that daunt us—any more than we let the evil spirits who rule the *Miqačin* frighten us out of fighting them when they crossed the Yalu to attack our tributary tribes."

He caught the eyes of both. "We are Mongols. We are descendants of the Ancestor. When we ride to war, our hoofbeats shake the earth. Whatever we find here, we will *use*."

Gansükh drew himself up and threw out his chest. "The Noyon wishes!" he said.

"You should be the one to speak with the Montivallan Queen, mostly," she said thoughtfully.

"Why?" Dzhambul said.

Börte is not shy, nor does she take a step back unless she must, he thought.

"Because you are so brainlessly honest that the power this Sword gives her will not matter much," she said.

Gansükh coughed and covered his lower face with a hand, turning his eyes aside again. Dzhambul looked ruefully at her.

"How have I survived uncorrupted this long, surrounded by oil-tongued flatterers like you, my sister?"

She threw the bag of *airag* at his head, and he caught it and drank.

"And besides," she said sardonically. "You are the handsomest of us. Perhaps you will charm her! You will make her heart flutter with love and she will accept that the Ancestor gave us the right to rule the world!"

Dzhambul chuckled.

Gansükh made a face. "There are things you cannot rightly ask of a man, even for the kingdom and the Kha-Khan," he said, and shuddered. "Death in battle or by torture, yes . . . but not that. She is *hideous!*"

Dzhambul laughed again, uneasily. "Yes, I am better fitted for diplomacy—our sturdy warrior here is even more blunt and honest than I."

"Or a complete idiot," Börte said. "Pass the skin."

CHAPTER EIGHTEEN

"Well, that settles the question of whether they're going to stand and fight," Órlaith said tightly, tapping their location on the map with a gloved finger—it was cold enough that their breaths were smoking even inside the big command tent. "They're not, except for these sacrificial rearguards that protect their withdrawal."

"It makes sense," Thurston said. "Since we couldn't take Pusan or its forts. They may be trying to draw us in, cut us off from our base."

Reiko nodded thoughtfully. "The forts we have attacked have fallen," she said. "But the cost is always high."

Órlaith looked over at Dzhambul. The Mongol prince was looking down at the map, his bluntly handsome face frowning in thought. The evening light and the overhead lanterns lit his face through the gauze windows of the tent.

Not any sort of a fool, she thought. *Quite clever. Straightforward, earnest, but clever. His sister's twice the politician he'll ever be, but I think he'd make a good commander. Or a ruler, with her to advise him. For example, right now she's keeping in the background and absorbing everything the way a piece of hot toast does butter.*

Dzhambul's finger moved on the map. "We've come a long way," he said, tracing the route up from Pusan, past the ruins of Seoul, and farther north. "You've dropped off a lot of troops to cover the enemy fortresses."

Órlaith nodded. "We want to end this war as quickly as we can," she said. "That means . . . well, when my father fought an enemy ruled by the same . . . force, entity . . . in our own land, destroying its central node, its passage into the world in Montival . . . left the rest to die like the body of a headless snake. He told me once that all the battles and marches were *preparations* for that, not ends in themselves as they might be in a war that was strictly one of human-kind."

"You mean, we must kill their ruler?"

"Yes," she said. "And with the Sword of the Lady—though the Grass-cutter would probably do as well. I'm fairly certain he's like the Prophet of the Church Universal and Triumphant was in Montival. The central . . . channel. Deepened over time; more deeply here, because there has been so much *more* time."

"They do not let him be exposed to danger," Dzhambul said. "He does not lead armies in the field; in fact, our reports are that he virtually never leaves his citadel of *Majimag bam-ui geulimja*, of which we know little. No living man who's seen it has ever fallen into our hands . . . and no scout we sent has returned alive."

Órlaith's mind absently corrected his terrible mispronunciation of the Korean words, and then she felt a flush of irritation at how automatic that was . . . automatic in a literal sense. The name translated roughly as *Fortress of Eternal Night*, though her Sword-given knowledge of the modern form of Korean suggested overtones of *Peace* and *Final Rest* in the last part of that. Or possibly *sacred nonexistence*.

The Mongol prince went on: "And what of the other magicians? They have many."

"If we kill the living nexus, it will cut off that part of them that is linked to the dark Power. That will wreck their minds, at the least—leave them like children, the children they were before they were corrupted, in the bodies of men. Some will die. Doing that won't turn the subordinate military commanders into good men, but it will free them of the grip on their souls that keeps them loyal. They'll become warlords and fight one another."

"Evil warlords who treat men as cattle," Dzhambul said, clearly remembering his trip southward; he'd described it to her. "The grip of the *kang-hsinmu* has lain long on this land, and corrupted everything it touched."

"Yes, but there are evil men everywhere. You Mongols can fight ordinary local warlords however wicked they are; and in any case those you fight won't have enough unity of purpose to threaten Japan, not after a few raids from the sea teach them better."

She dropped into Japanese and repeated the exchange. Reiko nodded grimly, and beside her Egawa Noboru wore an expression that a deer might see on the very last wolf it ever met.

"Japan does not wish to rule this land either," she said. "We did rule here once, in the early part of the last century, but nothing good came of it, and we have better uses for our men now. We can even forego revenge . . . beyond what this war brings, and I suppose what a Mongol invasion does."

Órlaith repeated that to Dzhambul. He shrugged.

"Well, we don't actually want to *live* here ourselves," he said. "Not enough grazing, for starters. And if there were no farmers, it would grow up in scrub and then forest. We do want a safe border here because it's on the edge of our tributary provinces in Manchuria and our treaty-allies like the Ussuri Hetmanate. I know my father has considered settling other folk here afterwards—and we don't want any of the Han successor-states meddling here either. There are those who speak Korean but whose ancestors fled and never submitted to the man-eaters, living in Manchuria under our rule; they're just ordinary farmers. They might be best."

Órlaith nodded. It would be a hard problem; this place had people living in it, and cultivated fields, but underneath it wasn't like a normal country of villages and peasants at all, more like a bad dream. Fortunately it wasn't *Montival's* hard problem.

"Montival isn't here to build an empire either," she said.

"We're here to end a threat, not to establish bases or garrisons. Once that threat is gone, we'll maintain our new alliance with Dai-Nippon, perhaps send a ship or two every year for a cruise with their navy, or help with pirate problems, and other cooperation as seems necessary. And there will be more trade in this part of the world without Korean piracy; with us, with Australia and the realms in between."

Which as far as trade with Japan is concerned, Reiko intends to regulate closely. And we will help them enforce those rules—nobody's going to treat her country's lost cities as a happy hunting ground, for example. That will benefit Montival too in the long run.

Órlaith looked around the ring of commanders and sovereigns. "I think that covers our immediate problems? We'll keep following the main enemy force as quickly as is prudent; presumably they'll stand when we get to their ruler's citadel. And we'll consider further attempts to establish contact with the Mongol army to the north if the current ones don't yield results within the next week. Dismissed for now, then."

Reiko, Dzhambul and Börte walked with her out of the tent, all of them donning hats with earflaps. The *Tennō's* inevitable attendants were minimal, and followed at a distance. Órlaith glanced back at them with sympathy; Reiko was enjoying a respite from the cocoon of ceremony which encompassed her at home, compared to which this was absolute freedom.

"I hope the officer you sent made it back to your army," she said to Dzhambul, absently repeating herself in Japanese so Reiko could follow the conversation.

"Gansükh? He is an excellent scout," Dzhambul replied. "And we're not nearly as far south as we were, and the enemy is disorganized by your advance and my people's. It's highly likely he will make it through. May the Ancestor aid him!"

The command *ger* of the Mongol army was made in the same form as the home that Gansükh had grown up in, a cylinder of withes tied together and covered inside and out with a lashed-on lining and covering of felt, topped by a conical roof of more poles and the same exterior, with a

smoke hole pierced by a sheet-metal chimney at its apex. A fire burned
in a metal stove beneath it, leaking a little tang of woodsmoke into the
air. He shivered as he hadn't in the cold, simply from the contrast—there
had been no campfires for him, not moving through the man-eater lines
to get here.

The difference between this and his *ger* at home was in the size—the
command *ger* was fifteen meters across and four meters high at the lowest
points around the edges—and a few little things like the clerks and the
typists and the man working the adding machine, the stacked document-
boxes that opened in front to turn into filing cabinets when they were
brought in from the backs of packhorses, and the colorful appliqués that
writhed with monsters and animal-shapes and scenes from legend across
the white felt of the interior. The floor was polished hardwood planks,
built to be knocked down into pack-loads too, and there were cushions
and rugs on the floor for sitting.

Toktamish was sitting cross-legged on one, hand clenched on the
jeweled hilt of the fine Chinese-made saber across his lap; he wore a
knee-length deel coat of dark blue silk with a padded lining, fastened
high on the right shoulder and at the neck with a set of silver clasps, and
bound with a broad black sash; his trousers were tucked into red-dyed
pointed boots tooled in intricate designs. A woman Gansükh didn't
recognize—and who didn't look like a Mongol, really, though she wore
a Mongol woman's long embroidered deel—was sitting not far from his
left hand.

Gansükh had tried to keep his report crisp and objective. Just listening to himself made him fear it was more like a lunatic's babbling or some
storyteller's fancy, and the general's face grew darker as he went on.

"Silence!" Toktamish roared as he started to tell of the meeting with
the Montivallan leaders. "Seize him!"

Gansükh felt shock paralyze him, more than exhaustion or gnawing
hunger. By the time his mind cleared, the iron hands of the commander's
personal guard were clamped on his arms.

Toktamish's square brown face was flushed, and Gansükh realized with another shock like a blow to the belly that this was a man in a killing rage. He hadn't had much contact with the army's supreme general before; when you were a hundred-commander in an army of three full tümen—thirty thousand men, counting only the Mongol cavalry and not the auxiliaries—you didn't.

"This liar and coward tries to cover up the death of the Kha-Khan's children with this nonsense tale! Take him out and behead him. Beneath the horse tail banner, that the *Tengri* may see his shame and the Ancestor spit on him!"

Gansükh surged against the hands that held him. "You break the Yasa, Noyon!" he shouted back frantically. "I am a free man, an officer and a Mongol of the Bayad clan; you cannot kill me without trial, like some Han peasant!"

Toktamish bared his teeth like a wolf staring at a sheep through a fence, looked around to see dubious glances from his staff, then gathered himself and shook his head.

"Bind him, then, and take him to await his fate. And gag him if he tries to speak!"

The guards brought a fetter—an iron rod with circlets for the head and both wrists—and clamped it on him, taking his weapons. When he opened his mouth their officer raised his riding crop in threat, holding it so he would strike with the weighted handle, easily enough to break a man's jaw and teeth.

Gansükh glared as he was marched away. There was something very wrong here. He had half-expected disbelief, but . . .

No. He does believe me. He is afraid others will believe.

He did hear a mutter from the general: "That whey-faced whore's get will not take what is mine. Never!"

The Montivallan camp was in what Dzhambul had told Órlaith was one of the few parts of this realm that wasn't ugly and barren; the old maps called it the Demilitarized Zone, which she thought was suitably ironic now that the allied armies were here and the main enemy field force was hovering off to the north and west, preparing to block yet another narrow pass.

The command tent was on a flat-topped hill, with the Guard regiments around it. As she left she stopped and watched the camp spread out below. The observation balloon was just being winched down, and cookfires were being lit; for once they had *nearly* enough firewood, and the scent of it and of baking and stewing added to the less comely but fortunately cold-suppressed smells of the mobile city that an army was. The canvas of the tents glowed in rows stretching almost to the edge of sight, amid vehicle-parks and rows of field-catapults and supply-wagons and horse-corrals. Whetted steel blinked where a patrol of Bearkiller lancers trotted by below the hill, back from making sure no substantial enemy force was close by.

"What a show of power!" Reiko said from beside her. "I never dreamed that we could march into the enemy's heartland; all my life and my father's we were on the defensive, with no more than the odd raid to strike back."

Egawa grunted agreement behind her, his eyes glowing. Then he added, in the tone of a man forcing himself to be realistic.

"Marching in is one thing, winning another, Majesty."

Órlaith nodded. "Your General is right. So many willing to die for us . . . it's a heavy thing. I'm glad there is . . . may be, we'll know soon . . . an alternative, even if it's risky and dangerous."

"We must be ready to sacrifice others," Reiko said. "For the greater good; it is our responsibility to make such decisions, the fate our birth gave us. But I would prefer to risk myself."

Órlaith nodded. "This is the price of power. We are the kings who die that their blood may safeguard their folk, the sacrifice that goes consenting, walking to their fate with open eyes."

Reiko gave one of her rare grins. "True. Though I would very much prefer to *fight victoriously* for my people, my friend," she said, and Órlaith laughed agreement.

"I have many plans that require my own presence," Reiko said. "For my people, and myself. My sisters are young women of strong talents and excellent character and they will serve Dai-Nippon well, but I have experience they do not. Still . . . karma, *neh?"*

She took a deep breath and made a sweeping gesture with her *tessen* war-fan, taking in the camp and the wide world beyond it.

"The thought that every moment may be our last gives a keener savor to the ones we have, at least."

She paused, then spoke:

"Natsukusa ya—"

Egawa gave the next line:

"Tsuwamonodomo ga—"

And his liege completed the haiku:

"Yume no ato."

The Sword of the Lady was not always a burden; one of the delights to Órlaith had been a command of *Nihongo* sufficient to appreciate Matuso Bashō's work. The High Queen of Montival murmured in her own tongue:

"Like grasses in summer
The warriors' dreams
All that is left."

Egawa bowed his head. "So a warrior must think, Majesty," he said.

Órlaith made a gesture of agreement and nodded towards the vast encampment.

"And if we succeed, so many who might have died will march . . . and sail . . . home again, to their hearths and loves and the fields that bore them. With a tale to tell on a summer's afternoon, their grandchildren about their feet and the harvest in and the leaves turning to gold above their heads."

She grinned. "Though they may leave out the blisters on their feet, and digging slit trenches for the latrines."

They turned towards Órlaith's own pavilion. The army had been perennially short of firewood, but she'd had the stand of oaks on the top left intact, and her pavilion pitched there, the blue-white-green stripes of Montival's colors showing through the bare branches. It was only a gesture of respect to the Lord and Lady of the wildwood, but gestures mattered and sometimes they were all you could do.

The tent was big but not enormous, but she'd discovered she genuinely needed it.

Not physically, she thought.

She'd gone on plenty of trips where she woke up in the morning to find snow inches-deep on the greased-leather exterior of her sleeping bag, and while she wasn't one of those who thought that was more fun than blossoming meadows in spring it didn't bother her. But she found she needed someplace quiet and private to sit and think and study maps and reports. And that was in essence her job.

Not far from the tent, knights of the Protector's guard were sparring. Heuradys and her brother Diomede d'Ath stepped up and an older knight spoke, one in the black armor with his visor raised and a white baton to mark his office in his hand.

"This is a match for chivalry, the sake of skill at arms and to the credit of the honorable estate of knighthood," he said. "It shall continue until one party concedes or I pronounce it ended. Fifth match of five, each party with two victories to their credit."

"Take stance . . . make ready!"

The wand went up and then slashed down.

"Fight!"

John was sitting nearby on a log in a suit of plate complete, his helmet on his knee and his shield leaned beside him, still sweating heavily from his turns. Behind the fallen log Toa stood, unhappy in the cold despite being warmly bundled in a way that made him look more gigantic still, and leaning on his spear.

Pip sat beside her husband, sipping at a cup of hot tea and looking comfortably elegant in her Association lady's winter travel garb . . . which with a few differences of detail, happened to be exactly what Egawa

Noboru was wearing, a few paces behind them. Órlaith and Reiko exchanged a glance and did not smile as they came to stand beside them.

It wasn't that contemporary Japan absolutely forbade the sexes to wear each other's customary clothing, the way some places she'd seen did. Reiko was clad in the same combination of *hakama* with padded lining, leggings, low boots, and double kimono jacket with long-sleeved knit undershirt that Pip wore herself; that was fairly common in modern Japan if the woman in question was doing something in the nature of war or rough travel. It was the fact that in the PPA's territory that was *specifically* women's garb, which Associate men did *not* wear, that Nihonjin men like Egawa found profoundly annoying . . . not that it would affect his expression in the slightest.

Reiko likes him greatly and trusts him wholly, but she enjoys teasing him a little, now and then . . . very subtly . . . sometimes, Órlaith thought. *He was the stern and masterful teacher for a long time in her childhood, and very hard on her once her brother disappeared and she became the heir.*

The *Tennō* of Japan and her bannerman watched with keen professional interest as the two knights circled, four-foot shields up under the visor-slits of their helmets and swords held hilt-first above their heads. The weapons were round-tipped practice models with blunt edges, but you could swing them very hard indeed when you were sparring with someone armed cap-a-pie.

"I have always been a little surprised that your *knights*"—Reiko pronounced the word carefully, because she had always used it as an example of why English spelling was an insane mess—"use shields at all. Didn't shields fall out of use when this armor of plates was first made in Old Europe? There is little a sword can do against a suit of plate in any case; a *naginata* or a war-flail might, perhaps. Certainly not a cut from an ordinary sword in a one-handed grip."

"Oh, I think *your* sword could accomplish a good deal," Órlaith observed dryly, and they both chuckled as the High Queen tapped her palm against the moon-crystal hilt by her side; Reiko's was already on the yellow cords of the Grasscutter's grip.

And the Sword of the Lady can, Órlaith thought. *You can't keep a steel blade razor sharp, and you can't slam it full-strength into plate armor many times either, not without damaging it to uselessness . . . but the Sword of the Lady is always sharper than a scalpel and* nothing *hurts it; you could put one edge on an anvil and beat the other with a sledge until the anvil was cut in half. I can parry edge-on-edge against an ordinary sword with this thing too, and just notch my opponent's blade until it looks like a saw, or outright cut it in half.*

"And a hard thrust to the eye-slit or armpit or groin or the back of the knee will work, that's why stiff blades with long narrow points came in, when my father was a child," she went on aloud. "But I think you're right—the shields were kept because they're useful against arrows and crossbow-bolts. And I'd rather stop a hard-driven lance with a shield than my breastplate, too." She smiled. "And the horseman's version of that armor leaves most of your seat exposed."

Reiko snapped her fan open and used it to hide a smile. "Scarred buttocks! Most embarrassing! Hard to explain in the baths!"

Egawa chuckled too.

"The foot-combat version has different tassets and fauds."

There was a loud dull *crack* as the shields met out on the practice ground; with bodies and weapons and armor totaled together that was just under five hundred pounds slamming into each other. Heuradys backed three slow steps as their blades locked and he pushed at her . . . and then suddenly pivoted and went down on one knee, neat as a dancer and sliding the shield out of contact so swiftly that it was like a door bursting open while a man pushed with all his might.

Diomede staggered three steps. He recovered quickly and cut backhand at her visor, but the shield had come up over her head in time to catch it with a hollow thud. His own was too far out to bring the tail back in time to stop a blurring-fast thrust into the mail grommet at the back of his right knee, and he went down on it in turn . . .

. . . but with a snarling grunt of pain, and when he rose he tested the limb in a gingerly fashion before ruefully bringing his sword up in salute. The referee raised his baton and then slanted it towards Diomede's sister.

"Lady Heuradys d'Ath is victor of this bout. The match is in her favor, three to two. Sir Diomede d'Ath concedes."

The pair of them handed shield and practice swords to Diomede's squires. He had two, currently; one a brown young man from County Molalla in his late teens and nearly due for the accolade and hoping for a battlefield knighting in this war, and the other a blond fourteen-year-old newly graduated from page status, gangling and with hands and feet that promised inches in the future and made her a little puppy-awkward now.

She was blushingly excited to handle the arms of the head of the High Queen's riding household, the more so when Heuradys gave her an absent word of thanks as she helped her unarm and reverently put her armor in the padded wraps and stored them in a stout leather bag and ran off with it towards her quarters.

They were all close enough that Órlaith could follow their conversation as they donned long fleece-lined wool coats, buttoned them to their throats, swung chaperon hats on their heads and buckled on their sword-belts.

"I have *got* to stop trying an overrun with you!" Diomede said.

His eyes were bright-blue in a flushed face; even with the cold it was streaming. They both mopped theirs on the towel the senior squire handed them.

"How many times have I fallen for that?" he added ruefully.

Heuradys laughed. "Dear brother, how many years have I heard you making the same promise to yourself? It works with other people or you wouldn't have developed the habit. Besides which, you knock me off my horse as often as not when we joust. You're at least as good as I am with a lance."

"With swords it's as bad as fighting Mother was when I was a new squire," he grumbled. "You *are* as fast as she ever was . . . faster than she was then. Well, duty calls. Good to cross blades with you again, sis."

They embraced, and then Diomede came to attention, thumped his fist to his chest and bowed to Órlaith and Prince John, and walked away with an abstracted frown. Several military functionaries were waiting for him, some of them eagerly holding document-boxes.

"Thank God for that man," John said fervently. "I'd never have a moment off if he weren't my chief of staff."

"You wouldn't need so many moments off if you weren't still working on that epic," Pip said.

"*Chanson de geste,* my sweet," John corrected. "Song of Great Deeds. The *content* is epic, I grant you. I just squeeze in a few minutes here and there as a change from paperwork."

"Your *paperwork* is epic and I do most of it," she said.

Then he groaned slightly as he stood erect to let two headquarters pages take his armor off.

Your own fault, Johnnie, she thought. *In weather like this you're going to get stiff if you don't disarm right away.*

"You're deft, Herulin," he said gently to one. "But no palms on the plates—fingertips only."

The boy flushed and hastily polished the tasset with the sleeve of his coat to remove the offending smudge. Órlaith's brother and sister-in-law bowed to Reiko and then a little deeper to her, the type with a knee bend in it that was a symbol of kneeling, and exchanged the kiss of greeting— letting someone kiss you on both cheeks was an acknowledgment of their high rank even if it wasn't equal to yours, and Pip was handling the Association courtesies faultlessly now, albeit Órlaith thought she was still rolling her eyes in the privacy of her mind.

Which I don't mind in the least because I do that myself.

John's voice dropped a little. "Deor and the others are back," he said to her.

"Good," she replied.

The Archers snapped to attention as she and her companions walked towards the pavilion; it wasn't one of the days on which member-realm contingents shared the guard duty for honor's sake. Two of the kilted troopers drew the leaf of the tent back; there was a small antechamber, and then it was blessedly warmer inside the inner portal, because the gear included several light-metal portable stoves. Those were also useful for keeping food and drink warm, and the smell of supper filled the air pleasurably. An orderly had brought a bucket and basket of the evening's offering up from the nearest communal cookfire.

Also inside were Deor Godulfson, his lover Ruan Chu Mackenzie, Thora Garwood, Susan Mika and the Dúnedain pair, in the underlayers of field scouting gear for this frigid time and place, and all looking a bit worn. Folding chairs stood around an equally portable table, and they sat and handed things around with the informality of field service; she thought Egawa Noboru was a little put-out that there wasn't more ceremony for his liege, but he had been a soldier for a long time. The food was boiled rice—Australian rice—camp-bread, cheese and dried fruit and a stew of salt pork and desiccated vegetables and beans that was savory enough.

She said so, and Heuradys replied:

"Or at least it's salty, thick and brown, Orrey, which is much the same thing in an army cook's opinion. Oh, well, the weather makes us hungry."

She was right about that; the hard work of campaigning would do that anyway, and if you threw in constant subfreezing weather you had to eat more or steadily lose weight.

The Nihonjin passed by the butter and cheese, politely hiding their disgust, and simply took a little more of the rice; the stew was similar enough to their native *butajiru* to be easy on their rather parochial tastes, though they used it as a garnish for the rice as they pulled out the little chopstick sets they carried in their sleeve-pockets. Those were slightly awkward when the rice was this type, less sticky and given to clumping than their own variety.

The Mongols loved dairy foods, preferred meat as their staple, and were familiar enough with rice if not enthusiastic about it. She'd observed that it was evidently a point of pride with them not to be fastidious and they spooned everything up with relish.

Deor and his companions were simply ravenous and would be for days after their ordeal. Órlaith and Heuradys and her brother John and Pip weren't, but they were solidly hungry, since in terms of sheer demand for fuel their day-to-day life involved the equivalent of a full day's work by a farm laborer.

"This is hard country to travel in by winter," the Mist Hills scop said after he'd finished a second bowl; he looked on the thin side of wiry now, hard and drawn and every day of his mid-thirties. "Doing this sort of thing was easier for me ten years ago."

Susan Mika chuckled. "You coastal types are spoiled," she said. "Now up on the *makol* . . ."

". . . the snow doesn't melt until June, and then it's hot enough to melt lead and one prairie fire after another until it freezes in September, but you don't care by then because you've been trampled by stampeding buffalo," Thora said dryly. "Try it on someone who hasn't spent a winter on the Trondheimsfjorden, girl. *And* a hot season in Darwin; I fried an egg on a pan laid out in the sun there once, for a bet."

Órlaith leaned to one side and murmured a translation of the byplay to Dzhambul. He'd been trying to pick up some spoken English, to go with the basic acquaintance he'd gotten as a child with the written form, but it wasn't nearly good enough yet to follow humor. He chuckled, and spoke softly in his turn, near her ear:

"We do that too—folk from the Gobi go on about their sand-blizzards stripping faces to the bone, and then we northerners will tell stories about hairy monsters that wander in during the snowstorms to eat people, or men and horses frozen solid like statues. Though that *does* happen sometimes, but not often."

Órlaith waited until one of the junior Archers came in and took the bowls out, and then whistled softly. Edain Aylward Mackenzie stuck his head through the flap.

"*Sea, Ceannas?*" he asked.

Órlaith swallowed. Suddenly hearing her father's old comrade say that—the simple *Yes, Chief?* she had heard all her life, but to her rather than him—made that looming absence almost unbearable once more for an instant. A slight change in his face as their eyes met told her that the same thought had struck him.

Instead of speaking she moved her hands in Clan Mackenzie battle-sign; the three gestures meant *secure the perimeter*, and *no entry except in crisis*.

A spirit lamp kept *sake* warm, and there was a bowl of some thin crisp crackers flavored with seaweed and powdered shrimp they'd picked up in Japan, where an enterprising trader had unloaded a warehouse-full on the quartermasters in return for a shipload of dried ramen. She nibbled on one; they were extremely tasty, once you were used to the combination of flavors, and for some reason the Japanese didn't usually eat rice and drink their national rice-based liquor at the same time.

Then she raised her cup to Deor.

"To our scouts—and to the scout who went beyond the light of common day. To Deor the Wide-Farer, Deor Woden's-man, *waes hael!*"

He raised his and replied to his people's toast in their fashion:

"*Drinc hael, Cwēn!*"

They all sipped, though John and Pip crossed themselves as well, and Deor and Thora signed the Hammer; down in Baru Denpasar they'd followed those disturbing gray eyes through the veils of the worlds. Ruan Chu Mackenzie, emptied his cup, leaned his head against Deor's shoulder and yawned enormously.

"I know my task if this goes where Deor thinks," he said; he was a physician as well as a warrior. "And if you'll excuse me . . ."

Deor grinned and they exchanged a wrist-to-wrist handgrip and a hug.

"He was up all last night," he said.

There was quiet pride in his voice as the younger man curled up in a corner and dropped off immediately with the ease of someone who'd been in the field long enough to take sleep when he could get it.

"One of our horses started favoring its left fore, and he put hot packs on it. We'd have been back later, if he hadn't, and believe me, by then another night in the open was nobody's wish."

Órlaith nodded. "Now, to business," she said, and unrolled a map on the table.

It showed central Korea; the old ruined capitals of the North and South Kingdoms, Seoul and Pyongyang, and north of that the massive complex of fortifications that housed the current *Sinseonghan jidoja*, the Divine Leader—or perhaps *Perfect Embodiment* was better—whose grand-father had conquered the peninsula in the wake of the Change. She had that odd feeling again that meant the Sword had given her more than one form of a language. The latter term was from the dialect used here and now by the Divine Leader's followers.

"We got just close enough to produce these," Faramir said. "It was . . . difficult. The *yrch* have hidden observation posts all over the area and constant patrolling."

"*Bayar khürgeye!*" Börte said.

Which meant more or less *congratulations* or *well-done* in Mongol. She'd managed to follow the English a little. In her own tongue:

"We've never managed to get anyone that close. They just . . . don't come back."

"The same with us," Reiko agreed.

Faramir nodded soberly. "We couldn't have done it without Deor. The *yrch* had . . . seers. Sniffers, rather."

Morfind silently laid out a series of sketches; they were drawn to a scale marked by the side, helpfully done in the meters the folk of this part of the world used as well as the feet and yards prevalent in Montival. All of them leaned closer to study it for long moments. Several looked in-credulous, Toa whistled, and then Egawa grunted:

"That is worse than rumor painted, for once," he said, then shifted to hideously mangled English: "Velly bad. Bad, bad."

"I don't see how you could build walls that high—that outer parapet alone is taller than the Silver Tower at Castle Todenangst," Heuradys said. "And the inward batter . . . odds are they just took a mountain and *carved* it. Those are retaining walls, not free-standing curtains. Mount Angel back home is something like that. But not nearly as big."

Órlaith nodded; that was the home and headquarters of the warrior monks of the Order of the Shield of Saint Benedict; after the Change they'd planed away the sides of the hill the monastery was built on and encased them in thick stone and concrete. That and Todenangst were the strongest fortresses in Montival, and there had been a joke back in the old wars that fifty thousand troops commanded by Saint Michael the Archangel and with Vulcan for a siege-engineer would still need divine intervention to take either. This was worse.

"Your bannerwoman is correct," Egawa said, when Órlaith relayed the comment. "We in Dai-Nippon used the same technique for building castles in the Sengoku and the early Tokugawa era . . . and when we invaded Korea the first time, about four hundred years ago . . . but never so big. That wall is unscalable. And where are the gates?"

Faramir arranged the sketches to give an all-round view. "There aren't any gates. It's just this moat—about half bowshot across—then a smooth wall, hundreds of feet high; then on the platform it encloses there are successive inner keeps, each higher than the last and big as major castles in their own right—probably that was part of the mountain-sculpting, successive spurs, which is why they're placed irregularly. And I suspect the construction involves a lot of steel, with reinforcement running into the living rock, and a maze of tunnels running from top to bottom."

Deor nodded. "See here and here and here? These are projections . . . towers and overhangs . . ."

"Machicolations," Heuradys supplied.

That meant the overhang beneath the fighting platform of a castle, so that you could raise metal trapdoors and shoot or drop things straight down.

Deor's finger moved. "The roads and railroads from the approaches terminate in this ring of forts on lower hills . . . small mountains, actually . . . around the greater one."

From the drawings, they did have gates, though well-defended ones; they were built into the base of the tall hills, and would be easy to seal with multiple solid steel portcullises, and each of them was a major fort in its own right.

"Tunnels," Órlaith said; she had that odd books-being-filed sensation that the Sword gave her when it was drawing conclusions. "Those outer-works are connected with the main fort by tunnels . . . probably some of them have railways . . . and they'd be easy to block. By dropping metal or stone slabs, for starters. And if you did manage to break through one set of obstacles, there would be another, and then flooding . . . pumping in burning napalm . . . cutting the ventilation . . . and then trying to fight your way upward through a maze of *more* tunnels. . . ."

Dzhambul bared his teeth. "There will be a good water supply, with reservoirs carved into rock, and pumps. And any amount of stored food and munitions. You could besiege it for *years*."

Órlaith looked at the sketches and then at the map.

"Worse than that. The subsidiary forts crowd any approach, and there are probably other tunnels into these mountains with concealed en-trances, possibly miles away. It would be impossible to stop all traffic in and out, so they could keep in touch with the other forts and bases we've bypassed and screened. And we know they have good catapults. The main citadel and the forts will all mount heavy throwers, heavier than anything we could bring up and with the advantage of height and care-fully prepared range tables."

Egawa grunted again. "So you could not concentrate your own siege engines on one of the outlying forts without your whole force being under fire from the central citadel and several of the others."

John leaned close to Pip, conferred in murmurs, and then spoke:

"This is militarily impossible, Orrey. Just can't be done. Not without years and years of reducing this country acre by acre and then starving that monstrosity out."

Dzhambul snorted. "Perhaps you will have to reconsider your strat-egy of driving straight for the enemy leader!"

Órlaith sighed. *I really wish I didn't have to do this, but . . .*

"There is another way; I've discussed it with Deor, and the *Tennō*. It involves great risk for us . . . and I mean us, personally, here."

Egawa stirred. Reiko turned to him, and touched the wrist of his sword-hand with her *tessen*.

"I have four sisters who can carry my blood forward, General, if worst comes to worst. There is no price too high for victory and there is no victory without risk. I took great risks to recover the Grasscutter, and so we must do here, to end this war and give our people peace. You will not object to what I consider that I must do."

He subsided, and Órlaith went on. "It's an idea I had, but based on what happened to my brother last year in the Ceram Sea, in Baru Denpasar. Deor? You're the expert."

"Scarcely an expert." The scop sighed and put a hand to his brow. "I make and sing songs . . . but I also studied *seidh*, wreaking . . . what most call magic."

He touched the Valknut at his throat. "I am Woden's man, and He is patron of music and *seidh* both. It is a power he gives some, to guard Midgard against trollcraft and ettin-work. I studied with Lady Juniper, the High Queen's grandmother. And elsewhere."

Egawa's tough scarred face was still as stone, but it had a sheen of sweat on it when that was translated. He turned and bowed to Reiko.

"Majesty, I am your loyal vassal, serving you as my ancestors served yours. It was a torment to me that I could not accompany you when you fought against evil spirits for the Grasscutter in the lost castle. Now that I may fight by your side, I am content, though the fight be in strange and dark places. Command me!"

Deor went on: "That place . . . it isn't just a fortress. Lady Juniper described to me what the Prophet's capital in Corwin was like when she visited there to help cleanse it. How it felt to her, how it looked to an eye that sees beyond the light of common day. I've felt places like that myself; most lately and most strongly in Baru Denpasar, where Carcosa was like an oozing sore in the fabric of the world. This was like that—a different flavor of wrongness, but the same feeling that something had burrowed through the walls. Only here it was ripped wide."

He hesitated, and bowed to the two monarchs. "And in a very different way, there is something of the same about the blades you bear. They don't feel hostile, or evil; but they are also . . . interventions. A finger from elsewhere in the Nine Worlds, stretching into Midgard."

The Christians in the room looked a little uneasy. Órlaith didn't, and the Japanese were even less so once Reiko had murmured a translation to her bannerman. Like hers, their faith encompassed many Powers; and some were hostile or dangerous to human-kind. Even Reiko's personal name was shared with the Ghost Fox, whose sly presence was perilous to mortals.

"Melkor has many servants, and his power was woven into the music of Arda from the beginning," Morfind said. "The Dark Lords always return."

"Like Han and the Double-Faced Woman," Susan nodded, her lips tight and the usual smile absent from her eyes.

"What we did in Baru Denpasar was a journey of the spirit, into the place where the enemy . . . that enemy, the King in Yellow and his servant the Pallid Mask . . . kept Prince John's spirit captive. I think we can do the same here. The shadowed fortress is very strong both here in the world of common day and in the Otherworlds, but its very nature, its *dual* nature, opens a way, if we dare to take it. But remember! Our bodies may be safe . . . but in that place, we will face real peril. We can perish there; and then we will never return to our bodies, and they will die in truth."

John's lips quirked. "Hurrah, I get to go to Hell, literally, twice." He crossed himself again. "Saint Michael, aid me!"

"And the Lord and Lady be by my side," Órlaith said, and Heuradys touched her owl amulet. "I don't think we have any real choice. Not when we think of what the cost of *not* doing this may be."

Dzhambul sighed. "I don't like depending on foreign magics," he said, looking at the sketches again. "But I don't want Mongols dying under those walls, either—and I am afraid my uncle would drive many to do so, for his own credit's sake."

Börte nodded vigorously. "He would, brother. You know it."

Órlaith looked around the table. "Is there any disagreement? No?

Then . . . let's say three days. That will give a little more time for Prince Dzhambul's messenger to get to his army and for word to return to ours. If nothing changes, we'll try it then. Our cover story will be that we're praying together for the success of the army . . . and I suggest you all do just that in the interim, as well as resting. Because we're going to need all the help we can get."

They rose; Órlaith caught Heuradys' eyes, and saw perfect understanding as she flicked them towards the exit. That made collecting Dzhambul's attention without attracting too much of the others' relatively easy—and she suspected that like Heuradys, if not in exactly the same way, he was used to the games you had to play around Courts and other crowded venues to have a little privacy.

Usually a monarch didn't have any more than a peasant in a tiny cottage in a village where everyone knew everything everyone did—only those in the middle levels of society could go unnoticed, particularly if they lived in a city. If you were the heir to a throne at least three people and a brace of bodyguards knew when you were so much as going off to empty your bladder and probably discussed it among themselves afterwards.

You didn't have any privacy at all if you didn't have close-mouthed, loyal and skillful friends ready to run interference for you. She thought that Reiko's brow cocked ironically as they bowed each other farewell, and let one of her eyelids droop just a fraction in reply.

When they were alone and the door-flap was fastened, Órlaith poured Dzhambul another cup of the sake, lifted hers, and said:

"*Sláinte!*"

He hesitated a moment with the cup raised. "Slan-cha?" he asked.

"A toast. *To your health*, in one of our languages."

"*Erüül mendiin tölöö*," he said, and drank.

Which meant exactly the same thing in Mongol.

She leaned back in the chair and put her stocking feet on the table; he'd removed his boots, as she had, when he came in. That was only courtesy if you walked around where livestock did, and the Japanese had the same habit. The thought of courtesy prompted an impulse; she stood, went over to the sword-stand by the entranceway, took the Sword of the Lady down and carried it into the store-chamber at the rearmost of the pavilion.

"There," she said when she returned and sat again. "Now you can lie to me, Dzhambul."

He laughed and filled her cup in turn. "But you can still speak Mongol."

"Oh, that's in my head, not the Sword. If I need a language, I have it as if I'd grown up speaking it, and it never goes away; there must be . . ."

She stopped to think. "Let's see . . . English, Old English, *Gaeilge*, *Español*, *Français*, *Lakȟótiyapi*, *Nihongo*, *Hànyŭ*, Mongol, *Ivrit*, Sindarin, Quenya, Hangul, Wolof, *Norrænt mál* . . . quite a few, in fact. Thanks be to Brigid and Ogma of the Honey Tongue, I don't keep the other, the truth-telling, unless I have the Sword by me."

"Convenient! But anyway, Börte says I'm so stupidly honest that the Sword is no threat to me."

Órlaith laughed. "Brothers and sisters! Perhaps she meant your commander."

"Oh, Gansükh," Dzhambul said. "He's a good tricky soldier, and brave as a bull yak. And about as thoughtful as a bull yak about anything off the battlefield, too."

He emptied the cup. "And I shall continue to tell the truth, Oor-la," he said. "I shall praise your beauty to the skies; I've already done that for your wits and courage, and you *know* that's my true thought."

She laughed. "Now you are being tactful . . . or dishonest. I know people of my looks don't suit a Mongol eye, there not being any like that on your ranges. I seem strange and odd to you."

He grinned. "Oh, but my mother was Russki. She didn't look much like most Mongols either."

"How did that happen?"

"It was a marriage of state, between the Kha-Khan's family and that of the Hetman Nicolai of the Ussuri Host."

"Not all that far from here . . . I think I'd heard of them, but hadn't kept the details."

His face softened. "She was homesick for her own people and their songs and their tongue, often enough—and their food! She missed the mountains of her homeland, too; often she spoke of her birthplace, Dalnerechensk, of the green flowery meadows by the river and the sound of the bees and smell of the cut grass in summer, the tall pine forests, and the Sikhote Mountains where the great tigers roam."

He lifted his cup. "I drink to her spirit. May the merciful Bodhisattvas bring you to your home again, my mother, Darya Nikolaevna Rodchenko, and to fortunate rebirth by the banks of the river you loved."

Órlaith began to lift her cup to join the toast, hesitated for a moment as a bolt like the fabled electricity of the ancients ran through her, and then continued it. There were certain things you couldn't tell an outsider.

Even if . . .

She looked at him again and remembered the pathway up from Lost Lake, and the earnest comely face of the woman her own age, her daughter.

Yes, it could be. Very likely could be . . . and perhaps that was part of the Queen-making too, what I learned from her? But the years and the Gods tell many stories. It doesn't have to be . . . if that makes any sense at all. Even the past isn't fixed, much less the future, and isn't that a thought to keep you wakeful of nights!

"You recognize the name Darya?" he said, not surprising her.

"Yes, many *Russki* settled in the lands that became Montival, and their names endure. Faramir's father was named Ivan, for instance, and the commander of the Lakota with us here bears the same, as well as Brown Bear. Darya would be a bit rare among us, but not enough to be out-landish."

She felt a prickling tension, and drank once more to give her hands and eyes something to do.

"Do I resemble her, then?"

"Oh . . ."

He examined her carefully; she thought he flushed, though his olive coloring made that a little hard to see. When he spoke it was with as much care as her glance.

"Not really. You're much taller; she was a little shorter than me, about Börte's height; tall for a *Russki* woman, very tall for a Mongol. Her skin was pale, but didn't show the blood beneath it as much as yours. And she was fuller in her figure, and her hair was brown, the color of deep polished beechwood. And her eyes were gray. Börte got that from her. Her face was more like ours, too. Short nose and high cheeks, and flatter. Perhaps because one of her grandmothers was Han, and they resemble us."

"Ah, well, I'm a beanpole even by Montivallan standards, and was as a girl too—they said my feet and hands were a sign of it, even newborn," Órlaith said. "I was teased about it sometimes."

"They dared!" Dzhambul said with a laugh.

He has a good laugh, she thought. *And good teeth. And kind eyes, though he's obviously a man of his hands and a tried warrior. Let's take the bull by the horns . . . or rather . . .*

"Dzhambul," she said. "We're going to be risking our lives, and souls for that matter, in three days' time, and there's something I'd like to do first. Or before you return to your country and I to mine, as well. Nor is there much time for gentle hints."

"I was hoping you were going to say something like that," he said, grinning a young man's grin. "But I didn't dare speak!"

She rose and extended a hand; and he did and gripped it.

CHAPTER NINETEEN

"I don't expect this to take very long," Órlaith said quietly to General Thurston three days later, as the standard afternoon staff meeting broke up.

She drew on her gloves as they walked out between the guard of Boisean legionnaires who came to attention with a clank of accoutrements and a thump of javelin-butts on the hard dirt.

"It's not as if we're in a hurry," she added, looking up at the gray louring sky.

It won't take long because Deor says time is different where we're going, she thought but did not say aloud. *Though I don't envy you, General, if this goes wrong! Still, you're perfectly competent to fight this war as war of human-kind. . . .*

"I and my 'tru brethren have managed to find a genuinely surplus-to-military-needs horse for a Blót ourselves," Thurston said, referring to the sacrifices his faith made.

"Please don't disturb us unless absolutely necessary," she added, then touched a finger to the pommel of the Sword. "This is a matter of . . . special circumstances."

Thurston's tough brown face was calm, though he touched his valknut ring himself, the three linked triangles that marked him as Odin's follower, as most of his family and many in his realm were.

"Yes, Your Majesty," he said.

Then with a fleeting grin: "I remember your father saying pretty much the same thing several times."

She could smell more snow coming. And . . .

"I think something's pushing that snow at us," she said.

"It's the time of year for snow, of course," he said.

"Yes, it is, General. And . . . interventions . . . sufficient to upset the cycle of the seasons are, thanks be to all kindly Powers, rare. Thought I've seen them; and I assure you that report of what happened on the beach at Topanga wasn't in the least exaggerated."

Thurston looked understandably grim and signed the Hammer. Reiko's appeal to her Ancestress had been answered . . . in an absolutely unambiguous manner. The fact that the result had been good for Montival didn't mean it wasn't enough to make the bravest uneasy, when such things walked in the light of common day.

"But even short of that level, it's not necessarily the *day* for snow," she added.

"Ah, I see your point, Your Majesty." He shook his head. "We thought the weather was suspicious, a couple of times, fighting the Prophet. This is worse."

"Doors that were half-open then are more so now," she replied. "The Change was a beginning, not an end. The Wise One knows what it'll be like in my children's time. Or maybe even They don't."

The oak trees sheltered her pavilion from most of the wind. Within bedrolls were stretched out in a circle. She took a deep breath and entered.

Deor closed his eyes for a moment after Órlaith entered the tent and nodded briefly to him. In this state he *felt* the presences with him. It was easier, because he had done it before with some of these. . . .

No, he thought. *It's not that, or not just that. It's because of what those two carry, as well.*

The two great Swords prickled at the edge of his consciousness at the best of times. Now he came perilously close to seeing them as they really were, and a human mind was not made for such knowledge. They were like *ideas*, but ideas so strong that they could overwrite the story that was the world, or possibly just rip apart the page they rested on. As a story-teller as well as a practitioner of *seidh* he feared that.

I am in no danger of the Christian sin of envy! he thought. *I have felt a burning curiosity to know more of these mighty things, but to carry those is a burden. And a perilous one.*

He focused on the people instead.

"Understand, all of you," he said aloud. "We will have to journey to the heart of the enemy's realm; to that part of it which stands on the border of worlds, and so partakes of both. A human's spirit is not a single thing. Parts may be absent, though the man walks and speaks and eats. If enough is gone, then the body is an empty shell . . . but always until death bound to the spirit with a cord that some eyes can see and follow. We will leave only that cord and our bodies, because for this we will need all that we have."

Deor felt them all. Thora's spirit, strong as steel, comradeship refined down through a generation of wandering and wild faring until it was a bond close as kinship, closer than most mated pairs. And by their common love of the daughter who was not blood of his blood, but tightly bound to him nonetheless.

"You join me first, oath-sister," he said aloud to Thora. "And you, Ruan, my heart, are the link back here. You do more than tend our bodies. You are my guide, for the return."

"Yet tending the body, sure and that is needful too. Ever will I guard your back."

Pip made an enquiring sound. "You and John next, and Toa."

John crossed himself and murmured a prayer to Saint Michael. That was no hindrance; it built the power.

"Then you three," Deor went on to Faramir and Morfind and Susan.

His gaze shifted to the Japanese. "Then you, Majesty, and your bannerman."

He could sense the iron bond of loyalty between them. And something else, something washing back through time; a blood link that was not yet there, but would be in Reiko's children and Egawa's grandchildren. Something not yet real, but a real possibility becoming more and more so as it approached through time, harder and more definite by a tiny fraction as each second passed.

He blinked in surprise. *That* was something he hadn't felt before.

And it was as if he could also see a long line of figures stretching out *behind* Reiko as well, receding, deeper, deeper, to a shamanness in an antlered headdress and hide cloak who turned and *looked* at him and somehow saw or sensed this moment herself, over inconceivable gulfs of time. And behind *her*, a roaring torrent of raw Power—a cave, and a figure within—

But I haven't dealt with something like the Grasscutter before, either. How it burns! Focus, Deor Godulfson. Those are not your mysteries, though they touch the thread of your life and land.

He wrenched his attention back to the here and now, feeling sweat rolling down his forehead and flanks. Deor had seen the riders of the surf-waves in Hawai'i and Australia, though he'd never had time to master that arcane skill. It must feel a little like this, not mastering the might of Ocean but dancing with it through each shift of body and balance, flying shoreward only a single misstep between you and disaster.

I have undertaken something at the very edge of what my might and my main can do, he thought.

That stiffened him.

"Heart must grow harder, courage the greater, as our strength lessens!" he murmured, from a poem old among his folk.

He spoke aloud to Órlaith: "Then you and Lady Heuradys, and Prince Dzhambul and his sister, Your Highness," he said firmly.

One eyebrow lifted as his focus sharpened. In her womb, tiny but intense . . .

Dzhambul's child.

He wasn't surprised that he could sense that; he had before, in like circumstances, with Thora and Pip.

But again vision flared: a dark-haired woman with the High Queen's blood-legacy in her face and that of the Mongol prince as well. The Sword of the Lady was in her hand, and she shouted defiance as it flared against something huge hidden in shadow amid tumbled ruins ancient beyond ancient. A ship, a star, a cyclopean palace amid the waves, and a darkling presence awaiting her whose countenance was like tentacles of ancient night weaving a scream of madness as they danced. . . .

And by her side a young woman whose yellow hair flew in a wind that lashed with cold salt spray, a woman with Thora's eyes and Thora's sword in her hand, and his harp cased across her back. . . .

And behind them was Órlaith's inheritance, the High King and Queen he had known and followed, and Juniper Mackenzie his teacher, and more and more.

No! The Sword is cycles within cycles, and perilous to one like me, a man whose lust is to know. That is for another day. Everything is linked, but not everything is as important as the other, not to us, not here and now. The work of the day is to be done!

His eyes opened and met Órlaith's, and they shared the knowledge.

Thus I repay Lady Juniper's teaching, and the High King who stood as my friend when I was a youth from a little place in the wilds of Westria, alone at the glittering court of Montival, he thought. *You are my Queen and liege, and for you I fight—with sword, and with craft.*

"Lie down and compose yourself, everyone," he said. "Time is . . . different, where we're going, but it won't be a matter of seconds here. We're all rested and fed. Keep yourself warm."

They lay and covered themselves, absurdly like guests settling in for the night back in the hall of his father, back in Mist Hills.

I will see my home again. Thora and Ruan and I will tend our land and raise the daughter of our souls.

He paced around the chamber in the pavilion, pausing at each corner to reach out to the spirits and pour a little rice-wine on the floor.

"Wights of this land," he murmured, "hail to you. Bless and ward our work today."

He looked at Ruan, where he sat in a chair; beside him were hypodermics and other gear. "Be careful, my heart, as I told you once before. To bring a spirit back untimely . . . that may mean the spirit is forever maimed. Or it may leave an emptiness that invites . . . other things."

He tried a few taps on the hand drum he had brought from Montival; it throbbed with a staccato beat that sank into bone and blood as his skilled fingers evoked the rhythms at the heart of life. All life was one, all one, all the beat of the heart every day of life—and before that in the womb, when your mother's heart was the beating of the heart of Earth itself.

Egawa grinned. "A priest's drum, like a shrine at home."

"Be close; take each your neighbor's hand."

"Or my stump," Egawa said.

He seemed to regard the fact that few of them spoke his language as a license for wit, but it was good to see a man so lighthearted facing peril to spirit as well as body. Reiko took his stump in her hand, after an admonishing tap.

"You are linked as closely as by blood, now, all of you," Deor said. "You are battle-comrades. You fight for your lands and peoples, and you do it together. This is a mighty thing! Feel the strength of each that is the strength of many."

Deor arranged himself cross-legged in the center of the circle, a posture that his trained body could maintain even without his waking mind to guide it. He began to tap on the drum, locking his muscles into the rhythm.

"If you need them, spirit weapons will come to you," he said. "Remember the weight of your sword and it will come to your hand. And those Swords will be ever with those who bear them."

"A sword made of thoughts?" Órlaith said, her voice distant.

"Your Sword is a thought in the mind of the Lady of all things, High Queen of Montival. And where we go, thought takes form and walks for all of us, not just those whose line has the special blessing of the Powers."

She nodded soberly, and he continued: "And all of you, call on your allies. Mine is a Meadowlark. You may see him when we're in the Otherworld. Thora's protector is the Bear, the Grizzly. Pip's is the Lion. . . ."

"Mine's the Bushrat," Toa said unexpectedly, chuckling like gravel in a bucket.

Tha-ba-da . . . tha-ba-da the drum spoke, sinking into bone, into blood, into pulse and gut.

He relaxed his throat muscles, let his voice go smooth. "Sink down . . . let each limb relax . . . The floor is Earth, our guards protect you, the wights—"

He reached out. Again he blinked. At first it was faint, and then a savage joy, as if he'd freed something long chained and it rejoiced in it and called him to war. The land-wights, the spirits of place as the Mackenzies called them, the *kami* of rock and tree and beast, were still here beneath the lifeless emptiness that had troubled him. And they longed for release.

"—grant permission for our work this day. Let your eyes close. . . ."

As he shut his own he felt awareness begin to alter, at once expanding and shifting focus.

"Láwerce guide me . . . Woden guard me . . . all kindly Powers, we are Your children."

He began to build up the visualization of the path, the cold and dread he'd felt as they scouted the fortress of shadow, the way it crippled the very earth with its weight.

"So—"

He began to tap a little more quickly.

"Let us fare forward. We steal into the enemy's fortress. Into the very heart of darkness, and there we bring light."

The Sword of the Lady shone in the eyes of his mind, the light of the Moon made blinding-bright.

"There we bring the cleansing fire."

The sun Herself answered, arcs of flame vaster than worlds spinning from Her fingers as she danced through space that was not an emptiness but a singing presence, and gave it life.

His expanded awareness could feel each of them behind him now. Toa added a bass note to it, something deep and massive, scarred by wounds within but stronger for it. A fluttering rose around him, as of a bird with a white body and a red beak. And something peaked out from behind a crevice, something with beady eyes full of cunning. A lioness snarled, an Eagle shrieked, a fox with many tails and deep russet eyes wound among rocks . . . wings and eyes and swords, a vast blue form on the ramparts of Heaven . . .

"See in your mind's eye the coldness of the mountains. Feel the land rebel against the bane wrought upon it, against the crushing power of the troll-grip, against the malice of the ettin-kind. Be there."

Deor could smell the scents of rock and earth, the dustier tang of cut stone and poured concrete. And as they went farther a cold reek that was like the acidic residue of despair. There was flagstone beneath his feet, but no light struck his eyes. He could feel that he was in Mist Hills dress, a linen tunic and cross-gartered hose, leather shoes and seax and sword at his belt and his harp in her case of tooled boiled leather slung over his back.

Light came from nowhere, though he was not sure that he was seeing with his eyes at all. An endless tunnel of moist rock stretched ahead of him, groin-arched above, with pillars of rusting steel set into the walls.

And somewhere . . . somewhere that started very distant and ran to-wards him, or *oozed* towards him . . . an *attention* was turned. He could feel its *fimbul*-cold rage at being diverted from an endless contemplation of nothing but it itself, an existence so complete that it had no present, had *never had* a present, nothing but an infinite past that was equally nothing where nothing had ever been.

I . . . see . . . you.

"Come to me, comrades," he said, feeling the strings of their fates in the fingers of his mind. "Come to me in my need!"

A meadowlark circled about his head.

"Come!"

"Well, here I am, oath-brother," Thora said.

She was in a simple brown Bearkiller jacket and trousers and boots, unsheathing her sword and looking around, but the strength of a she-grizzly was in it.

"Come!"

A lioness snarled, a gaping pink-and-white yawn. Pip—not in Associate garb, but as he'd first seen her, in round-topped black hat, white shirt and shorts, suspenders and boots and knee- and elbow-guards, the kukri-knives and slingshot at her belt and an ebony cane with two silver-gold heads. A circle of black makeup marked one eye.

"Crawling through a bloody chilly dungeon this time," she murmured, looking around. "Suddenly, changing nappies and arguing with the cook back home seems like a fair chav."

"Come! Come!" Deor called.

The drum thundered, but not in his ears. It was a heart beating at the center of all things.

The Maori was there, leaning on his spear and panting. John, in knight's armor. A glimpse of someone with a coyote's head, grinning in deadly humor, and Susan Mika leaned panting against the wall, in her fringed leathers, face painted for war. A pair of amber-eyed cougars, and Faramir and Morfind were there in their Ranger garb, the white Tree and seven Stars and the Crown above it glowing for a moment in white on their jerkins before it faded.

"We're in the dungeons of Barad-dûr," Faramir murmured.

Morfind put a gentle hand on Susan's shoulder for a moment, and then they all drew their swords, standing with their backs to one another and looking about.

"Or Angband," Morfind said.

"What is it with these evil Dark Lord types and the huge buildings and the buried pits?" Susan said, her voice slightly plaintive; she didn't like being confined. "Why not villains on nice open plains?"

A glimpse of a rampant boar, tusks lowered to gore amid foam and gnashing, and then Egawa Noboru, looking exactly as he had, even to the lost hand . . .

Of course, some distant part of Deor's mind thought. *That loss, each scar upon his face, are badges of honor—what he has sacrificed for his liege, what he is in his heart's heart.*

"Come! Come!"

They all stumbled back. A sinuous dragon coiled before them, for an instant luminous as pearls, and stark fire of yellow and red billowed. Then Reiko stood there in her armor of lacquered scarlet, her hand upon the hilt of *Kusanagi-no-Tsurugi* and the chrysanthemum *mon* of the Yamato house on her brow.

"Come! Come!"

The wings of a great Golden Eagle beat the corridor's air, and around it circled a Snowy Owl, the keen-eyed and beautiful white-and-black hunter of the northern woods.

Órlaith stood, and extended an arm for Heuradys to steady herself with.

"Come!"

For a moment the tunnel was bright with dawn, soft with sunset, lit with light the deep endless blue of a summer's sky or the sharp cutting color above an endless waste of snow. Everyone exclaimed and set their backs against the walls. A panting and a thud of paws came with the sound, and a rank scent, and then the sky-blue wolves poured past them. A flood of the beasts, so real he could feel the brush of their coarse fur, but blue save for the yellow eyes and the white fangs over which tongues lolled. A breeze from the high steppe came with them, the crackle of dry grass and hard earth and the ozone of thunderstorms. . . .

And Dzhambul and Börte were with them, in their blue deel coats and point-toed boots, hands on their hilts.

"Ancestor . . ." Dzhambul said, wonder in his voice. "I felt him, the Ancestor. For an instant we were one!"

CHAPTER TWENTY

CHOSŎN MINJUJUŬI INMIN KONGHWAGUK
(KOREA)
MAJIMAG BAM-UI GEULIMJA
(FORTRESS OF ETERNAL NIGHT)
DECEMBER 18TH
CHANGE YEAR 47/2045 AD
(PLACES OUT OF SPACE, AND TIME)

Reiko pulled *Kusanagi* from its sheath in a snapping *iado* movement. A shape writhed down the blade for three-quarters of its length, as if the steel had been chiseled in a *horimono* and inlaid with the thinnest film of burnished gold. The inlay on the blade was an abstract pattern, seeming at one moment to be curling leaves of fire, another an elongated form dancing, then nothing that human eyes could interpret at all. When you looked more closely you could tell . . . somehow . . . that it was not gold in the form of flame.

It *was* flame, in some entirely nonphysical way.

She looked up; there were globes for a biogas lighting system at the peak-points of the groin-arched ceiling. She whipped the sword back and then forward in a long cut. The globes lit, and a low yellow light flooded the passageway. Though with it came a faint tang of old death that made you wonder what fed the gas-pits.

Órlaith drew the Sword, and the world *flexed*.

She was in Mackenzie kilt and plaid; evidently that was how her mind conceived of herself. Experimentally, she lifted her weight on the balls of her feet and down again. It felt . . .

Like rising on the balls of my feet, she thought. *Muscle, sinew, balance . . . but those things are lying on a pallet in my tent!*

Deor grinned at her.

"When you feel your feet upon the ground in the waking world, your body sends the feelings to your mind," he said. "Do you think your mind forgets now? You're not a ghost yet, High Queen."

She nodded, and then simply opened and emptied her mind. "This way," she said, and pointed.

"The feeling of . . . wrongness is greater there," he said, nodding in the opposite direction.

"Yes, but the Divine Leader is this way," Órlaith said.

Toa grinned. "And we're just going to chop the boss cocky?" he said. "'Strewth, I like the sound of it."

Órlaith nodded; she did too. As her father had said, fighting evil usually involved killing a good many whose only crime was to be born in the wrong place. Some of the songs her brother loved had armies meet and then the leaders settle things on their own. It didn't happen often, but it did happen now and then; her father had killed the Prophet Sethaz on the steps of his Temple in Corwin, though only after beating his armies.

I'll be very content if I can do better than that this time.

Órlaith looked to Deor. "Can they see us here? Can they feel us, strike at us? Or we at them?"

Deor nodded; it was an excellent question. "They can and will just so far as they have become part of the thing, the Power, that rules this place. You will see men; if you see them as other than men, or as men who are partly something else, they are of the enemy."

"As when Frodo saw the Nazgûl and Lord Glorfindel at the ford, when he was nearly on the other side of the curtain to the wraith-world," Faramir said softly, and his cousin nodded.

Deor looked at them, and Órlaith could tell he was surprised.

"Very much, Ranger of Eryn Muir. Very much indeed. Your Historian spoke more truly than many think."

Including you, Órlaith thought, as the two Dúnedain nodded. Then she noticed something else.

"Wait a minute," she said. "Faramir just spoke in Sindarin. Do you know the Noble Tongue, Deor?"

He shook his head, his thin face growing keen. "Only a little. The rest of you? What did you hear?"

"Mongol," Dzhambul said, and his sister nodded. "Rather flowery and formal and with some names I didn't recognize, but Mongol."

"Nihongo," Reiko said without turning.

"Bugger!" Toa said. *"Te reo Māori!"*

"Lakȟótiyapi!" Susan blurted.

"We are not speaking with our mouths, then," Deor said. "Or hearing with our ears."

"But we'd better keep a good eye out," Órlaith said. "Rangers first."

Time hardly seemed to pass as they made their endless way through the tunnels. Susan Mika fought hard not to let the sameness lull her into incaution, and the effort paid off as a faint far-off noise suddenly made sense in her mind. She put her hand up in Ranger battle-sign for *halt and hide;* she'd learned that quickly. Toa was well back of her and her partners, and Pip behind him; they'd relay the message.

This section of the tunnel had open doorways every thirty feet or so, including one not far from the junction ahead. They ducked inside into an empty storeroom that measured ten yards by thirty, plastering themselves against the wall on either side of the door, on hewn stone still rough with the pick-marks of the laborers who'd built it. The iron sound of boots striking the flags in unison came louder and louder. Susan dropped flat, and Morfind reached down to hand her a mirror on a collapsible rod, all the metalwork done in a soft dark matte gray.

Rangers do have the best gear, she thought, and extended it.

She got a good view of feet. A column of thirty men was marching down the way; by tilting the mirror she could see the spears and bows over their shoulders. They were in the standard steel-studded leather gear of the enemy, and looked ordinary enough . . .

Except for the guy in charge, she thought with a shudder, pulling the mirror back.

He was perfectly ordinary too. Except that there were tendrils of black growing out of his back and seeming to vanish somewhere, and at the same time loom like wings. And that his face was normal, but when you looked at it carefully the lower part was drawn out into a near-muzzle. And the edges of his mouth and the underslung lower jaw were formed in wedges like a saw-edged beak.

And his eyes were empty holes. It looked like the ordinary man was drawn over what she was seeing or sensing beneath, like a mask over a dancer's face. Except that the normal face was the false one, and she suspected that if she weren't here . . . irregularly . . . all she would see would be the human being.

Like there was a man there once, and he was eaten out from inside like one of those wasp grubs.

The thudding stamp of the boots died away. Susan handed the mirror back to her partner. . . .

And the enemy leader leapt through the doorway in a blur of deadly motion. His sword was drawn, ordinary steel that dripped dissolution. Susan rolled frantically as it slammed down towards her. Sparks showered off the stone . . . and though they were light, when they struck her they were freezing cold.

Susan shrieked, pulled the tomahawk out of its loop at the rear of her belt and threw it, with the same horrified reflex she would have had waking up and finding a worm coiling on her lip. The sword knocked the hatchet aside . . . and it was gone. Faramir and Morfind had their bush-swords out and shouted as they hacked:

"*Lacho calad! Drego morn!*"

That was the Ranger war cry: *Flame light! Flee night!*

The *thing* parried in a blur of steel, the familiar unmusical clang; but he didn't seem to bleed when the edges struck him. Instead he *leaked* light-swallowing blackness, as if the thing inside him was swelling and oozing. Susan rolled backward and flipped herself to her feet, sweeping out her saber and dancing around to the left to get them on three sides of the . . . thing.

That made the feeling of cold die down a little. What didn't was a sensation of not caring. It made her fearful; how could you not care?

I'm fighting a monster in a cave under the fortress of a demon king, she thought. *But when the sun goes out, who'll give a damn . . . does it really matter . . . is it worth the effort?*

Someone loomed in the door to the corridor. Someone huge, and a contorted tattooed face shouting as he lunged:

"Ke mate! Ke mate!"

She knew what that meant: *It is death! It is death!*

The palm-broad head of the Maori's spear smashed into the enemy's back and broke out through its chest. The thing looked down at it, then threw back its head and roared. As it did the black threads vomited out, and the three companions backed and struck frantically at the tendrils lunging towards them.

Reiko struck in the hall outside, visible in an explosion of fire. The blade of *Kusanagi-no-Tsurugi* passed across the half-seen, half-sensed cable of nothing that linked the man to whatever its source was. Where he had bellowed before, now he screamed; Susan could hear the physical voice among the tumult in her head, and it was agony such as she had never heard in her life.

He turned and stumbled, still screaming, into the corridor. Then he fell. Pip was there, hammering with the silver-and-gold head of her cane at something that crawled out of his eyes, striking over and over again with hysterical vigor. The sluglike thing whimpered as she struck, crying in a voice like a baby.

Órlaith extended the tip of the Sword of the Lady and thrust it home.

The scream cut off and silence fell. The body was vacant now, just a man. Then it began to collapse in on itself, until there was only a flaccid skin lying on the stone.

Susan leaned against the wall, panting, feeling as if a layer of wet felt had been unwrapped from around her mind. She also felt a stinging on her skin, and saw welts where spatters of . . .

Well, it wasn't blood, exactly, she thought.

. . . had landed.

"There is great evil here," Deor said quietly.

"You think so?" Pip half-yelled. "You think so? Do you really bloody *think* so? I'd never have suspected there was *evil* here. Sod all, we really needed a magician to figure *that* out at this point!"

Toa bellowed laughter at her expression of indignation. "Let's get on with it."

Reiko nodded sharply and pointed with the Grasscutter. "The . . . whatever it was I struck . . . linked the . . . man, I suppose I must say . . . in that direction."

"Yes," Órlaith said in agreement. "There is a sense of . . . center-ness there. As if that was a limb, and the brain lies there."

Pip raised the cane above her head. There was more traffic in this part of the . . .

Warren of bloody tunnels, she thought. *Ant-farm of demonic minions? Holiday spa for orcs?*

Her other hand came out in the *hold in place* signal. The passageways were better-lit here, and better ventilated; the slight draft on her skin spoke of some sort of convection system. There were also cooking odors and a disgusting reek—the tunnels managed to be unpleasantly bare and give an impression of filth at the same time.

The door beside her opened, and she heard the creek and wobble of casters, some sort of cart. Then more noise; it was a series of the carts moving in a convoy. Two soldiers came through first, swaggering along with their hands on their hilts and eyes rigidly front—you didn't expect trouble when you were guarding a meal delivery in a palace. Then the carts, with open tubs of some sort of very odorous pickled cabbage and covered trays of meat.

Heuradys d'Ath was on the other side of the door. Pip started to move, and was almost startled out of it as the knight's sword blurred into the left-hand guard's throat first. D'Ath was recovering into guard position even as the serrated knob of Pip's cane smacked into the face under the other helmet. Both men collapsed limply. Pip whirled and lunged like a fencer; the knob punched the throat of the first cart's server. The knight cut at the second, and then the third was fleeing, eyes bulging in terror and tongueless mouth gibbering.

Pip dropped the cane and had the slingshot off her belt in the same motion. The arm-brace snapped open and the curved metal snugged home just inside her elbow; she had a ball bearing nearly the size of a golf ball in the pocket and stretched the tough rubber back as her left hand pushed forward.

Thock.

The ball struck the fleeing servitor in the back of the head and he dropped limply forward, face plowing into the roughened stone planks of the floor. Thora and Deor ran past them, through the swinging door where the food carts had come, and Reiko and Órlaith trotted up the sloping corridor. Pip just had time to notice . . .

"No blood," she said, looking down at the bodies.

They were *dead*, there was no doubt about that. But she'd been cracking in faces—the blow to the face had been full-force and right into the skull just above the man's nose—and crushing throats, while Heuradys ran the narrow point of her longsword through a throat. Yet the bodies were curiously unmarked.

The one who'd fled was bleeding, but only where his face had struck the stone.

"That's damned—" Heuradys began, when Deor and Thora backed out of the kitchen-storeroom-whatever.

The Mist Hills scop was white-faced, and Thora was holding her free hand over her mouth. Pip's brows went up. She'd been in action or around the pair of adventurers for a year now, and she knew they were . . .

Not squeamish. The opposite of it. Bodies don't bother them.

"Don't go in there, Pip," Thora said. "Nobody should see *that*, but especially not a new mother. We . . . took care of the cooks and . . . butchers."

Pip looked at the food-carts, and judged the size of the salver covering the main dish on each.

"You were right, Deor," she said; there were things you imagined that you couldn't get out of your head either, but it was better than actually seeing. "Let's go."

"They were headed this way," Órlaith said. "That was for a lord's banquet. It'll give access to the hall of this place's master."

"This is a service elevator," Órlaith said grimly. "Everyone in!"

"I'm not usually one for chasing down evildoers," Pip replied; Órlaith thought she looked rather drawn. "But I'll make an exception for this."

They poured in. It was a bit crowded, but only slightly so. The sides were a metal lattice showing the carved rock and cement and rusted steel of the shaft's sides, and at the rear was a large crank sticking from a cylinder two feet across and man-tall. The cable from above ran through it, and the handle was brass worn shiny with use. Toa leaned his spear against the side, and John sheathed his sword and slung his shield over his back, and they gripped it together.

"Annnnnnddd . . ." the prince said.

"Go!" the Maori replied.

Huge muscles bunched and rolled beneath the tattoos of his arms and shoulders, and he grinned a gargoyle grin of effort and pride. John's lips were hard as he added his strength to the mix, and there was a slight lurch. The gears whined in the mechanism, and they began to rise as the two men kept up their constant motion.

Do we really need to do this? Órlaith thought.

Something gibbered above them. Then there was a thud on the sheet-metal ceiling of the elevator. Everyone tensed . . . and Órlaith knew what would come of that, with the pack of wolves she had along; she threw out a hand to keep the reaction in check. Toa and her brother labored at the crank, but it went slower and slower as they strained. There were more thumps, and the metal above them began to bulge and creak.

"I don't know what that is, I don't *want* to know, but I don't think it likes us," Susan said; lightly, but her teeth were bared.

"Together," Órlaith said, and Reiko nodded.

They drew their weapons, and the elevator lit . . . as if they had been in darkness before, and were only now aware of it.

"*Sutoraiku!*" Reiko snapped: *Strike!*

The Sword of the Lady punched through the ceiling of the elevator with less effort than she would have felt with a shield-cover. The Grass-cutter did the same less than a yard away. What was *beyond* the metal re-sisted; a soft feeling that was enormously dense as well. The scream that followed was entirely without sound, but the elevator shook violently; even the trained reflexes of her followers couldn't keep all of them on their feet. Heat and light blossomed across her face, and then the motion stilled.

When they withdrew the blades, *something* dripped down through the slits the Swords had cut. It wasn't black, or any other color; more of an absence than a presence, but you could see it.

Or at least, we can see it, as we are now. Is it like this for Deor all the time? I sincerely hope not, Órlaith thought.

"Back! Don't touch that!" Deor said sharply.

"I have absolutely no desire to touch it," Pip said sincerely. "Would you gentlemen care to get us moving again?"

Órlaith's breath stopped for a moment as the gears groaned beneath the strain, and then the cage lurched into motion once more. As it did there was an odor that might be decay, but wasn't exactly like anything organic—more of a sour acidic taint, and they all felt a piercing chill. Frost blossomed on the metal above and where the . . .

. . . *whatever it is* . . .

. . . had dripped with a dry crackling, and after a while dust flowed down rather than the liquid seeming matter.

She and the *Tennō* looked at each other, and Órlaith knew they shared a thought: it was time and past time that this was done.

There's something ahead of us. Something that's pushing, pushing at our minds, pushing at all minds everywhere, but we're getting closer and closer. Above us lies the heart of the enemy . . . no, not the heart. More like the brain, or the spinal cord.

"This is right," Reiko said. "Not the slow grinding of armies, but a single swift strike."

"I wish it were even swifter," Órlaith replied.

Not long after the elevator jarred to a halt. Egawa Noboru and Toa started to shoulder forward. Reiko put out her fan, and her *hatamoto* stopped in surprise.

"Not now, my faithful *bushi*," she said, tucking the *tessen* back in her sash and taking the Grasscutter in the two-handed grip. "The High Queen and I must lead, because of what we bear."

"Everyone else, follow closely," Órlaith said. "We're about to hit them where it hurts. If this can't be done quickly, it can't be done at all, so don't stop for anything."

Órlaith took the long hilt of the Sword in both hands, with the point down to her rear and right, the *neben* stance of the ancient swordmasters, to complement Reiko's overhead *Jōdan-no-kamae*. Toa leaned forward around them—and she admired the courage of it even then, to put that massive arm close to *these* edges—and gripped the knob that opened the sliding doors. He threw it back.

"*Morrigú!*" Órlaith called, her voice an eagle's shriek as she invoked the Battle Hag, the Threefold Doom who drove her House forward in battle.

"*Dai-Nippon Banzai!*" Reiko shouted.

The door slid back, and Órlaith saw a great antechamber. Some distant part of her mind took in a change from the inhuman bareness they'd seen below, a luxury of gilt and ornament and carving . . . but dusty and neglected, as if it was something that had been put aside, dropped, no longer of concern.

A startled guard's face confronted her, beneath a spiked helm—someone who'd been expecting to escort a train of food-carts. Órlaith had just enough time to realize the guard was a woman, though with nose and lips and ears removed that was hard to tell. The enemy spear drew back, and the Grasscutter whipped it to the side and struck in a curving upward stroke to the neck. Where the gift of the Sun Goddess met flesh, flesh *burned*.

Ash drifted away, and armor and weapons fell and clanked on the pavement.

More crowded forward. Órlaith struck, and ruin flopped away from the supernal keenness. They stepped forward together; their followers were behind them, Heuradys to the left of Órlaith and Egawa to Reiko's right. A wind built behind them, mingled of fire and beams of moonlight like spears of ice. Órlaith felt herself carried beyond herself; part of her was fighting, a thing that struck and struck and struck as the enemy pressed them desperately. Part was full of a raging pity, the sorrow of the Mother of All at the pain of Her children, even these. The battle cries rose behind her, then to either side as the others fanned out in a wedge behind the two monarchs:

"*Athēnē Promachos! Alala!*"

"*Ho, la, Wotan! Wotan!*"

"Thor with me! *Hakkaa päälle!*"

"Saint Michael guard!"

"*Te mate! Te mate!*"

"*Flame light! Flee night!*"

"*Hoka hey,* you bastards!"

Shapes towered into dimness as they broke through the antechamber and into a vast vaulted space. A hammer flashed, ravens circled a single Eye, a winged warrior wielded a sword that was the blue of the sky, a tall shape held up a shield that bore a Gorgon's head and wielded a bitter spear that pierced like understanding.

"*Morrigú!*"

"Toktamish!" Dzhambul exclaimed in astonishment and horror.

His uncle started up from a bed of cushions. That was near the swollen feet of *something* that sat enthroned. Sprawled, for it was swollen and pale and rippling, until even the shape of humanity was lost except for the features of a face more moon-shaped than a baby's. The face screamed through pouting lips, waving limbs tiny and plump.

His uncle's face was recognizable, hard and angry, but there was something trapped in his eyes, something that begged. The woman beside him snarled instead, drew a curved blade and leapt at Dzhambul. Börte surged between them, and the sabers clashed. Dzhambul's own blade was in his hand, but he hesitated.

"Uncle," he said. "Let me help you—"

"Die!" was the only reply.

He blocked a cut to his head from his uncle's blade and stepped into a thrust. Fighting his kinsman was like fighting himself in a mirror, the product of the same teachers. As he drove him back he saw what lay gnawed on a platter, and at last anger filled him. Cut, beat aside a downward slice at his leg, and then—

Something leaked from his uncle's eyes and mouth and nose and ears as Dzhambul's curved sword slammed up under the breastbone and out his back. Hands clutched at the blade, and Toktamish staggered backward . . . but no blood flowed. The older Mongol looked down incredulously, patting at himself with his left hand, and started to giggle dreadfully. . . .

And then looked up, up and over Dzhambul's shoulder, and screamed:

"*Ancestor!*" and turned to run; the word was horrified recognition rather than prayer.

Shapes bounded past Dzhambul, blue fur and white fangs, hairy shoulders as tall as his. The snarling of the Sky-Blue Wolves sounded, the forefathers of the *Mongol ulus*, the time of legends come again. Toktamish made only a dozen steps before they were on him, and the screams died down to a gurgling and then a ripping and tearing.

Now there was real blood, smoking on the flags and tattered rugs, and then it was gone along with the Wolves of Heaven.

That was his soul, Dzhambul thought. *I just saw the Ancestor's emissaries devour a man's soul.*

The guards were retreating, massed in front of their charge. Arrows were arching over his head as some of the others in his party unlimbered the bows cased across their back; arching towards the great pallid shape that thrashed and squealed. The skull-grinning guards flung themselves between, and fell and died—*they* were of the Thing, and he could see the severed cords of their connection to It recoiling as they died.

They're just its hands and feet, Dzhambul thought with revulsion. *It is fighting us . . . but through them.*

Others grabbed the swollen shape and helped it along, on feet and legs far too small to bear its naked bulk.

"Don't let that thing get away!" a voice shouted; Órlaith's, he thought.

"Don't let that thing get away!" Órlaith called. "We can't lose it in this warren!"

Guards threw themselves between their master and the attackers, with a courage she would have admired if there had been more of humanity in their eyes. Órlaith cut, and cut . . . and bodies died, though she suspected their souls had long since. Behind them doors opened in the monolithic stone that backed the throne, graven with symbols that she could have read with the Sword's help, but desperately did *not* want to understand. The pale shape bawled and sobbed as arrows were plucked out of it, but it could not, would not die so. The doors began to swing shut again in their faces.

"Strike!" Órlaith shouted in her turn.

She and Reiko did, ignoring the black-dripping steel that threatened them as the last rearguards died trying to keep them from the gates.

The Swords struck together.

The doors froze for an instant, as the glyphs on them glowed like black pearls in a universe of blackness. Órlaith felt a weight heavier than worlds against her arms, constriction like steel bands squeezing at her head and chest. Reiko strained by her side. Forces balanced for a long moment, and then both of them gave an endless shout and something *yielded*. It felt the way a cord did as it stretched and then snapped, but one that might have upheld a world.

The gates turned moon-white and then shattered into gravel beneath a rush of golden fire. Beyond the pale shape thrashed and whimpered. Behind them the last guards fell, as the companions guarded their monarch's backs. Órlaith and Reiko stepped forward with their blades raised and—

Time froze for a long instant. She *felt*, she *knew* what would happen as they struck. The Thing before her was the rotted husk of a man, but it was a gateway too; and that gateway was open to the Powers that she and Reiko bore. Energy exploded through the fabric of things into infinite emptiness.

That energy could not fill the void, or make it live. The glowing concentrated *life* of it, the torrent of possibility, could disturb the Void, trouble it . . . the concept was utterly inadequate, but they could make that endless emptiness *fear*.

As its channel died, the Void fled and pulled the connection between its home and this cycle of the universe closed.

Beneath them, the rent in the fabric of things ceased to be, and the Change-thinned wall of the world was restored. Órlaith and Reiko stopped and looked at each other. The obscene bulk of the Thing remained, oozing real blood, but now it merely evoked . . .

Pity, if anything, she thought. *That was a child, once.*

Some of the guards behind in the throne-hall had collapsed when their master died. The others were attacking still, faces contorted and howling in grief. And the stone beneath their feet began to shake. The hairs on the back of Órlaith's neck struggled to rise, as she sensed . . .

A bear. And a Child of Heaven. That which was usurped returns, and Dangun Wanggeom *returns to the kingdom He founded in the time before time. And I do not think he will be merciful to this place, or anything in it.*

"We need to get out of here! Now!" she said.

Deor's voice was sharp, raised to carry across the noise of battle.

"Yes, and quickly! This place was built with ettin-craft as well as the labor of men's hands. Ettin-craft sustained it, against the pull of earth and the anger of the Powers truly native here. We have destroyed the force that kept it upright. We must return to our true selves in the light of common day, or die with it!"

Órlaith flogged her mind back to functioning. They were in a passageway about twenty feet across and as high; the ruins of the doors lay behind them, and the surviving guards of the Divine Leader were climbing over it. Deor had sheathed his sword, and taken up his hand-drum. The first notes were faint, but it built, demanding, pulling.

"I will hold them, Majesty," Egawa said.

He stepped forward before them. The blade of his katana flashed; or the dream of it did, the spirit-image of the Hojo Masamune that lay by his side in Órlaith's tent. It glittered, and the curved wakizashi that fitted over his stump was almost as bright.

"You and me, mate," Toa said, whirling his spear around his head.

"No time for argie, Pip," he said over his shoulder. "I promised yer mum, and that's it."

John threw his shield in front of her and used it to pull her back; the others of the party formed a rank behind the two men. The drum sounded louder, but louder still was the squeal of tortured stone groaning.

Egawa shouted, his voice and face towards the enemies he had fought all his life . . . and Órlaith thought towards the memory of the *Tennō* he had not saved, Reiko's father, at whose side he had grown to manhood:

"I am General Egawa Noboru, Commander of the Imperial Guard of the Sovereign Majesty of Victorious Peace, victor in eight pitched battles, thirty-nine skirmishes and ship actions, and four duels! My father was Egawa Katashi, leader of the Seventy Loyal Men, who saved the dynasty and our nation! His father was Egawa Osamu, who dove his aircraft into a Beijin battleship! His father was Egawa Takeo, who lost his right arm leading his men in the storming of Mukden! For uncounted generations, the Egawa have served their Emperors and Dai-Nippon! *Tennō Heika banzai!*"

Then in their own language, just before the first reached him:

"Come to us and die, filth!"

"*Te mate! Te mate!*"

Reiko cried out in wordless protest, and then the drumming carried them away. Órlaith gasped, half-screamed, shot upright against a body chilled and stiff. When she came to herself, all were stirring . . . except the Maori and the samurai.

Pip rushed and fell to her knees beside Toa's unbreathing form, and Reiko beside her retainer. Órlaith turned her head aside, to give them the privacy of tears.

"All who are born will die," Reiko said after a moment. "Few so well, or for such good reason. Farewell, Egawa Noboru. Farewell, and fortunate rebirth, and eternal honor. I will bear your ashes to your family, and tell them how you died."

John laid his hand on Pip's shoulder. "He was a brave man, and he died for love," he said.

She nodded, and the tears flowed. The rest of them slowly stood, and looked at one another.

We will rejoice, Órlaith thought; they had won a victory for all of human-kind, and spared the lives of nameless thousands. *But not just yet.*

EPILOGUE

"I must return quickly," Dzhambul said awkwardly, his face framed by the earflaps of his cap; the sun was well up now, but the cold was bitter. "The army will be in confusion, and only I . . . well, only Börte and I . . . know what has truly happened."

"And we will have to figure out what to tell people," Börte said tartly, obviously meaning *I will*. "So that we won't be thought mad."

Órlaith nodded, smiling and hiding a slight wistfulness.

"Go, and the kindly Powers go with you, Dzhambul, my friend," she said. "The seas are not so broad as they were. Perhaps we will meet again; certainly, we will exchange letters."

"I wish we could visit your Montival," his sister said suddenly. "I wish *I* could visit!"

"And perhaps that will happen, too, someday," Órlaith said.

The Mongols bowed, and she returned it—giving him the monarch's honors she was fairly sure would be his in truth someday. Then they mounted, flowing into the saddle and reining about; the whole party and the escort she'd provided trotted north, across the night's fresh snow.

Órlaith watched for a while, sighed, and turned to walk back towards her pavilion. Heuradys had spent the last few days scrounging and scheming to lay on a feast, celebration and wake for the dead all in one.

"It'll take a month or two to make sure of things here," she said to Reiko.

"And then back to Japan," the *Tennō Heika* replied. "There will be the *Sokui no rei*, the Enthronement. And then my marriage. My faithful *bushi's* line will live, even if he does not see it, and that blood shall mingle with mine and rule as long as the Land of the Gods endures. We will remember him, and each year at the Obon festival all will remember him, and his deeds and his honor and a pride stronger than death."

They walked a minute in silence, and then Órlaith grinned. "I'm invited to the wedding?" she said.

And to herself: *And I will make my own offering to your spirit, Egawa Noboru, and to yours, Toa the wanderer, the strong, the faithful.*

"Most assuredly! Did I not say once that we must watch the cherry-blossoms together on Sadogashima? And for that, you must stay until spring. You will meet my family, and they will be extremely polite and not cry out in horror at their first sight of you."

"I think I can endure that," Órlaith said. "We shall watch the blossoms fall and the moon rise and recite Bashō in your bannerman's memory. Then home . . . and a surprise for my mother. And my grandmother Juniper, who'll be happier still at being a great-grandmother once more, since she's not a Christian."

She looked down at the camp, and across the years to come. "It's an ending, I suppose. And a beginning . . ."

"Both are illusions, my friend," Reiko said. "There is only life. That, at least, cannot change even in this world the Change has left us."

"And let's go drink to that!"

CHECK OUT THE FIRST NOVEL IN
S. M. STIRLING'S BRAND-NEW WORLD WAR I
ALTERNATE HISTORY SERIES.

BLACK CHAMBER

OUT NOW FROM ACE!